— Book 3 —
VERITY CHRONICLES

ON THE RUN

T S VALMOND

A K DUBOFF

Published by Dawnrunner Press
Cover Copyright © 2020 A.K. DuBoff

ISBN-10: 1954344074
ISBN-13: 978-1954344075

0 9 8 7 6 5 4 3 2

Produced in the United States of America

TABLE OF CONTENTS

KEY TERMS, CAST, & LOCATIONS

KEY TERMS

Taran – The race of all people in the Taran Empire; synonymous with human

Tararian Guard – The primary military force for the Taran Empire

Tararian Selective Service (TSS) – A quasi-military organization with Agents specializing in telekinesis; a complement to the Tararian Guard

Jump – Faster-than-light travel through subspace

Beacon Network – The navigation method for subspace jumps, maintained by SiNavTech

High Dynasties – The seven ruling families of the Taran Empire, collectively a governing council

Lower Dynasties – Influential families throughout the Taran worlds, second only in power to the High Dynasties

CAST

Verity Crew and Passengers
Iza Sundari – Captain of the *Verity*
Trix – Lynaedan android companion of Iza
Joe Anderson (AKA 'Jovani Saletas') – Undercover TSS Agent
Braedon Valtteri (AKA 'Devon Arvonen') – Pilot and VR gamer with a gambling problem
Cierra Quetzali – Healer and Braedon's ex-girlfriend

Apex Enterprises
Karter Hyttinen – Lower Dynasty heir and starship salesman
Becca Drejas – Karter's right-hand and assistant

Iron Dog Crew

Marten Douketis – Captain of the *Iron Dog* hauling freighter

Sydney Reis – Second-in-command of the *Iron Dog*

Additional Key Characters

Desirae Hyttinen – Failed TSS Agent turned Enforcer; cousin to Karter

Victor Arvonen – Head of Arvonen Dynasty; father to Braedon

Viper (AKA 'Abby Quetzali')– Competitive gamer and engineering genius

Yeaga – Leader of the miner revolt on Hubyria

Ian Mandren – TSS Sacon Agent Division Lead; Joe's direct supervisor

Raquel Calveras – Old friend of Karter, now working with Victor Arvonen

LOCATIONS

Tararia – The central planet of the Taran Empire

Lynaeda – Technologically advanced central world, specializing in AI and cybernetics

Beurias – Middle world with significant shipping industry, including headquarters of Apex Enterprises

Galminus – Dusty outer colony world; transit hub

Hubyria – Outer colony planet specializing in ore mining

Leveckis – Outer colony planet; home to Cierra

Phiris – Prosperous middle world

Sarduvis – Asteroid housing the Sarduvis Penitentiary

1

VICTOR ARVONEN STOOD with his fists clenched and breath held, praying to the stars that the nebula would be enough to hide them from the TSS ship scanning the area.

They'd been jumping between remote planets and nebulous clouds since their unfortunate incident with the *Verity*, when all of his careful plans had suffered an unfortunate setback. Captain Iza Sundari, the key to using the Gate, was also an unbearable nuisance. She'd almost ruined everything. If it hadn't been for his forward-thinking guard, they'd have been captured by the bumbling Enforcers. He needed Iza to work with him willingly if they were going to make any progress, but an alliance was impossible so long as she was aligned with his wayward son.

"They're moving off, sir," the helm officer reported.

Victor breathed a sigh of relief. "Good. Keep a close eye on them and alert me immediately if you see any more Agents or Enforcers nearby."

He took his seat at the center of the flight deck, trying to focus on the sights outside the viewport rather than the interior of his once-glorious ship. Since the attack on the *Arvonen One*, the ship had been in a constant state of disrepair. Exposed wiring and damaged bulkheads peppered the ship like they'd been in the middle of a warzone. Those bandits, with the help of his youngest son, had broken through the ship's defenses and pulled Iza and the sphere from his grasp. Victor was determined to not let it happen a second time.

"Sir?" The mousy woman at the communications station raised her hand as if she were a child in school.

He gritted his teeth to keep from roaring at her. The last time, it had only made her timidity worse. If she wasn't the best communications specialist he could find, he'd have thrown her out the airlock ages ago. "What is it?"

"It's the resonance signal—the one we've been searching for. I think I found it."

Victor crossed the flight deck in three strides and leaned over her chair to stare at the console. "Where?"

"Here." She indicated the position on a holographic map.

The planet was nothing remarkable on its own, but Victor admired the small, brown world like it held the greatest riches in the galaxy. In many ways, it might. They'd been searching for months, hoping to find additional evidence of the alien tech that was so critical to his plan. Now, for the first time since his run-in with the *Verity*, they had a solid lead on a new artifact.

"When did the signal appear?"

"A few moments ago. One minute, nothing. Then, all of a sudden, it was there."

They had no time to waste. Few others would know what it was, but it would no doubt attract attention. "Helm, how long until we can reach the coordinates of that signal?" Victor asked.

"If we follow a covert path to the destination, avoiding the TSS patrols, it will take at least eight hours."

He frowned. "How long if we take the direct path?"

"Three."

"Make it happen."

The helm officer shifted in his seat. "Sir, with the TSS in the area, I don't recommend—"

"Circumvent them! Do what you have to do," Victor roared, cutting him off. "I want to get to that artifact before anyone else does. Understood?"

"Yes, sir," the crewmembers on the flight deck said in unison.

Victor snapped a finger. "Bring me the digger."

Several minutes later, a guard returned with Raquel Calveras. Calm and confident as always, she strode in with her blonde hair loosely tied and draped over one shoulder of her lab coat. Had Victor been a younger man, he might have entertained thoughts of testing their DNA for compatibility. A successful pairing between them would bear him tall, intelligent children. Maybe they wouldn't be such a disappointment as Devyn.

"We've found a signal," he told her without preamble.

"Really?" Raquel's ocean-blue eyes lit up. She stepped over to the console to verify the signal as he had. "This may be the break we've been waiting for."

"Indeed. It's far stronger than the signal we observed with the previous artifact."

The side of her mouth lifted. "Is that so? Where is it?"

"It's a place I believe you know well. Uephus."

She faltered the slightest measure. "I see."

"I thought you'd be excited," Victor said. "Some might consider it quite an honor to have their homeworld play such a pivotal role in future history."

"Of course. It's just that we were there not that long ago, so we should have picked up something then." She studied the information on the screen for herself, composing her face. "Based on these readings, a portal must already be active. A big one. But who opened it?"

"Any chance it's your *Verity* friends?"

Her eyebrows furrowed and her lips drew into a pout. "No, I doubt it. They can't have gotten the other artifact back from the TSS, and this is the first evidence we've seen of another."

He smiled. "Then the only reasonable explanation is that the creators have decided to finally make contact."

She took a slow breath. "I know we've been hoping beyond hope for exactly this, but I can't help wondering what we're going to encounter when we do meet them. It would be wise to be prepared for anything."

"Oh, my dear, I am."

She nodded. "Of course. And I stand ready to assist."

"Where are we on the DNA sequence?" Victor asked.

"The synthetic process is lengthy and complex. The scientists we have left aren't experts in this field. Their limited knowledge of the exact process is slowing us down."

"That is unfortunate. Have we found anyone with a genetic match?"

"No. And considering Iza was orphaned at such a young age, it's not surprising."

"Keep looking. Iza Sundari can't be the only one. She's connected to the artifacts, and I want to know why."

— — —

Iza lay beneath the console of her old shuttle, mumbling curses as she beat the underside with a wrench. The interior wires spilled out in a rainbow of colors to either side of her face. She groaned, slamming her foot down on the floor.

I can't deal with this right now. She pulled herself out and stormed off the shuttle into the *Verity*'s cargo hold, where Trix stood staring out one of the viewports. Today she wore her blue and white jumper, and she'd pulled the perfect waves of brown hair together and bound it at the back of her neck so it hung between her shoulder blades.

"You need assistance," Trix said without turning. The Lynaedan android's voice was monotone and matter-of-fact by choice.

"No, I don't."

Iza kicked at an empty crate and watched it fall to the floor, where her dog Atano moved in for the kill, barking with excitement as if it were a game. Iza wiped her sweaty brow with the back of one hand, brushing aside the stray curls that refused to stay off of her face.

"What are you doing, hovering out here, anyway? Waiting for me to fail?"

"I was thinking."

Iza moved behind Trix to peer out the viewport, straining to see over the android's broad shoulders. Trix had changed since her encounter with the alien virus. She'd softened and become more reflective. Meditation wasn't something she used to do. Trix seemed determined to double her efforts to be more like her organic companions.

"What are you thinking about?" Iza asked.

"I am contemplating the quantity of dying stars between us and Lynaeda. At the same time, I am monitoring the ship's systems for any abnormalities, and I found there is a small leak in one of our intake lines, which I will correct. In addition, I am making slight course corrections in our trajectory to avoid debris from a comet that passed through this space sixty-eight minutes ago."

Iza peered up at her, waiting for her to get the point.

"You did not want that much detail into my thought process, only why I was looking out at the stars."

"It's fine. If I'm not used to your quirks by now, I never will be."

"I believe we should discuss the Joe Anderson situation."

Classic Trix non-segue. No way I'm getting baited. Iza cleared her throat and headed back to the shuttle. As much as she didn't want to work on the repairs before the next job, she'd rather suffer through that than discuss Joe. It was painful enough to think about him without others making their own observations.

Against Iza's wishes, Trix followed her over to the shuttle. "It has been exactly three months, two days, and seven hours since he was taken into Enforcer custody and turned over to the TSS."

Iza stopped short. *Has the eternity since our last kiss only been three months?* Her restless nights often contained scattered images of her tearful goodbye. By now, he'd been sent to Earth on the other side of the Taran Empire.

"We should be working on a way to retrieve him as soon as possible," Trix said as she took two steps to stand in front of Iza.

"Why is that?" Iza asked, forced to look up at her.

"You are adversely affected by his absence."

It doesn't matter how I feel. A rescue attempt so close to TSS Headquarters was risky under the best circumstances, and they were already on the TSS' watch list. Even so, she'd heard from almost everyone individually about their desires to figure out a way to bring Joe back. It was no surprise Trix had a reason of her own.

It also wasn't surprising that Trix's motivations were tied to ensuring Iza's happiness; she'd always been Iza's greatest supporter. "I appreciate your concern, but I'm fine."

"To the contrary, in the last three months, you have not slept a full night, waking up either screaming or crying."

"Have you been spying on me?"

Trix ignored the question continuing in her evaluation of Iza's 'adverse effects'. "You have lost almost twenty pounds due to lack of appetite and have visited the gym less than seven times total."

"That has nothing to do with him," Iza said, shaking her head and reaching for the necklace around her neck. "I have a lot of things on my mind."

"Not only that, you have been short-tempered with everyone and avoid sitting down to eat with the rest of the crew."

"Personal choice," Iza grumbled as she climbed back into the shuttle. The mess of wires made her want to turn back around again.

Trix followed her inside, preventing her escape. "You insist on making repairs on your own instead of allowing the crew to help you."

"I like doing things on my own. You never had a problem with it before."

Trix moved to the console and handled the wires with care while she sorted them returning them in neat bundles to their correct locations.

Iza crossed her arms and silently watched the android work, not sure how to reply to Trix's assessment of her mental state. She was probably correct, but Iza didn't want to get overly analytical about herself. She knew she missed Joe. She cared about him, deeply. But none of that changed the fact that she had her own problems to deal with before she could think about rescuing him from the primitive planet where he'd been banished.

Atano, having finished his morning explorations, bounded to Iza's side, rubbing his white fur over her calves. Her black pants collected the short hairs, and she half-heartedly brushed them off. They always proved harder to get off than she'd have thought possible and clung to the oddest of places. She'd found two wayward strands just that morning woven into her braid.

Trix completed putting the shuttle's innards back in order and stood up to face her. She picked up right where she'd left off with their conversation, "Most of your time is spent either here on the flight deck or locked in your cabin avoiding everyone on board other than Atano."

Iza sighed. "Atano's a good listener, and he doesn't bother me with conversations about things that can't be changed."

He leaped up at his name and danced in front of her until she bent down to scratch behind his ears, prompting him to rub against her pants again.

"Speaking of the flight deck, it's time one of us was up there." Iza gave Trix her most intimidating glare.

Trix stared back at her, unblinking.

Iza huffed out a breath. "Fine, *I'll* go."

The flight deck wasn't as empty as Iza had expected. Braedon sat at the helm, biting his lip as he doodled on his tablet. His wavy chestnut hair had grown unruly, falling into his eyes. Cierra was bent beside him, her tight curls bound on top of her head with loose tendrils falling in a cascade to frame her face.

When she spotted Iza, Cierra gracefully turned toward her, unsuccessfully trying to use her near to see-through sage-green shift to hide the hydroponic plant that she'd tucked next to Braedon's chair.

Iza usually made an ongoing point to warn her about the dangers of walking barefoot around the ship, but today she shrugged it off, focusing on the more important matter. She pointed at the plant. "No. I said no plants on the flight deck, and I meant it."

"Joe said that sometimes you say things you don't really mean." Cierra's silky tones grated on Iza's nerves. Her gray eyes never shifted from Iza's face as her lips curled into a measured smile. Even with no makeup, the girl had the best skin in the Taran Empire.

"I don't care what Joe said. Get that green off my flight deck or I'll be shoving it down your throat."

"Speaking of Joe, when are we going to pick him up?" Braedon asked. "It feels like it's been long enough––hasn't it been long enough? The TSS hasn't been around in months, and I haven't even seen an Enforcer ship come up on our display in weeks. I think we could make the attempt. I know it won't be easy, but I can't be the only one thinking it."

Is this a coordinated assault? Iza groaned. "No. Not this again."

He whirled around in his seat, revealing an expensive navy shirt and over-styled pants like something out of the Sensationals' Rich and Famous fashion feature. "I mean it's been three months and no word," he continued. "I'm sure he's suffered enough on Earth. Besides, if he were here, we wouldn't have had half the trouble we did on that last job."

Iza threw her arms up in the air, letting them slap against her thighs before circling the room. "Everyone wants to eat, but no one wants to do the work it takes to get it. You all want a free place to sleep, but no one wants to put in the time on repairs. Everybody wants Joe back, but no one has any bright ideas on how to do it."

"We could do what we normally do—just take him," Cierra said as she lifted one perfectly arched black eyebrow.

Iza met Cierra's gaze, glancing down at the plant in her hands and then back up. "Still here, are you?"

"She's not wrong," Braedon said. "It wouldn't exactly be the first time we've taken something, or someone, for that matter. Remember those scientists my dad nabbed? Wacky fun." He chuckled to himself.

It was easy for some highborn to say, never having to want for anything. *You can take the boy out of the dynasty, but you can't take the dynasty out of the boy.* She knew Braedon had come a long way since they'd first met, but he was still prone to wishful thinking and a desire for instant gratification. Not so unlike his father. Victor Arvonen's quest for power had forced them into far too many close calls. Though rescuing those scientists *had* gotten her a pet. She glanced down to her left where Atano sat at attention awaiting orders; he was the only one smart enough to be quiet.

"Am I the only one with brains this morning?" Iza asked. She looked at each of them in turn, giving them each a chance to respond. When neither answered, she continued. "The only reason the Tararian Selective Service agreed to let us go on our merry way is because we put Joe in our rearview. If we don't keep our noses out of trouble, and they get a whiff of it, they'll confiscate our independent jump drive and haul us all to a TSS holding cell faster than you can say, 'Joe I miss your—"

The doors to the flight deck slid open and Trix entered, giving Iza a quizzical look.

"—'face'," Iza concluded.

Braedon and Cierra exchanged a knowing glance. "Uh huh," he said.

Trix tilted her head. "Have you all been attempting to convince Iza to listen to reason so we can rescue Joe?"

"Yep. Still working at it," Braedon replied, swiveling back and forth in his seat. "She's a stubborn one."

Iza placed her hand on Trix's shoulder. Standing this close, she could see the circuits hiding in her iris. "We can't go back for him, not even if we wanted to."

Trix looked down at Iza sadly. "You have never been in as good of spirits as you were when he was here. I fear that you will regret this choice."

"Agreed," Cierra said.

"I hate to say it, Iz, but it's true. You've been more volatile lately. If you ask me—"

"I didn't," Iza cut in. "It wasn't my choice, remember? He's the one who made the deal. I had nothing to do with it."

"Perhaps if you told everyone that your engagement to Karter was a ruse, it would make you feel better." Trix held her expression sincere and neutral.

"It's not, and it never was a ruse," Karter said as he stepped onto the flight deck, taking advantage of the open doors that hadn't been closed after Trix entered.

"What did I tell you about barging in here uninvited?" Iza clenched her teeth, trying not to bite off her tongue in the process.

"What, and miss the party?" At Iza's glare, Karter held up his well-manicured hands in defense. "I believe you said something about 'emergencies only'." Fabricating such a situation was probably what he'd been doing back in his quarters when he was supposed to be figuring out how to get a new fiancée.

Karter Hyttinen was a sleaze of the highest order, and he'd somehow weaseled his way on her ship as a long-term passenger. Despite his lean physique, even brown features, and dynastic heritage, he was more trouble than he was worth. She determined a long time ago it was time to drop him off. The engagement had been made in haste to save her crew, but it wasn't meant to be a lasting bond.

"And what is this emergency?" The building frustration pressed against Iza's ribs. She had to focus on her breathing to calm herself down.

"I wanted to request a short visit to Beurias. I have some business to attend to there."

"If we go back to Beurias, you're getting off—

permanently."

Karter stroked his chin, as if debating. He'd already made his intentions clear; he was going to try to wait out the contract forcing her to marry him, despite their mutual lack of love. Lower Dynasty heirs and their politics were enough to give Iza a raging headache.

"I need to formalize a few deals, and they require my presence. It shouldn't take long. We can arrange it for a time that coincides with one of your jobs, if you like. I only wanted to bring it to your attention."

"So, not an emergency at all." Iza waved him away.

"Captain?" Braedon's tone had turned all business.

"What now?"

"I'm picking up a general distress call for any ships in the vicinity," he said.

Iza moved back to the center of the flight deck. "Pull up the message."

The stars in the viewport morphed into a white background, where a woman with smooth black hair and darting black eyes faced the camera.

"My name is Luxi Song. I don't know if this is going to reach anyone, but if you're in the area of Uephus and receiving this message, then you're close enough. Something has gone terribly wrong here, and we need your immediate assistance. Please, it concerns all life as we know it."

The looped message continued until Iza ordered it to stop.

"Locking in coordinates and preparing to jump," Braedon said as his hands flew over the smooth console.

"That's not your decision to make!" Iza protested. "What makes you think we can do anything to help them, anyway?"

"We have the *Verity*, and we may be the only ones close enough to do anything. Besides, it's not that far off our current course." His hands hesitated over the console waiting, for her go-ahead.

Iza wasn't so sure. The distress call was far too vague. Anything concerning 'all life' sounded way beyond their capabilities to address.

"We might be their only hope," Cierra added.

Iza didn't like it. The last thing she wanted to be was anyone's only hope. Yet, all of her crewmembers' gazes were fixed on her expectantly. She sighed; it was useless to argue.

"Fine, set a course for Uephus. I guess we're going to play the heroes."

2

AS THE *VERITY* approached Uephus, the crew admired the view of the marbled forest-green planet floating against the starscape.

"This doesn't look anything like the Uephus I remember." Braedon leaned forward, squinting. "I swear the whole world was a desert planet—hard to grow anything. It was known for its caverns."

"Yes, it was," Karter said staring at the viewscreen.

"It's beautiful," Cierra said, smiling. "This is the kind of world we're trying to make on Leveckis. If only more people would consider the benefits of agriculture over technology."

"I do not believe this transformation is natural. I will continue running scans," Trix said.

"Anyone else in the vicinity?" Iza asked.

"No one," Braedon replied after checking the scan data for other ships.

"Well, let's take a closer look," Iza suggested. "Clearly it's not an arid rock anymore."

"The *Verity* isn't equipped to handle whatever's going on down there," Karter said.

"Neither are the people who live on this planet." She'd

almost forgot Karter didn't like to do anything that wasn't of immediate benefit to himself.

"I hesitate to align myself with Karter, but in this circumstance, he is correct." All eyes turned to Trix as she spoke. "I was in favor of responding to the distress call, but that was before I had information about the state of this world. The surface of the planet is undergoing severe tectonic shifts, which could pose an extreme hazard to the *Verity* if we land."

"What about the shuttle?" Iza asked.

"The shuttle has a faster ignition sequence and can be controlled by me remotely. It is an acceptable alternative, though I must emphasize there are still risks," Trix said.

For the past few years the AS-225 shuttle had been Iza's home. The second-hand transport vehicle she'd picked up from Apex Manufacturing had the aged look of a well-used vessel. Though she'd never admit it to Trix, the shuttle had more sentimental than re-sale value. *Perfectly safe for a tin can in space. Isn't that how Joe had described it once?*

Iza pushed her thoughts of Joe aside and spoke to Cierra. "Get a medkit together and be prepared to help with the injured."

Cierra inclined her head. "I'll do what I can, of course. But, as you know, my healing abilities have their limits."

"I'm aware of that, but whatever you can do will be better than nothing at all. The survivors are going to need you, from the look of the place."

—

Twenty minutes later, they were piled up in the shuttle and headed for the surface of Uephus. Iza sat behind Trix and Cierra behind Braedon as they maneuvered the shuttle down to the surface. Iza had locked down the *Verity* as a precaution, to prevent someone from scoring a free ride if they happened upon the ship while it remained in geosynchronous orbit. At first, Karter insisted on staying aboard, but when Iza threatened violence, he chose life over a slow and painful death. Insisting he had no intention of helping, he sat on the bench in the rear cargo area and stayed quiet.

Braedon peered out the front viewport. "Where are all the cities? There were millions of people on this world," he said. "We should be right above the capital city. There should be shops, restaurants, homes... Even the transport station is gone!"

Iza let out a forced breath. She glanced over and caught the wonder in Cierra's eyes. She seemed more fascinated than disturbed by the apparent changes to the planet. "I suppose you don't see a problem with this?" she asked, her steely gaze on Cierra's round gray eyes.

"I assume you mean plant life? I do not. I think if it were possible, every planet in the Taran Empire would be better off with this kind of ecological development." Cierra pursed her lips.

"Redevelopment," Trix corrected. "This planet was already engineered by Tarans from its natural state to support colonization. However, it has now been redeveloped. Transformed. The process is unlike anything in my database. And the changes are not only on the surface. The crust of the planet has been reshaped."

"What could possibly transform a planet so quickly?" Karter asked from the back of the shuttle.

"It is beyond known Taran science," Trix replied.

Iza held in a swear. She'd known better than to respond to the distress call, but they were here now. There was no way the others would leave without getting answers. "All right let's focus on making contact with the people down here. Keep us low."

"You got it," Braedon said and banked to port, dropping them to just above a row of crumbled buildings with trees sprouting from the rubble.

"These trees show years of growth," Cierra observed.

"Are you sensing anything?" Iza asked.

Cierra closed her eyes then shook her head.

"Of course not; that would be too easy. Trix, just put us down as close to the distress signal's origin as you can manage."

"That is going to be very difficult."

"Why? Don't we have the coordinates?"

"The coordinates now read at sixty-four meters below the surface of the ground. There, near that large body of water."

Braedon gaped. "This planet didn't have any oceans—just the underground water reservoirs in the caverns. What's going on here?"

"It might be a good time to invest in the new waterfront real estate," Karter said in a flat tone that Iza couldn't tell was a joke or not. "What was their primary industry?"

"Uephus had very few exports," Trix said. "Their primary industries were textiles manufacturing and archaeological research."

"Diggers?" Iza asked.

"Yes, and notably, the homeworld of Raquel Calveras."

Iza ground her teeth together to keep from saying anything more about the woman. Three months ago, she'd betrayed them to Victor Arvonen, kidnapping her and turning her over to the man for his sick experiments. *How had I missed the signs?* Rachael had come on so strong, it should have given her away. She'd made Iza feel like she'd been missing something, not having another woman as a close friend with whom she could share her feelings. But that friendship was a ruse; her real goal had been the sphere.

Iza had to pull herself away from the tarnished memories

to focus on the lush foliage of the trees and the grass growing wild as if it had been there for decades. The only evidence of the old Uephus were the tops of several crumbling buildings sticking out of the ground. They'd once been the tallest buildings in the city.

"Is it safe to land?" Karter asked.

Trix evaluated the newest set of readings. "The tectonic activity appears to have subsided. However, I advise we continue monitoring the planet's climate, since we do not yet know the cause of the changes."

"Let's keep this visit short," Iza said. "Put us down there." She pointed to a small clearing surrounded by trees.

Once they were safely on the ground, Cierra was the first to climb out of the shuttle with her bag of medicinal supplies. As her bare feet touched the grass outside, she closed her eyes and took in deep breaths.

Iza followed her out with Atano on her heels, curled tail wagging. When he saw the grass, he started dancing around, anxious for permission to explore. "Go on," Iza said, pointing toward a nearby clump of trees. The dog didn't hesitate dashing off, the curl of his white tail an identifying flag in the distance while he kept his black nose to the ground.

"It's real," Cierra said with wonder as she touched the leaves of a nearby bush.

"It's hot." Iza removed her jacket and tossed it back to Braedon, who was still on the shuttle.

"It may not have happened the same way, but it feels as real as the gardens on Leveckis," Cierra continued as if Iza hadn't spoken. "The leaves and the trees are all doing what they would if they had been planted here, but they aren't native to this planet. In fact, most of the plant life here is not native to this part of the galaxy."

"So, where did it all come from?" Karter asked, his pulse

handgun out as if ready to confront any unknown adversary.

Cierra eyed him. "What are you worried about? Getting snuck up on by a tree?"

Karter seemed to realize his mistake and returned the gun to its holster.

Iza stood still, listening to the light breeze that lifted the ends of her hair. Strange that a planet so lush had no other sounds on the wind. It was as if it were plucked out of the pages of an old book. It was exactly like the small colony that Cierra had settled and cultivated. No wonder she was smiling and practically dancing for joy in the meadow where they'd arrived.

"How many people are supposed to be on this planet?" Iza asked.

"This planet is home to over three hundred million people and seventeen thousand species of animals," Trix answered.

Iza didn't like the way things were going. "Scan for communications signals. We need to find those people."

"Isn't it obvious?" Karter held out his hands. "There's no one here."

"I hate to agree with Karter as much as the next guy, but maybe a tree ate them."

"I never said—"

Iza cut off his next words, her nerves on edge. "Well, the Enforcers should be here, at least. An entire planet can't just be transformed without anyone knowing about it!"

"We must be the first ones to receive the distress signal," Braedon said. He turned in a slow circle. "Hello!" His voice died on the wind.

Iza strained to hear a response, but none came. The sweet smell in the air and the light breeze should be comforting. Yet, the world was too eerily quiet and still. There wasn't a bird or insect in the sky.

Her shoulder's tensed, and she called the dog as they began

to roam away from the shuttle to look for clues. She walked along the edge of the meadow with the dog trotting at her side until she saw something that didn't seem to fit.

Braedon moved to pick it up. "Is that a—"

"A child's shoe." Cierra took it from Braedon. She held up the small red shoe with two fingers to examine it, then she looked around as if the child it belonged to would step out from behind a bush with one barefoot.

"I don't like this," Braedon said. "What if whatever happened here happens again?"

Iza's thoughts circled the same question. Whatever had caused this level of change might return to finish the job of wiping out every bit of life left.

"There is a faint communications signal coming from the building ahead," Trix announced, pointing in the direction.

"Lead the way," Iza said, and the others fell into step behind.

"How long should it take to alter the environment of a planet like this using current technological processes?" Iza asked the android.

"Decades, most likely. So, when it comes to Uephus, I am aware of no technology that could have so rapidly reshaped this world. This is what scientists call a catastrophic event of epic proportions."

"This place was engineered." Cierra dug her toes into the dirt and sighed. "The design elements are obvious. There isn't enough of the wild visible in the landscape or the formation of the tree lines. Walking barefoot, you get used to certain things——pebbles, jutting rocks displaced by animals, plants pushing upward in their fight for life. This feels new, untouched, unnatural."

Cierra halted, holding up a hand to indicate they should all stop. "There's someone here."

IZA AND THE others followed Cierra as she glided around branches and over bushes, careful not to disturb anything larger than a blade of grass. The strange distress call and the altered planet with no wildlife had warning bells going off in in Iza's head, driving her to keep a more cautious pace as she trekked toward the unknown.

Cierra led the way through the dense and eerily empty trees toward the buildings in the distance. She stopped at the tree line, and the others fanned out to her sides. She whistled for Atano to stay close at her side; she wanted him nearby in case there was trouble.

Several meters from where they stood, a half-swallowed building jutted out of the ground. Vines and leaves clung to the bottom and snaked up the sides to the second row of windows. Based on the architecture, the   building must have once scraped the sky. Most of the windows were missing or broken, and Iza thought she saw a small pale face in one before it darted back into the shadows.

A small group of people covered in gray dust, dried blood, and tattered clothing spilled out of one of the archways leading into the building. Iza was grateful to see their hands were empty. They were probably in shock and hadn't thought to protect themselves against anyone who might be coming to take advantage of their misfortune.

Iza chastised herself for thinking the worst; living in the Outer Colonies her whole life had made her jaded and cynical.

She raised her right hand in the formal Taran greeting as the group approached. "Hello. We received a distress call from Luxi Song. Is she among you?" Iza asked scanning their shocked faces for the one she'd seen on her holodisplay.

"Yes." The response came from a woman at the back of the group. The people in front of her parted to make room as she limped forward, leaning on a long metal pole for support. The metal vibrated with a slight clang as it led her across the fresh grass. "I'm Luxi Song."

Like the others, Luxi was covered in gray dust from head to toe. A trickle of blood had dried and crusted on her temple, where it then trailed down the side of her narrow face. If she hadn't come forward, Iza wouldn't have recognized the woman even close up.

Luxi coughed into her hand, and Cierra stepped forward to offer her a canteen of water. Luxi drank it down without hesitation.

"Thank you." She wiped her mouth with the back of her hand. "We haven't even organized a group to collect water yet. There are too many wounded." She nodded to the gathering crowd pressing in behind her, looking thirstily at the empty canteen. Many more were coming out of the shelter of the building.

"Trix, test the local water and begin collecting a few barrels so these people can have something suitable to drink," Iza instructed.

"Aye, Captain."

"There's a large barrel inside," Luxi said, but shook her

head and moaned. "Filled with water, it's too heavy for any one person to carry. I'll send some of the men with you."

"If someone can show Trix where to get the barrel, she can take care of the rest."

Luxi let her eyes linger on Trix. "An android? I've never seen one up close."

Iza nodded to a man who raised a finger in the air, indicating he knew where to find water. Then, she turned back to Luxi. "I'm Captain Iza Sundari. We retrieved your message and came straight away. What happened here?"

"Your guess is probably as good as any we have. Perhaps we should go inside where we can all sit down." She took a wobbly step.

Cierra handed off her supply bag to Braedon so she could assist Luxi. "My name is Cierra Quetzali," she said as she took Luxi's arm to support her. "I'm a Healer. Where are your injured?"

"I'll take you to them. Follow me." Luxi pulled away from Cierra, shifting her weight to the pole, even though she clearly needed medical attention herself; her hastily bandaged leg bore a patch of blood.

Two doors hung off their hinges on the front of the partially engulfed building. The hallway beyond looked like a school; both sides of the corridor were lined with doors to classrooms. Iza recognized the institutionalized setup from the years she'd attended before her mother Left.

As Luxi led them through the first level, her metal pole clanked against the tiled floors. She'd tied off the pole's end with cloth strips, but it did little to soften the echo.

She paused at a wide staircase on the left, which led to the upper floors. "This used to be the labs and upper study floors of the University's science buildings. This is all that remains. The injured are recovering here."

She pointed to a classroom on the right filled with people. A dozen men, women, and children waited in chairs, lay on tables or were resting on the floor. All of them were covered in gray dust and were actively bleeding or covered in dried blood. Some of their arms or legs were in makeshift slings and splints.

Cierra pushed up her sleeves and directed Braedon to put the bag down on one of the empty tables. She didn't waste any time setting up at the end of the room closest the window. Most of the patients had edged away from the exterior windows, where the vines and brush had taken root, blocking the sun outside.

Luxi limped further down the hall, and Iza nodded to Karter and Braedon to stay and help Cierra.

"What about you?" Iza asked as she hurried to catch up to the woman. "You need treatment."

"I'm fine for now. Let the Healer help the others first," Luxi said. "Come with me."

Iza followed Luxi to the end of the hall, where two doors still on their hinges were propped open. The windows here also were half-covered in ivy and moss. Someone had pushed a large desk, the only unbroken furniture in the room, to one side to make room for a circle of ten chairs. The seats were occupied by five men and four women. Another chair was brought into the circle for Iza, while still others stood lining the walls of the room.

Iza took in the group of dusty and bruised adults as she sat down. The arrangement of chairs and the absence of children gave the impression they were the ones making the decisions for the survivors.

"We're all that's left of the University. We're mostly lecturers and professors, but there are a few businesspeople and local government workers," Luxi explained. "The others among us are students, staff, or visitors on campus."

"What happened here, exactly?" Iza asked loudly enough for the others in the circle to hear.

"What happened is that you're too late!" a gray-haired man replied, slapping his hand against his thigh.

An older woman seated next to him put a gentle hand over his, and he clamped down on whatever else he'd planned to say. He sat back in his chair, crossing his arms.

The woman spoke to Iza. "Sorry, we appreciate you coming. It's only we're still grieving over what we've lost. It happened so fast."

Another man with dark features and a cut on his bald head spoke next. "One minute the ground was solid beneath us, the next, grass started sprouting up everywhere we looked."

There were murmurs of agreement as he continued.

"You have to understand, at first the sight of all that green was breathtaking. We had no idea that Uephus could sustain anything so lush and alive. But it didn't stop. Soon, bushes were popping up as if they'd been there all along. The ground started to reshape itself. Our scientists gathered themselves virtually to determine what was going on, but everything changed so quickly they couldn't keep up. When entire cities started to be swallowed whole…" His voice broke.

Luxi Song took over the narrative. "The trees grew as tall as buildings and the air became so thick with humidity it was like being smothered by a heavy wet blanket."

Another woman from the opposite side of the circle, with short curly hair and a dusty gray lab coat spoke up. "Our people are accustomed to an arid climate. Between the fear and the rise in humidity, it was impossible to have a coherent thought."

"The ground came up over the ridge and engulfed most of this city in a matter of minutes," the man with the dark features continued. "The water springing up out of nowhere became an ocean. It drank everything the shifting land had left behind.

There was no escaping it. We've always been reliant on outsiders for transport, so we didn't have ships of our own for escape."

"Are you all that's left?" Iza asked. She wasn't sure she was prepared for the answer. When Trix walked in the door, Iza breathed a sigh of relief that she'd be there to hear it, too.

Luxi hung her head. "We don't know, we haven't been able to locate or contact any others. We believe our world leaders retreated underground and are buried there."

"We might be able to help there. We can use the *Verity* and my shuttle to see if we can pick up anyone sending out a latent signal."

"The *Verity*? What kind of ship is that?"

"H3X-Z500 Legacy Class cargo ship. Its drive is—" Trix started to answer.

Iza raised her hand to stop Trix from giving out all of her ship's specs. "What we have is at your disposal."

"Thank you. We appreciate any assistance you have to offer."

The sight of their hopeful faces made Iza uneasy.

Braedon hurried across the room to her; she hadn't seen him approach the doorway. When he reached her, he put a light hand on her shoulder and leaned down to whisper in her ear. "You're doing great, Iz. Want me to join the search party?"

Iza nodded, both relieved and distressed he could read her expression from across the room. "Take Karter with you and maybe a local who knows the area. I need Trix to remain here for now."

"Got it. Where will you be?"

"There's something strange going on here, and I intend to find out what it is."

Iza folded her arms across her chest in thought while Braedon went on his way to help with the rescue efforts. *What could cause the changes to this world? And why would anyone want to?* She'd never heard about a planet in the Taran Empire with a similar experience. "Do you have any information about where the transformations began?"

Luxi carefully stood, using her chair for support as she favored her injured knee. "Come with me. I was getting to that." She grabbed her pole and nodded to a young man Iza hadn't noticed standing near the door.

He seemed to be Braedon's age and as tall as Joe. He moved with the confidence of someone twice his age. His face and tattered clothing, like everyone else, was dusty gray. He disappeared into the corridor somewhere ahead of them.

"She is unwell," Trix whispered to Iza.

"I know. Since she refuses to visit Cierra, we might have to bring Cierra to her."

"She seems determined to injure herself further," Trix continued. She raised her voice just loud enough for Luxi to overhear. "Emergency protocol dictates she care for her injuries before attending to the needs of others."

"Right now," Luxi said, "my biggest worry is that this could happen again or continue happening. We need to know what we're dealing with, or no one is going to sleep tonight."

Iza gave Trix a raised eyebrow and a shrug. This wasn't her call, but she respected Luxi for having the courage to make it.

They followed Luxi up the flight of stairs they'd passed by earlier. Due to her injuries, it was slow going, but Luxi was determined to move and function on her own.

"What's your role here?" Iza asked as they slowly ascended the steps.

"I'm technically a student," the woman replied. Her breathing was shallow, and she needed more breaths and pauses as she climbed. "I was serving my practicum here to receive my accreditation to teach here as a professor of planetary science."

When they reached the next landing, Iza and Trix followed Luxi through the doors to an abandoned corridor. Above them, Iza thought she heard the sound of children.

"That is the current nursery," Luxi said in answer to her confused expression. "We keep most of the children there, so they don't overhear anything too scary for them to process. It's been hard enough, as most of them are missing at least one parent."

Luxi turned left to where the young man who'd proceeded them was waiting. She held up one hand. "This room has all that's left of our communications equipment, and it's our only lifeline to the rest of the Empire. There's a backup power system in the room that wasn't damaged, but we don't know how long it will last if we don't get power to the rest of the building. Though the communications array appears to be malfunctioning, the records stored on these servers might be all that's left of our world's history. Since we've been unable to contact others, we are currently operating as though we are the only survivors of this catastrophe."

The young man opened the door to allow them to pass through.

It took a moment for Iza's eyes to adjust to the dark room, but she recognized the angry gray-haired man who'd spoken out earlier.

At Iza's hesitation, the man took her hand into his; the calloused palms and worn fingers were warm against her skin. "I apologize for my outburst. I thought yours was the same ship that had come and gone hours ago, back when it may have made a difference. I was wrong, and I wish you no ill will. My name is Jaxon Davarro. My friends call me Jax."

Iza let the man apologize while holding her hand.

He suddenly released her, gaping at Trix. "She's an android?"

"She's a very sophisticated AI from the planet Lynaeda, and a member of my crew."

He nodded in understanding but didn't take his eyes off of Trix, as though taking her in a centimeter at a time. "Amelie, my wife would have been fascinated…" He shook his head, his eyes filling.

Iza didn't have to ask what happened to his wife. This time, it was her who reached out, placing a light hand on his shoulder and nodding.

Luxi turned back to business. "With the damaged communications, we've been unable to interface with the surveillance satellites to get details about the event. Perhaps your ship could access the records? We can provide the access codes."

"Yes, I can remotely interface," Trix confirmed.

Luxi provided her with the required credentials. "We'll need at least the data from 09:00 to 11:00 Adjusted Standard Time today."

Iza's eyes went wide. "This all happened in less than *two hours*?"

The large holodisplay broke into six sections as Trix relayed the requested information via her remote connection to the *Verity* and the satellite link.

Iza's mouth fell slack watching in horror as whole communities were swallowed up by the ground and replaced with ocean or forests. Another continent jutted out of the ground, rising into the sky until it seemed to touch the clouds. The violence of the transformation was so intense Iza had to turn away, tears filling her eyes.

"This is impossible." She shook her head in disbelief. "Trix, where are the Enforcers?"

"I am scanning the subspace communication logs, one moment." Trix's gaze looked distant as she processed the information. "It appears the planet's orbital communications hub was accessed by someone else before we arrived. They used an encryption code unassociated with the Enforcers or the TSS. I believe that the subspace link was disabled by them shortly after we picked up the distress call; that would explain why no other ships have responded."

Iza's heart sank. "Why would someone disable it?"

"They don't want us to get help," Luxi said bitterly.

"Or they're covering their tracks," Jax suggested. "Either way, it's too late now. We need to identify where the changes began and why."

"Can you restore the subspace communications link?" Iza asked Trix.

"Yes. I have also updated the distress call with the planet's current condition and the status of survivors."

"Good. Speaking of which, can you use the surveillance feed to pinpoint the epicenter of the event?"

"Processing."

While she waited for Trix's report, Iza regarded Luxi and Jax. They seemed to be doing a lot of the leading among their group. She admired them for stepping up into role; it certainly couldn't be a position Luxi would have wanted as an aspiring professor, though she realized she knew nothing about Jax's background. "What were you and your wife doing here, Jax?" she asked.

"I'm a maintenance worker," he replied. "My wife and I split the building, and she was working downstairs today of all days." Tears welled up in his eyes and he let them fall down his worn cheeks.

"Oh, I'm sorry. So the woman in the other room…?"

He wiped at his face with the back of his hand. "Oh, that's Pam. She's a chemistry professor. When everything happened, I was standing outside her classroom and got her to safety before it was too late. I'm glad I was able to save someone."

Luxi cleared her throat and wiped a tear from her face. "When I woke up this morning, I certainly didn't think I was going to be the spokeswoman for a remnant of survivors."

"You rose to the occasion, and that counts for a lot," Iza told her.

Trix came to attention. "Captain, I have located the epicenter of the event."

"What have you found?" Iza asked, eager to get any answers about the bizarre transformation of the planet.

"From the data received, it appears that the event emanated from a location in the southern hemisphere."

"That's all water now," Luxi said.

"I have synthesized the available data about the event, but, unfortunately, I cannot draw any conclusions based on the limited information collected from satellites," Trix stated. "The new ocean is approximately three-thousand six-hundred eighty-eight meters deep at its center, and I believe the cause of this planet's change originates there. A closer inspection will be required."

"Well, I guess it's time to go swimming," Iza pulled out her handheld. "Braedon, where are you?"

"Picking up a group of survivors with Karter."

"You're using the shuttle?"

"Yes, and don't bother yelling at me about not asking for permission first. We both know that you won't let these people suffer any more than I would." He wasn't wrong.

"Are there any more people that need to be brought in?" she asked.

"This is the last of the group that the locals know about right now. There are probably more, but there are weird energy readings that are making it difficult to tell people from the bushes, trees, and whatever else. It might be better to do a flyover at night and spot survivor groups by their campfires—assuming they build them."

It was smart thinking, though she hadn't considered they might still be here by nightfall—let alone needing to chase the planet's night around the globe. However, with the subspace communication beacon reactivated, the Enforcers should pick up the message and arrive soon; they would be equipped to offer proper assistance. The *Verity* only needed to stick around until then.

"You're doing good work, but we'll need to take a detour in a bit. We might have a lead on the origin of the transformation."

"Okay. Give me an hour to finish getting these people settled."

"All right." She turned to Trix. "In the meantime, can you figure out how to best get readings underwater? I don't know if the shuttle's sensors will do it, or if we'll need an underwater ROV, or…"

Trix nodded. "Luxi, do you have a robotics lab in this building that is still accessible?"

The woman bit her lip in thought for a moment. "I think there might be some accessible storerooms."

"I would appreciate the use of any parts you may have."

"They're yours. We want answers."

Iza nodded. "While you're working on that, Trix, I'm going to find some people to gather firewood. These folks are going to need to keep warm overnight, and without power, they'll need a fire for cooking."

The android tilted her head. "Cook what? There are no wild animals to hunt for food."

Iza scowled. "Well, let's tackle one issue at a time. I'll keep an eye out for potentially edible fruit or vegetation, though Cierra or one of the local scientists should lead that effort."

"I would gladly assist, but she will not want to work with me," Trix said, her voice had a hint of disappointment.

"Yeah, I know. She'll see you as a person eventually." Iza put a light hand on her shoulder. "If she doesn't, she'll get booted out of the airlock."

Trix smiled. "I doubt that, Mrs. Robin Hood."

"Don't you start with that mess, too. Let's get to work."

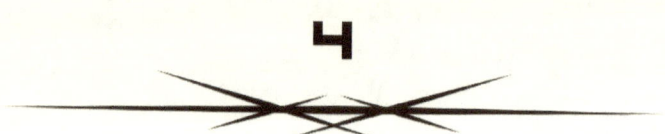

4

IZA DROPPED ANOTHER bundle of firewood near the camp that was beginning to take shape near the former University building. The branches were all too fresh and green to be good for fuel under normal circumstances, but she couldn't think of what else to offer the desperate people.

The distinct sound of a shuttle flying overhead drew everyone's attention.

"Finally, more help!" someone in the crowd shouted.

In the sky, Iza could just make out the distinct markings on the side of the landing shuttle, tying it to a very familiar ship.

"You have to be kidding me. *Them*?" The *Iron Dog* always seemed to be in the same place as the *Verity*. She wouldn't put it past Karter to have hired them to trail her ship.

Luxi, who was overseeing the organization of salvaged supplies nearby, looked at her questioningly.

"I hope that's not who I think it is," Iza said before she jogged to the grassy meadow.

"You recognize them?" Luxi asked as she limped over after her.

Iza kept her attention on the landing shuttle. "Our paths have crossed before. He's known to have shifting priorities, so don't get too excited about them being here to assist."

Once the shuttle was on the ground, the hatch opened. Captain Douketis and three members of his crew, including the pink-haired Reis, stepped off and onto the grass.

As he surveyed the people who'd run over to greet them, he immediately picked out Iza. "I'm surprised to see you here, Scrap Rat," he said.

"I'm sure you are," she said flatly.

"Why is it that whenever there's trouble, it's the rats that are the first to arrive?" Reis asked looking over the crowd with disdain before letting her eyes fall on Iza.

Atano, who'd been silent as he followed her up until now, growled at them. Douketis looked down at the dog with some confusion.

"Captain Douketis, what are you doing here?" Iza kept her tone dry and uninterested, though her heart was pounding in her chest. Her hand twitched at her side over her holstered pulse gun.

"We saw the distress call and came right away to see if these folks needed any help."

"Is that so? I didn't know you were so charitable."

Douketis chuckled like she'd made a joke. Iza ignored it and continued monitoring their movements. Their last encounter had ended with Iza making away with the goods and his crew being left behind for the Enforcers. She had no doubt the event was still fresh in his mind, even three months later. Reis smoothed her pink hair to one side. She sneered at Iza, not bothering to hide her true feelings the way Douketis did. The other two men seemed to be scanning the crowd for something. Iza looked behind them into the shuttle to see if they'd brought Viper, but there was no sign of her.

"What are you really up to?" Iza asked.

"No need to get your hair up." Douketis waved his hand

dismissively. "You're not the only one capable of helping these people."

'Capable', no; but 'willing', yes. I'd bet my ship that my crew is the only one here without an ulterior motive. Iza glared back at him. She'd had too many run-ins with the *Iron Dog* recently for it to be a coincidence that there were now here on this world. The implications were unpleasant any way she looked at it.

Luxi Song stepped forward, as if on cue. "My name is Luxi Song, and we're in the middle of rescue efforts and preparing for our first night on this changed world. We're happy for any assistance you can provide. At the moment, we're trying to track down the cause of our rapid global climate change."

Douketis put on his most charming smile, which only emphasized his dog-like features. "As soon as we got the distress call, we headed this way. When we arrived, we noticed a strange signal coming from the southern hemisphere. We tried to track it down, but it was underwater. I think the only way to find out what's really going on is to get under there and see for ourselves."

Already on it. Why in the stars is he really here? Iza evaluated him through narrowed eyes. "So, looking for others to do the hard work for you, as usual?"

He gave her a casual shrug. "We just don't have the equipment for deep-sea diving. We figured the people around here needed more immediate help. Let the Enforcers investigate. Isn't that their job, anyway?"

A few people in the crowd listening closely nodded and uttered their murmurs of agreement.

Iza didn't believe his innocent, altruistic act for a second. Nonetheless, she was curious to find out what may have caused the planet's transformation.

"I'm not willing to put my trust in Enforcers, who haven't

even arrived yet, to know for sure that whatever happened here isn't going to happen again in the middle of the night," Iza said, raising her voice. Then, she caught the terrified look of a mother and two children cowering in her arms. *Why can't I keep my big mouth shut sometimes?*

"Fine, then it's settled. We'll do some of the heavy lifting around here while you go deep-sea fishing," Douketis said, slapping her back as if they were old friends. "Be careful out there, Scrap Rat. You don't want to get eaten by some giant fish." He tipped his hat toward her.

Was this his intention all along—to get me away from here so he can take advantage of the situation? She couldn't say the words aloud, so she gave Luxi a look that might be interpreted as 'keep an eye on him'. Luxi seemed to understand because she gave an almost imperceptible nod.

"Great, let's get started," Douketis said as he rubbed his palms together. "Let's see if we can get some of this debris cleared and essential systems back up and running."

Reis inclined her head in response while two of his larger men followed her.

"Is my sister with them?" Cierra asked; she'd crept up on Iza's right shoulder from the trees. Iza was starting to get used to her barefooted stealth.

"I imagine so, though she didn't come down with the shuttle. Keep an eye on things around here while I'm gone," Iza instructed.

"Where are you going?"

"The southern hemisphere, to investigate what started all of this."

"I've seen to the worst of the injured other than Luxi. The new arrivals seemed to be more shaken up than injured."

"At least there's that little bit of good news."

The people on Uephus faced a difficult path ahead.

Rebuilding the infrastructure of cities and such could take decades, with the limited resources of the outer rim for a reason.

Iza went to meet Braedon, Karter, and Trix at the *Verity*'s shuttle. When she walked up, Braedon was seeing off the last group of rescued survivors. He turned his attention to Iza.

"Was that the *Iron Dog*'s shuttle I saw?" Braedon asked, his cheeks flushed an angry red.

"Yes, unfortunately. Douketis came down on a shuttle with three others to 'help out'," Iza said raising one eyebrow.

Braedon wrinkled his nose. "How in the stars were they, of all people, the next closest ship positioned to respond to the distress call?"

"I've been asking myself the same thing." She sighed. "At any rate, he confirmed what we already knew about the underwater disturbance in the southern hemisphere."

"You think he's actually here to help?" Braedon asked.

"Not in the least," Karter said.

Maybe it wasn't him who has them trailing us, after all. Iza nodded her agreement.

Karter shook his head pensively. "He's after something else but helping these people is a more urgent concern than dealing with Douketis."

Iza looked at Karter in surprise; she hadn't expected those words to come from him. "We should hurry. He might be helping out now, but he's no doubt here because there's something he can haul or steal off of this planet."

"They don't have anything left. You've seen these people," Braedon said with a wave of his hand.

"Yes, but look around," Karter said with an all-encompassing wave of his arm.

Iza took in the lush greenery, pristine and untouched beyond the building ruins underneath. The beauty of the place was unmistakable. However, she already knew what he meant.

"This place is untapped for its new natural resources," Karter continued. "They're looking for something other colonists would pay for, and we need to find and protect it before they do."

Of course, that's what they were doing. If there was something here in the rock or the water that could be sold, they wanted to be the first to find it for whoever it was they really answered to. However, with the pressing needs of the planet's people, it might delay them a little.

She glanced down at Atano. "Are you staying here, this time?" she said. The white dog stared up at her expectantly, wagging his tail, but didn't move. "Good choice."

"Karter, it might be better if you stay here with Atano and Cierra. But I'm warning you, if anything happens to my dog, I'm holding you personally responsible."

"You have my word." Karter raised his hands in the air; they were covered in dirt, as was the rest of his fine clothing. His cream-colored shirt bore wet stains under his arms, and the green vest and matching pants had various smudges of dirt as if he'd been lying on the ground at some point. A sheen of sweat still shown around his brow. Perhaps he'd already done more to help than she'd given him credit for.

"Oh, and Karter," Iza said, "take a shower. You're starting to smell." She couldn't hide her smile.

THE LAPPING WAVES of clear blue water were divided from the edge of the new southern continent by a sharp and jagged line. It looked as though the water filled up a gaping hole of land.

High above, the shuttle soared out toward the middle of the new ocean into the twilight.

Iza didn't have to see below the surface of the water to know there were no fish or any other signs of animal life. She had a bad feeling about the whole thing. Something was off about this planet, let alone the strange coincidence that she and Douketis had received the distress call but it had been shut off before the Enforcers could respond. Trix had reinitialized the signal over an hour ago.

Where are the Enforcers? This was a planet on the outer fringe of the Taran Empire, yes, but they were still citizens in need of assistance. *Where is their help when people needed it most?*

Braedon was like a little boy with a new toy as he looked over the underwater remotely operated vehicle Trix had constructed using parts salvaged in the University building. "I can't believe you built this so fast, Trix! Granted, it's not the prettiest thing, but—"

Iza pinched the bridge of her nose. "Braedon, please spare us the rundown of its specs."

"I was just going to ask about the camera—"

"We've reached the designated coordinates," Trix said, thankfully cutting off his chatter. "However, there's something wrong with the shuttle's instruments."

"How so?" Braedon put down his device and moved back to the pilot's seat. "We were having a few issues locking onto signatures earlier, but overall…" He stared at the read-out. "Oh no!"

"What?" Iza said standing up and looking over his shoulder as if she could read the code herself.

Braedon turned to stare at her. "Remember that alien virus we contracted back when we were carrying the sphere?"

"The one that disabled my ship and almost broke Trix? Of course, I do!"

"It's back."

They both turned as one to look at the android.

"Trix, how are you feeling?" Iza asked her.

"I'm feeling fine. How are you?" She didn't seem to pick up on their concern. Her eyes were focused on the shuttle's instruments.

"We need to hurry," Iza said. "That virus only ever showed up in the presence of the sphere, which means there's alien tech here. If that's what's causing these planetary changes, we can't stay here long."

Trix stood up from the pilot's chair, keeping her hands on the controls. "Braedon, please hold the craft in this position while I deploy the ROV."

"You've got it." He took over the flight controls.

Trix went to the back of the shuttle and opened the hatch.

Braedon kept the shuttle level, but the waves below lapped about in different directions contrary to their subtle movements. Iza's stomach did a nervous flip at the sight of the water below them, the black of it revealing nothing below the surface. She swallowed hard, focusing on the horizon instead of the drop.

"How long do you think it will take to find something?" Iza asked.

"Unknown, but I will work as quickly as possible." Trix turned on the ROV and it whirred to life. She dropped the mechanical drone into the water.

It sank below the waves as they watched on the holodisplay as Trix guided it remotely. Whatever had started this planetary change wasn't visible from the surface. The ROV's searchlight was bright, and Iza could see the glow of it on the surface for a few seconds before it disappeared from their view and she had to look at the monitor again. As suspected, there was nothing in the water itself. No fish, no fauna, nothing alive.

Until they got to the ocean floor.

The first mangled face that flashed in front of the camera's view startled all of them. The rest of the person's crushed and ruined body drifted by. Then another. And another—barely recognizable as people under the crushing weight of the ocean at that depth.

It didn't take long for them to realize that the ocean had formed on top of one of the cities. All of its residents, dead.

"How much farther to the signal's source?" Iza asked, unsuccessfully trying to quell the queasiness in her stomach as the corpses bumped against the drone.

"We're almost on top of it," Braedon replied, "but it's hard to pick up anything, there are so many bodies and destruction. The debris is thick here at the bottom."

Iza bit her lip. She'd been looking at the monitor for all of a minute before she realized she couldn't anymore. Then an idea came to her. The alien sphere had glowed brightly when it was activated as a gateway. Maybe the other tech did the same.

"Turn off the camera's light," she said.

"Navigation will be difficult without illumination," Trix objected.

"If you turn off the camera's light, you'll be able to see if there's anything glowing down there."

Braedon perked up. "So, you're working on the assumption that whatever is emitting the signal has some kind of radiance of its own. Interesting theory, though it's highly unlikely that we'd be able to see it through all the destruction."

Trix nodded. "I will caution, there is an increased risk of damage to the ROV's camera without clear visibility of its path."

"It's worth the risk. If we're right on top of it, like you said, we should be able to see *something*."

Trix cut the light. She then pivoted the ROV in a slow turn. Three-quarters of the way around, a blue glow filtered through several darkened objects.

"There!" Iza pointed on the holodisplay to the faint light pulsing on the other side of a fallen structure. "Can you move us in closer?"

"Yes, I will try," Trix acknowledged.

She alternated between the ROV's light and the illumination to create a route to the signal's source. Iza watched her maneuver the device through a collapsed building. A piece of debris fell just in front of the ROV.

"Look out!" Iza warned.

"Yes, I have it," Trix said calmly. She deftly maneuvered the drone around the threat.

Several more minutes and two more close calls and they were through the building. The light was brighter, though they couldn't make out the source. But what it illuminated made Iza gasp.

Here, buildings rended from their foundations were twisted into crumpled knots. Corpses and household items floated amidst the structural ruins. The amount of death and destruction concealed under the artificial ocean made her sick.

Trix kept her focus on controlling the ROV until they could see the light's source.

Braedon's eyes widened. "What is that?"

An oval field of light was nestled between toppled stone columns, rippling slightly like a pond within the ocean. Positioned on a nearby column was an unmistakable form the size of Iza's fist.

"A sphere," she murmured, and swallowed hard.

Braedon paled. "There are more of them?"

"Maybe? Or the TSS lost control of the one we handed over."

Trix moved the drone closer, and the small sphere turned like an eye looking back at them. Iza shuddered.

Braedon stared at the light with wonder. "Does this mean that's a…?"

"A Gate," Iza confirmed. She couldn't shake the feeling of electricity that enveloped her, just as it had when Raquel had pushed her through the Gate on the *Arvonen One*. She'd wound up on the other side in a cool, dry cavern—alone, or so it seemed. Perhaps it had been a monitored location at one time, but she hadn't dallied in the cavern before trying to get back. It was the return trip that had been the most trouble, when a force had grabbed onto her and tried to prevent her return. If Joe hadn't been there to pull her through, she might not have made it.

Iza tensed as the drone neared the event horizon to get a better look at the sphere's etchings. "Careful! Don't get too close." The words were out a second too late.

As soon as the small device was close enough to read the

inscriptions, it was swept up into the ring of light. The camera feed cut out. Iza had no way of knowing if the drone would be disintegrated like the people Victor Arvonen had forced through, or if it would make it through to the other side. Either way, the drone was lost.

"Guess, we're not getting that back," Iza muttered as the video feed from the drone went dead on the shuttle's front display.

The shuttle bucked and a gust of air rushed through the open hatch in the rear, which had been left open when they released the drone. Iza's skin tingled, sensing a change in the atmosphere. She was quick to recover and scrambled toward the back of the craft to close the hatch with the manual lever.

"The climate is under flux," Trix reported. "Gale-force winds originating from this area are sweeping north, along with seismic activity affecting all continents."

"What?" Iza ran back to the front of the shuttle and strapped in. Red alerts were flashing across the console and holodisplay. "Get us out of here and back to the survivor's compound!"

"That is going to be difficult," Trix warned. "The intensity of the winds are extreme enough to blow us off course. Navigation control will be compromised."

"We've gotta set down. These winds could tear the shuttle apart," Braedon said.

Iza didn't like the look of the electrical storm around them. If the shuttle was struck, it might cripple them permanently. The risk wasn't worth the trouble. They wouldn't be able to help anyone if they needed to be rescued themselves.

The hairs on her arms stood on end as one of her dreams from when she had the sphere came back to her. A storm cast a black shadow over everything. The sight outside now was so close to the dream that she gaped at the menacing clouds, everything else around her disappearing.

"Iz!" Braedon's frantic voice pulled her back from the memory. He was fighting to control the ship.

She snapped back to the present. "Find a place set us down. Keep scanning for any transmissions. We need to warn the others."

"I believe it is too late for that. The planet has already started to transform again."

Trix and Braedon fought the storm all the way to the shore. They managed to set the shuttle down between two clumps of trees. A small rock formation to the east thankfully blocked some of the wind and debris, offering just enough protection to avoid being swept away in the gale.

"We should maintain cover here until the changes to the planet's surface subside," Trix said.

The shuttle shook as the ground heaved under them, and Iza's worried gaze met Braedon's.

"Is there any chance we could be swallowed up whole here?" she asked.

Trix was quick to answer. "Yes, there is a—"

"No!" Braedon and Iza both yelled at the same time.

The last thing either of them wanted to know was the actual percentage chance of their demise. Instead, they huddled together in the shuttle as it rocked back and forth while the wind whipped new tree branches, pebbles, and dirt against the hull and the ground shook from distant quakes.

After fifteen minutes, the shaking stopped.

Iza let out a long breath. "Wow, that was—"

Without warning, the shuttle powered down, all displays going dark. At the same moment, Trix jerked and then froze.

"Trix, are you okay?" Braedon asked.

"Trix?" Iza gently shook her shoulder. The android's head was tilted at an odd angle and her hands were down at her sides. Iza turned to Braedon, hoping for an explanation. "Were we hit with something like an EMP?"

"No clue." Braedon tapped on the controls but they were unresponsive. "I can't—"

The main console sprang to life again, flashing with scrolling code and alien characters.

Braedon swore. "It's the virus! Looks like it's progressing through the ship's systems."

Trix's head suddenly lifted. Her eyes were blank as she spoke. "You have broken the treaty. The Gatekeepers have returned." The creepy monotone accentuated by the lower octave.

Iza and Braedon looked from each other back to Trix.

Iza reached for Trix. "Who are you?"

"We are the Gatekeepers. This vessel is serving our purpose. Your actions are an act of war, and your kind will be wiped out now, the way they should have been before."

Iza didn't have a chance to back away before Trix's hand gripped her neck. Trix stood up, lifting Iza into the air until her head was pressed to the roof of the shuttle. Iza could feel her airway being cut off as she kicked and struggled to get free. Every move she made only tightened Trix's grip on her. The tightness of her larynx brought tears to her eyes. Soon, her vision blurred and a cloud of black closed in from her peripheral vision until all she could see was Trix's determined face.

Then, she was dreaming again, like before when the sphere had been on the ship with her all those months ago. The colors in her dream were so vivid that she struggled to take them all in. The breeze on her skin lifted the hair at her neck. Chilled, she went to rub her arms but then two arms embraced her, cradling her and providing warmth. The solid frame behind her was Joe; she'd know him anywhere. The scent of his soap made her smile as he kissed the spot in her hair closest to his mouth.

"You can't do this alone," she heard him say with a sigh, picking up like they'd been deep in discussion.

"I don't have a choice," she replied—an automatic response, even in her dreams.

Joe turned her to face him, still keeping his arms wrapped around hers. He rested his forehead on hers. "Yes, you do. I'll always stand with you. Promise me you won't do this without me."

Iza turned her face up to him. His blue eyes bored into hers with all the hope and promise he'd shown the day he'd been taken away.

"Besides look what will happen if you don't." Joe pulled away, his hands sliding down her arms to take hold of her hands.

For the first time, she saw they weren't just standing on the top of some random mountain. Under them were bodies. Dead bodies with blank stares for as far as she could see. She made out Braedon and Cierra before she caught a glimpse of Trix lying dismembered only a meter from where they stood.

"Promise me," Joe said, his insistence pulling her attention back to him.

Iza tried to swallow the bile in her throat before she whispered the words. "I promise."

Pain shot up the back of her neck and Joe's hands let go of hers. She reached out for him while at the same time she groaned as the movement made the pain worse.

When her eyes opened, there were still stars swimming in her vision. Braedon sat at her side holding the plastic oxygen mask over her face. She breathed in the air deeply, but her neck was so sore and her body so weak she couldn't lift an arm to hold the mask herself. He was whispering something soothing.

"Iz, are you okay? Can you hear me?" Braedon tilted her head toward his and his light brown eyes stared back into hers with concern.

"Don't get any ideas," she croaked.

He hugged her and his body relaxed against her with relief. Then he let out a laugh. "I thought she was going to kill you."

"What happened?"

"I don't know, but when her voice changed, I knew it had to be the virus. I ran the debugging program while she was talking. It took a minute to reach her system. I'm sorry."

Iza tapped his arm weakly to signal she was ready to try and sit up.

"Take it slow, you hit the ground before I could reach you. You banged your head pretty hard."

Iza managed to get on all fours and hold back the nausea that swept over her, though it made her sweat. When the room stopped spinning, she got her feet under her and Braedon helped her to the bench seat. Trix stood in the middle of the floor with her hands now down at her sides and her head tilted to one side. Her eyes were blank and her body lifeless.

"Why isn't she back to her old self like before?"

"I don't know. The virus is out of her system and we've got power back to the shuttle. She should be fine now."

"This is all connected to that bomaxed sphere," Iza said, her hands balling into fists. "Get us back to the settlement. We need to see if everyone else is okay."

"Do you think the reason the planet started transforming again was because of us?" The guilt was already there in Braedon's eyes, and Iza figured it was also on her own.

She looked back at Trix, still blank-eyed and unmoving. "I don't know, but whatever the reason, we should help these people. Do you think there's a way to jam the sphere's signal the way you do with the virus?"

Braedon blinked twice at her. "I don't know, I've never thought of it that way."

"I want you to try. Contact Douketis and let him know that Viper should be working on it too, though I can't guarantee he'll see reason and allow you to work together. In the meantime, I want Trix protected from this virus. Now!"

"You got it, Iz." Braedon turned to the console and typed in the coordinates to get them back to the settlement. "Should I let them know we're coming?"

"Yes, connect me with Luxi."

Braedon frowned. "I'm not getting a response."

"Okay, just get us back."

Once the shuttle was airborne, Iza looked out the viewport and down at the new damage to the planet's surface. New hills had thrust upward in some places, and chasms had opened in others. Even now, foliage was rapidly growing over the newly exposed ground.

Her amazement turned to horror as the approached the settlement site.

"Stars! Look at that," Braedon exclaimed.

Iza gaped at the new valley that led from the new ocean back to the settlement. The University building was now split in half along two sides of the chasm.

"Cierra." Braedon breathed her name as if he'd been holding it in.

We left her and Karter behind. Were they still in the building when this happened? Iza could only hope not. Though, that is where they'd left the injured.

"I'm sure she's okay, but if anyone was in there, we need to get them out."

"Hold on, I'm getting a call from Douketis," Braedon said.

"Ugh, he always has the worst timing! Can you handle him and then start working on a signal blocker for the sphere? I'll go and check for survivors."

Braedon swallowed, staring down at the console and then back at her. It was clear he didn't want to be on the sidelines of the rescue, but she imagined he also didn't want to be the one to find Cierra's body if she'd been killed.

"I'll find her," Iza said, forcing the confidence she didn't feel into her voice.

He nodded faintly as he moved the shuttle into position to let her out.

Iza looked Trix over one more time. She was clear of the sphere and the virus, so why was she still shut down? Iza didn't have time to figure it out. There were other people in more immediate danger. Maybe her system needed to reboot itself as it had back on Hubyria when the EMP went off. They'd just have to wait.

She hopped down from the shuttle. Iza was becoming accustomed to the eerie silence after the climate changes here. The shuttle's engine quieted enough for her to hear something in the trees to her left.

Iza waited, unsure of what was making the sound but not ready to turn her back on whatever it was. Then the bushes parted and Atano limped out, his left paw gingerly tucked close to his chest. Iza rushed forward and closed the gap between them, worried he'd do something foolish. When she reached for his paw, he pulled back. He started limping away from her on three paws, heading for the western half of the building.

"Atano, wait, you're in no condition to run," Iza called after him, but he didn't turn at the sound of her voice nor did he stop moving toward the building. The building had been in shambles when they found it earlier that day; now it was almost completely devastated.

Oh, no! What about the children and everyone that was in the building? Did they make it out?

Iza stamped down her worries as she followed Atano to the safest-looking entry at the new ground level, careful to avoid the steep-walled valley; it was deeper than it had looked from above. The damage to the building was more extensive than she imagined from the outside; it could fall on top of her any minute.

"That's far enough, boy. Go on, I'll find them." Iza pointed back out the door and held her stance until he obeyed. He sat down in front of the gap, holding up his injured paw.

She stepped further inside and cupped her hands on either side of her mouth and called out. "Hello, anybody in here?"

Iza's voice echoed back to her, but there was nothing else.

She was about to venture deeper when several loose chunks of concrete cascaded down the rubble toward her. She stepped aside to avoid them just in time to hear a cough from inside.

IZA SCRAMBLED OVER the debris covering half of the first floor as she moved toward the coughing. "I hear you. Where are you?"

"Here." The voice was distinctly male and familiar, though he couldn't seem to get another word out due to the coughing.

She turned into one of the rooms. Dust was floating all around, and a small fire burned in one corner. Karter lay in a heap against the opposite wall, trapped under collapsed segments of the walls and ceiling.

"Hang on, I'll get you out," Iza said shoving away a heavy structural beam that had pinned him to the spot. Smaller chunks of concrete had pummeled his body, but she didn't see signs of any massive trauma.

"Did they get out?" he asked, his voice faint and raspy from the dust and smoke.

"Who?"

Karter coughed through the smoke. "The others."

"I haven't seen any others. Atano led me the entrance and I came straight here when I heard you coughing. Are there more people inside?"

"No, we saw it coming. Got everyone out," Karter tried to fight off another uncontrollable coughing fit. "We were the last."

"We?"

Karter shifted, and that's when Iza saw the little girl. Her eyes were closed, but she was breathing.

"Take her and get her out of here," Karter said, cradling his ribs. He slowly started to stand using the ruined wall for support, but it was obvious he'd need assistance to navigate the treacherous rubble.

"Take it slow," Iza said. She lifted the limp girl into her arms, her slender limbs dangling.

Iza had taken no more than a step when the building shifted again, causing more dust and debris to rain down. She looked back at Karter. She couldn't get them both out.

"Go," Karter said, waving at her to escape with the child.

If only Trix was here, then we could get them both. Where is everyone else?

Iza shifted the girl to her shoulder so she could use her other hand to keep them upright over the debris. When she reached the door, she saw Braedon running toward the building, his eyes filled with worry.

For once, Iza was relieved that Braedon hadn't followed her orders. "Karter is still inside!" she yelled.

"Douketis is on his way," Braedon told her as he ran without hesitation into the building.

The little girl slung over Iza's shoulder had become heavy, and now she couldn't carry her any further. She gently put the girl down on the grassy ground. Her small chest was moving up and down, but her eyes were still closed.

Iza sat down to catch her breath. She looked up as Braedon emerged from the building with Karter leaning against him. Karter's leg was bleeding underneath the fine suit pants that now hung in tatters around his calf. He limped along until they reached Iza. Braedon eased Karter down and Iza took a closer look at his leg.

"You're going to need that cleaned, and soon," she said.

Karter winced and nodded. The effort it had taken to get outside had left him drenched with sweat.

The building shifted again and there was a large collapse inside, blowing out more dust and debris. They were far enough not to be injured as the structure started to fall in on itself, but the dust cloud whooshed out to envelop them. Iza covered the girl while Braedon did his best to shelter Karter.

A cry sounded from the trees. People streamed out of the brush and ran toward the ruined building. A woman with long blonde hair and dirt smeared on her face fell to her knees in anguish and sobbed into her hands. None of the people in the crowd had seemed to notice the four of them sitting down on the grass.

"Cierra?" Braedon stood up and called into the mass of people.

Tense moments passed as Braedon continued his search through the grief-stricken crowd. Then, Cierra stepped forward trembling, dirt and blood staining her delicate green shift. He ran to her and lifted her into his arms. Their display of emotion so touching Iza had to look away.

"My baby!" The woman with the long blonde hair who'd been on her knees came rushing over when she saw her daughter where Iza had set her on the ground. Still sobbing, she lifted the girl into her arms and rocked her unconscious form back and forth.

The girl coughed and her eyes fluttered open. "Mommy?"

The mother was so overcome with emotion she couldn't speak, but she nodded without taking her eyes off of her daughter.

Braedon released Cierra from his embrace, but he kept his fingers entwined with hers as they approached Iza and Karter.

"Let me see to your leg." Cierra knelt down in front of Karter.

"Iza, your neck," Karter said. It must have been bruising already. "Did this happen where you were, too?" Karter winced as Cierra began tending to his wound.

Iza took in a deep breath and nodded. "We think we know what's causing the climatic shifts on this planet."

"Good, because I'd love to get off this planet and back to the ship. We've done enough heroism for one day." Karter looked like he'd been trampled by hooved beasts in a stampede. She couldn't blame him for wanting to be off this world, but she had to tell them all about the sphere.

Before Iza could elaborate, she saw Luxi limping toward her, covered in dust. Based on the grim expression on the woman's face, there must have still been lots of people inside the building when it went down. Iza glanced over the crowd and didn't see the old man Jax.

"Did Jaxon...?" Iza asked dreading the answer.

Luxi shook her head.

Iza noted the familiar stone in her gut. *Why does everyone around me get hurt?* She tried to focus, biting down on the inside of her cheek at the disappointment.

"What happened to your neck?" Luxi asked.

Iza gestured for Braedon to head back to the shuttle and continue with the coding project he should have been working on already. Then she lifted a hand to her neck; it must look pretty bad if everyone was noticing it.

She figured Luxi wouldn't sit unless she did, so she gestured to the grass and sat down where she could watch Cierra tend to Karter's leg. Atano decided he was ready to be held and scooted in so she could wrap an arm around him, though he still held his paw gingerly out of reach. Luxi joined her and Iza began her story. It took much longer to recount their expedition due to interruptions of hacking and coughing. At some point, someone brought Iza some water and she gulped it down, the coolness easing her aching throat. Luxi listened without saying a word, finally allowing Cierra to tend to her injuries from hours before.

When Iza finished, Luxi nodded once. "This could happen again, and we aren't safe here." She glanced over her shoulder at the others gathered outside the building. "Any of us."

"I don't have the space to evacuate you," Iza told her. "There may even be more pockets of people that haven't been found yet. I'm not sure what to do."

Luxi looked over to Douketis, who was approaching from the field, which was now two hundred meters from its original location. He was escorting a group of survivors from the shuttle.

Iza sighed. As much as she didn't like the man, he did seem to be following through on his promise to assist, at least a little. She waved.

Douketis sauntered over, not a speck of dust on him.

Luxi gave him a weak but grateful smile. "We appreciate all you've done." When Iza raised her eyebrow questioningly, Luxi added, "Douketis used his shuttle to get people off of the upper floors of the building before it collapsed. We couldn't have survived without him."

Douketis bobbed his head. "Just doing our part."

"I'm sure." Iza rolled her eyes, still not convinced he had altruistic intentions.

A roar sounded overhead. She looked up to see three sleek shuttles descending toward the landing sight.

"Looks like we don't have to worry about anything else now. The Enforcers have finally arrived," Karter said.

"Well, I guess that's our cue to leave," Douketis said. He tapped two fingers to his hat and winked at Iza. "See you around."

"Douketis," she replied with a curt nod.

"Scrap Rat," Douketis said as he turned on his heel.

"Scrap Rat?" Luxi asked.

Iza waved the question away with a hand. "It's a long story." Iza stood up, lifting Atano and hugging him to her hip so he wouldn't attempt to run after her.

Douketis and the limited crew who'd accompanied him on the *Iron Dog*'s shuttle jogged back to their craft and lifted off moments before the Enforcers touched down.

"I better go and see who's in charge," Iza said. She walked over to meet the Enforcer who stepped out in front giving orders.

He removed his helmet while the others stood in formation, awaiting further instruction. Their tailored gray uniforms with black accents seemed out of place against the backdrop of bright, vibrant green.

Iza held up a hand in the formal greeting. "It's about time you got here. These people have been waiting for aid for almost a day."

His brow furrowed at her sharp tone. "I'm Captain Brontes. And you are?" the man asked.

"Captain Sundari, of the starship *Verity*. We were passing through when we got the distress call from these folks requesting help."

"We'll take it from here, Captain." The man brushed past her.

"Really, with one Guard ship?" Iza raised an eyebrow. "I'd think you'd want all of the help you could get."

"Under most circumstances, yes," the officer replied. "But we pulled your record, and you have some... history. These people don't need any more taken from them."

"I would never—" Iza started to protest.

"Thank you for your assistance thus far, Captain. As I said, we'll take over now," Brontes said. He turned his attention to the crowd, ignoring Iza's choked response, "Is there someone who can speak for your people?"

"I'm Luxi Song. We require evacuation, Captain. I hope you can accommodate us."

"Before we discuss evacuation, we'll need to get up to speed on exactly what happened here," he said, speaking around her. "Mathers, Saelin, get any information you can from their communications array. Korsek, take your team to see if there's any equipment that can be salvaged. I want to know exactly what happened here."

Iza cleared her throat. "I might be able to help you with that, Captain."

He glanced down at her and eyed the dog with disdain. "I thought you were just passing through? Your work here is done."

Iza was about to correct him and explain the strange message that had been relayed through Trix, but the man's attitude grated on her. Saying anything would make it just as likely that she'd end up in a jail cell rather than be thanked for passing on critical information. So, she kept her mouth shut as the Enforcer office began barking out orders to his team.

"Baelsen, lead the distribution of water and food to the survivors. Alani, I want your team on transports—find any other pockets of survivors on the planet." Captain Brontes didn't wait for Iza or the others to even say goodbye. "We need shelter for these people. Trent, see if you can find any buildings still intact, and we'll begin moving the survivors there."

Iza huffed before turning back to Luxi. "I wish you and your people the best. If you ever need me, just reach out."

"I will, Captain. Thank you again for all your assistance." Luxi lifted her hand and Iza did the same.

Then, with a nod to Cierra, the two of them helped Karter up and headed back to their shuttle. They set Karter down on the bench in the back.

"Time to go. Any luck?" Iza asked Braedon, who was hunched over the console in thought.

"I finally got in touch with Viper on the *Iron Dog*, and she's working on the virus, too. We'll try to figure out if we can use the antivirus to disable the sphere so it can't do any more harm to the planet."

Karter looked over from his place on the bench and noticed Trix, still rigid and vacant-eyed. "What's wrong with her?" he asked.

Iza sighed placing Atano on the floor next to Karter. "This bomaxed alien virus is dead-set on ruining my day, that's what," Iza grumbled, then stepped gingerly around Trix's lifeless form in the middle of the shuttle, followed by Cierra, who seemed even more unnerved by the android than normal.

"Once we get to the *Verity*, we can run a diagnostic," Braedon said as Iza sat down in the seat beside him.

"Then what are you waiting for?"

— — —

Ian Mandren viewed the latest report on his viewscreen in disbelief. He ran his fingers through his light-brown hair and pulled out his handheld.

"CACI, a message for the High Commander: We need to meet, now."

"Message sent," the AI replied.

Ian shook his head again at the reported death toll. He'd requested an update after one of his Initiate trainees from a small, dusty planet in the outer colonies informed him that her parents were missing. She'd been in his office crying most of the morning, and once he'd seen the report from the local Enforcers, it was clear this was something the High Commander needed to know.

The ping on his handheld came a minute later, and he gathered himself to go and meet with Wil Sietinen in his office. Even after years of Wil holding the position of High Commander, it still felt odd to meet with him in such a formal way. Ian had trained directly with Wil as young man, part of the first team of Primus Elite Agents in the TSS. Looking back, it felt like eons before the Bakzen War. A lifetime ago. It was a thrilling time—studying alongside their new commander—the Cadicle himself—as he taught them to reach beyond all previously set limits, in a desperate bid to save the Taran Empire. Ian's life had forever changed, and he didn't regret it for a moment. But he'd thought that winning the war would be the end of it—not that new threats to the galaxy would keep popping up. Then again, true peace would be rather boring.

Almost to Wil's office, he remembered the gift sitting on his desk. Wil and Saera's wedding anniversary had been the week before, and he'd already forgotten the present twice. Admittedly, he wasn't good with that kind of thing, but he'd known them since the beginning, and he beat himself up for not remembering it.

When he reached the High Commander's office, he found one of the large wooden doors open. Ian stepped inside to and find Wil staring at the holodisplay above his desk, rubbing his chin in reflection. He'd chosen to keep the leather couch and the carved wooden desk that his father had used when he was High Commander, which had also belonged to the High Commander before him—a close family friend. It suited the office more than it suited Wil, though Ian couldn't imagine the room without it.

"Did you see the report I sent you?" Ian asked without preamble.

"I did. Have a seat."

Ian took a breath. He'd already barged into the man's office without even a greeting. "I'm sorry, I've had a devastated Initiate in my office worried about her missing family all morning. This thing has completely derailed my day."

"Were she any more advanced than an Initiate, I'd worry about her disposition."

"Yeah, she's still green. But her potential is off the charts," Ian said.

Wil raised an eyebrow.

Ian realized his mistake in wording. "Not *actually* off the charts like you, but high. Above 9, easy. Anyway, it was a task just to get her to stay at Headquarters and not go running off to Uephus to find her family."

Wil nodded but remained silent.

Does he know something? "Any idea what's going on?"

Wil stared at the wall behind Ian as if he could read the answers in the rustic landscape holopainting. "No. It's unnatural, and it's wiped out a planet of people. We need to keep an eye on the Outer Colonies. The people out there are going to be frightened and confused. We don't have the resources to cover every planet and watch for transformations."

"It's bizarre. Has there ever been anything else like this?"

"Not to my knowledge, but there's a lot that was lost during the previous Revolution."

Though Ian knew it was unfair to expect Wil to immediately have all the answers, he certainly felt better when that was the case. For now, it seemed he'd have to wait.

"Do what you can for your Initiate," Wil continued. "You

were right to keep her here. It's too dangerous for her to return to her world before we know exactly what's causing these transformations."

"Yeah, I'll figure out something to tell her."

"Remember when we first met?" Wil asked after a moment. It seemed out of nowhere, but Ian knew better; Wil had always been wise beyond his years, and he didn't ask questions just to hear himself speak.

"Yes, like it was yesterday."

Wil folded his hands on the desktop. "You may recall that one of the first things I told you and the other Primus Elites was that I'd do anything for the person I loved most, Saera— though I didn't give her name at the time. I think half of you thought I was crazy for leading with that."

"It did set a tone," Ian said.

"What I didn't say then is why I felt that was important information to share. Yes, it was in the context of the biases I may hold and how that could impact me as a leader, but that's not all there was to it. Every single one of you Primus Elite trainees came to the TSS with strong ties. It was one of my selection criteria, in fact. It's been my long-held belief that you'll fight harder for something specific than you ever would for a vague idea. Parents, a friend, a lover—it's the people closest to us that come to mind in the dark moments when we need a reminder about why it's worth it to push through the pain. Those people we care about can be our greatest vulnerability, but they are also our greatest source of strength."

"I agree. But what does that say about a perennial bachelor like me?" he said with a smirk.

Wil smiled. "Clearly, that you have an unhealthy infatuation with your work and need to get laid more often."

Ian laughed. "That is undoubtedly true."

"Anyway, my point is that your Initiate is emotional

because she cares deeply for her home and loved ones. That kind of passion is what makes the best Agents. Teach her to harness those feelings as motivation to accomplish mission objects, and she'll be unstoppable."

Ian nodded. "I'll do that. Thanks." Ian rose from his chair. "Oh, speaking of Saera, how was your anniversary?"

"Busy."

"I understand," Ian said. He did understand. Wil's normalcy in life could be counted on one hand. He and Saera had done right by raising their children on Earth where they could have a more conventional childhood.

"By the way, how's Joe settling in on Earth?" Wil asked.

Ian's eyebrows drew together. He knew his friend wouldn't read his mind outright, but there were times he seemed to pick up his stray thoughts as if they were floating in the air between them. He sighed, picturing the look on Joe's face when he'd been sent away. Joe had shown some promise as an Agent, but his stubborn disposition had proved to be too much to overcome. "He's found employment, though it won't be satisfying to someone even at his level. He made a lousy TSS officer, but he'll be bored to tears on that planet. I can barely keep the officers tracking him engaged."

"It doesn't matter. Keep monitoring his situation. I believe he's still a target."

"A target?" Ian's eyebrows rose to his hairline. "Why?"

Wil shook his head. Ian wasn't sure if that meant he didn't know, or he wasn't going to say. "Let me know if anything changes," Wil said without elaborating.

"Yes, of course," Ian said. In his mind, he stumbled over the overabundance of questions that sprang up.

It seemed that was all Wil was going to say on the matter, so he changed the subject. "I've got an anniversary gift for you in my office; it's been there for two weeks. One of these days

I'll remember to give it to you."

"Is that a subtle hint that I should come by and visit you next time?"

"No, but I'm just saying it out loud, so maybe I'll actually remember to bring it." Ian smiled as he left. He didn't expect Wil to come to his office. The High Commander was far too busy saving the universe.

7

KARTER DIDN'T LIKE how Iza was looking at him differently—like he'd finally earned a measure of respect in her eyes. It made what came next that much more difficult.

The small shuttle that they'd been using had seen better days, but it managed to get them back to the *Verity* without any problem. Their departure from Uephus had been expedited by the local Enforcers, who'd decided that there was only room for one set of heroes. They weren't wrong so much as greedy. Karter knew a little about that.

"Why don't you go get cleaned up. There are booster nanite injections available in the infirmary," Iza said, her voice echoing off the empty cargo hold as they exited the shuttle.

Karter followed her, leaning on Braedon for support. *Why does she care whether or not my leg falls off?* There could only be one explanation for it: what he'd done for the little girl. He still remembered the feeling of being buried alive as he held onto the child, shielding her tiny body with his own.

"I'm fine." Karter let go of Braedon as if to prove it. "We don't need to use up our resources on something that will heal on its own in a few days."

Iza stopped short and turned to glare at him while Braedon

and Cierra hurried past, neither of them making a sound. Even the dog seemed to give them a wide berth as he trotted over to wait at the foot of the stairs.

Iza used her height to her advantage, squaring her shoulders and tilting her head back so she could look down at him. It was one of her favorite postures, but he tired of it. "What do you mean by 'our' supplies?" she asked.

"I didn't mean to imply anything." Karter had learned not to respond when Iza was threatened. "We should talk about what's next."

She raised an eyebrow in question but didn't speak as she folded her arms.

"Like it or not, we're still engaged," he continued. "It would not be wise for me to make any major changes that might scare off my business investors, considering my delicate situation at present."

Iza sauntered forward until they were almost nose-to-nose. "Let me be transparent about something," she said through gritted teeth. "I don't care a bomaxed flying fruit what your investors think. You and I are *not* getting married. In fact, this engagement contract is going to come to a swift end when I throw you out the airlock."

Without her android friend for backup, the threat didn't bear any teeth. But, Iza was resourceful, and it was clear she'd made up her mind about him a long time ago. No singular redeeming action could warm her to him, only elevate him to the status of a person rather than a parasite.

"There is one way you could get me out of the contract," he said.

"Yes, I know. Find you someone else. I think you and I both know you're into your assistant, Becca, and there's no one else willing to tolerate your ridiculousness."

"Yes, I think we're in agreement there." Karter noted the

slight widening of her eyes.

"So, you're finally willing to admit it? Well, that's a start. How soon can we get you two together and get you off of my ship?"

"Although I'll admit to having more than platonic feelings for my assistant, I cannot for certain say that she's equally as interested, or willing, to live out her days married to someone as insufferable as me."

"Stop with all the false modesty. She's into you, and we both know it. All you have to do is grow a pair and ask her." Iza gave him a light poke to the shoulder then refolded her arms over her chest.

"It's not going to be so easy. My mother has been trying to turn Apex investors away from me for months, and the one thing I have on her is you at the moment. If I drop you for someone else, it will give the impression I'm as fickle-minded in my business dealings as I am in my personal life. Not to mention, Mother made it clear that employees aren't spouse material."

Iza dropped her arms to her hips. "So, what exactly are you proposing?"

"I think it will go over a lot better with my business associates if there's some reason for them to sympathize with me—a man whose fiancée has gone off after someone else might be a bit more sympathetic than one who trades one woman for another."

Iza bit her bottom lip in thought. She had no idea how attractive it made her. He pushed the thought down reminding himself of the larger picture.

"I see. You want me to play the bad girl so you can come out looking like the innocent."

"I convince people I'm heartbroken. Then, I turn to my assistant who's always been there..." He left his thought unspoken so she could fill in the rest.

Iza nodded with understanding. She was quick to figure things out; that's one of the things he loved and hated about her. As long as he could keep the rest of his plans to himself, everything would work out. But maintaining that measure of secrecy was difficult with a telepath around. There was a hard line between not thinking about something and drawing attention to something by trying not to think about it.

"Fine, then. Let's go get my boyfriend so I can get rid of my fiancé," Iza said. "Braedon you can come out now."

Braedon stepped back into view at the top of the stairs. To Karter's horror, it seemed he and Cierra had been listening out of sight the entire time. Karter tightened his jaw, biting down on the anger that swelled up in him at being so violated.

"Set a course for Lynaeda," Iza instructed, unfazed. "Once Trix is better, we're going to go on to Earth."

"You got it. But I don't think we'll need to stop at Lynaeda."

"Why not?"

"Because Trix is up and running again."

"How do you know that?" Iza asked.

"Because she's right behind you." Braedon pointed behind them.

Karter turned to see Trix standing at the entrance of the shuttle, as if waiting for them to address her.

"Trix! Are you all right?" Iza raced to the android, looking her over.

"Yes, my systems are functioning normally again. The virus is gone."

To Karter, she looked as she always had. Her brown hair was pulled into a perfect plait and her eyes took in her surroundings, missing a measure of depth he'd expect to see in a person.

Braedon jogged over to get a better look at her while Iza stepped back. "What took you so long to come out of it this time?"

Trix looked up at him as he approached her. "After the virus took control of my systems, I created a backdoor, which, if triggered, would roll back my systems to my last backup. However, I needed to be back on the *Verity* in order for the system to fully restore. Before that, I detect that I underwent a hard shutdown?"

"You had Iza by the throat. I had to," Braedon said his voice apologetic.

Could she really have hurt feelings? Karter watched with interest as Trix described her sentience being pushed to one side while the alien virus animated her body.

"You acted appropriately by shutting me down," Trix assured Braedon. "It prevented further damage and allowed an error log to be made of the virus' activities. Using this information, I have been able to write in code to protect me from being used by the alien virus again to hurt any one of my friends."

Karter stared in wonder. She was remarkable, but something about the way she casually said she rewrote her system's programming made the hair on his arms stand on end.

"Well, I'm just glad you're okay." Iza gave her a hug.

"Would you be willing to let me take a look at your new code?" Braedon asked. "It might help us solve another problem we've been working on."

Trix paused for a moment as if measuring his trustworthiness. Then she nodded. "That is acceptable. I am available to assist with your project in any way that would be useful."

"Good, we can work on it while we're underway."

Braedon's eyes lit up. "If I heard right, I think we're about to go on a side quest?"

Iza nodded. "Sure, I guess we can call it that. Set a course for Earth. It's going to take us some time to get there, and I'm going to need to read up on Earth's culture before we arrive."

"Yes, Captain," Trix acknowledged.

Braedon clapped his hands together. "Earth! I can't wait. Boy, is Joe going to be shocked when we show up…"

"Or upset that we did not come for him sooner," Trix countered while the two of them walked up the stairs toward the flight deck.

Iza seemed to remember Karter was still there. "Well, I suggest you get ready for departure, because it looks like we're picking up Joe sooner than we thought. Let me know if you need help packing," she said.

Despite her attitude, there was a slight shift in her eye when she spoke about heading to Earth. She was worried about going there. It wasn't like they were free to enter orbit and then fly to his front door and knock.

"Don't worry, I'll help you get around the TSS patrols once we get to Earth."

"Who's worried?" Iza shrugged and strolled away.

She might not admit it now, but they would need more than her usual finesse to get her precious Joe back. They'd need someone with connections. Someone like Karter.

Cierra helped him to his cabin and promised to bring him new dressings for his leg. After she'd gone, Karter saw he had a video message waiting for him from Becca. He settled onto his bed an opened it. Though his mood lifted just looking at her face, he was concerned to see that her features were filled with worry for him.

"I hope you're well and that you're fitting in with the crew. I know how much you detest following orders, but I'm sure you're doing better than you imagine. Things here are unchanged. The investors are still asking questions, but your mother has not been able to move them to take further action against you.

"Their distrust of your mother is the only thing keeping them where they are, for the moment. Though there are rumors that someone else is trying to make a play for the business. I haven't been able to track down the source of the story, or the facts, but you'll be the first to know if I do."

Becca looked off-camera, and he knew she could see into his office from her desk. It was designed in such a manner so that she'd be able to anticipate his needs.

"Your office is very empty without you here. Everyone misses you and is hoping that you are able to return soon. This may be a lot to ask, but I hope you'll do something for me. While you're there, make a friend. You need more allies in your life. Becca out."

The screen went black, and Karter found himself reversing the video until her face was back on the screen. His chest tightened at the sight of her full lips pressed into a tight line, eyes pleading. Karter couldn't imagine wanting anyone more. His mother had complicated matters. No one else knew about the clause in his father's will that said his dynastic inheritance was dependent on his son marrying 'a woman worthy of him'. His mother's interpretation said he couldn't be with someone who wasn't highborn. Others who knew his father's heart had offered another interpretation—one that was more lenient, as it would have been between a father and son. It was a matter of character, not blood.

Nonetheless, with his dynasty in danger, Karter had to make a choice. His mother would use the clause against him, should he choose Becca. His only chance was to keep Iza as his fiancée until the matter of his father's will could be addressed or challenged. Unfortunately, it was becoming increasingly difficult to conceal her true lineage from her. He'd kept every other secret at the forefront of his mind in order to keep that one thought hidden. The injections helped.

Karter opened his suitcase and pulled out the vial of green liquid and injected himself with what the black market salesmen called a 'Thought Blocker'. It kept his passive thoughts to himself, making him unreadable to high-level telepathic gleaning. However, under anything more intense, he'd have trouble, which was why it had been a good thing that Joe was no longer on board. Once he was back on the *Verity*, Karter would have to find something else to keep the ex-TSS Agent from digging into his buried thoughts.

"CACI?"

"Yes, Karter Hyttinen?"

"Pull up all relevant data pertaining to the current state of affairs on the planet Earth."

"Please narrow your topic of choice."

"Current news reports on Earth in the location of Minneapolis, Minnesota, United States of America."

BRAEDON WAS UP to his eyeballs in work. While they made the trek to Earth—stopping for cool down breaks to maintain the appearance of having a conventional jump drive—he, Trix, and Viper collaborated remotely on a way to neutralize the sphere's effects on Uephus. The issue with the virus had always been its rapid adaptability, making any signal blocks a temporary fix. For the planet to be safe for the survivors, they needed a way to fully disable the sphere and its ability to create a connection with wherever that Gate led. No doubt, it was that open portal that had precipitated the planet's transformation; the sphere itself was just a glorified map. Something powerful was controlling the changes from the other side, and it wouldn't be safe to attempt to move the sphere or get close to it until the Gate was closed—permanently.

Between messages to Viper, he doodled on his comic. He had enough other work to keep him busy, but the creative project was a release from the stress. He could paint himself the hero. As silly as it may seem to others, it gave him a little more confidence that he could help save the day in real life, too.

Cierra peeked at it from behind him. "It looks good. You

have a real gift for drawing and story. I can't wait to see when it's finished."

Braedon lifted one shoulder and let it drop. "It sort of relaxes me. Someday, I want to create a virtual-reality version of it. People could follow my character through the story and then make their own decisions and choices along the way. More like a game than a story," he added for clarity.

Cierra nodded. "Like the ones you and Viper play," she said. There was nothing on her face to give away her bias one way or the other, only a blank look.

The front console beeped. He glanced down and saw it was a new code snippet from Viper. At the sight of Viper's contact card flashing across the screen, Cierra stiffened. He and Cierra walked a delicate balance between friendship and the potential for more, but every time he spoke to her about Viper, he had the distinct feeling she didn't like it.

"I have to go through this message," he said. "It will probably take some time."

"Did you have to bring my sister in on this?" Cierra asked.

"Aside from myself, she's the best coder I know. Look, I don't want things to be awkward with us. I get that you two don't see eye-to-eye on a lot of things, but—"

"The two of you have a lot in common," she interrupted. "She gets you when it comes to the technical stuff. I get you when it comes to the emotional stuff. I trust you know what's more important." She glided out off of the flight deck, leaving Braedon staring after her.

I don't think I'll ever understand that woman. Is there an issue or not? He had no clue, but there wasn't time to worry about it while he had the issue of the alien virus to solve.

Viper had sent a video message along with the code this time. He played it.

"Ping me for a live chat when you get this. We're on a stop

planetside for a while, and I've got some ideas I think we should discuss. This back and forth is getting ridiculous."

Braedon couldn't agree more. Without delay, he sent a communication request to the *Iron Dog* and had the flight deck route it to Viper's quarters.

"What have you got for me?" Braedon asked the moment her face was visible on screen.

"Don't rush me, little lamb. I'm doing the best I can with what I've got. You know I've got jobs to pull in between helping you storm the castle." Viper had dark smudges under her eyes as if she'd been working all night.

"Well, don't kill yourself. I can do it on my own, you know." It was wishful thinking, but she didn't need to know that. "I just thought you might enjoy the challenge. Who doesn't like a good mystery?" Braedon asked.

"Uh huh. Sure." Viper still had a spark in her eyes, despite her exhaustion.

"Whatever. Are you going to talk me to death, or are we going to figure this out?"

"All right pull up that latest segment I sent you," Viper said, sitting back in her chair. He could tell by the way she shifted in her seat she had tucked her feet underneath her. "I cross-referenced the code that was messing with your ship and Trix when you had the sphere on board before and compared that to the signal code you gathered on Uephus. It has the markers of being the same language, but this new code is a lot more complex… and it goes beyond what's written. Like there are 'things' coming through the open portal."

Nothing about that sounded good. "What do you mean?"

Viper shook her head. "The technology they're working with is some kind of hybrid between electrical and something I've never seen before. I don't understand how they're using it to manipulate matter."

"But it all comes back to the Gate that's opened using the sphere," he said.

"Yes, that much is clear."

"Well, then all we have to do is figure out a way to close the portal and then get the sphere off of the world so they can't open it again."

Viper raised an eyebrow. "Tell me something I don't know."

He cracked a smile. "I think we might have a key."

"What makes you say that?"

"Remember what Iza said about the sphere being DNA-coded?"

"Yeah. Which is why your father needed Iza."

"Right." Braedon hated it whenever people made the connection between him and his father. He was nothing like him.

"And he must have tried *everything* before her. He's got some serious reach."

"What do you mean?"

"I mean there's no business in this sector that your father doesn't touch. And it seems that he's determined to get his hands on more of these spheres. We've already turned down a job, an all-call for haulers, earlier this week. But Douketis knows better; he's aware of how your father rewards the people that help him. Though it hasn't stopped him from making other dumb decisions."

Braedon's face flushed. He knew all too well his father's methods firsthand.

"Sorry, no offense."

Braedon shrugged. "Don't worry about it. I know what kind of man he is. I don't want to be anything like him, so we're on the same page there."

"So, what were you saying about a key?" Viper asked.

"Well, Iza said that they needed her to make the Gate work. They were able to 'power on' the sphere, if you will, and get the doorway to appear, but no one except for her made it past the event horizon. So, what if closing it is DNA-keyed, too?"

Viper sat back in thought for several moments. "That's a good point, and the logic follows. But that does bring up another question."

"Which is?"

"If Iza opened and closed the Gate last time, then who opened it this time?"

Braedon's heart sank. "I have no idea."

"Maybe she has a long-lost family member?" Viper suggested.

"Actually, she does. Her mom's sister and her cousin. She won't really talk about them, so I don't know what's going on there."

"Family is complicated. Of course, it doesn't leave us with a lot of options."

"Don't I know it." Braedon sighed. "But maybe there's a way to get the sphere to listen to Iza and force it to disconnect?"

"Even if that's possible, it's under three thousand meters of ocean. There would be no way for her to make contact with it without moving it first."

"And if we get close, it'll destroy our systems."

"Exactly. It means we're out of plays." Viper sat back in her chair stretching her arms across her chest.

Braedon tapped on the console. "I guess we need to keep working on a new antivirus that can counteract this more complicated signal."

"I'm not giving up, don't worry, but that's enough for today," Viper said, cracking a smile. "You've got me locked into this mystery now; I won't let it beat me."

"Good thing you hate to lose as much as I do."

"Yeah, that's true. At least when it comes to tech-related problems. Relationships and people? Forget about it. I'm not even in the game."

"Cierra was saying something like that the other day. What's the deal with you two, anyway?"

"No deal," Viper replied. "We're just like you and your father—complete opposites. It's a hard bridge to cross most days."

"Cierra worries about you sometimes. I don't know what to tell her."

"Tell her I'm fine and I'm not a baby that she needs to check up on. I thought she'd have her own life by now."

"She does, but I think we both like knowing that wherever you are, that you're okay."

Viper tilted her head to one side and then grinned. "Look at you, caring about me and stuff. Don't get too attached. I'm nothing like my sister; you'll get your little heart broken."

Braedon waved a hand at her. "It's not like that and you know it. After all we've been through, I'm just looking out for you, we're on the same team now. It's nice knowing which players have your back."

"Aww, the little lamb is playing the shepherd."

"Ugh, forget it. I should go look over this new code with Trix."

"Speaking of looking over things, when am I going to get to see this comic of yours?" Viper crossed her arms over her chest and kept her gaze on his.

Braedon faltered. "How do you know about that?"

"Let's just say I have my sources."

"Your sister." Braedon cursed Cierra in his mind, preparing what he was going to say when he saw her next.

"Sprout? No way," Viper smirked. "I have more reliable sources than her. But anyway, I heard it was good. It sounds like something that would be perfect for VR interface. Have you thought about doing that? You know, once we're not trying to save the planet."

"Actually, I have," Braedon said with some surprise. He didn't know what he was expecting, but it wasn't this. "Have you ever done anything like that before?"

"You mean create a comic from scratch and then turn it into of virtual reality game? No, I can honestly say I've never done that before." Viper smiled. "But there's always a first time for everything, and it's your game and I'd love to try it. Maybe we can come up with something better than the garbage they've been putting out lately. Even on the Dark Net the games are getting stale."

"I've been avoiding the Dark Net these days. It's got me into some trouble lately. I'm surprised you're still dipping in."

"A girl's got to make her own credits. I can't be an *Iron Dog* underling forever. Sure, Douketis got me out of some trouble, and I owe him, so I'm gonna work it off. But I won't be here forever," she said, looking at him intently.

Where does she see her future? For that matter, Braedon didn't know what to envision for his. Certainly, it wouldn't be the life his father would have designed for him. "Okay, I guess I better get back to solving this little problem of ours. Let me know if you find anything else."

"I will. And send over that comic; I want to read it for myself."

"I'm not really sharing it with anyone at the moment. It still needs some work." Braedon chewed at the inside of his lip.

"Of course it does. That's why you need me! I'll help you get it into shape. No judgment, just constructive critique. Then we can start building this game," Viper said.

Braedon liked the sound of that, but he wasn't sure if he was ready for whatever kind of commitment that would require. Especially since he was still torn between what to do about her sister. Things were getting complicated, and fast. "As soon as it's ready."

"Okay. Viper out," she said signing off with a mock salute.

Braedon watched the screen go from black to the stars again and found himself staring out for a while. Viper was a good kid. Maybe there was something he could do to help her and her sister make amends.

IT WOULD HAVE been easier to storm a High Dynasty palace with a pellet gun and dog than it was going to be to get Joe from Earth. Though Iza learned from her research that the planet didn't have a planetary shield or orbital weapons that would pose a threat to a starship of her size and capabilities, the problem was the proximity to TSS Headquarters located on Earth's moon. It wasn't clear why the TSS had picked such a remote, backwater world to serve as their central administrative office and training center, but she wondered if they were regretting the decision now that the planet's technology had advanced to a point where it must be difficult to keep the locals ignorant of Tarans roaming the rest of the galaxy.

They were on what was scheduled to be their final fake cool-down stop, a short jump away from Earth, when Iza made her way on to the flight deck with Atano trailing behind her.

"All right, no more throwing around hypothetical ideas. How are we going to get Joe off the planet?" she asked.

"Their planetary defenses are more focused on domestic conflicts than dealing with an outside threat," Karter replied. "And as advanced as they may think their tech is, the H3X's shield can shrug off even their most powerful nuclear missiles and lasers, based on the specs I've read."

Braedon nodded. "Yeah, I found some guides on the Dark Net about Tarans who like to go mess with the locals for fun. Draw doodles in their fields and stuff. Don't ask. But anyway, the only weapons that could *maybe* damage us, they won't risk firing back toward the surface of the planet. So, it's getting *away* that will be the most dangerous. Getting down, we just need to be fast. In and out before the TSS or local military try to intercept us."

"Would they really fire on a stranger before trying to talk?" Cierra asked. She was becoming a permanent unwelcome fixture on the flight deck, like the vines in the galley.

"Yes, they would. There's a reason they're not already a part of the Taran Empire," Karter continued. "Any Tarans living there know to keep their true identities hidden, and there's no unauthorized contact between Earth and the other worlds using subspace communications. Which is why the Taran government has taken great pains to ensure that the TSS provides another layer of protection for the planet."

"We can't get the ship through, but we could bring a stealth shuttle," Braedon said.

Iza rolled her eyes at the ridiculous suggestion. "Yeah, if we happened to have a covert ops military ship at our disposal."

Braedon glanced at Karter. "What about a Q Maximus?"

"What's that?" Cierra asked.

The other man nodded. "Yes, that could work, provided we landed in a remote area and kept the comms dark."

Iza wasn't familiar with that particular craft, but it sounded like just what they needed. "Could you get access to one?"

Karter gave her a broad smile. "I told you I'd get you past Earth's defenses. Give me a day to arrange it."

Iza nodded. "All right. We'll go down before their sun rises and leave after the sun sets that night. A day should be plenty of time to find Joe and get back to the shuttle."

"I believe that timing will provide you with the minimum amount of exposure," Trix assessed. "However, there is a thirty percent chance that you will be seen."

"I'll take those odds. It's for Joe," Iza said.

"Captain, if I may…" Cierra began.

"What is it?"

"I want to see you reunited with Joe as much as anyone, but I think you're making a mistake by going about it this way. If you kidnap him from Earth—"

"Who said anything about kidnapping?" Iza interrupted. "We're just going to check on an old friend. If he chooses to leave with us, that's on him." She held her hands up.

"I pointed out the obvious to you months ago, and you continue to ignore the fact that Joe will undoubtedly be under surveillance by the TSS. He's been banished from the Empire. He might—all of us might—end up in a jail cell for life for trying to 'liberate' him from Earth." Cierra looked squarely at Iza, her eyes wide and serious. "Do you want that on your conscience?"

Iza had thought about the consequences of bringing him back on board. She'd considered it and dismissed it when she realized what would happen to them all if he *wasn't* on board. "I have another scenario for you. I'm getting him whether you like it or not."

"What if he chooses to stay behind?"

"Then he'll stay behind." The burn of doubt coated her throat. What if he did choose to stay on Earth? There was no guarantee that the dream version of Joe and the real Joe would be in agreement. She might have to convince him.

"He made his choice when he defected," Cierra continued as if Iza had spoken her doubts aloud. "That's why he was sent to Earth. Going back for him now is reckless."

"I'm the only captain here," Iza said, glancing around as if taking inventory. "If what we're doing here is too risky for you, you're welcome to get your own ride home." She let the threat hang in the air between them, waiting for Cierra to make up her mind.

There was a crackling to the quality of the air as Cierra gathered up the loose portions of her outfit. With her chin lifted, she left.

"Q, hang on…" Braedon half-heartedly started to protest.

Iza knew the consequences. She was putting the others in danger of being apprehended by the TSS. However, they didn't have all the facts. They didn't know about the dreams. She had to take them seriously. Yes, it was a risk, but it was a risk she was willing to take. Anyone who didn't want to take that chance didn't have to go along for the ride. That included their Healer—the stuck-up, self-righteous snob.

Iza turned to Karter. "Make the arrangements."

—

As promised, a day later, Karter arranged for delivery of the specialty Q Maximus shuttle. It was even smaller than her own, fitting easily in the *Verity*'s cargo hold. She didn't know how he got it, or who owned it, and she didn't want to know.

"This is a *loan*, he emphasized." The urgency in his tone made Iza suspect that he'd had to hand over a substantial deposit to get use of the craft. She still didn't like the guy, but she had to admit that he wasn't all bad.

"It's really something." She admired the matte black finish the craft and ultra-sleek lines. For being so small, it was impressive that it was equipped with a jump drive. "I can't wait to see how it handles."

"I'm going with you," Karter said.

"No, you're not."

"Don't start that again. This was my financial contribution and I'll stick around, if you don't mind, to see that it's returned in one piece."

"Whoever is coming, I suggest you leave all of your weapons and identification here. That includes your handhelds. If we are caught transmitting, we will violate Taran law," Trix warned.

"Are you sure you want to go through with this?" Karter asked.

It's a little late for a change of heart now that we have the Q Maximus, isn't it? Iza dropped her voice so that only Karter could hear her. "Yes, regardless of our—" Isa didn't know how to finish that sentence, "contract, it seems that Joe is a part of my life. I want him on board. He's an asset to me and my crew, and we're not leaving him behind."

Karter seemed to accept her explanation for the moment, though his pinched facial expression said otherwise. Despite everything he was doing to help reunite her with Joe, it seemed that part of him hadn't gotten over the fact that she had no desire to marry him.

But she wouldn't lose the man she loved. She loved Joe. She'd realized that after Inspector Desirae Hyttinen had hauled him away to be handed over to the TSS.

Iza had seen enough tumultuous relationships to realize that what she had with Joe was something special. The bond that kept them together had only grown in their proximity. Having him so far away was heart-wrenching in the literal sense. It'd taken her a week just to get out of bed, and another just to be able to think straight without him. From what she understood of such resonance connections between Tarans, it was two-sided. Whatever she was going through, he had to be experiencing it, as well. That gave her some comfort that he'd jump at the chance to return to the *Verity* with her.

"Braedon, how's our gear coming?" Iza asked him over the comm.

"Just finishing up now. Be right there."

He arrived a few minutes later carrying three devices that reminded her of handhelds. "All right, I think these should do the trick. I had CACI fabricate some 'cellular phones' in one of the popular Earth models."

Iza took the device when he handed it to her.

"You'll need them to communicate with each other if you get separated and if there's a problem," Braedon explained, handing the other two to Karter and Trix.

"Can you communicate with us on these?" Iza asked.

"Yes, but it would risk drawing unwanted attention, since any offworld calls would require relaying a signal through the shuttle. For that matter, I'd suggest limiting any communications, even to each other, unless it's a dire emergency, because the government has been known to monitor calls."

Iza frowned. "Noted."

"You can use the devices for electronic payments, too—I set up a digital account with a little local currency," Braedon continued. "I also did you the favor of adding a language translator from English to New Taran; you should be able to understand their speech, though it might be a little awkward at first. There are plenty of different languages and dialects of Earth, so if anyone tries to talk to you, using the translator on the phone won't raise too many flags."

Iza gave Braedon a light pat on the shoulder. He'd gone above and beyond, and she wasn't sure exactly how to thank him. "Good work. Keep the *Verity* safe while I'm gone. And take care of Atano for me."

The dog lifted his head at the sound of his name. Cierra had tended to his injured leg using her natural medicines, but it wouldn't be completely healed for another day.

"Of course. Be careful," Braedon cautioned. "I tried to make everything look as native Earth as I could, but our onboard fabricator used off-world materials. If the authorities on Earth find anything that leads back to us, it could put the Taran government in a tight spot. If we care about that kind of thing." He shrugged one shoulder.

It was clear where he landed on the subject. The Lower Dynasty heir of a madman, he had made his choice quite clear. Braedon cared nothing of governments or their actions. He had his agenda, and he was happy to be helping where there was a need. He didn't care what it took.

"What about her?" Karter asked with a nod toward Trix.

"What do you mean?" Iza questioned.

"She can't come. She stands out as an android. They do have synthetic AI on Earth, but nothing as advanced as her. If they discovered Trix, that's a whole other can of worms."

The expression sounded strange to her ears. "Are you trying to sound like Joe?"

"No, only adopting some of their common speech."

"Why would anybody want a can of worms?" Iza asked. "Doesn't matter. She'll stay on the shuttle to pilot it. If there's any trouble, I want her to be able to get the ship out of view and away from the authorities."

Karter didn't look convinced, but he inclined his head.

Iza headed for the Q Maximus shuttle. "Let's go play among the Earthlings."

— — —

The *Arvonen One* made its last jump, dropping out from

subspace near Venus. The planet would offer cover for the large ship, though there was still the risk of a TSS patrol stumbling upon them. They had to work fast. After the debacle on Uephus, they had some catching up to do.

Victor barked out orders to the crew while Raquel waited patiently behind him. She'd been troubled after they'd arrived at Uephus and found what the Gatekeepers had done to the planet. Victor was intrigued. He now knew the sphere's power as a Gate had even more possibilities. Transforming Taran planets from one climate to another hadn't occurred to him, but the financial potential was astronomical. A planet with no potential for crops could become a farming community. A lush planet with a local government that refused to bend to his will could quickly become a barren rock.

He had no idea he'd been smiling until Raquel mentioned it.

"Something funny, sir?"

Victor waved a hand in dismissal. "No, nothing. I was just daydreaming. Where are we on the location of the rogue Agent?"

"We have the information you requested. however, I have to emphasize that retrieving him in this manner will draw attention from the TSS. Even if they don't want him back, it is unlikely they will just let him go with us."

Victor nodded as he continued to constrain the excitement. "No, we won't be here long. Crew deck, prepare for immediate departure. I want to leave the engines running and as soon as the man is on board. We will leave this uncivilized system and its people behind."

"We could wait until nightfall; it might be less conspicuous," said the pilot.

Victor turned a glare on him that could melt metal. He had no intention of waiting for anything. The people of Earth were hardly advanced, and the TSS wouldn't be expecting him to show up on their doorstep after all the trouble he'd gone into hiding from them.

"No. Prepare the shuttle and take him with you." Victor pointed at one of the other crewmembers.

The large man inclined his head before leaving. Victor liked the deference, and he couldn't wait for the rest of the Tarans to bestow him the same respect. He'd earned it, after all. He'd done so much to bring his family's name to a place of dignity and to ensure his grandchildren would have the name and recognition they all deserved. However, his youngest continued to disappoint.

There was a time, many years ago, when Devyn had bounded into his office and declared he'd do more for the dynasty than his older brother, his light eyes set and his lips in a thin line of determination. He'd only been five years old, but it felt like yesterday. He'd ignored his father's busy scheduled and marched in, climbing onto Victor's lap to state his intentions. Where had those days gone? Would the boy ever learn to embrace his station instead of dragging the Arvonen name down? His eldest would take the reins, but Victor wished that Devyn's energy and charisma had been bestowed on his older, more obedient son. Instead, he simply followed after his father, sniveling all the way.

Devyn, meanwhile, had turned away from his dynastic purpose with relish, instead focusing his time, money, and attention on black market games. It was ludicrous, but he'd continued to stay on his father's radar as long as he ran with the crew of the *Verity*. He'd taken the ship with the Gate generator in the first place, making a mess of everything. However, uniting the Gate with the key had been, at the time, a happy coincidence. Now, Victor knew better. Iza was different; in some way, she was connected to the Gatekeepers.

Perhaps, like himself, it was her destiny to find the Gate and go through, showing him how it was done. She'd been the first to venture through the Gate and return whole. After so many failed attempts, she'd solved the mystery he'd been trying to find. If he wanted to secure the Gate's power for himself, he'd need her genetic code. Until he could replicate the component of her genetics that allowed her to interface with the Gatekeeper technology, he would need Iza to serve as his key to operate the Gate.

It was unfortunate they hadn't been able to retrieve the sphere that had appeared on Uephus; that would have been the answer to at least one of their problems. They'd done everything they could to set themselves up for its retrieval, upon identifying its presence—disabled the distress beacon and then had made quick work of getting to the surface. Unfortunately, when they arrived, they'd made the frustrating discovery that the Gate was under water. Without anything to counteract the effects of the active portal, they had been unable to retrieve it. And, the mystery remained of how it got there and why it was activated in the first place; Victor has been unaware of any other Gate generators, aside from the sphere that had been seized by the TSS three months before.

However, all was not lost. If everything went according to plan, he'd have another Gate generator and the key in short order. This time, Iza was going to come to him, and he'd be waiting for her.

Raquel approached Victor on the right of his periphery. "Sir, I have news." She hadn't quite been the same since their visit to her home planet. She seemed more driven somehow—not that it mattered. She'd be of use until she wasn't.

"What is it? Have you found him yet?"

"Oh, yes, he's gone to work for the day, but we have his schedule. As soon as he crosses the threshold, we'll have him.

But this is about something else. I've discovered there may be another with the same gene sequence as Captain Sundari," Raquel said, speaking rapidly and waving her hands. "At first I didn't think it was possible, but then, suddenly, there it was right in front of me! The same unique markers."

The contagious excitement in her eyes was enough to force Victor to clear his throat. "Another key? Who?"

"A blood relative. I believe he is a cousin. Do you want to pursue him?"

"No, not yet. Track him, but I want to put this plan into action first. He's no use to us without it, anyway." Victor turned his attention to the two brutes who did the heavy lifting for him; they were larger than life and looked almost as intimidating as they were. "Prepare the shuttle to go down to Earth."

10

THE ALARM BESIDE his bed startled Joe awake before dawn on Thursday morning. He groaned and turned it off before he planted two feet on the floor, digging his toes into the plush rug he'd purchased. It had been the same routine every weekday morning since he'd gone back home to Earth.

He'd arrived at the end of fall, the perfect time to find an apartment as the rents were cheap and finding work during the school year seemed to be easier than in the summer months. Now, nearly three months into winter, he was glad he'd rented an apartment with central heating in the St. Anthony district near downtown Minneapolis.

The city was as it had been when he'd left to join the TSS: quiet, unassuming, and the kind of place no one much cared to visit in the winter. There had been minimal advancements in technology, medicine, or social economics during his decade-long absence. It was like going back in time. He couldn't imagine a worse place to live out the rest of his boring days.

The news for the last three mornings had been continuing coverage on another series of riots. He had forgotten how violent Earth had been. It was no wonder the government leaders weren't ready to admit they were not alone in the universe. There were still far too many things to deal with in their own backyard. Introducing not only more people, but more laws and rules that people would break, would be an overwhelming task. Joe slipped into his street clothes, a pair of blue jeans and a navy-blue button-down shirt. The shirt had been a gift from his adoptive aunt and uncle, who thought they'd never see him again. They'd become close friends of his parents when they'd gone down for their undercover TSS assignment on Earth. Technically, they were his godmother and godfather, but he and his sister had grown up calling them 'aunt' and 'uncle'. When they'd asked about where he'd been, he'd evade the question, saying that he had been in the military and the details were classified.

Though his aunt and uncle had done their best in the absence of his parents, in the end, he'd resented them more than he could ever love them. Their initial reunion had been short, but he'd kept to his promise to come for dinners every Sunday, and that seemed to appease them. They were all the family he had left, after all. He was forbidden to contact any of his TSS friends or family. Not that he had any means of contacting them even if he wanted to, since his handheld had been confiscated before his exile to the planet.

Gone were the days of being an elite TSS Agent. He couldn't even use his Gifts. Stars, how he missed using telekinesis.

Their most recent Sunday meal had been a repeat of the others, as routine as his tedious workdays. After the obligatory greeting hugs, they asked him about his week, like they always did. As usual, he had nothing interesting to say. Thankfully, the food was ready, and they'd ushered him to the table for the meal without asking about his dating prospects again.

They made small-talk throughout the meal. He tried to give them real answers when he could, but the truth was that talking about the weather made him want to throw himself out an airlock—if only he had access to one. At this rate, stargazing on a mountaintop was the closest he'd ever get to space again.

"Being back here can't be all that bad," his uncle said as he reached for the butter to accompany the final bites of his roll.

Joe made a noise in the back of his throat akin to agreement as he chewed the last of his meatloaf.

"I hope you left room," his aunt said, leaping up from the table. "I made your favorite."

She came back with a rectangular glass dish with what smelled like apple pie and looked like apple crisp. It wasn't his favorite. It was Skyler's, but he didn't correct her as she'd gone to the trouble. Instead, he smiled and took the plate she dished up for him.

"I know you can't talk about everything that happened while you were deployed, but did you meet any interesting people?" his uncle asked.

Joe had to swallow hard to get past the apple crisp and the lump in his throat. *Why can't I stop thinking about her?* He stabbed at another piece of the crumble but didn't lift it to his mouth.

"I did, I met some interesting characters."

"What were they like?" questioned his aunt. "You don't have to give us names just describe them to us."

"Well, I met a young pilot from a wealthy family who reminded me a lot of Robin Hood. He had a tendency to get into trouble, but it was usually for a good cause."

"Sounds like a good kid. Must have come from good parents like you," his uncle said.

Joe didn't have to pretend to smile as both his aunt and uncle were looking down at their plates. They didn't know the half of it. If they knew what he'd been through with Braedon's father, they'd wonder if the apple didn't fall too far from the tree.

"Did you meet any young ladies?" His aunt gave him a wink as she tried to cut him another slice of crisp.

Oh, yep, here we go. Joe held up a hand, insisting he couldn't eat another bite. He was stuffed to the neck and he was sure he only had room for the hot coffee she'd poured him without asking. "Yes, I met a few women." Joe smiled at her and she seemed satisfied.

It was his uncle that spoke up. "Anyone special, or lots of friends?"

Joe found it hard to smile when he thought of Iza and how he'd never see her again. No wonder she was always on his mind; everything always came back to her. She was more than just a friend. Iza was more than anything he'd ever had in his life. The connection he had with her had taken months to fade, and when he thought of her, the pain wasn't gone, only dull with her absence.

He cleared his throat to speak. "There was one special someone."

Most days, he wondered about Iza and what she might be doing now. Did she get away safely, as was their deal? Was she still engaged to Karter? How was the ship faring? Had the TSS caught up to them and forced them to give up the independent jump drive? He had loads more questions with no answers.

"Did you get the chance to tell her how you felt?" His aunt had reached her hand across the table toward his. He grasped it, knowing it would make her happy.

"Yes, we didn't leave anything unspoken. Though things are a bit complicated now."

His uncle nodded, seeming to understand his meaning. There was a sheen in his aunt's eyes that he wished he could unsee.

"If it's meant to be, you'll get together again. I promise you, the universe will bring you back together again," she said. "Let me pack you up some leftovers."

Leftovers wound up filling several bowls that she placed in a bag for him to take home and return the next week, as he'd done every week since his arrival. They usually lasted a day or two and filled his lunches with something other than sandwiches.

"Thanks, I appreciate it," Joe said and meant it.

He was grateful for them welcoming him home, despite him being evasive and distant. It gave him new appreciation for his parents' judgment in character; they'd picked genuinely good friends. But his aunt and uncle's hospitality didn't change that Earth was only his planetary address, not where his heart wanted to be.

His lack of commitment to the place was evidenced by the sparse furnishings in his one-bedroom, one-bathroom apartment. There were no decorations or personal effects decorating the surfaces. In fact, there was nothing in the place that made the apartment look like more than a temporary pitstop. Maybe because that's how he viewed it. He had no pictures of loved ones or anything of material importance. He'd turned everything over to the TSS and he hadn't collected anything much on the *Verity*. He ground his teeth at the thought that he hadn't remembered to leave something of himself behind.

He returned his thoughts to getting through the rest of the work week. Thursday meant he only had two days left before Saturday—the only day he didn't have obligations—and then the routine would reset anew with another Sunday dinner that would no doubt be identical to every Sunday for the past three months.

Joe snatched up his gray backpack and slipped it over his shoulder. About to walk out the door, he remembered to grab his coat; he had to keep reminding himself that it was winter now, and he'd freeze without one. Normally, he'd walk, but the winter winds were picking up and he didn't want to risk frostbite.

Working in downtown Minneapolis was as close to being in a high-tech environment as he could find in the area. It was funny now, thinking about anything on the planet as being remotely 'advanced'. Joe remembered the looks he used to get at TSS Headquarters when he told other Tarans he was from Earth; now, he understood how they viewed the isolated blue and green globe. Looking at the blank faces of those around him on the bus into downtown, it was clear that they were going about their business with no clue about the expanse of the universe or the people that lived among the stars.

After he hopped off the bus in the city just beginning to wake for the morning, Joe lifted the collar of his jacket and crossed the street to the IDS building where he worked as a security guard. It was once the tallest building in the city, which Joe found hard to believe at only fifty-seven stories; it had long since been dwarfed by the buildings around it, though it remained a central hub for several large businesses in the area. He'd applied for several jobs in security, knowing it was the closest thing to being an Agent without taking a job in the government. It had been made clear to him that any such posting could put him, and others, at risk. Keeping a low profile while back on Earth was paramount to his continued ability to roam free.

When he had turned his back on his mission, choosing to side with Iza and her crew despite their involvement in some necessary but illegal business, he'd committed treason against the Taran Empire. They could have thrown him in a prison cell for life. He knew he was fortunate to have any freedom at all. Or, maybe the TSS knew that an existence here was more punishment than being locked up—not confined but trapped all the same.

Joe traversed the manmade park in the middle of the Crystal Court, the open first level of the tower with seven floors, to reach the elevators. He smiled at the young lady with ginger hair and a scatter of freckles over the bridge of her nose sitting at the reception desk. He couldn't imagine doing her job—being at a desk all day, or worse, answering phones. Having to speak to people put his teeth on edge. At least security work meant, on occasion, that he could lay hands on someone who was out of line rather than having to smile and nod even when they were being an idiot.

There was a locker room in the basement where he began and ended each day. He changed into his uniform, a black pair of pants and matching shirt and boots. On the left breast pocket of his shirt, he attached the metal name pin with his last name ANDERSON spelled out.

"Don't ever have kids! I don't think I've slept more than two nights through in a row." Charlie Stevens was the other security guard for the IDS on the day shift, and he had declared himself Joe's friend from day one. He was chatty but knew how to mind his own business. Joe liked him immediately.

"You and Jesse have plans this weekend?" Joe asked.

"Nothing special. You're still welcome on Saturday. Jesse is on my back about having another baby again. I keep telling her we can't afford it on my salary, but really, I just want to sleep. Haven't I earned a good night's sleep?" He opened his wide-set eyes pleadingly, wrinkling the dark skin on his forehead.

Joe laughed, knowing his friend was prone to over-exaggerate his situation in order to garner sympathy. Just the other day, he'd mentioned wanting a boy in order to have an even playing field with his wife and daughter.

"Quit your bellyaching or you'll end up with another daughter," Joe said with a grin. He threw the words Charlie had used to describe his daughter back at him, "What's worse than one cinnamon cherub with big eyes begging you for another toy?" Joe raised two fingers in the air and wiggled them at Charlie.

Charlie's eyes grew wide in shock at the idea of two little girls, then he shrugged. "That's what Uncle Joe is for," he said and gave Joe a punch in the arm.

They went to relieve the graveyard shift guards. Charlie was tall enough he could look Joe in the eye as they walked over.

"Speaking of girls, when are you going to take out that little receptionist?" He wiggled his eyebrows at him.

"Nancy?"

"Yes, the red-haired temptress that lights up at the sight of your bright blue eyes and killer smile every morning."

"Give me a break, Charlie," Joe said without meeting his gaze. He'd swapped out his brown contacts for a blue closer to his natural shade, though they still blocked the bioluminescence from his abilities. Still, whenever someone looked too intently at him, he worried they'd notice something was different about his eyes.

As they walked by the reception desk, he glanced at Nancy. She was hard to miss, and she made sure of it. The low-cut tops and the bright red lipstick only highlighted her best features, but she wasn't Iza.

"What? You look like a prince from a Disney movie. You've got a steady well-paying job. What's not to like? Take my advice and date her. If Jesse finds out your taste, she'll be throwing single women at you every week."

"No way." Joe shook his head.

"I'm serious. You don't know how hard it is to hold her

back from inviting strange women to our Saturday college football evenings."

"Please, tell her I'm fine on my own."

"That won't work. Jesse is notorious for matchmaking. Like a dog with a bone, she won't leave you alone." Charlie rubbed at his chin. "Are you still getting over the one that got away?" He didn't wait for an answer, "I understand. I'll tell her you're not technically available. She'll understand."

They punched in and started rounds, working their way up from the first floor. The early-morning office workers were just beginning to filter in. Joe always liked the quiet mornings; it helped ease into the day.

"You *are* coming on Saturday, right?" Charlie asked as they walked.

"Sure, I'll be there."

They completed their first round on the building, checking in all the usual places for vagrants and mischief, starting with the loading dock where they pushed off an unwashed couple bundled under blankets sharing a cigarette. Joe called in a work order for the graffiti they found on the outside wall facing Nicolette Mall Avenue; maintenance would be out there half the day scrubbing away the three colors of ink.

"Everyone thinks they're the next Picasso," Charlie said, shaking his head.

The contrast between life in the Taran worlds and Earth was jarring to Joe. He considered the outer colonies more civilized than the selfish and egocentric attitude that permeated Earth. Maybe it was just 'grass is greener' thinking, but he couldn't help it.

Mid-morning, Joe went to take his first break for the day. He had just finished up in the restroom when he got a buzz on his walkie-talkie.

Charlie's voice came over the speaker, "Security to Crystal

Court, we've got a ten-thirty-two. Requesting assistance!"

Joe bolted toward the building entrance. There was an armed intruder in the lobby.

He found Charlie staring down the barrel of a handgun wielded by Crazy Bob. Neither of them seemed to notice Joe's approach over the screams and commotion on the floor.

Crazy Bob was a regular, a homeless man with a history of mental illness. He often wandered inside of the building disturbing the patrons, but he'd never before posed a violent threat. He was more a nuisance, since he hadn't bathed in months according to the smudges of dirt on his white skin. His graying beard and hair had yellowed and matted together in disordered clumps from the lack of care. He'd never brought a weapon before, nor had Joe ever seen him with one until today.

"Come on Bob, you don't want to do this. I've got a wife and kid at home," Charlie said, keeping his hands at his sides unthreateningly and his voice even, though his eyes remained steady on him and his hand. "Put the gun down, and we'll all have a nice night. We'll get you some help, a warm meal, even a place to sleep."

Joe crept along the wall from the elevator to the line of trees just behind Crazy Bob. He was wearing the same clothes as always, an old worn through jumper with black stains at the knees and the rear. His boots were new, probably a gift from one of the shelters, and he wore a black coat with a hood that fell to one side held on by three snaps instead of five.

Joe peaked around the tree to get a look at his partner. Charlie's face was serious, perspiration running down his neck to his collar. Joe focused on what Crazy Bob was trying to say.

"They're here! I'm telling you, I saw the ship with my own eyes. Aliens! They're taking over everything, man," Bob said, pulling at a clump of hair while waving the gun in Charlie's direction. He was known for his theatrics, but this time he was over the edge.

Like Charlie, Joe had to assume that the weapon was loaded until proven otherwise. Any sudden moves and the gun could go off, shooting anyone in the crowd.

Someone must have called it in, because two squad cars with flashing lights and sirens, and then three, pulled up to the building on the Nicollet Mall Avenue side. They would breach the building soon. Joe had to be ready to take Bob down if he made a move to fire the gun.

"I saw them flying around last night while everyone was asleep. They were trying to blend in like us, but I know the truth," he said, turning around to face the crowd and waving the gun in their direction.

The people who'd stayed, thinking they were going to get a good show, suddenly backed off with startled exclamations. Didn't they realize anyone with a gun was dangerous? The last thing they needed was more casualties.

While Bob was distracted by the arrival of the police, Joe made his move. If he could distract him enough to pull the gun in his direction and away from Charlie, they'd both be able to walk away from this thing.

"That's enough, Bob. Time to call it a day," Joe said. He tried to keep his voice level, even though his heart was racing. He noticed gasps above him and realized there were more bystanders on the upper levels watching Bob spiral out of control. One slip and any one of them could be injured. Joe kept his eyes on Bob, just as Charlie had done.

"Police! Drop your weapon and get down on the ground, face down and hands behind your head!"

Joe noted that the officer with the gun trained on Bob didn't have a clear shot. Charlie had his back to the police. If he was still with the TSS, he could use telekinesis to disable Bob in an instant without harming anyone. The unfairness of it washed over him as he tried to focus on Bob's shaky right hand.

"It's all right, Bob, you can come with us. We'll take care of you," Charlie said.

"You don't understand, they're coming for us! If they didn't mean us any harm, they'd tell folk they're here instead of sneaking around."

"Okay, Bob," Charlie said, turning to wave the police back. "We'll look into it, but you've got to work with us and put that gun down. You might hurt someone, and then it won't matter if it's an alien invasion."

"Aren't you listening? I saw them land the ship in the park, and then they came walking around here. They were looking for something—or someone. Talking a funny language I've never heard before."

Joe hesitated. *Could Iza have come here to get me…?* He might just be hearing what he wanted to hear.

"They could have just been tourists, Bob," Charlie said.

Bob pawed at his head with his free hand. "No! Kept saying 'taran' this and 'taran' that. They looked like they'd never seen anything before—pointing and laughing! Sure, they were trying to look like us, but they didn't fool me. They were aliens. You've gotta believe me!"

Taran? Joe's heart jumped in his chest. Laughing about antiquated Earth tech did seem like something Iza would do. *But if she's on Earth, then why hasn't she reached out to me already?*

The police were fanning out and getting into position, pushing the crowd back and away from an increasingly agitated Bob.

"You guys stay away from me! Any one of you could be one of those aliens," he said, waving the gun at the crowd again.

He has no idea. Joe could sense that the man's mental state had shifted, and they need to deescalate the situation quickly before he acted.

"Come on, Bob, we'll protect you. You've just gotta come with us." Charlie took a step forward.

"You're working with them, aren't you?" Bob pointed the gun at Charlie's forehead.

Charlie's face fell in realization. Joe heard his thoughts as if they were his own, *"Don't do this to my daughter."*

Joe raised his hand out of instinct. "No!"

11

THE GUN WENt off, but Joe was already charging forward. He had Bob on the ground with his knee in the man's back before Charlie hit the ground.

There were screams up above from the crowd, and then it was over. The police moved in smoothly, two coming in and cuffing Bob and another calling in an ambulance for Charlie in one quick motion.

In a matter of seconds, Joe was able to run over to his partner. Charlie was lying on the ground, bleeding out, while the female officer held her hands pressed down on his chest where the bullet had gone in.

Joe swore under his breath. "Bomaxed bullet." He ripped off his black uniform shirt worn over his own bulletproof vest to press against his partner's wound. He could've stopped the fight in the first place—used telekinesis to knock Bob to the ground or telepathy to command him to stand down. But it was too much of a risk that Bob would end up shooting someone else. Someone who wasn't wearing a bulletproof vest. Instead, Joe nudged Bob's hand just as he'd pulled the trigger to aim the bullet downward, intending for it to hit Charlie's vest, but the trajectory hadn't change enough. It wasn't the fatal headshot it would have been, but it had still struck him just above his vest near his clavicle.

Charlie tried to speak but it was a gurgle. The bullet might have penetrated his lung, making it hard for him to breathe.

"You're going to live. Hold on, partner. I can't tell Jesse that you got hurt on my watch. No way she'll never set me up on a date, then." Charlie made a movement as if to laugh, but no sound came from his lips.

Joe made room for the first responders to come over and help his partner onto a gurney. "I'll be there as soon as we get things locked down here, and Jesse will meet you at the hospital."

It was a shame he couldn't do more for him. Nanites would've taken care of that injury in a matter of minutes, had they had access to modern Taran medicine. It was just one of a million things that annoyed him about being on Earth.

Since Joe had to deal with the fallout after the shooting at the IDS Center, he'd have to wait to see Charlie until later. The custodians had been called, the spectators had been cleared, and the crime scene secured with caution tape. The police officer who'd led the squad came over to take a statement from him. The man was large for a police officer, probably played ball in college and kept himself up.

He lifted the blue police cap and ran a hand over his sweaty, bald head. "Did he say anything about why he had a gun?"

Joe kept his face and voice neutral. "No, I suspect he's off his meds." Joe wouldn't give them any more information than they already had. If he told the police that there was any credit to Crazy Bob's rantings, they might find the shuttle before he did.

"Some of the witnesses say they heard him talking about aliens," the officer said.

"Yeah, that's new for Bob. But that doesn't explain where he got the gun."

"True." The officer looked down at his notes. "Well, I think that's all for now. I'll get a statement from your partner when he's up to it. No hurry. This seems to be only a little atypical for Bob."

"Yeah, outside his normal but not far from it. He's in here at least once a week harassing the patrons. I hope they get him the help he needs if he's starting to see little green men."

The officer smiled. "If you think of anything else relevant, let me know." He handed Joe a business card that read Officer Martin Dolan.

With his official duties completed—and the building was temporarily closed for cleanup and so the police could complete their investigation of the shooting, anyway—he was released for the day. First, he needed to see that Charlie was okay and then he needed to investigate the shuttle sighting. If Iza was here for him, he'd find her.

—

Joe took the indoor skyways as far as Fifth Street then walked the rest of the way to Hennepin County Medical Center, where Charlie was recovering. He hadn't gone home to change, as his uniform would get him through hospital security faster than his ID. By now the incident had already reached the news and he caught snatches of whispered conversation as people passed him and stared.

He played over in his mind again what he was going to say to his partner before he potentially disappeared from his life. Charlie had been a daily comfort and a friend over the last few months, making Joe's exile tolerable. Given their relationship, he still couldn't exactly tell him the truth. Going back on the

Verity with Iza meant leaving behind his new life and friends, but it also would mean putting his friends on the *Verity* in potential danger, if the TSS came looking for him. No matter what, it seemed like he may end up hurting someone. However, nothing was more important to Joe than being reunited with Iza.

The fourth-floor rooms were quiet, and the smell of cafeteria food was in the air. When he reached Charlie's room, he swore under his breath when he caught the heavily Jamaican accented voice of Charlie's wife, Jesse, in the room with him. Saying goodbye to Charlie was bad enough, but his wife had a way of seeing right through him that was uncanny for all but a trained telepath.

"There's my hero," Charlie said as soon as Joe came through the door of the room. Joe noted they'd given him a private room—a small luxury in a place that often had more patients than space. The couple's four-year-old daughter was tucked into a chair beside the bed and covered with a blanket she'd brought from home, which left only the top of her tight curls visible. Charlie looked good, the glint had returned to his brown eyes and his right arm was wrapped up tight in a lightweight sling.

"Enough of that," Joe said. "I just came to see if you were still alive or if your wife needed a new husband." Joe winked at Jesse, and she giggled.

"That's right. You could have died and left me everything, including your handsome partner," Jesse said with a nudge of her husband.

"I'm sure there are plenty of women your speed in the morgue. This one's taken." Charlie reached out for Jesse's hand and then winced.

"That's enough," Jesse said as she moved to interlock her fingers in those of his free hand. "You'll hurt yourself and then you'll be stuck in the hospital for another day. You heard what the doctor said," she scolded him. Their daughter stirred in the chair, whimpering in her sleep. "I'm going to take her out. Are you going to be okay for a minute?" Jesse glanced between Charlie and Joe.

"I'll be fine, woman. Go." Though he said the words, he didn't release her hand right away, and something unspoken passed between them. Joe didn't have to look into their minds to know it was love.

Then, Jesse carried their four-year-old daughter out of the room. The girl's legs dangled to Jesse's small hips and her head cradled into her mother's neck to avoid the light.

"She's getting so big," Joe said as soon as she'd left the room.

"Don't I know it."

Joe raised an eyebrow. "Sure you don't want another?"

Charlie shook his head and chuckled softly. "No way! I can barely handle that one."

The two fell silent, reluctant to talk about what had happened. Even so, Joe needed to tell his partner everything. After tonight, he'd probably never see him again. He'd never had a close friend other than Emery. Charlie didn't have a lot of other friends, either, since they'd moved from Chicago a year ago. Joe knew his sudden departure would be hard on the man, but he hoped his near-death experience would give him a new appreciation for his life and loved ones, softening the blow in some small way.

"What did the doctor say?" Joe asked.

Charlie winced when he instinctively shrugged one shoulder. "The bullet nicked my clavicle but managed to exit out my back. A clean shot, except for the muscles it tore through. My right arm is no good to me until it's healed."

Joe nodded. Charlie would probably want to know how

things went down after he'd been carried out.

"Crazy Bob's going to spend the few months in jail," Joe began, "and I imagine they'll give him a psych eval."

"That's the least they can do. It's obvious he shouldn't be wandering the streets on his own." Charlie shook his head and winced from the pain. "The man's lost everything. He's been crazy for years; maybe he'll finally get the help he needs."

It was a sad situation. Joe knew on other Taran worlds there were those with mental disabilities and problems, too, but those people were rarely left out on the street for an extended time. On Earth, it seemed as though there were more of them and fewer options for care. Crazy Bob would probably end up staying in some kind of locked-down mental facility getting three meals a day while he was pumped full of mind-numbing drugs. He'd live out the rest of his days bored to death, surrounded by full-time caregivers and other people who'd lost their minds.

"How many days off are they giving you?" Charlie asked.

"Only two." It wasn't a lie, but Joe had only requested the two days. He would be gone tonight if he was able to track down Iza before the TSS Agents tailing his every move caught up to him.

"I wondered if you'd take the mandatory." Charlie nodded in understanding.

Joe didn't correct him, letting Charlie believe that he needed the mental health time after the shooting before returning to work. His aunt and uncle had thought the same thing when he told them that he was going to be taking some time off. No one could know he was leaving, or it might jeopardize his escape and put Iza in danger.

"I guess after that," Joe continued, "I'll be working with whoever they get to cover for you."

Charlie smiled. "You're not gonna get anybody as good as

me."

"Exactly! I'm looking for someone better. I've been suffering long enough," Joe said with a laugh. "How long is your rehab?"

"The doctors say a couple more days and then I can go home. I'll have to take it easy for two weeks. If I had a desk job, I could go back then. Given what we do, I'll probably be out for three altogether."

"Hey, take the paid leave while you can."

"Oh yeah, I'm going to milk it." Charlie's eyes lit up. "Speaking of me being stuck here, what did you bring me?"

Joe furrowed his brow, not sure he understood the question. "What do you mean?"

"I'm in the hospital, man. You didn't think to bring me some contraband? You know the food in here is lousy," Charlie complained.

Joe didn't know anything about the food; he hadn't been in an Earth hospital since he was born. Once he joined the TSS and was introduced to medical nanites, he'd never had much need for a hospital. That was, until the mess with his arm. In that case, though, the hospital on Beurias was like a resort spa compared to most medical centers on Earth.

"I'm sorry, I'll have some flowers waiting for you when you return to work," Joe told him. "It was a busy morning. Had to clean up your mess, take care of the receptionist, come over here and make sure you're doing okay without me to watch your back."

"How is Nancy?"

"She's shaken up; they sent her home for the rest of the week. Who can blame her?"

"Sure, sure. Well, maybe when she gets back you can ask her out instead of hitting on my wife. And don't forget to follow up on those aliens." Charlie winked.

I plan to do just that. "Did the police get your statement yet?" Joe asked.

"Nah, I was still unconscious when they came by. I'll give them a call in the morning."

"Don't worry, I've already given my statement. There's not much else to do but get Bob some help," Joe said.

Charlie's wife Jesse returned a moment later. Their daughter, now standing on her own two feet, was gripping a small yellow flower.

"Hi there, Jasmine. You're wide awake now," Joe said, stating the obvious. The little girl ignored him, barely sparing him a glance. That answered the question of whether or not he was good with kids. He was just happy to have mastered the ability to have social relations with people without wanting to punch them in the face.

"For you, Daddy." Jasmine held out the wilting flower to him, and he grabbed it with his good arm. "I picked it all by myself!"

"Thanks, baby, it's beautiful."

His wife placed a loving hand on his good arm. "I need to get her something to eat and you need the peace and quiet."

"Mommy, I want pizza," Jasmine insisted while speaking over her mother.

"I better let you rest," Joe said, seeing a good opportunity to make his exit. "But hey, it'll be nice being able to sleep in tomorrow." Though even as he said it, Joe's throat tightened at the prospect of never seeing his friend again.

"That's right go home to day-drink and then have your TV dinner. And don't forget to turn off the TV before you fall asleep," Charlie chided him.

Joe gave him a fist bump. Then, he gave Jesse a light hug and waved to Jasmine. Her head tilted up as if she suddenly recognized him and decided that he was the most interesting thing in the room.

"Bye, Uncle Joe," she said to his back.

Joe took a step toward the door and then turned back to them, realizing he wanted to say something. "I know I never told you this before, but I think of you as family. Don't ever change."

They stared back at him a moment before Charlie broke the silence. "I knew you were going to miss me, man. But come on, not in front of my wife."

They all laughed, and he waved to them as he walked out the door.

EARTH WAS NOTHING like Iza had expected it to be. She'd always heard people talk about it as a backwater world that was technologically archaic, but it seemed that humanity had come a long way in recent years. On the surface, at least, the architecture and transportation network were comparable to some of the Outer Colonies, or even a few Middle Worlds. What she found most interesting was that she recognized shades of the cultures found throughout the rest of the Taran Empire. *Funny how our common ancestry is still evident, despite thousands of years of being estranged.*

Trix had piloted the Q Maximus stealth shuttle the short jump to Earth and then flown it down to the surface as quickly as possible. Even at night, there was a high risk of the craft being spotted. Trix had landed it in a treed area outside the city, where the winter-bare tree limbs would provide more cover than nothing at all. As long as the shuttle remained powered down and Trix didn't engage in any outside communications, there was no reason for anyone to suspect it was there.

Using their phones, they had summoned a taxi, which took them to the address Braedon had found for Joe.

The taxi ride to Joe's gave Iza ample time to rehearse in her head what she wanted to say. It would be the first time they'd laid eyes on each other in months, and she wasn't even sure she looked presentable. She glanced down at her clothing and her dirty boots and wondered if she should have worn something more feminine. She could have blamed it on their trip to Earth and trying to fit in, but she rarely wore clothing that wasn't fit for running.

The building Joe lived in was situated off of a place called St. Anthony Main. The boulevard was divided by a continuous island of manicured trees and brush. People here were comfortable walking the street, and she saw more than one person with a dog. It made her think of Atano. He'd given her his version of disapproval at leaving him behind, a short bark followed by a whine. The animals with owners all had dogs tethered to leashes. Atano would be as miserable as Joe on this planet.

As soon as they exited the taxi, Iza pushed past Karter as she raced to Joe's apartment building. The loft apartments didn't look like much from the outside, but from a glance around the neighborhood, it was clear this wasn't a family or economically poor area. Iza pushed and then pulled at the door to the lofts but it was secured. She hadn't anticipated the outer doors having security.

Iza leaned into the box and spoke the two words that didn't require proficiency in the native language, "Joe Anderson."

When nothing happened, she stared at the keypad, wondering how to work with the interface.

"It won't work on verbal commands, try the little buttons," Karter said pointing to the keypad she'd overlooked.

There was one button with the label 'ANDERSON' typed out next to it. She had practiced reading his name in English characters enough that she recognized it on sight. Her finger lifted to the button and pressed. A corresponding buzzing signaled it had worked. Again, nothing happened, and she turned to Karter who was staring at his hands doing his best to appear uninterested. Iza pressed the button again but there was still no answer.

"Well, we tried. I'm ready to go back if you are," Karter said.

Iza bared her teeth as she spoke, "We are *not* going back without Joe. If you don't like it, you can wait in the shuttle with Trix." She pulled out her new Earth cellphone.

"Wait, what are you doing? Any comms risk alerting the TSS of our being here."

"Thank you for stating the obvious," she said. "If he's not here, then he must be at work. Braedon compiled all the research." She waved the phone with the note displaying the address for the office building where Joe worked security.

Karter rolled his eyes.

She smirked. "Let's go."

The taxi driver, an older man with brown skin like her own but more wrinkles than she'd ever seen, talked all the way to their destination. Even though neither Karter nor Iza answered any of his questions or even pretended to listen, he rattled on nonstop. Since the place where Joe worked was in a high traffic area of Minneapolis, according to the map software on the phone, the driver let them out two blocks away.

"What now?" Karter asked as soon as they'd paid the fare and sent the taxi on its way.

"I guess we walk the rest of the way," Iza said her teeth beginning to chatter in the cold winter air.

Karter wrapped his arms around himself. "Well, it's ice cold, so I'm not going to stand around here all day just waiting."

"You were the one who wanted to come." She fixed him with a level glare as she stormed off in the direction of Joe's work building

For once, Karter took the hint and kept his mouth shut.

When they reached the building where Joe worked, they were greeted by a large monument in the center courtyard, surrounded by saplings with white trunks and bright green leaves.

"Where do you think he is?" Karter asked.

As silly as it was, she'd been hoping that maybe she'd just step inside the building and feel his presence somehow and know where to go. Now, she stood looking around at the near empty atrium as people rushed to work, ignoring the two lost people on the main floor. Karter started off and she scampered to follow. He was walking toward a young man wearing a headset and sitting at a sleek half-moon console near a set of glass elevators. It reminded Iza of Karter's reception desk. He must have been thinking the same thing as he strolled up and leaned one elbow on the desk.

Using his translator, he asked, "I'm looking for a security guard name Joe Anderson."

The man used the manual interface in front of him before he raised one hand to his mouth. "Oh, he was in the shooting."

There was a delay while the translator read out the words and Iza gasped as her heart plummeted to her knees. Iza swallowed hard. *Would Joe let himself be shot?* He wasn't completely without skills; he still had telepathy and telekinesis. *Wouldn't he use it to save himself?*

"Where is he being treated?" Karter asked.

He raised his hands palms out as if in Taran greeting. "I'm not allowed to talk about the incident. Check the local news."

Again, Karter and Iza waited for the translation.

Iza's eyes flew to Karter's. "Ask him where we can find this news."

Karter used the translator and the man smiled politely.

"Uh, just look it up on your phone."

"Any other way?" Karter asked through the device.

The man glanced down with a frown and then back at them. "Well, there's a library downtown, to the northwest from here. They've got a ton of free computers over there if you prefer to watch the news on video. If you have any trouble, you can speak with the librarian; they'll be glad to help you."

Karter inclined his head to the man and turned from the console to Iza. He must have seen the worry in her eyes because he put both hands on her upper arms and stared down at her.

"We don't know yet what happened. Relax. If you start crying on me, I'm going to drag you back to the shuttle."

It was enough to snap her back to the moment and out of the worst-case scenarios running through her mind. Iza's eyes cleared before they narrowed into slits. "You wouldn't dare."

Satisfied she was in control of her emotions again, he released her arms and turned away mumbling. "I might."

Iza led them north on a street called Nicollet Mall Avenue, as the map showed the library in that direction. The people in the city came in all shapes and sizes and colors. Some of their clothing styles were bizarre, and she and Karter found themselves pointing out the most absurd of them. It wasn't anything stranger than she'd seen on Taran worlds, but the fact that it was something on Earth made it more entertaining.

To her surprise, there were several dirty and ragged-looking individuals shuffling along the street, carrying sleeping bags or pushing carts. When one such man came up to her with his hand out in the universal sign for begging, she shook her head.

"Sorry, I haven't got any credits on me," she replied in New Taran before remembering that it was a foreign language to the locals. "Bomaxed rogue worlds and their lack of a standardized language," she muttered to herself as she got her local phone out to use for translation.

"We really do take New Taran's ubiquitousness for granted," Karter agreed.

Once the translator was running, Iza repeated her response. "Sorry, I'm not from here. I don't have any credits on me."

"Oh, I'm not asking for your credit card, lady," said the man, holding up his hands. The translator showed a text transcript of his reply in near real-time. "I was just seeing if you had any spare change. Maybe your fancy friend, here, has a few cents he can spare?" He looked over Karter from head to toe.

Karter ignored the man and walked off.

"Guess not," the man said, giving Iza a wink. She laughed. If she had some physical currency, she would've given the man some just for being so entertaining.

Iza started to turn away. Then, she remembered the food bar in her pocket. "Hey, are you hungry?"

"Am I living on the streets?" He snickered.

Iza tossed him the wrapped bar. He looked at it suspiciously. That's when she realized her mistake; the bar was like nothing they had on Earth, but maybe he wouldn't notice.

"Yeah, not from around here, you said?" His eyes narrowed as he studied her, looking her over as intently as he was studying the wrapper.

That's the understatement of the year. "Nope." She waved him farewell.

"Guess Bob was right," he muttered as he walked away.

"Really smooth, Iza," Karter said with a smirk on his lips as they walked away. "No Tarans here. Nothing to see!"

The Minneapolis Central Library building was the most progressive architecture they'd seen so far. They proceeded to the information desk where a woman stood helping an older lady.

"Let me do the talking," Karter said, putting a hand in front of Iza with his translator open on the screen of his phone.

Iza stared at the hand and then up at Karter with some significance.

"Can I help you?" asked the woman standing behind the desk when her previous patron departed.

"Hello, we're new here," Karter began, with the phone translating for him. "We require a computer to do some research."

The woman had her hair divided into two braids and wore bright red glasses. It was as if she was trying to draw attention to the fact that she couldn't see. Iza found it somewhat disturbing.

She looked them up and down. Karter was immaculately dressed and Iza was dressed in less formal attire, but there was nothing about their appearance that didn't blend in with the community around them. The woman gazed at Iza's boots a little bit longer than she would've liked.

"Sure, I can help you with that," she said at last. "I'm just going to need a little bit of information from you first in order to get you set up with a library card. Can I get your current identification showing your address in Minneapolis or one of the surrounding cities?"

Karter glanced at Iza and she stared blankly back at him. They didn't have anything of the sort.

"I'm sorry, we've been recently robbed, and they took our ID. And our foreign phones don't have a connection to the Net, which is why we need a computer here," Iza jumped in.

"Oh dear, I'm so sorry. Sure, let me set you up with a computer so you can get on the internet and get everything sorted out. You'll only have an hour to use the equipment on a guest pass. I'd be happy to make a call to the authorities for you to report the robbery," said the young woman.

"No, that's okay, thank you," Iza replied. "We've already contacted the authorities about our situation. The computer is all we need now. An hour should be fine. We appreciate your help."

The woman behind the counter pulled out a slim piece of paper and wrote an alphanumeric code on it below the word 'visitor'. She handed it to Iza and directed them toward the row of computers for public use.

"Are you sure about this?" Karter asked. He seemed concerned that they were going to be conducting their search in the middle of public space.

"We don't have much of a choice, aside from contacting the *Verity*—and I'm not desperate enough yet to take the risk." She sat down at one of the open terminals and pointed to the chair next to her. "Grab a seat. We need to work fast."

The interface seemed strange to her. It didn't help that everything was in a foreign language. She had to hold up the phone to look at the translated text on her screen. Even then, she didn't know how to do what she wanted. *Where's Braedon when I need him?*

"I have no idea what to do with this," she admitted after staring at the various icons. The translation didn't help. "This is like nothing I've ever seen before." She leaned into the computer display and spoke, "CACI, I need to run a records search."

The screen didn't move and there was no response. The text box in the middle of the screen with a blinking line taunted her as if daring her to figure it out.

"They won't have CACI here," Karter said.

A man about Iza's age with blue spiked hair and black eyeliner came in and sat down a couple of terminals away. He quickly signed in and began navigating the interface.

Karter shook his head at Iza, indicating she shouldn't talk

to him, but they were stuck. Without some help, they would never find Joe. She scooted closer to the young boy and spoke into her phone for translation.

"I'm sorry to bother you, but could you help us?" Iza asked, hoping the use of a translator would make their need understandable. "We're not from here, and we're trying to find the local news. Can you help us understand this interface?"

He looked around as if surprised she were talking to him and then shrugged.

"It's not that hard." He hadn't taken his eyes off his screen.

"Can you show me, please?" she asked holding out the slip of paper the woman had given her.

He sighed and rolled his eyes. "Fine."

Iza stood up from the chair, bumping into Karter as she made room for the young man.

With expert hands, he clicked on an icon and navigated to a dialogue box. "Which local news outlet and how far back?"

"One that covers events in the area of downtown Minneapolis within the last day or two," she said.

"Really?" He stared at her like he didn't believe it.

"Yes, why?"

"No reason," he shrugged. "I was expecting something more complicated, I guess. Is there a particular story you're looking for?"

Karter leaned forward placing one palm flat down on the table. "A shooting at the IDS building." His translator keeping up with his words.

"Oh, the shooting yesterday?" He brought up a news article. His eyes widened and he cracked an amused smile as he read it over. "Yeah, I saw this on the news! Some guy was in there yelling about aliens, of all things. Shot up the place. One of the guards was hit, but they haven't released his name."

"Hit with what?" Iza asked.

He turned to stare at her with some confusion. "A bullet. You know, shot. Like from a gun," he said, holding out his hand thumb up with a finger pointed at her chest.

Iza slapped his hand away, feeling foolish for not understanding the translation, but liking even less that he seemed to be making fun of her. The young man frowned as he pulled his hand back into his chest. Karter gave her quick shake of his head, to which she lifted one shoulder in quiet assent.

"We need to know where they took him after the shooting," Iza said.

The blue-haired man nodded his head as he used the manual interface pressing on the keys without looking down. Then he started reading off the screen. "The Minneapolis Star and Tribune reported that after the security guard was shot yesterday, they took him to HCMC."

Iza eyes darted to Karter but he kept his features neutral.

"What is an HCMC?" Iza asked.

The young man looked from Iza to Karter and then shook his head. "It's Hennepin County Medical Center—a hospital."

"Is it a secured facility?"

"As secured as this place."

Iza looked from him to Karter. They'd barely made it to a computer without the required identification.

The young man continued as if they'd been waiting for him to explain. "You just check-in at the front desk."

"How far is it from here?" Karter asked.

"A couple of blocks west of here." He pointed vaguely toward the door and then returned to his computer, leaving them to decide what to do on their own.

"Thank you for your help," Iza told him, but he had already put in earbuds.

She turned away from the row of terminals and walked out with Karter on her heels.

"It might not be him," Karter said in New Taran. The words almost comforting in their matter-of-fact delivery.

"I know, but since it's the only lead we have, we need to be sure."

13

IZA AND KARTER hurried the two blocks east to the hospital and raced into the lobby. Now that they had more pertinent details about the shooting, it couldn't be too hard to track Joe down. Since the shooting was the day before, it would make sense that he wasn't home, since he would likely still be in the hospital convalescing.

The hospital emergency room was a flurry of activity. It seemed there were people constantly coming and going, but there was a quiet area near the reception desk. It was as good a place as any to start.

"Excuse me, I'm looking for someone who might've come in recently," Iza said using the translator.

The man gave them an odd look at the use of the translation device, then returned his attention to his computer screen. "Name?"

"Joe Anderson," she said.

"Sorry, we don't have a patient by that name here."

Karter leaned forward over the desk. "Perhaps he's using a different name to protect his identity. He was involved in the shooting at the IDS," he said.

The man looked at him with some question and

skepticism. "I can confirm that a security guard who was hit in the incident was admitted here yesterday."

"Is he still here?" Iza asked.

"We're not at liberty to give you that information."

"He's a good friend of ours. We need to see him," Iza said. "Please can you help us?"

"Only family is allowed at the moment. I suggest you reach out to his relatives to get an update on his status." Assuming that the conversation was over, he turned away from them and looked over their shoulder toward the next person in the queue. "How can I help you?"

Iza and Karter were brushed aside as the next family visiting someone in the hospital approached the desk. They gave their names and their identification forms and were admitted in.

Now what? Iza was beside herself. They were so close to finding Joe, and they were steps away from having the access they needed.

Karter jerked his head to one side, indicating they should step away from the desk.

"What?" Iza asked.

"I have an idea."

"Does your idea involve sneaking in on our own?"

Karter nodded.

"Then I would say it's the best idea we've had all day. Let's have it," Iza said.

"See those doors over there?" Karter asked. Iza looked over his shoulder toward the doors. The family that had been admitted just after them were going through them. "Doesn't look like anyone's guarding them, does it?"

Her eyes darted around the waiting area. There wasn't a sentry in sight. In fact, there wasn't any hospital staff other than the man at the desk. "It looks like he's buzzing them in with the button on his side," Iza said.

"That means we need to get him away from the desk, and then get someone to push the button to let us in." Karter raised his eyebrows.

"I guess you're indicating that it should be me," Iza said, rolling her eyes. "Of course you are. I have to do everything."

That's when she caught sight of the kid—the one that belonged to the family who'd gone through the door. They'd accidentally let the door close between them and would have to re-open it to let him in.

"Come on," Iza said through her teeth, rushing toward the doors. As if on cue, they pushed opened the door and the child ran in after his mother. Karter caught it from closing, opening it just wide enough for him and Iza to slip in behind.

"It looks like they've got a monitoring system here," Karter observed, pointing to the black sphere in the corner above the door. "We need to hurry."

"We don't even know where we're going," Iza said.

They raced along the hall. When they encountered a sign overheard, Karter stopped and pointed his phone translator up at it. "It says 'Emergency' is that way. That's where I'd look for someone who's recently been shot."

"Good point," Iza warned.

When they arrived at the emergency room, it was more chaotic than anywhere else they'd been on Earth. People were being rushed through the doors and into rooms, while the staff seemed more concerned with their patients than anyone walking through. In fact, there was no one to even ask the question.

"How we can find anyone in all this mess?" Iza asked.

"Darling, have a little faith. We just need to be persistent," Karter said.

"Call me darling again, and it will be literally the last thing you ever say," Iza shot back.

Karter snickered as he led her toward a room that had been recently abandoned. There was a sweater with an identification sticker still on it. He removed it and put it over her jacket. Then, he scooped around for another, and found a trashcan, which seemed to be full of them. He unrolled one and carefully smoothed it out before putting it over his left breast pocket.

"There, now we won't stand out so much."

Iza stared at the crumpled sticker on his chest and then to Karter and back again. "Oh no, Mrs. Myrtle. No one would ever think you didn't belong," Iza said with some sarcasm, covering her laughter with the back of her hand.

Karter said. "Come on, it doesn't look like he's here."

"Now what?"

"I guess we better ask someone," Karter said. He looked around again and found a harried nurse standing at one of the stations.

He spoke into his phone for translation. "Please Miss, can you help us? We seem to have lost our family member. He was the victim in the shooting at the IDS yesterday. Can you direct me to where he is?"

"Oh, Charles Jones? Yes, I remember him. Let me see where he got moved." She said racing to a terminal typing in the information. "You can find him on the fourth floor. Room... 4102."

"Thank you so much." Karter gave the woman a slight bow and then turned to leave.

"Hey, wait!" The woman called after them, causing Iza's blood pressure to spike. "You're going the wrong way." She pointed in the opposite direction toward the doors. "You'll have to take the elevators. That's the only way to get up there."

"Sorry, it's our first time here. Thank you again," Iza said, keeping the translator open in case they encountered any other questions.

"Charles Jones?" Karter said with a raised eyebrow as soon as they were beyond the nurse's earshot.

"Even if it's not Joe, maybe he knows him."

They made it to the elevators without incident. When the elevator arrived at the fourth floor, Iza approached the nurse sitting behind what looked like a reception desk.

"Hello, I'm a relative of Charles Jones. May I see him?"

The woman barely glanced up from her paperwork. "He's there down the hall, last door on the right," she said.

Iza exchanged a surprise glance with Karter. *That was easy.*

They walked together down the hall to the end of the corridor. There were voices coming from the room, and Iza was about to step into the doorway when a woman stepped out.

"Oh, hello. Sorry I didn't see you there. Can I help you with something?" The woman looked her up and down curiously, wondering what she could be there for.

Iza had prepared for this, though it might be a tough tell with her speaking a foreign language into a translator. "I am a friend. I'm here to see Charles Jones."

The woman looked her over again and stared at Karter for second before turning her attention back to Iza. "A 'friend', huh? All right, I'll let him know you're here." The woman said turning about and returning to the room. "Charlie, this woman says she knows you."

"Probably thinks you're his exotic mail-away mistress," Karter whispered jokingly in her ear. He narrowed avoided getting her elbow in his ribs.

Iza stepped into the room after the woman. One look at the man lying in the bed, with his arm around a small little girl, confirmed that Charles Jones was definitely not Joe.

"I'm sorry, this is awkward," Iza said. She'd just told the man's wife that she was overly familiar with her husband.

Clearly, she wanted some answers, and Iza didn't feel like trying to come up with another lie so she decided on the truth. "I'm actually looking for Joe Anderson; I thought maybe he was admitted under a different name. I heard he was working as a guard at the IDS building, so I thought he may have been involved in the shooting."

Despite the translation delay, the woman's expression changed from suspicion to relief. Then, she smiled widely, showing a mouth full of bright white teeth before standing up to shake her hand.

"Oh, yes. My husband and Joe work together," she said. "I'm Jesse, and this is our daughter, Jasmine."

Jasmine, at the sound of her name, put her arms up to her mother to be held, but Jesse instead directed her to a paper notebook and a set of colored sticks on a chair.

"Yeah, everything happened so fast yesterday," Charlie said. "I was the one who was hurt while he was stuck cleaning up the mess." He looked Iza over, casting a quick glance to Karter hovering outside the door. "How is it you know Joe? You look familiar, but I get the impression from the translators you're not from around here."

"We met abroad," Iza replied cryptically.

A spark of recognition flashed in Charlie's dark eyes. "Are you his mystery girl? The one who got away?"

Iza's heart skipped a beat. *So, he does feel the same way.* She took a breath to steady herself.

"Oh my goodness, I should have seen it before. Look at her face, babe," his wife said.

He did and nodded. "That's why she looks so familiar."

Iza was embarrassed by all the attention and quickly turned the conversation back to the point.

"Do you know where I can find Joe now?"

"He came by yesterday but maybe he went into work,"

Charlie replied.

"No, we went there, and he wasn't in. They wouldn't tell us anything that's how we ended up here."

Iza could feel the anxiety of the morning's events creeping up on her as she waited for the translator to interpret his response.

"He owes me a gift for taking a bullet for him. He said he was taking some time off. If he ran out of food, he might be at the grocery store," Charlie said letting out a chuckle. "Though, I wouldn't trust his cooking. You two will have to come by our place for a decent meal while you're in town."

Not if I have my way and we're off of this planet tonight. Iza liked them, but she doubted she'd ever see them again.

His wife gave him a light slap on the leg. "Don't say things like that about his cooking. She doesn't know your joking."

Iza forced a smile even as the desire to be on her way made her fidget. "It's urgent I speak with him. Do you know how I can find him?"

"Have you tried calling him?" Charlie asked. He wiggled his fingers at his wife, and she passed him a small device that resembled the cellphones Braedon had manufactured on the *Verity*. He held it up to his ear, and it rang four times before Iza heard Joe's voice.

"Hi, this is Joe."

"Hi." Iza stepped forward, excited to speak with him.

"I'm not available at the moment. Leave a message and I'll get back to you."

Charlie ended the call. "Nope, he's not answering his phone."

Jesse met Iza's eye and there was sympathy there. She seemed to understand Iza's urgency. Then, she leaped up and moved to the small cabinet on the other side of the room.

"Honey, didn't he give you his spare apartment key for

emergencies?"

"Yes," Charlie said, uniting in his wife's excitement. "It's in my pack, side pocket, white key fob."

Jesse lifted it out of the pack and waved it at Iza. "Found it. You can use this to get into his apartment. That way, you won't be standing out in the cold waiting for him to finish his errands."

Iza took the offered key fob from her. "Thank you so much. We'll leave you to rest."

Charlie smiled. "No worries. I'll always take extra attention."

Jesse sighed. "Well you have fun. Charles is gonna be here at least one more night for observation. Maybe you can join Joe at our place for supper in a few days?"

"I'm not sure how long I'll be in town," Iza said, "but thank you for the offer. Have a good night, and I wish you the best with your recovery."

Unexpectedly, both Charlie and Jesse reached out to shake hands with her. Charlie's good hand was warm and calloused. His wife's hand wasn't soft, but it was cool to the touch. Their daughter slid down from the chair and held up the picture she'd been working on in silence for Iza to take.

"Oh, thank you," Iza said. The image Jasmine had drawn was of two people holding hands. She assumed it was her parents, but she asked anyway. "Is this your mom and dad?"

Their daughter Jasmine shook her head vehemently as if the thought to draw her parents hadn't crossed her mind. "No, that's you and Uncle Joe."

Then, Iza looked again and saw the distinct curl in the hair of the woman and the bright blue of Joe's eyes. Jasmine had done her best to put hearts all around their heads, and Iza's eyes filled before she could stop them. She bit down hard on the inside of her cheek to control the rush of emotion. *Was I ever so insightful as a child? Did I ever draw pictures?* Iza couldn't remember ever having done so, since her earliest memories of her home with her parents was a blur. She'd forgotten her father's face, but she'd never forget how safe and warm she was in his arms. That never really went away.

"That's so sweet," Iza said when she'd gained control of her face again. She carefully rolled up the picture up in one hand. She couldn't wait to show it to Joe. He would probably love it as much as she did. "It was a pleasure to meet you. Thank you again."

Charlie and Jesse waved as she passed through the door, and Iza couldn't help feeling sad that they probably wouldn't see Joe again after tonight. They seemed so nice—the kind of people you'd miss.

She followed Karter through the corridor along the path of glowing red signs leading to the nearest exit.

"Seems like Joe has a good life here," Karter said. "What makes you think he'll want to leave?"

Iza placed the rolled-up picture in her inner jacket pocket next to her heart. "You wouldn't understand."

—

Joe's street was much as she'd left it earlier. At this hour, there were more people strolling along the walking paths and more traffic. Now that the large, yellow sun was dominating the sky, it wasn't as cold. People even smiled at them as they passed.

Iza slid into the building and Karter was right behind her until she held up a hand. "If you don't mind, I need to do this part alone."

"What am I supposed to do? Sit on the steps and wait for your return?"

Iza shrugged. "Or across the street. I noticed a small café, where you can sit down and have a coffee until we come out. Either way, I'm going the rest of the way alone. I don't need you for this part."

"What if he's still out?"

"Then I'll wait. If you get bored, head back to the shuttle. Trix can be very entertaining," she said, not bothering to hide her smile.

Karter's lips firmed into a line. It was clear he didn't like the idea, but it wasn't as if he had a choice. "Fine, but don't leave without me."

Iza tapped the key fob on the palm of her other hand. The unit number was '5b'; she'd memorized it. She took a deep breath. *All right, Joe. Hopefully you'll be home and happy to see me.*

14

JOE KNEW SHE was close as soon as he reached his apartment building. He could feel her. Carrying his bag of groceries procured on a quick trip to the store, he ran into the lobby. He expected to see her waiting for him there, but it was empty. As he took the stairs up, he sensed he was getting closer to her.

With his heart pounding in his ears, he flung open his front door. There, sitting in the seat facing his television, was Iza.

"Hi," she said. It was the simplest of greetings and said as if they'd spoken no less than a few hours ago. She stood up and moved toward him like she'd just strolled over from the apartment next door, not from a distant star system.

"Hi," he said trying to match her tone. "Were you in the neighborhood?"

"As a matter of fact, I was. I thought I would check out this place that they sent you, to see how you're holding up." She looked around the bare walls and sad decorating style. "I see you've settled in."

"This place could never be home without you." Joe ran to her.

Iza wrapped her arms around his neck and leaped into his arms. He held her up while she entwined her legs around his waist.

He held her close. "How are you here?"

"That doesn't matter right now." It was clear she had only one thing on her mind.

He clamped his lips against hers, tasting the sweet warmth of her. Since she was already in his arms, he thought he'd show her to his room.

Joe dropped her onto the bed. He slipped out of his shoes and unlaced her boots one at a time until he could pull each off and toss them across the room. She reached up and pulled off his shirt, then drew him closer to her. He gave in, like he had since the first time they'd met.

He'd missed the bond between them. There had been so many nights he'd spent with the ache in his chest keeping him awake, wondering how she was faring. Now, she was here in front of him like he'd always imagined.

"You're not mad at me?" he asked.

"I came all the way to *Earth* for you, didn't I?" Iza smiled and let out a light giggle as she wiggled out of her pants. He loved the sound.

Then, while he worked on his pants, she unbuttoned her shirt. "I was mad, but not anymore. Having spent half a day in this place, I can see you've been punished enough." She was leaning toward him now a breath away. Her shirt open as she caught her breath her chest heaving.

He slid onto the bed beside her and entangled his fingers in her long black curls. "I was lost without you."

"Does that mean you're willing to leave here?"

"I'd go anywhere if it means being with you." He let his lips fall to hers.

—   —   —

The mental manipulation device was working flawlessly. Victor Arvonen smiled down at the former TSS Agent. The retrieval from Earth had gone perfectly the day before. Now, Victor had Joe—and more importantly, his mind. The young man was practically obsessed with Iza. Now that Joe was in the induced dream-state, extracting information about Iza may be easier than Victor had anticipated.

"Mr. Arvonen, we're in. He's fantasizing about Iza Sundari," the technician confirmed, pointing to the wall-mounted monitor behind Joe Anderson's head; the subject was secured to the angled observation bed in case he woke up and tried to fight back again. The readout on the monitor wasn't an exact representation of what Joe was seeing in his unconscious mind, but the interface allowed them to guide his thoughts. The technician could barely curb his enthusiasm, tapping his foot anxiously.

Joe had resisted at first, no surprise for a former TSS Agent, but Victor was patient. After months and years of bringing his plans to fruition, the delay had been nothing more than a minor inconvenience.

The aftermath of the shooting at Joe's work had been a perfect diversion for capturing him and bringing him back to the *Arvonen One*. The irony wasn't lost on Victor, since it appeared that the shooter only perpetrated the act because he spotted one of the shuttles Victor had sent down with investigators to look for Joe. But, everything had gone according to plan with his eventual capture, and that's all Victor cared about.

Victor's attempts to locate another accessible Gate sphere had hit a dead end, and with a confirmed Gate now active on Uephus—too dangerous to retrieve—time was running short. Joe's relationship with Iza, the key, made him Victor's best lead. While Joe had no doubt handed the sphere over to the

TSS, it was possible his memories held some clue about where it may be held longer-term. More importantly he might be of some use to him in dealing with the key. However, it would only work if the man's mind was pliable.

Now, Victor and his team just needed to trace their way back through Joe's relevant memories to the part of his mind that created new ideas so he could plant a few of his own. Unfortunately, Joe's frequent mental tangents about his parents' death kept getting in the way. This was the first breakthrough they'd had since they'd connected him to the device.

Victor smiled. "How long can you keep him in this fantasy?"

"The mind is a strange thing," the technician replied. "As far as he's concerned, everything that's happening is real. If we try to redirect him, the mental link can be broken and we'd have to start over. I suggest we let him play the fantasy through to its completion. Then we can start working backward through his memories to the last moment he saw the sphere and Iza Sundari. We'll know everything about them and have a better chance of being successful."

"We'll do whatever it takes. He's our best lead, and if his mind is malleable, we can get him to do even more."

"He's been highly trained as an Agent; his mind is going to be very difficult to fool. We'll have to take our time with this or it could all backfire."

Victor moved to the technician's side and studied the monitor behind Joe. Strapped down and unconscious, the former Agent didn't seem threatening in the least. "We don't have the luxury of time. Things in our galaxy have already become unstable. I need you to work as fast as you can," he said.

Victor then turned to Raquel, who was working at the

console on the opposite wall of the compact lab room. "Any progress on your end?"

"No, sir." Her eyes shifted away from him and toward Joe strapped to the inclined bed. "But I'm concerned this won't work."

"Let me worry about whether or not this is going to be successful. I was asking about your assignment. Where are we on getting through the Gate?"

"I can't replicate what Iza did without access to a sphere. But, if my original findings were correct, I think it has more to do with her genetics than we realized."

"Then we'll get her," Victor said without hesitation. "That's why we have him." Victor turned on one heel and left the lab behind.

He smiled to himself. Soon, he'd have everything he wanted and his legacy would be safe.

— — —

Joe woke up in his bed and reached out beside him for the familiar shape of Iza, but she was gone. He sat up, preparing to go find her when he heard the flush of the toilet. Iza glided back into the room wearing one of his button-up shirts. She hopped back on the bed beside him, looking as content as he'd ever seen her.

"This place is so different," she said, nuzzling up against him. "I don't know how you do it."

He smiled back. "I'll be honest, at first I didn't know how I would. It took a long time to get used to that dull ache in my chest." He touched the place where it hurt when she wasn't there. It had faded now, like it had never existed.

Iza nodded. It was obvious she felt the same as she reached up to touch the identical place on her own chest just over the heart. "We're together again now."

Joe reached up to brush the side of her face with his fingertips. "It's so strange seeing you here. I can't get over it."

She turned into him and kissed his hand. "You don't need to get used to it, because we won't be here for long. I suggest you pack." Then, she looked around with a frown. "That is, if you have anything worth keeping. Otherwise, get dressed. We'll take the shuttle back to the *Verity* tonight."

"How did you get down here without detection, anyway?" he asked.

"I have my ways," she said with a coy smile.

The details didn't matter to Joe. All that he cared about was that they were back together.

"Iza, if I'm going with you, I do have one condition."

"Which is?"

"We need to get rid of that fiancé of yours."

She laughed. "Well, obviously!"

"So, you're admitting the whole thing was a sham?"

"Publicly, no, but I know you've always known the truth. I so wish I could have told you from the beginning, Joe."

His heart still leaped every time she said his real name. "I should have trusted you more. Trusted what we had. I let Karter get to me."

"Well, he's an ass, so I can't fault you."

"What were the terms of the agreement that you'd go along with that insane marriage plot?"

She shook her head. "Let's not get into it now. Suffice to say, you're the only guy I'm interested in being with. I'll ditch him as soon as circumstances allow it."

He nodded reluctantly. "All right."

"Now, pack!" she urged. "Or say your goodbyes. Whatever you need to do. As soon as it's dark, we're out of here."

WHEN IZA REACHED the door marked 5b, her heart was pounding with anticipation for seeing Joe. She knocked first.

There was no answer. *Where is he?* She swiped the key fob over the reader, and the door unlocked. She walked into Joe's apartment and straight into a trap.

Uh oh… Iza was about to make a run for it, but it was too late. The moment the door opened, she found herself standing face-to-face with two TSS Agents. They weren't dressed as Agents, but their dark clothing and way they carried themselves reminded her too much of Joe when he'd been trying to blend in as a civilian.

However, the Agents weren't alone. There was also an older couple standing with them, who looked to be Earth civilians. Instant recognition filled their eyes when they saw her.

"Yes, I'm Iza," she said holding up a hand in formal greeting to them both.

"Oh, we know," the older man said. "My name is Mark, and this is my wife Shirley Ann, Joe's, aunt and uncle. Please, dear. Come in."

The older couple beckoned her into the apartment. They clearly wanted the Agents to leave as they did so, but the two black-clad individuals instead followed the couple into the living room.

What in the stars is going on? Hesitantly, Iza followed the older couple's lead while giving the two Agents as wide of a berth as she could in the compact space.

The small apartment had a table against one wall before opening up into a small seating area. Joe hadn't bothered to put much decorating into the place; it was as bare as his cabin had been on the ship. He'd chosen black and gray furniture and the varying shades of it echoed her current mood. She'd expected to find something of him in the space, but there was barely any warmth in the small apartment. The uncovered windows throughout the space were the only thing that gave the room any depth.

Iza looked around the room, scanning for any clues about what Joe's life had been like over his last three months on Earth. It felt like a violation to be in his private space with so many strangers. *Where is he? Why isn't he here?*

"I always wondered why he'd never been interested in anyone. It all makes sense now," Mark said with a wink toward Iza.

"Did he tell you about me?" Iza's heart leaped at the thought.

"Not in so many words," Mark said clearing his throat and casting his eyes in the direction of the living room wall next to the TV. Iza turned then and gazed up at the painting that took up most of the wall space just above a short bookcase with a scattering of books, and knickknacks. An outline painting of herself looking back at her. A hand brushed line of soft curls framing the face and a playful grin lit up the eyes that stared up in a way she wasn't sure she'd ever done before. It was the most stunning portrait she'd ever seen. The hairs on Iza's arm stood on end when she saw her name painted in a brushed script black at the corner.

She couldn't take her eyes off of the painting and wondered
who had created it and how they managed to capture such a
realistic expression. Something she'd never seen in the mirror,
but that Joe had seen and then brought to life in the painting.
Is that how he really sees me? Am I that beautiful in his eyes?

"Where is Joe now?" Iza asked, ignoring the Agents who
stood staring at her.

"We don't know," Shirley said. "He called yesterday after
the shooting at work to say he was all right and not to worry—
told us he would call again this morning. When he didn't, we
came over to check on him. Instead, we found these two here
snooping around." She glared at the two black-clad men
wearing tinted glasses.

"Ma'am, we understand your concern, but we're looking
into it. Please, return to your home and allow us to complete
our investigation."

"No, now you hear—" Mark started, but one of the Agents
removed his tinted glasses and looked him square in the eyes.

"Please, sir, return home," the Agent repeated. The glow in
his irises was unmistakable.

Without another word, the older couple left the apartment.
Iza had heard about Agents using mental influence in that way,
but she'd never seen it firsthand. Not for the first time, she was
grateful to be immune to telepathy.

Then, the Agent turned his eyes on Iza. She was sure he
was expecting something to happen, but she stared unblinking
back at him. The two Agents stared at each other in the way
that said they were telepathically communicating before they
turned back to her.

"Captain Iza Sundari, you'll come with us," the second
Agent stated.

She kept her expression blank as she answered. "I doubt I
have a choice." They might not be able to mentally control her,

but they could certainly physically overpower her. If they'd been local Enforcers, she'd have made more of fuss, but she'd seen what Joe could do back on Phiris. His telekinetic abilities alone were more than the average civilian saw up close. She wasn't willing to test these Agents' relative abilities by resisting.

The two Agents led her out of the building and down to the street, where an unmarked black van waited. They opened the rear doors, and Iza saw Karter was already apprehended, the stasis cuffs on his wrists resting in his lap. Once she was seated, they put cuffs on her, as well, and without a verbal word the van was in motion.

"Is anyone going to tell us where Joe is?" Iza asked.

The Agents remained quiet. She thought of asking them where they were going but she recognized the protocol of an arrest, and they were no doubt taking her to a holding cell until someone with more authority could question her. Being on a planet that wasn't recognized as part of the Taran Empire didn't change procedure much.

They rode in silence out to the countryside, where the van pulled into what looked like a typical hanger at a civilian airfield. Except, housed in the building was a matte black TSS shuttle that had all the stealth capabilities she'd dreamed of and more. She was strapped into the back passenger area across from Karter, who stared at her as if willing her to read his eyebrow signals and blinks. Iza rolled her head, this wasn't a movie vid, and she had no plan for out running or escaping the TSS. It would be ridiculous to try, and Karter should have known better.

"We depart at nightfall," the first Agent said.

"And where are we going?" Iza asked, though she already suspected the answer.

"TSS Headquarters."

—

The ride in the stealth shuttle from Earth was one of the smoothest flights Iza had experienced. She had to admit, she was curious to see the TSS' base of operations up close, after everything Joe had told her.

First impressions did not disappoint. The large spaceport tucked on the back side of the moon as a beautiful piece of engineering, with sweeping sculptural lines and fine materials typically not seen outside the wealthiest of the Taran central planets. The small stealth shuttle—breathtaking in its own right—paled in comparison to the fleet of TSS ships.

The shuttle arced past the spaceport and landed directly at a surface port on the moon, situated at the bottom of a crater in the pitted, gray surface. She and Karter were then ushered into an elevator, which descended deep underground.

When the doors opened again, Iza was reminded of the stylish interior at Apex Manufacturing—dark tile flooring paired with natural wood accents. Her lip lifted at the sight of the small plants encased in glass along the walls and potted plants in designated places; they must have someone like Cierra in the place making sure they can all breathe clean air.

Iza was directed out from the elevator, but the escorts held Karter back. Before Iza could look over her shoulder at him, the doors closed between them. She was led to the left down a corridor, and she found herself wondering if these were the same halls Joe had once walked. The thought lifting something inside her a little. *What if Joe is already here? Are they taking me to him?*

However, Iza knew the moment she was brought into a small, white lab and pushed into an exam chair that this was neither a reunion nor questioning. They were about to do something to her, and despite what she already knew of the

Agents' abilities, she fought with all she had. Yet, without even laying a hand on her, she was immobilized, and restraints clicked around her wrists and ankles, with another at her waist.

"What are you doing to me?" Iza shouted. "No, I'm a Taran citizen! You can't do this without my consent!"

The two Agents stepped back, and an older woman of medium height in a white lab coat came up next to Iza. Her light green eyes, complimenting her dark hair and olive skin, peered down at Iza and frowned. The woman's voice was soft and warm as she spoke like they were old friends. "I'm Sheila Wescot. I'll be examining you. This won't hurt a bit. We're just taking a blood sample and performing a couple of scans. Please don't resist; if you do, I'll have to sedate you. Unless, you would prefer to be asleep."

Iza swallowed. Being awake meant she'd know exactly what was going on and be able to see for herself. She didn't trust them with her eyes open, so she certainly wasn't going to give them a reason to put her out. Iza forced her breathing to calm.

Iza kept her eyes on the woman's movements during the entire process as she collected blood and tissue samples. At one point, she stepped back and a bright red line of light scanned her from head to toe. The whole thing took less than ten minutes to complete before they were unstrapping her and putting her back into the stasis cuffs. Iza didn't have time to give the woman a proper glare before the Agents led her out of the lab and to another part of the building.

They brought Iza into a conference room where a female Agent waited at the far end of a large oval table. Her brown hair was swept across her forehead and clipped at the nape.

"Welcome, Captain. I've heard a lot about you and I'm glad we get to be better acquainted." She gestured to a seat on her right in one of the black fabric-covered chairs nearest her.

Whatever their intentions, they seemed ready to talk now. Iza raised her cuffed hands in question. The woman nodded to the Agents who stood on either side of her. The one on her right released the cuffs from around her wrists and they both moved to stand at the door as they'd done in the lab.

Iza rubbed at her wrists absently before she joined the female Agent at the large table. They sat down in unison. There were no decorative pictures or accents in the room, and no clues as to what she might be here to do.

"I'm sure you have questions, but I'm hoping you'll hear me out first."

"Who are you?" Iza asked. She'd already decided her own questions were more important at the moment.

"My name is Agent Skyler Anderson."

Iza choked and then gathered herself again. *That lying, cheating, no-good—* A litany of curses were rolling through her mind and she stared at the woman keeping her expression as blank as she could. *Married? Joe was married and to this woman.* Iza did a mental comparison of their differences that took less than ten seconds. They couldn't be more opposite. *What did Joe see in her?*

"I can see by the way you're controlling your facial muscles that you've never heard of me. I'm Joe's older sister."

Iza then remembered a few months back when Joe had talked about his sister. They struggled to get along, according to him. He hadn't given her name or said she was also an Agent. Instead of saying so, she waited for Skyler to continue.

"If you're worried about your fiancé you needn't. He's sitting quietly in a cell. He hasn't been harmed and he's cooperating with us for the moment. Can I ask you to do the same?"

Iza bristled at the mention of Karter as her fiancé. Agent Anderson held Iza's gaze until Iza sat back and crossed her arms over her chest and nodded.

"Good, now first things first. I need you to contact your ship and tell them to meet you here."

"Why would I do that?"

"I want to see my brother, Captain, and I don't really care if you're hiding him, but—"

"I'm sorry, what?" Iza's hands dropped to her sides.

"Please," Agent Anderson leaned forward over the table and placed her hands on it palms down, "I need to see him."

"I haven't seen Joe since Enforcers escorted him off my ship."

"I don't believe you." Anderson's eyes went from pleading to hard in an instant.

"Stars! I don't care what you believe. You can't blame me for the fact you two haven't talked." Iza's back straightened. She didn't know much about his sister, but she wasn't afraid to use what little she had on her.

"Do you have any siblings?" Iza could see Anderson's jaw tighten.

Iza shrugged. "No, I don't."

"Then you don't understand what it means to be family even when you don't get along. He's my little brother, and I'll do anything to get him back."

Iza's mouth opened to answer, but then the door opened between her two escorts and another Agent entered. He took in the room and frowned before moving to the table. He spoke aloud even though he could have used telepathy.

"Agent Anderson, I thought I told you, I would send for you when it was time." His tone was deep but disapproving and Anderson bristled.

"It's Joe," she said as if that explained away her actions.

Something more passed silently between them before the older Agent turned to Iza.

"If you'll excuse me, Captain Sundari, I'm Agent Ian Mandren, Sacon Division leader, and I apologize for my tardiness," he added the last part with a look at Anderson that read he wasn't tardy at all.

Knowing now who she would be meeting with, Iza suddenly had the feeling this was more than an update. Any close friend or colleague of the High Commander of the TSS wouldn't have come all this way only to question her about being on Earth. It even commanded Iza's attention, and she held a less than favorable impression of the Taran elite.

"He reported to you," Iza said.

"Yes, I trained him."

Iza looked him over, attractive for a man of his age. "Don't take this the wrong way, but you didn't do a great job."

Agent Anderson choked back her shock before her eyes flew to Mandren's face, which was passively calm as he spoke.

"Joe didn't love the training and struggled in many of his classes. I was one of a few instructors who pushed him to do better. Demanded he improve himself. To be an adequate Agent was all I ever wanted for him. That was my mistake. Now he's gone."

Iza watched the older man's face twist into something like regret. The way he talked about Joe made her wonder why he'd ship him off to Earth.

"Well, if you missed him so much, why did send him away in the first place? It's an easy enough problem to fix. Get a shuttle back there, pick him up and bring him home."

His hesitation gave her hope. Perhaps that's why they'd brought her here; they were planning something exactly like that and needed her cooperation.

Something in Ian's eyes warmed, and he smiled down at her before sitting in the seat at the end of the oval table closest to her.

"Interesting you should say so. In fact, we did send for him. However, we found you instead. Perhaps you can help us with something," Mandren said without preamble.

"You can't find Joe and you think I have him," Iza answered. "Well, I can save you some time. Like I told Agent Sky here, he's not with us."

Iza could see the hackles rising as Agent Anderson shifted in her seat and glared at her.

Mandren eyed her for a moment as if making up his mind about something before speaking again. "He's in love with you, you know."

The muscles in her limbs turned to mush at his words. Iza heard his sister's quick intake of breath. She wasn't sure what Mandren saw in her own reaction, but he nodded slowly. Anderson relaxed for the first time as she sat back in her seat and watched Mandren. Iza kept her expression as blank as possible but her limbs tingled as they regained feeling. Her thoughts went to the drawing in Joe's apartment. *Had he seen it?* She clamped down on her tongue and waited.

Mandren spoke again in that same calm resonant tone, "You are correct, Joe is missing, but that is not the only reason you're here. We would like you to bring in your ship, Captain. What we need to discuss will concern them, and I believe you're the type of person who's capable of deciding without them, but we would prefer to have your people with you."

"This is about the sphere," Iza breathed.

"What about my brother?" Anderson said, keeping a threadbare rein on her temper.

Mandren didn't respond to her but kept his eyes on Iza. "Do we have your cooperation?"

"Yes."

He pulled out a handheld and slid it across the table.

— — —

Braedon sat on the *Verity*'s flight deck monitoring the TSS comm traffic. His eyebrows were drawn together in concern as he chewed his bottom lip. It had been almost radio silent when they'd arrived.

"Any word?" Cierra said from behind him her hand resting lightly on his shoulder as he stared at the readings on the console.

"No, but they're due back any minute. We'll know soon enough."

The comm chirped, and he answered.

"Yes, I got you Iz. Hurry, things are getting exciting down there."

"Iza and Karter are not with me," Trix answered. "They did not make the rendezvous and I fear they have been apprehended by the TSS."

"Stars! What do we do now?"

"Prepare for docking. We cannot leave this shuttle behind. It has a value near to priceless according to Karter."

"Understood. You're all set, Trix."

The shuttle was a marvel, and Braedon could hardly contain his excitement at the sight of it a second time. Its amazing features were similar to the *Arvonen One* his father had procured. He'd tried to get his hands on it once, but he paid dearly for his act of rebellion. It had taken him almost two years before he'd been able to get his hands on another of his father's ships.

The *Verity* hadn't had a name back then. The H3X-Z500 was a special ship, and he couldn't let it go to waste sitting in his father's docks, so he'd nabbed it. Braedon wanted to enter a few more Dark Net virtual game tournaments, and the ship had made excellent collateral; he'd planned to return it after he'd collected his winnings. However, the ship ended up impounded after a significant loss, and someone else had gotten it out and sold it to Karter. Running into Iza and finding the ship again had been a remarkable stroke of luck. Now, he stared at the Q Maximus shuttle with the same longing to run. Then, Cierra stepped forward and took his hand.

She grounded him in every way possible, and he couldn't imagine a life without her anymore.

"What are we going to do?" Cierra asked.

"We wait, as instructed," Trix said. "Iza will signal us when she can. For now, we are safe where we are."

"True, no one knows we're here. But if they were to start looking nearby, we should have a plan."

"There are several possible coordinates where we can jump that will help us to avoid capture. I have a preset sequence charted in the case of an emergency."

Sometimes Trix amazed him, and he said so. "You're amazing, Trix. I can't get over how well you're able to plan ahead. I know you've got the capability. When are you going to admit you'd rather sound like the rest of us?"

Trix stared at him as if about to shrug.

"It's fine if she doesn't want to blend in with the rest of us. It makes her unique," Cierra said. "She's still a machine."

"If I were to speak as you do, you'd hardly know the difference between me and a more organic species. Does that bother you?" Trix asked smoothing out her vocal processing to an eerily perfect Taran register.

Cierra took a step back her eyes wide.

"Why are you more afraid of me when I speak this way than when I speak in a more robotic way?" Trix asked, her voice still altered.

"It's confusing. You're an android; I don't want to think of you as anything else," Cierra said.

"That is intriguing," Trix said, reverting to her regular tone. "To answer your question, Braedon, I once cared for someone so deeply that when they abandoned me, I needed to protect myself from ever having such a close bond again."

"That's cool," Braedon said.

"No, it's creepy." Cierra turned up her nose in disgust. "We should go to the flight deck and await a signal from the captain," she said as she climbed the stairs.

—

Three hours later they got the call from Iza.

"Hey, Iz, glad to see you're alive. Where are you?" Braedon asked.

"It's a long story, but I need you to come and get me. I'm at TSS Headquarters."

"TSS Headquarters?" Braedon looked at Cierra and then Trix. "Are you sure we should go there?"

"Yes."

"Captain, would you like me to refuel the shuttle before we arrive?"

Iza smiled as if Trix had told her a joke. "No, I refueled it before I left. I'll see you soon."

The call ended and Braedon turned to Trix. "The PEMs don't need fuel. Was that code?"

"Yes."

"So are we getting her or not."

"Yes, she is fine. We can meet her at TSS Headquarters."

"That's a good idea—to have a code. Why don't we all know it?"

"She has always trusted me with her life and her ships. You are all relatively new. Perhaps one day she will depend on you, too."

Braedon nodded but Cierra stood looking at Trix thoughtfully.

— — —

Though Iza had told them she didn't know where Joe was, they'd tossed her ship anyway as soon as the *Verity* docked at the TSS spaceport. The crew had been questioned, but as promised, they were not detained. Once it was all done, Iza had been escorted back to her ship, where Agents Skyler Anderson and Ian Mandren were waiting in the cargo hold along with her crew.

Braedon and Cierra dominated the steps to the flight deck level, sitting with their heads together while Trix stood on one side and Karter on the other. Atano raced to greet Iza; it was good to see him hopping up and down again, his leg completely healed. She'd have to thank Cierra for that, too, she supposed.

"I trust everything is as you left it." Mandren inclined his head in her direction.

Iza scoffed. "I told you we didn't have him," she grumbled.

"Yes, and I believed you," Agent Mandren raised an eyebrow as if in challenge.

"Then why did you have to have your people crawling all over my ship?"

"Every ship that comes to Headquarters that doesn't belong to us is searched. And you, in particular, have some experience with the Gate. We wanted to be sure there were no more spheres or alien technology hidden on the ship."

"We don't. I would know," Iza said, crossing her arms over her chest.

"Yes, we know that now, too. Your genetic analysis yielded interesting results. You have the natural ability to resist telepathy and you seem to have a special connection to the

Gates."

"I do." She swallowed hard. She'd been sitting on the knowledge of the bizarre experience in the shuttle on Uephus, when Trix had been taken off. She hadn't trusted the Guard, but maybe the TSS would go easier on her. "They keep finding me, it seems," she began.

The Agent gave her a questioning look. "Have you communicated with the creators of this technology?"

"Maybe? I don't know. My android friend was temporarily taken over by them. They spoke through her." She paused under his intense gaze, waiting for her to continue. "They called themselves the 'Gatekeepers'. They said our actions are an act of war, and our kind would be wiped out now, like we should have been before."

Mandren muttered under his breath, and Iza was pretty sure it was a creative string of profanities. "I'll pass on that information to the High Commander, thank you. As troubling as that is, there are other urgent matters. We believe that, based on Joe's abduction, you may be the next target."

Iza snapped to attention. "Wait, what are you saying? What abduction?"

Agent Mandren shifted his weight before answering her question, his eyes wavering only a brief second between herself and Braedon. "We believe Joe's been taken by Victor Arvonen."

EVERYONE STARTED TALKING all at once. Braedon, Cierra, and Karter all began asking questions. Iza had only one, and her voice carried over all the others.

"Why?" she asked.

"We don't know." Agent Mandren's eyes passed over Braedon briefly before returning to her. "We think it has something to do with the Gate technology he's been so obsessed with obtaining. Joe was the one who handed the sphere over to the TSS, so maybe Arvonen thinks he still has access to it—which should be obvious he doesn't, given the banishment."

"But, you think he'll come after Iza again," Karter said, understanding dawning on his features.

Agent Mandren nodded. "She has the strongest connection to the sphere, regardless of whether it's presently in her possession."

"What do we do?" Cierra asked. "Arvonen's a madman; we've already seen that. He'll kill Joe if he determines that he's of no value."

"We've come to the same conclusion. However, we haven't been able to find him for some time." Agent Mandren's amber eyes rested on Iza again and she understood.

"You want to use me as bait," Iza said.

"No way, that's craziness." Karter stepped out in front of her. "Please tell me you have a better plan than dangling her in front of a psychopath."

"If I didn't know any better, Karter, I'd think you really cared," Iza said with a raised eyebrow.

Karter huffed. "If he's coming for you, then he'll be coming for us all since we're all on this boat with you. Personally, I have more to live for than Joe Anderson."

"There it is—that Karter self-preservation." Iza rolled her eyes.

Ian's expression suggested that he was silently questioning what had possibly endeared Joe to the crew enough to give up his TSS commission. He shook his head slightly. "I'm here to level with you, because we're, admittedly, in uncharted territory regarding this alien tech. You, Iza, have had more contact with it than us—and seem to have an ability to interface with it in a way no one else can. So, in the interest of expediency and the well-being of everyone on these planets that are finding their worlds being inexplicably transformed, we need to trust each other and work together."

"Wait, *planets*? As in plural?" Iza's heart dropped. What she'd witnessed on Uephus was horrific, but to think of it happening on other worlds, as well, was too awful to imagine.

"Will you help us?" Agent Mandren asked without answering her question.

She nodded.

"And your crew?" He looked around at the concerned faces nearby.

They gave grim nods of assent. There was no choice, really.

The two Agents exchanged a glance, and Mandren continued, "The technology that Arvonen is using comes from a race we call the Gatekeepers. Before you ask, we hadn't heard of them, either. It took a *very* deep dive into the information archives with the Aesir to get a handle on what's going on. According to the Aesir's records, the Gatekeepers and another unknown race had a run-in with Tarans sometime in ancient history. The information about the conflict itself are frustratingly vague, but we know that there was a treaty signed by all three sides, agreeing to avoid each other. Use of Gatekeeper tech seems to have violated that treaty." Agent Mandren waited for the significance to sink in before he continued. "It's imperative we keep Arvonen from any further use of this technology, as it may have already started something that we can't fight."

"The planet transformations," Iza murmured. "It could be retaliation by the Gatekeepers for using their tech?"

Mandren smiled; he seemed pleased she'd made the connection. "It certainly fits with the information you just shared, about the message."

"Let me talk to him," Braedon cut in. "He's my father, I might be able to reach him." His face was determined, though his shoulders slumped forward. He had the bad habit of taking responsibility for his father even though it wasn't his fault.

They all turned to regard him. Iza watched Agent Mandren's eyes intensify the way Joe's did when he was using his abilities.

"It's worth a shot," Braedon insisted when no one replied right away.

Cierra put a hand on his arm in quiet sympathy.

"We've tried that before, if I recall," Karter said.

"Yes, but this time will be different. I know what my father wants and why. I can use that to try and reach out to him." One side of his mouth lifted.

"Is that all you plan to do?" Iza asked.

Braedon winked as if she'd found him out. "I also thought it might be a good time to see if I can triangulate his position. With a little help from Trix, I think I might be able to do it."

Agent Mandren nodded. "You've got a good crew here, Captain. Not one of them has expressed interest in leaving despite the dangers."

Iza looked around at them and realized the truth of his words. Not even Karter had talked about leaving, though now, with the extra shuttle on board, he could.

"That's why I'm sending Agent Skyler Anderson with you."

"What?!" Iza and Anderson's voices clashed in an eerie unison.

Agent Mandren smiled at Iza, ignoring Agent Anderson's incredulous expression.

"Yes, exactly. Agent Anderson is a capable member of the TSS with a vested interest in helping track down her brother," he continued over her squeak of protest. "You are potentially Arvonen's next target. It is likely that you'll find him long before a team of Agents randomly searching the Taran Empire will."

Everyone else remained silent.

Iza squared her shoulders, preparing her counter argument when Agent Mandren raised a hand.

"This isn't a request. We are perfectly within Taran law to hold you and your ship here indefinitely."

Iza bit down her protest and swallowed her arguments. If she didn't want to be stuck at TSS Headquarters in a cell, she had to comply.

"Take care of our Agent, Captain." Agent Mandren swiveled on his heel, turning to leave, then called out over his shoulder, "I expect regular reports on your progress, Agent Anderson."

Iza wanted to choke Agent Mandren with her bare hands. He'd taken Joe away from her and allowed him to be abducted by the crazed Victor Arvonen. To top it all off, he'd dumped Joe's older sister on the ship, as if somehow that made it okay. They were using her to lure in Arvonen. *With all their tech and abilities, they should have the old fool by now.*

Iza stomped up the stairs to the flight deck. As she passed Trix, she spoke to her. "Are you okay. Did you have any trouble back on Earth?"

"None, as soon as you missed the rendezvous, I returned to the ship."

"How many times am I going to get arrested because of you?" Karter demanded, following close behind Iza.

"Me? I haven't done anything wrong."

"Not yet."

"I'd say of the two of us, you're the one with the most dirt on your hands."

Karter glanced at his fingernails and shrugged his shoulders. "Perhaps."

"I never did hear how they caught you," Iza said.

Karter opened his mouth to speak when Cierra and Braedon joined them.

"I knew nothing good would come from us going to Earth to get Joe. Didn't I say it was too dangerous?" Cierra spoke to Brandon loud enough for the rest of them to hear.

"It's Joe. What were we supposed to do, just leave him here to rot? That's not what fam—" He stopped short, remembering Joe's sister following behind them.

"There were Agents watching the apartment," Karter continued speaking over their interruption. "They took me because I identified myself as Taran to give you a chance to find a place to hide or get out. I didn't have time to come up with a more intelligent play."

"You sacrificed yourself to get me out?" Iza was trying to make sense of the gesture.

"Not that it did any good, as you were caught anyway," he said as they reached the corridor leading to the crew quarters.

"But they kept you in a holding cell the entire time," Braedon said, eyeing Karter with suspicion and dropping his voice to a loud whisper. "Were they able to get into your head? You must have given them something."

Karter was quiet for a moment. Agent Anderson was following them to the flight deck, and Iza saw him imitate Braedon's gesture looking back at her trailing behind Trix.

When he spoke, he lowered his voice, too, even though he knew the Agent could hear him if she wanted to. "What I gave them has nothing to do with any of you, since I hardly know you. It was my business alone. Nothing they can use, either; only I know the details of my mind in that way."

Iza noted the twitch in Karter's cheek as he spoke. The sudden stillness of his body. They got something out of him, and she couldn't help but wonder what it was that rattled him.

She stopped in front of Joe's cabin, letting the others file around her. Karter moved to his cabin and Cierra into hers. Braedon gave Cierra a peck on the lips before heading to the flight deck.

Trix caught up with Iza and stopped with the Agent behind her.

"Atano was quite distressed as the Agents searched the ship. I did my best to detain him."

"He was just doing his job. I'll have to remember to reward him," Iza said, keeping her voice dry and unbothered.

Agent Anderson seemed to be measuring her again but then looked away.

Iza continued addressing Trix, "Go on up to the flight deck with Braedon and prepare for our next jump."

"Do we have a destination?" The question had the hint of amusement, which was rare for Trix. Iza scanned her features to see if there was a smile to match, but the android's face was passive as usual.

"Not yet. Just get us out of this TSS dock and to somewhere we can regroup. See if you can help Braedon track down his father."

Iza waited while Trix passed her and Agent Anderson stepped forward. It was clear Joe's sister didn't like her, but it didn't really matter.

"You can stay in Joe's old cabin for now."

Anderson nodded but didn't move. Iza crossed her arms. If she thought she was going up to the flight deck, she had another thing to learn about being on her ship.

"You said you were on Uephus when they experienced the transformation event," Anderson said.

Iza's face relaxed but she kept her arms in place.

"That's right. We saw firsthand the devastation there, and then, of course, we were planetside during the second smaller event."

"Yes, I remember seeing the reports. However, they were unable to find the cause. Were you able to reach the source?"

"Nope," Iza said with a shrug.

Agent Anderson squinted at her. An expression so like Joe's that Iza had to force herself to exhale.

"According to your crewman, you believe that there is a Gatekeeper sphere on the planet. Is that so?"

"What if it is? We didn't put it there and we couldn't reach it."

"True. However, you could have informed us of this information earlier."

Iza's arms dropped to her sides. "Why, so you can blame us for not doing more? We were there tending to their injured for half a day before even one Enforcer ship arrived. We took nothing from those people and protected them from those who had planned on looting the planet for their new natural resources. We were doing your job, so you're welcome."

Iza tried to control her breathing even as the words she'd been holding back until now came tumbling out of her.

"I don't know what Joe told you about me, but I'm not the enemy. I'm here to render assistance should you and your crew need it, and to find my brother."

"What I've heard about you and Joe is next to nothing, which tells me all I need to know. You're here so the TSS can *claim* to be helping me while using me to track down a lunatic. We don't need you or your help. We've been doing just fine without you so far."

"I don't care what you think you know. Joe is my brother, and I'll do whatever it takes to get him back. If that means hanging out on a ship full of criminal delinquents, so be it. But you won't shut me up in here and expect me to obey."

Iza gave her the sweetest smile she could muster. "If you need food, it's down the corridor and on your left." Then she took a step forward until they were nose to nose. "Oh, and one more thing, stay out of my way."

Iza turned away, her eyes stinging with anger. Why did the woman have to remind her so much of Joe?

17

JOE'S MIND DRIFTED back to the day he'd left TSS Headquarters. The shuttle back to Earth had been as quiet and disgraceful as his trip to the Outer Colonies transport had been. This time, however, there was no mention of his disgrace, only the long interrogation. He'd managed to keep his anger in check even when they threatened to go after Iza.

"You don't know who or what she is." Ian Mandren had ran a hand through his hair, pacing back and forth. Joe couldn't remember ever seeing the Primus Elite Agent looking so frazzled. "You've jeopardized your mission in every way possible, and you still think keeping her hidden is the way to go. We can find her and bring her in. Considering what you've told us so far, we should."

"I'm asking you—begging you—not to, sir," Joe had said, sitting forward in the chair as Mandren paced. "I know what I did was wrong, but with my relationship with the crew being what it is, I think I did more good than if I'd gone by the book. You know what it's like in the field. Decisions have to be made, choices that at the moment can't be weighed against the better judgment of times without threat or danger."

Mandren had shaken his head. "It doesn't matter. I don't

know what the High Commander is going to do with this information. You did more than bring us information about Arvonen and the uprising on Hubyria. You used your training to aid this Captain Sundari in theft, extortion, and other illegal activity. You let her fiancé, Karter Hyttinen use you to gather more information to aid him in his nefarious business dealings. That's quite a list of offenses, despite your reasoning. All I know is, I can't protect you. You'll be exiled to Earth for this, and bringing in the artifact and this report isn't going to change that."

"I know. And for the record, so did she when she gave it to me. Iza didn't have to turn the sphere over to the TSS. She's being cooperative; she should get some credit for that."

"Credit? She's riding in an H3X with an independent jump drive that we provided. She's changed you. You were always quick to anger, but you've turned your back on the principles that made you an Agent, and I'm not sure sending you to Earth is far enough." Mandren had stopped pacing to lean forward to look into his eyes.

Joe wasn't sure what he had seen there, but he hadn't said anything for a full minute. It had taken everything Joe had not to shift in his seat at the scrutiny.

"The one thing you haven't admitted are your true feelings for this woman, Captain Iza Sundari. You're in love with her, aren't you?"

The conversation had been interrupted with the arrival of his discharge orders. It didn't matter that Joe hadn't answered the question. Mandren had a job to do, and he viewed Joe's lack of enthusiasm for the interests of the TSS as proof enough of his change of heart.

Joe had been given back his duffle, minus any Taran tech. He'd have to learn to fit in again on Earth. He was provided with the necessary credentials to begin his exiled life and there wasn't another word spoken about how he would manage or live.

The sight of the blue planet from orbit took his breath away. It seemed so small, but he knew it held places he'd yet to visit. He'd been gone for years; things might have changed, even progressed, in his absence. Going back to the Earth didn't have to be a punishment. The further he traveled, the deeper the ache in his chest became. Iza would see none of it. He couldn't imagine any kind of fulfilling life without her. Perhaps, one day, Earth would become an official member of the Taran Empire and they'd be reunited. He didn't want to die alone.

Maybe he could arrange to attend his sister's wedding. Then Iza could join him there. It wouldn't be so bad if he knew she'd be there. Seeing all of his old friends and former teachers would be tough, but with Iza at his side, he could brave the animosity they might feel for a TSS traitor.

— — —

"Sir, it's happening again. He's leaving the fantasy and drifting back into memories," the technician said as he watched the brain patterns on the monitor change.

"It's all right. Keep him focused on Sundari as long as you can. Monitor everything, real or imagined. There's plenty here we can use," Victor said. "Even if you have to move forward a bit in his timeline, keep him out of reality and inside the fantasy." He held out his hand over the controls and swiped his fingers over the thought patterns to the right.

"Yes, sir."

"Keep me updated on his continued regression. I'd like to be here when you break through."

"I'll do my best. As I said, sir, this technique... it's not an exact science. The mind is complex and layered. It does everything it can to protect itself. Any sign that these memories aren't happening in real-time and he'll try to force himself awake. The jolt could—"

"I know the risks, Doctor. That's not why you're here. You're here to get it done. If you have a problem completing this task, I'll get another brain expert in here to replace you. I think you understand my meaning." Victor held his gaze steady.

The man's shoulders slumped but he nodded before turning back to the monitor. "Yes, sir."

— — —

How different Joe's journey to Earth had been compared to his trip from the *Verity* back to Headquarters. He didn't want to leave Iza behind, but he wasn't going to put her in front of the High Commander with what he knew. If they chose to keep her there, Joe knew he'd do whatever it took to get her out, and that would put them both in compromising positions. The last thing she needed was to be on the run for the rest of her life. He didn't savor the idea himself.

Investigator Desirae Hyttinen put him in a holding cell like a common criminal, though she didn't force him to hand over the sphere. She didn't take her dark brown eyes off of him but didn't seem to want anything to do with the artifact he carried. Her straight, blunt hairstyle matched the sharp outline of her uniform.

"You'll be more comfortable here. Besides, from what you've probably done, this isn't so bad. At least you still get a view of the stars." Desirae pointed to the overhead viewport and the stars beyond it.

Joe looked up through the viewport at the stars, thankful

that whatever happened, Iza would be safe now. Arvonen would have more than a few repairs to attend to after their last bout and he had the sphere in his hand. No one could open a Gate without it.

18

TRIX WAS ON the flight deck monitoring the systems when Iza arrived. Braedon was sitting at the console with his tablet in his lap. It looked like he was sketching a new comic.

"Braedon, have you reached out to your father?"

"Yes."

"Any word?"

"No, nothing from Joe, my father, or anyone else of consequence." Iza picked up something else in his tone but couldn't name it before he continued, "A message came in from Apex for Karter, and I've already informed his Highness."

"All right," Iza acknowledged.

"Your heart rate is no longer erratic, but I believe this set back in finding Joe will be detrimental for you," Trix observed.

Iza caught the worried glance from Braedon before he averted his eyes back to the console. She rolled her eyes. "Just do what I ask will you and save the physical check-up for later."

"Are you all right, or is there something we need to know?" Braedon asked.

"No, I'm fine," Iza said waving away their worried looks of concern.

Iza ran a hand under Atano's black chin and he licked at

her fingers as if they were covered in meat sauce.

"I hear you did a lot of guarding while I was away. You're probably hungry." Iza didn't have to wait for an answer as he danced around her ankles. "Okay, then, let's get you something to eat. I'm going to my cabin after I feed Atano. Trix, keep monitoring comms, and let us know the minute we get a nibble."

Atano dashed to her side at the mention of his name, and he followed her to the galley. Inside, she found Cierra tending to her plants and Agent Skyler Anderson at the table, her hands folded in front of her as if she'd been waiting there the whole time. It was unnerving to come upon her unexpectedly, and Iza had to force her mind to remember why she'd come. Atano nudged her calf and she reached for his bowl.

"He's cute. What's his name?" Agent Anderson asked.

Iza answered without looking at her. "Atano."

"Speaking of names, you can call me Skyler. No need for all the Agent formality."

"All right," Iza muttered. But I rather like 'Agent Sky'.

"I made vegetable stew if you'd like some, Captain," Cierra snatched up her bowl, dropping the stew in before she could protest. Then, to Iza's horror, she reached for one of the plants and snatched several leaves off of it and topped off her bowl before handing it back to her.

As if she'd done nothing at all, Cierra sashayed out of the room, her pink robes whispering. Iza leaned back against the counter and stared down into the bowl for several more moments in shock before she looked up and met Agent Anderson's strange look.

"Did Joe ever tell you we had a cat?"

— — —

Karter detested sharing. Perhaps it had to do with being an only child.

His intention was to have it all—carrying on his father's legacy, as it had been done in the Hyttinen Dynasty for centuries. He had no idea what that responsibility had meant at the time. However, as he got older, he realized the root of most of his problems was the fact that he was required to, or someone insisted, he share.

He'd already tried to get rid of Agent Joe Anderson once before, but it had all gone awry. This would make things more difficult for him later on. *She'll be my wife like it or not.* Hadn't that been the mantra since he'd forced her to sign the contract?

It was entirely unfair and nothing like he'd imagined for himself as a child playing in his father's office. Thinking of his father reminded him that he still had work to do. Karter had chosen Iza for more than the mere fact she was interesting. He happened to know more about her than she knew about herself at the moment. He'd known about her aunt for some time and had to use that to his advantage when the time came. It had gone almost as well as he'd hoped. Though, due to Iza's hot temper, their reunion had backfired. Not only had she darted out without getting any meaningful information, but she also didn't seem inclined to even speak with the woman again.

That left Karter at a disadvantage, which wasn't a position he was used to playing. He needed something to go on if he was going to defeat Mr. Arvonen. The man was in league with several other Lower Dynasty heirs, and it was obvious that he was going to have to deal with the man sooner rather than later.

Mr. Arvonen was after those spheres, and that meant Karter needed to get to them first. It was a simple as that. He would not be outdone by the man or run out. The man had something over the other dynastic heirs, but he had nothing on Karter himself. The Hyttinen Dynasty heir ran his business with immaculate precision with an efficient team led by one of the best.

Becca had reached out to him, and he used his handheld to return her vidcall. "Becca, where are we with the most recent transactions and acquisitions?"

"Everything is going according to plan, Mr. Hyttinen. We've acquired the other two locations, as requested, and we have completed the financial transactions needed to secure them."

"And my mother?"

There was a pause as Becca looked off into the distance as if trying to figure out how to say what came next.

"I need you to be upfront and honest with me. What's going on? Have you heard from my mother?"

"Yes, she made a public statement for the Sensationals several hours ago. I was debating about how best to tell you, but maybe you should see it for yourself."

Becca sent the video file, and as soon as he received a notification of the message's arrival, Karter downloaded it to be viewed after the vidcall. He hardly wanted Becca monitoring his reactions.

"I'll be sure to look at it. But I'd like the highlights please."

"Your mother has aligned herself with the Arvonen Dynasty. She has spoken out openly against you, accusing you of going rogue, and insists that your investors are making a mistake by backing you."

Karter gritted his teeth. He knew his mother was intent on keeping the Dynasty to herself, but he had no idea how much. He looked back on all of the meetings she'd dropped in on, and the clients that she dismissed him from the room to speak with privately. Had all of those times been with Mr. Arvonen? Quite possibly. What did she hope to gain by aligning herself with a madman?

"Also," Becca sounded even more tentative, "it appears that she may have hired the *Iron Dog* to trail you."

"Well, that explains a lot."

For as long as he could remember, his mother had been behind him pushing toward his father's legacy—doing anything in her power to upset Karter's other dealings and force him back under her thumb. *When had things changed?* He tried to remember but his thoughts were interrupted when Becca called his name. She was asking him something that he'd missed.

"I'm sorry, what was your question?"

"How would you like to proceed?"

Karter was accustomed to dealing in options, but he preferred to be the one in control. This feeling of powerlessness was new. After discovering the true motivations of his friend Raquel, the archaeologist, he'd lost some of his confidence. *Had my mother prearranged that meeting as well?* Karter didn't want to entertain the thought that every relationship he had was based on his mother's lies. Iza was the only one untouched and untainted by his mother's ambitions and yet central to both their plans.

"What about my engagement party? Has it been confirmed—was my mother responsible for the robbery?"

Becca took a deep breath hesitating and then rushing forward to answer. "Yes, it has been confirmed."

Karter let out a slew of curses he usually kept under wraps around his employees. "I apologize. This has taken me by surprise. This is an impossible situation. If I have my way, then my mother will suffer the consequences of her choice in alliances. No one should have to decide between loyalty to their legacy and their surviving parent."

"Many must make that choice, sir. She knew what she was doing when she made her choice. The question is, will you do the same?" Becca's voice dropped and she leaned toward the camera. "Karter, you're not a child."

His eyes met hers at the familiar use of his name.

Becca's intensity didn't waver. "She's your mother, but this is your business and your livelihood. As much as she may have shown her love for you in the past, she will not live forever. You can't trust her to look out for the best interests of your legacy anymore. You're a man who is more than capable of handling his own future."

"Are you buttering me up like bread or what, Becks?"

She blushed, which made her green eyes sparkle even more. Then, she got control of her irresistible smile and spoke. "Absolutely not. I'd never lie to you," she said her expression serious.

He wondered if that were true. The sincerity in her tone made him want to believe it.

"I'll send you a file of everything I found, but I think the video will have most of what you need for now."

Karter nodded and flashed her a smile of his own. "Be careful, I'm not sure you're not in danger yourself."

"I know how to get myself home," she said with a wink.

Then, the vidcall ended, and he was left staring at the video she'd sent over to review. He opened the file and an image of his office appeared on the viewscreen. He watched his mother enter his office alone. Then, Mr. Arvonen came in and sat down in the sitting area of Karter's office opposite his mother and managed to look pleased with himself. Karter paused the video, looking away from the display, determined to calm his breathing. *How could she betray me in my own house?*

— — —

Once Atano was fed, he seemed eager not to let Iza out of

his sight and clung to her heels as she moved about the ship. Looking at the dog circling her feet as she was coming out of her cabin, she bumped into Karter. He was grumbling to himself, and he looked ready to punch something or someone.

"You look like you could use some good news."

"Why? Do you have some?"

"Sorry," Iza shrugged, "fresh out. What's going on?"

"I just got off a call with Becks—Becca—my assistant," he stammered. "Sorry, I'm a little thrown."

Why doesn't he admit his feelings for her? She's the kind of woman who would wait for him to get his affairs together.

"So, are you keeping your true feelings for Becca a secret from her, too?" Iza said.

Karter's head snapped up and he glared at her. "I don't know what you mean." His eyebrows furrowed.

"You haven't told her?" she said her eyes wide.

"I already told you, there are many obstacles to us being together," Karter said with a wave of his hand as if he could erase the conversation.

"We've all got obstacles. What are you going to do about it?"

"Do about what?" Braedon said coming down from the flight deck.

"We were just discussing Becca. Karter's very attractive and loyal assistant," Iza said. She smirked at Karter when he glared at her.

"What's going on with you and her, anyway?" Braedon asked.

"There's nothing between us. She's my assistant—not that it's any of your business."

"Nothing more because you don't want there to be anything more, or nothing more because there can't be anything more?" Braedon asked. He raised his eyebrows and gave him a knowing look.

Iza shifted her weight and narrowed her eyes back at Karter. "Here you've got me locked into this contract with you, doing your hardest to try to keep me here, and you've got someone who's head over heels in love with you. And from what I just saw, you are madly in love with her, too," Iza said spinning on her heel and brushing past Braedon to the flight deck.

Trix was standing to the right of Iza's chair when she arrived.

Karter rushed to catch up to her. "My feelings on the matter are irrelevant. I can't marry my assistant," he said between his teeth.

"Well, then can I have her, because stars, she's supernova hot!" Braedon wiggled his eyebrows suggestively and slid into his chair at the helm.

"Careful," Karter warned, his tone turning frigid.

Trix was next to chime in. "The contract between yourself and Iza clearly states that your romantic interest in another party constitutes grounds for dissolution."

Iza had to hide a smile behind her hand as Karter fought for control of the deteriorating situation.

"Becks— Becca is my assistant. There can be nothing between us," Karter reiterated, slipping his hands into his pockets. She wondered if he noticed that when he was in denial he tended to rock back and forth on his heels. "I rely on her to handle the business while I'm away. I depend on her for a lot of different things that doesn't mean there's something between us."

"Save the garbage sandwich for someone who'll eat it. You like her, like really like her. She's gorgeous, refined, and she's already in the family business. You'd be a fool to walk away from her," Iza said.

"You and I have an arrangement. I can't go back on my word," Karter said. "As I said to you earlier in confidence, my business interests would not look kindly on a sudden switch in my affections, but they might forgive it if you had another offer. Otherwise, you'll be forced to marry me. We can't be engaged forever."

Iza stood up and crossed to him in three easy steps until she could look him in the eye. Then she spoke through her teeth in a low hiss. "I wouldn't marry you if you were the last man in the galaxy. So, if you think you can out-wait me on this contract, you're sorely mistaken. We need to find you a wife, and soon. Becca is already in love with you, and if you don't see it, we'll arrange an eye surgery on the nearest civilized planet. But, either way, you and me in this contract are going to be done."

Karter let out a sigh as if all the air had been knocked out of him.

Why is he fighting me on this? He was so obviously in love with Becca. Neither one of them wanted to be together, so why was it so hard to separate? Her heart belonged to someone else, and he knew it. Holding on to her was delaying the inevitable. The reasons he had entered into the engagement in the first place no longer made sense. As far as she knew, his mother hadn't let up on her interest in taking over his legacy. He'd have to do more than marry to save his business. That left one reason he hadn't made his move on his assistant.

Karter, through with being the target of their teasing, left the flight deck with his head down and his shoulders slumped. Iza wanted to follow him but didn't want to make it obvious.

"I need to get something from my cabin," she said. Atano jumped up to follow her out the door.

Karter hadn't gone far. He stood in the galley facing the wall and hadn't noticed her approach. Iza debated whether to just leave him alone or voice her theory out loud. She took a tentative step in his direction, and he didn't budge. She walked into the galley and stood next to him with her hips resting on the counter behind them. She had her eyes on the floor as she spoke, not trusting herself to take it seriously if she could see his face.

"I get it. Putting yourself out there to someone who could actually care about you it's scary."

Karter was silent for a long moment. Without lifting his head, he spoke in a low whisper, "How do you do it? How do you open yourself up to someone who could turn around and hurt you?" He looked at her, the question in his eyes.

Iza could admit now that before he'd joined her on the *Verity*, they never really knew each other. Somewhere in his past, he'd been hurt by someone he loved. The betrayal was there in the set of his jaw as he asked the question. She knew that pain; she'd experienced that pain. Not with Joe—he'd been different. He hadn't been completely honest with her from the start, no. But he'd been under orders. Her own contract with Karter had put her in a similar bind. Iza wasn't going to let anything else separate them.

"It's hard at first. You start small. You let them in a little bit at a time. Then, the next thing you know, you're wide-open, accepting them for who they are, flaws and all. And believe you me, they always have flaws," Iza said with a laugh.

Karter only smiled when he shook his head. "Yes, but I have a lot on the line. If things don't go my way, I could lose everything forever. My Dynasty could be irrevocably destroyed; I don't know if I could take that. Even if she's everything that I imagine she could be, I might've already lost everything. What do I have to give her?"

"If she already loves you, she couldn't care less about the other things. The most valuable thing you can give each other is your hearts. The rest is just icing. But you'll never know unless you try. And you have to make a step in the right direction."

"What do you suggest?"

"Well, first, you need to nullify this engagement façade that you've been carrying around. Next, I suggest you let her know that not only is she an important asset to your business, let her know that she's also a contender for your heart. Invite her out to dinner. Have her over for movie night," she suggested. She couldn't imagine him anywhere other than his office. She tried to picture him slipping off his shoes and cuddling up to Becca on the couch; it was too ridiculous to consider.

"I don't know." He frowned. "It's a huge risk, and right now, I've got so many things going on. I let someone get close to me once, and they betrayed me. How do I know I can trust her?"

"You don't. You won't know if you can trust her until you try. But don't forget, she's trusting you, too. You need to show her that you're someone worthy of that trust."

Karter gave her a wry smile. Iza never would've thought a year ago she'd be having this kind of conversation with him. He was becoming tolerable, despite their past. He pulled his own weight on board and had come through when needed. Despite his self-interest when it came to his business, he had held up his end of the bargain. Only now, it was a matter of giving him the kind of advice that only another woman could give.

A year ago, she wouldn't have *had* the advice to give. Joe had changed all that, and now more than anything she wanted to be with him.

19

CIERRA AND BRAEDON were nose-to-nose when Iza reached the galley the next morning. She stopped for a moment to take in the scene, unsure what she was interrupting since both Karter and Skyler were also at the table. They bolted apart at the sight of her. Cierra held a spray bottle that she was using on the plants.

"Please don't use my kitchen for making out," Iza said as she entered.

"Thank you," Skyler said over a bowl of cereal.

"No one asked you," Braedon said with a sneer. He was more annoyed with Skyler Anderson than he'd ever been with Karter. It was odd.

Did I miss something? Iza wondered.

"I would prefer to have my breakfast without the show, as well, if my vote counts for anything," Karter said.

"It doesn't." Iza said reached for her own bowl. "However, I'm captain, and I say go to your cabin if you have to be all over each other this early in the morning."

Trix entered the galley and stood at the door, scanning them in her way.

"Stop checking my vitals," Iza grunted while she filled the

dog's water bowl and placed it on the floor for him.

Iza took the seat at the head of the table nearest Karter and furthest from Skyler. Cierra finished spraying her plants as Braedon sat down next to her.

"Don't worry, we'll find him," he said as if she'd spoken her concerns aloud. "Joe's tough, and he's gotten on and off the *Arvonen One* before. He might have escaped already." His tone wasn't as hopeful as his words.

Skyler was watching him with her eyebrows drawn together. "Your father has created quite the mess for everyone, Devyn."

Braedon fidgeted with his food under her scrutiny. "I've gone by Braedon Valtteri since my father disowned me. I can hardly call that man—that monster—my father."

Skyler made a face like she'd just sucked something sour before she pushed her bowl away. Iza didn't like the way she was looking at Braedon.

Cierra moved to stand behind him, resting one delicate hand on his shoulder, her heart-shaped face resolute as if preparing for the Agent to strike him. She'd swept her curls up on top of her head, though several curls were already escaping the binder.

"Braedon, any word yet from your father?" Iza asked. She needed to get control of the situation fast.

Braedon reached up and pulled Cierra's hand to his lips before he answered, and she seemed to relax.

"No, not yet. He's received the message, but he's not answering. I didn't mention Joe or that we know he was anywhere near the sphere on Uephus. Though I suspect he's aware of my hacking skills; I've used them against him before. If he wants to stay hidden, he might not answer." Then he held up a hand. "Before you ask, Viper and I haven't come up with a solution to blocking the sphere's energy using an antivirus. It just won't work since whoever put them there is controlling them from the other side."

Iza gave his words a moment of thought. "Keep trying to get through to the *Arvonen One*."

"There is an incoming message from Hubyria marked 'urgent'," Trix announced.

Iza's mouth fell open. *What could Yeaga possibly want with me?* The others stared at her as she rose from the table and started for the flight deck.

"Do you think she knows where Joe is?" Braedon asked, scrambling after her.

Iza hadn't even considered Yeaga before. What if she had something to do with Joe's disappearance? She might have liberated him from Earth for her own ends; she had a horrible crush on him.

"Anything's possible, but I doubt it. The TSS believes he's with Arvonen, because he's the only one who could have gotten to him so fast and not been caught. Yeaga doesn't have her own ship, let alone one capable of retrieving him right out from under the nose of the TSS."

Braedon jogged passed her and sat down at the helm. "Trix, bring up the message."

The front screen went from the stars to black and then bright as Iza's Aunt Reagan's terrified face filled the screen. Her dark eyes shifted back and forth as if looking beyond the display. Her once mahogany curls were dull and matted in uncombed clumps. Her clothing bore dirt stains and looked disheveled as if she hadn't bathed for days. "I don't have much time. They've taken your cousin."

"Reagan? What's going on?" Iza asked.

"He's missing. Your cousin, Jaidyn, is missing. I tracked him here to Hubyria, but he's nowhere to be found. I think they have him."

Her cousin was only a recent acquaintance, but what she knew of him was that he looked a lot like her and had the stealth of a trained assassin. If someone caught up to him, he didn't go down without a fight.

"Who has him?" Iza questioned.

Reagan shook her mass of matted curls. "We can't talk like this."

"I don't understand."

"Come quickly. We don't have much time. I'll tell you everything, but you must come."

Iza started to protest but the screen went black.

"It's only a few hours from here. If we hurry, we can make it just after lunch," Braedon said. He turned to look at her, his eyes bright.

"Does she have my brother?" Skyler asked. The glow of her topaz-blue eyes, almost identical to Joe's, shone from across the flight deck. Even without her uniform's overcoat or the tinted glasses, she was unmistakably a TSS Agent—and clearly felt entitled to be places she didn't belong.

Iza glared at her. "What are you doing on my flight deck?"

"I thought the call might have something to do with my brother. Can this woman help us find him?"

Iza saw the hope on her face and had to squash it. She shook her head. "No, this is a family matter."

"This might be a good time to remind you that the owner of the Q Maximus shuttle is going to want their ship back," Karter said from behind her. It seemed they'd all slipped onto the flight deck during the call. He continued, "Their people are on their way this morning to retrieve it."

"It's your aunt. There's really no choice here," Braedon said again with a significant look at Skyler. "Family doesn't abandon family."

Iza rolled her head. "Karter, tell the owner of the shuttle

there's been a change of plans. We're in route to Hubyria and to pick up the shuttle there."

He grumbled something about the price, but Iza didn't have time to hear him as she turned to Skyler.

"As soon as we get word of your brother, Agent Anderson, I'll fill you in. For now, you are not cleared to be on the flight deck. That goes for the rest of you, too. Trix plot a course."

"I should remind you, Captain, that you are not welcome on Hubyria," the android said. "Yeaga may still be angry about the auction."

"I'm aware, but it's not going to stop me from helping my aunt and finding my cousin."

—

Upon arriving at Hubyria, Iza had to make some decisions. If she took the *Verity* in, they'd have to ask for permission to land. If she tried to sneak in on her beat-up shuttle, there was a risk they'd shoot her out of the sky, but only if they were looking. It was a big sky. While debating which route to take, Trix spoke up.

"We are receiving a communication request from Yeaga," Trix said. "With some impatience, I should add." Though her face was pleasant, the tone suggested Trix was not happy with whatever language Yeaga was using on the other end. Iza watched her plans to sneak down to the planet disappear in a puff of smoke.

"Put her through."

"You better have a good reason for coming back here, Scrappy," Yeaga stated in her raspy voice.

Iza gritted her teeth at the strange amalgamation of the nickname Douketis and the other haulers had given her years ago. Despite her short stature, Yeaga's pale face and blue eyes filled the screen. She'd kept her blonde hair pulled up in a high ponytail the long strands of hair reaching below her left shoulder and off-screen.

"I received an urgent message from my aunt. She's tracked my cousin here, and it sounds like he might be in danger."

Yeaga shook her head. She lifted her eyebrows then and smiled as if they were old friends. "As much as I love when you come to call, I'm going to have to ask you to leave. Consider this a warning. If you set foot on this planet, I'll blow your transport out of the sky, as I should have done the first time you came here stirring up trouble."

"Yeaga, listen, normally I'd go back and forth with you and then let you have some time with Joe—Jovani," she corrected as Yeaga probably didn't know him by any other name. "But we believe he's been abducted by Victor Arvonen. I need to make sure my aunt and cousin are okay, and then we have to get back to the business of finding him. So, call off your weapons."

Yeaga stared back at her of over the viewscreen a moment before she shrugged. "Fine, suit yourself. I'll give you one hour, and not a minute more. After that, I get to play target practice with your ship, and I'm an excellent shot."

The front display returned to the view of the stars, and Iza let out the breath she'd been holding. "Trix prepare the shuttle and lock into the coordinates my aunt sent us. Braedon, you stay with the ship and look after Atano."

"No problem, Iz." To prove it he scooped up the dog into his arms. Atano, thinking it a game, lavished his face with long licks of his tongue.

Iza headed for the cargo hold, where she found Agent Anderson and Karter waiting. The last thing she wanted was a meeting with her aunt under threat of fire and these two tagging along. "No, no, no!"

"I want to meet my fiancé's family," Karter said. "You really shouldn't attempt to leave me behind. You might need me again."

Iza hadn't forgotten how Karter and Joe came to her aid the last time she'd been caught by Yeaga. Yes, it had been helpful, but this time was different. She didn't need him. "I appreciate this newfound concern over my well-being and the desire to make a family, but let me remind you of a couple things. One, this engagement is still fake, and we all know it, so drop the act. Two, you need to be here to facilitate the shuttle pick up; I'd hate for you to be losing more credits on it than planned."

Karter bit the inside of his cheek, it seemed he was weighing the options of having his way or losing more money than necessary. He didn't like his decision, but he seemed resolved to stay behind.

Iza turned to Skyler, who squared her shoulders and spoke before Iza had a chance to list off her objections.

"If my brother were here, he'd be going. I'll go in his place and provide whatever security you might need. Having a TSS Agent with you might be an advantage. This crew and my brother can't afford for anything to happen to you."

Iza could use the assistance of someone who might actually be able help. Though it was still a risk.

"The first time I brought Joe here, they snatched him *because* he was a TSS Agent. These are the Outer Colonies, Agent Sky. I don't know what they told you, but these people have as much respect for you as they do a dog."

"I'll take my chances. You shouldn't go alone."

"I'm not going alone. Trix is flying the shuttle."

When Skyler refused to leave, Iza shrugged. "Fine, but if they take you as a hostage, I'm leaving you behind."

20

IZA SAT IN the co-pilot seat beside Trix as they made their approach to the surface. Her mind was a jumble of questions, and unlike the last time she'd spoken with her aunt, she planned to get answers. After getting over the shock of her mother having a twin sister, it hadn't gone well. Iza could see where she'd gone wrong, that time. She'd blamed her aunt for not doing more, not reaching out sooner—but putting that on her hadn't made Iza feel any better. In fact, she'd realized too late the woman might be the last connection she had to her mother.

Like Joe, Skyler was pleasantly quiet on the way to the surface, allowing Iza to ruminate in peace. She'd chosen the seat behind Trix where Iza could easily see her, but when she glanced back, Skyler had her eyes closed as if she were sleeping.

Trix piloted their shuttle to the coordinates they'd been given. On the outskirts of town, the small property had been cleared of boulders and bore a small structure at one end. To call it a cottage seemed too generous. The sheet-metal shanty probably had only one room for sleeping. A stove made out of constructed blocks sat to one side of the structure. Primitive was putting it lightly.

As soon as the shuttle powered down, the small wooden door of the place flew open and her aunt ran toward them. Before Trix had opened the hatch, her aunt was there waiting and wringing her hands.

"What is it? What's wrong?" Iza asked reaching out to stop her nervous hand wrestling.

"They're almost here."

"Who?"

Reagan didn't seem to hear her and continued to mumble as she glanced around, then she focused her attention back on Iza. "They've found me, and I believe they've taken your cousin. I knew you'd come. If they find you here, they won't let you leave alive."

That got Skyler's attention; her head snapped up and she tracked Reagan's movements.

They followed Iza's aunt into the small hut. Inside, it was as Iza feared. A small bed covered in a dark gray blanket sat against the far wall with a square, two-drawer nightstand at the head; on top sat a framed photo of her aunt and cousin. One metal chair faced the bed, near the corner stove that would give off enough heat to warm the place on cold nights.

"If you're worried about someone finding you here, maybe we should go," Iza said as she looked around the room, concerned that it wouldn't keep out a stiff breeze let alone anyone else.

"Have you ever heard of the Gatekeepers?" Reagan asked Iza, her eyes focused.

"I've recently been acquainted. Short version: they hate us and are willing to take out planets to keep us from using their tech."

"That's what the government knows." Reagan waved a hand in the air in the direction of Skyler as she reached for a duffle and tossed it on the bed. "Your mother probably never spoke of them, though now I wish she had. If you knew about your past, you might have seen some of this coming. You see, I knew this would happen. I've prepared Jaidyn for this day ever since his father left."

"I thought he died?" Iza asked, looking over the woman as if catching her in a lie.

"You misunderstand me. Your father and my husband are Gatekeepers. They cannot die in the same manner as you and me. They are a physical manifestation of beings that exist on a higher dimensional plane, able to change forms by creating hybrid vessels for their essence in our reality. They cannot be killed in the manner we know."

Skyler listened intently to this information, no doubt absorbing every detail to bring back to TSS Command. Iza suddenly wished she'd asked her to stay outside.

"I don't understand. Are you saying my father was an alien… from another dimension?" Iza wanted to laugh at how ridiculous it sounded. She glanced at Skyler, but her glasses hid her eyes, and her mouth was set giving nothing away about her feelings

"He's an ancient and powerful being that took the form of a Taran man in order to study our race's development in recent years. Your father and my husband were sent to the Taran worlds to travel around from planet to planet, learning all they could about our modern culture and what has changed since the Gatekeepers last dealt with Tarans millennia ago."

"If these aliens are still around, then how come we haven't seen them?"

"The Gatekeepers are xenophobic by nature. From our vantage, their race is made of pure energy with the ability to take a piece of themselves to manifest in whatever form they choose," Reagan explained.

"Like taking off a finger and creating a clone of yourself

that can go off and does its own thing," Skyler said. "Huh, neat trick."

"Essentially," she said looking at Skyler as if for the first time. "The Gatekeepers, in their native form, have remained hidden. But the Taran hybrid clones—as you called them—that were sent to investigate are still out there in the general population. When they took our form, they also got our impulsive desires and need for connection. They fell in love. And that's how you and your cousin came to be."

Iza's stomach knotted. "Wait, you're saying I'm an alien hybrid myself?"

"The genetic markers are so minute, no one would know unless they knew what to look for."

Her mind was racing. "Is that why I'm immune to telepathy?"

"That was always a trait of my husband and your father. But there's no time to get into the details now." Reagan resumed pacing the shack, shoving random things into a duffle. She picked up the picture from the nightstand and slipped it inside.

Her movements reminding Iza too much of her mother. *Hadn't she been just like this the day she left? I can't remember, or maybe I don't want to remember.*

"Did you know about them being alien hybrids? Did they really just seem like normal guys?" Iza asked, her voice dropping to a whisper.

"We always knew they were special, but it wasn't until later we realized why." Reagan got a far-off look in her eye then. It was as if she was living back in that time when she first met her husband. "Your mother was enamored with your father— almost to the point of obsession. Wherever he went, she went, too. You have to know they loved each other, but your mother loved harder than most. It was a shock when we learned the truth about them. They insisted on telling us themselves and at the time, I'll admit, it was hard to accept at first. We knew nothing of the Gatekeepers' existence. When your mother and I had a falling out, we decided it was best we part ways for good."

"What did you fight about?"

"Nothing of consequence," she said, waving her hand in the air. Then, she continued filling the duffle. She grabbed a small blanket and a small journal she pulled from a drawer. "Looking back now, I can hardly remember. We were always fighting. I let it get the best of us, and I'll always regret that we never made amends before her death. If we had, perhaps we—" Reagan stared at Iza.

Does she regret not being there for me? What if my mother didn't leave by choice? It was the one answer her aunt didn't have but the one Iza needed most.

Reagan pulled another photo out of the small nightstand of her mother and her and slipped it into the bag before zipping it closed.

"You and your cousin, Jaidyn, are the same age. I did some overdue research after you left and discovered you were born days apart. Now, his life is in danger. Or, worse, he may already be dead. I didn't know who else to call."

"What was he doing out here?" Iza asked.

"He was trying to protect me. At first, he went in search of you, against my wishes. Then when he knew my life was in danger, he tried to lure them away." Reagan shook her head. "He didn't understand, I tried to tell him it was useless, but he wouldn't listen."

Iza shook her head and looked to Skyler to see what she thought of these ravings. The woman wasn't making any sense at all, but Skyler seemed to be listening.

"Where would they take him?" the Agent asked.

"I don't know," Reagan replied with a slight shake of her head, her eyes filling. "I can only hope that wherever they've taken him, he might be close to his father."

Iza's breath caught in her chest. "Are you saying they might still be alive?"

"It's a very strong possibility, but I don't understand enough about them to know for sure. As far as I know, you and your cousin are the only Gatekeeper-Taran mixed children in the universe. That makes you special—able to do things others can't. My husband never elaborated on what that would mean, only that we were to keep you hidden. If the Gatekeepers ever learned of your existence, it would destroy the delicate peace between our peoples established so long ago. Do you understand?" Reagan took her hands and stared into her eyes waiting for an answer.

"I think so," Iza said, though her mind still swirled with questions.

"I only wish that I'd known about you. I would've done something, been there. I can't make up for that now. You're a woman now. Please forgive me and help me find my son."

Iza didn't know what to say. The woman's hands were warm in her own. They were weathered with gardening and the life of a mother who'd raised a son without help. She had the face of her mother, down to the same lines. Everything about her, except her demeanor, was the same. She was asking Iza to do something her mother had not done. It was a lot to swallow, but Iza gulped around the knot in her throat. She nodded.

"Remember, you represent the one thing they fear the most: exposure. Your existence is a threat to that. It makes you not only a target but something for them to fear," Reagan said. "There's no place you can hide here, but there's something you need to take with you."

"I thought you said they already had my cousin?" Iza clarified.

"Yes, they do, but you can find him." Reagan held up a necklace with the symbol from the sphere. It was identical to the one Iza wore. "It's the one thing that his father left for him. I found it here on the floor; he must have lost it in the struggle."

Iza put a hand inside her shirt and pulled out her necklace, rubbing it between her fingers.

"Oh, that's wonderful. You have one, too." Her hand reached out and clasped the symbol on the bottom. "Good. Well, then, this one belongs to your cousin when you find him."

Iza glanced back at Skyler, who was standing rigid behind her. They were supposed to be tracking down Joe. She didn't have time to look for both men, but she slipped the necklace into the pocket of her pants.

"How would I even begin to find him?"

"You won't have to; they'll find you. They'll have a ship of some kind, not easy to pick up on regular sensors, I'd suspect. Don't deal with any of the ones walking around on the surface of the planet. Once they identify you, they won't ask questions, they'll just kill you. And they're coming for me. They can't find you here. You have to run," Reagan said as she pushed Iza through the small door toward their shuttle.

Trix was standing outside the shuttle transfixed. Skyler took two steps outside and stopped, looking up.

Iza did the same. Dark clouds had rolled in out of nowhere and blacked out the sun. A thunder rumbled from her toes and up her body, making her teeth chatter together.

Iza reached out to her aunt grasping her by the wrist. "Come with us."

Reagan shook her head. Then as if just remembering the duffle, she ran back inside and then shoved it into Iza's arms.

"When you see my son, tell him that I protected him until the end. I only wish I'd been there for you sooner. You've got to run and don't look back. I'll hold them off as long as I can, but if you don't hurry back to your ship, they'll take you."

Iza glanced back at the rundown shack. Hold them off with what—a broom? What was she going to use to fight off a hybrid alien being from another dimension?

The sky above them had turned an angry black. The clouds seemed ready to drop buckets of rain on them in seconds, but the charge of electromagnetic energy in the air was so strong it hummed all around and through her. She slipped the duffle strap over her body and behind her so she could start running.

"Hubyria isn't known for freak rainstorms," Skyler said looking around at the worrisome clouds.

Iza couldn't make her legs work as she stared up at the sky again. Remembering where she'd seen those ominous clouds before. In a dream, while she'd had the sphere. She'd been still holding Joe's hand and the feeling of immense joy fading at the sight of the dark cloud rolling in. The clouds hadn't been bringing rain, and she doubted that this one was either. She remembered looking down at their joined hands in confusion.

Something behind them crackled, and Iza felt the heat of it run down her back. Then another thunder crack. The sky opened up, and it was an ocean of water falling from the sky. So heavy it pushed them to the ground with the weight of it. Iza pushed herself up from the ground and looked back. Her aunt stood inside the shanty, the water already pooling inside. Skyler waded back to her then grabbed Iza's arm, pulling her toward the shuttle through the steady sheet of rain pounding on them from above.

Iza called out to Trix. She was as stiff as a board and her eyes were open as if frozen on something behind her. Iza looked back and she heard her aunt waving and yelling something; the water was up to their thighs.

"Trix!" Iza yelled.

As if on cue her eyes fluttered, and she looked down at Iza. "I apologize. I had to purge the alien signal from my system. We should leave immediately."

"Tell us something we don't know!" Skyler yelled as she pulled the duffle from off Iza's back and telekinetically levitated it up to Trix. "Get the shuttle prepped for immediate take off. Now!"

Trix obeyed, but Iza struggled to keep her feet under her as she waded to the open hatch through the water and mud at her hips. Her aunt had told her to keep going and not turn back, but Iza couldn't help herself. She yanked her wrist out of Skyler's grasp, forcing the other woman to stop.

As Iza turned to go back, her aunt and the shanty burst into a ball of flames.

IZA'S KNEES BUCKLED and she sank into waist high water, watching the debris drown under the weight of the water. The smoke blackened the sky, reaching up into the dark clouds above.

"No!" Iza's throat ached from screaming.

Skyler half dragged her, putting an arm around her as she awkwardly ran and swam to the shuttle.

Trix had control of the shuttle as it lifted up out of the water and through the onslaught of rain with the hatch open. Skyler used telekinesis to lift Iza into the shuttle and leaped in behind her. Iza was still in shock when the shuttle hatch closed.

"Head back to the *Verity*. we need to try and outrun this thing," Skyler instructed.

"The planet is currently being transformed. The signals are the same as Uephus. Someone should warn the inhabitants of the planet to seek shelter or cover and contact the Enforcers," Trix stated in her monotone voice.

"Yes. I assume you're capable of sending that message?"

"I am."

"Then do it! Let the *Verity* know we're coming in and that Iza isn't well."

Iza heard the exchange, but she couldn't bring herself to say the words that would make the horror she witnessed real. Her aunt was gone, and the Gatekeepers had killed her. Her cousin might already be dead. It was the one thing that her aunt hadn't wanted to admit, but after seeing what they could do, it was a strong possibility. It was then she noticed her hands had found the duffle bag. She clung to it, not wanting to put it down.

"Captain, I have contacted Yeaga and informed her of the situation. I will not repeat what she said, but it seems they are already aware."

Iza stared at the opposite wall of the shuttle, unable to focus. Inside, she screamed. Instead of taking one of the seats, she curled into herself, wrapping her arms around the bag.

Iza's body was numb and her heart broken for another mother figure she'd never know. She reflected on her aunt's last words; they hung in her mind like wisps of truth in a web of questions. *Did she say my father might be alive? Why didn't she try and leave with us?*

"We're docking," Skyler said, coming to her side.

She'd been kind enough to leave her alone for the ride back to the ship, but now Skyler pulled Iza to her feet with a strength Iza didn't know she possessed. She left the duffle for Trix to retrieve. Skyler's gentle yet firm hands guided Iza off the shuttle as if she were made of glass. Iza wasn't glass and she didn't need Skyler. It was Joe in the dream; he'd been the one to make her feel better, not his sister. She was about to say so when her knees gave out. She would have fallen face first onto the deck if Skyler hadn't been there to catch her.

"I've got you. there you go." Her voice sounding too gentle, too motherly.

Braedon was waiting for them. "Iz, are you okay?" He reached for her, helping her off the ramp.

"She just lost her aunt. We need to get out of these wet clothes. She's going to need something to help her sleep. Trix, we need to get the ship as far away from here as possible."

"Yes, Agent Anderson. I presume we do not have a destination at this time?"

"No, we don't. Just move the ship out of here, and fast."

"I'm sorry, who put you in charge?" Karter asked as he joined the others in the cargo hold.

"As the only ranking TSS officer, I did. If you have a problem with it, feel free to send your complaints to TSS Headquarters."

Iza would have enjoyed the banter if she'd been able to erase the image of her aunt disappearing before her eyes. Braedon must have dashed off, though Iza didn't see him leave. Trix was a blur as she passed them. Karter didn't struggle or rush as he took over from Skyler, helping Iza to her cabin.

"Put this in her room," Skyler said, handing off the duffle to him. "As soon as I'm dry, I'll come back to check on you."

Iza felt a light pat on her back. She made a noise to protest, but Karter shook his head.

"Let us take care of you. It's okay. Everything's going to be okay," he said. She liked how soothing his voice could be.

Cierra must have been informed because Iza could smell the garden scent of her as she walked just ahead of them with a satchel in her hands. Karter placed her hand on the biometric reader that opened her cabin door, and she was led inside where she collapsed on the bed. As soon as Karter let her go, she curled in on herself. Atano sniffed at their ankles the moment they arrived. When Iza didn't respond to his greeting, he leapt on the bed, snuggling up to her curved back.

"She's sopping wet. What happened?" Cierra asked, her voice barely above a whisper as if even the sound of talking might break Iza.

"Her aunt was killed. We don't have all the details yet. Agent Anderson was with her."

"What? Are we in danger?"

"Knowing Iza, absolutely," Karter said.

"Fantastic," Cierra said, though her tone of voice suggested it was anything but. She checked her pupils, holding up a penlight to her eyes, and made a tsk sound between her teeth. "She's in shock."

Iza lost track of the time she lay there listening to Karter and Cierra. At some point, Trix and Skyler entered and ushered Karter out. Skyler had changed into dry clothes and was helping get Iza out of her wet ones along with Trix.

Skyler spoke as she worked, "The Enforcers have arrived to help evacuate those who are in the most danger. Hubyria is continuing to experience severe storms and atmospheric changes. I've also sent a report to the TSS advising them of our current situation."

She said 'our' as if Reagan's death somehow affected all of them. Iza didn't correct her.

—

More time passed, and people came in and out from Iza's cabin. Eventually, she became more aware of the visitors. Trix was there at her bedside, and Skyler was kicked back in a chair.

"Where are we?" Iza asked. Her throat ached and head was throbbing.

"We are currently in orbit of Sarduvis Penitentiary," Trix replied.

Iza brought a hand to her head. "What? Why?"

"Captain Desirae Hyttinen has requested to speak with you, but I informed her you were unconscious to alleviate any further questioning. Also, Ava Brandis sent you a personal message."

That didn't exactly answer her question, but Iza was still feeling too overwhelmed to ask for clarification. "Thank you," she croaked instead. Trix was quick to grab her a cup of water. The coolness eased Iza's dry throat.

"Captain, can I get you something to eat?" Trix offered.

Iza shook her head. She propped herself up in bed.

At some point, they'd changed her into dry clothes and tucked her into bed. The entire departure from Hubyria and what followed was a blur. Her blanket had also been replaced with one of Cierra's homemade ones.

"Why are you still here?" Iza asked Skyler.

"Cierra left instructions for you to drink all of whatever that is in the cup by the bed."

Iza eyed the greenish drink with suspicion. She needed the sleep, but she wasn't sure choking down one of Cierra's famous plant drinks would be worth it. "Fine."

Atano leaped on the bed as if sensing she wouldn't put up a fight and nuzzled her hand.

"Trix is needed on the flight deck with Braedon," Skyler said. "I know you don't know me very well, but I'm not about to let you go through something like this on your own."

Iza wasn't sure how she felt about Skyler's easy grasp of command. It sounded like she was still in charge during her absence. *If Joe were here, wouldn't he do the same?* She had to admit he would. But Skyler wasn't Joe.

"I am capable of caring for Iza as well as monitoring the ship's systems." The offense carried even in Trix's robotic tone.

"No offense to you, but have you ever lost a parent or a close family member?" Skyler took the silence to mean she hadn't. "Well, I have. Iza is going to need someone to help her through this. I'm not going anywhere. If you don't like it, you'll have to remove me." Skyler crossed her arms over her chest and lifted her chin.

"I'll pass," Iza said. "I don't need anyone at the moment. This is the one time I'm going to listen to the Healer. I need rest and I can't get that with either of you hovering over me."

Iza drank the concoction Cierra had left for her beside the bed. It didn't taste half as bad as the vegetable drinks she'd pushed on her, but Iza still needed water to chase it down. Then, she curled up and pulled the covers over her head. Only when she was sure she was alone did she let out the moan she'd been holding back. The ache filled her stomach and chest forcing out the tears and grief until she cried herself to sleep.

—

Skyler was once again sitting on the chair, her bare feet propped up on the bed while reading something on her handheld, when Iza stirred awake. Atano nuzzled Iza's cheek, giving her a testing lick before backing down and waiting for her to respond. She reached over and rubbed behind his ears the way he liked before rolling back onto one elbow and watching Skyler. She seemed to be pretending not to notice she was awake.

Iza studied the lines of Skyler's face, looking for all the ways she was different from Joe. The delicate chin and hair tucked neatly behind one ear were signature to her alone. The way she moved, and her patience seemed to be something they'd both learned in their military training. Joe and his sister had inherited the same eyes and smile, and the determination was there in the set of her jaw as if waiting for a fight. Iza didn't have any fight left.

Skyler made a show of putting down her handheld then letting her blue eyes fall on Iza. "My brother probably never told you about how we lost our parents."

"He did," Iza said, not sure why she wanted her to know that Joe had confided in her.

"Oh. That shouldn't surprise me, considering his feelings for you, and yet, I'm still a little surprised." Skyler's chin dropped to her chest as she looked down, smiling. Then, she met Iza's gaze as she continued. "Though Joe and I were both raised on Earth, I always knew there was something more. Something beyond our world. You've been there, so you know how difficult that is, considering our surroundings. I didn't wait around for someone to tell me. I just knew deep down the way I know I'm a girl."

Skyler took a deep breath. "It made my transition into the TSS easy. I did well, and I eventually fell in love with another Agent."

"Joe's best friend," Iza said, doing her best to sound disinterested. If she wanted to retell her everything she already knew while she was half-asleep, then this is what she got.

"Yes, Joe's best friend, Emery. We fought about it of course, the way we fought about everything. He thought I'd plotted to take Emery away from him. Which couldn't be further from the truth. I think since he found you, he understands that a bit better. But it doesn't erase years of not talking and not dealing with the real problem." Skyler shifted her feet to the floor and crossed her arms. "I was the one that told my brother our parents were dead. It was like hearing it from me made it my fault. If I'd known that, I would have let the cold TSS Agent who had informed me tell him, but I didn't understand how Joe would take it. Ever since I uttered the words 'our parents are dead', I've been fighting with him for a bit of familial normalcy."

Iza closed her eyes a moment, not because she didn't want to hear anymore, but because the weight of sadness still pressed against her eyelids. She wasn't sure the shock had worn off entirely.

"I'll get to the point. When I boarded your ship, I don't know what I expected, but it wasn't this. I saw how everyone pulled together in a moment of crisis. You have a family here, like the one I always wanted for myself and Joe and couldn't provide for him. Your crew runs smoother than most hauler crews I've ever come across."

"Know a lot of haulers, do you?" Iza chuckled, just a slight movement in her chest and a smile.

"You're right, I don't know that many. But I do know a family when I see one. I don't know how, but Joe's found a place where he belongs. And I think you are the center of this family. I'm sorry I ever doubted you."

"I get that a lot."

Braedon's voice broke in over the comms in her cabin. "Captain, there's an incoming message for you marked 'urgent'."

Isn't everything right now? She pinched the bridge of her nose. "Who's it from?"

"I'm not sure, it's encoded."

"Send it here," Iza said.

Iza moved to sit at the end of her bed and watch the message.

"Do you want me to go?" Skyler asked.

Iza held up a hand. There weren't many secrets left on board the *Verity*, and she couldn't think of any reason why Skyler couldn't stay, especially if the message was from Arvonen or better yet, Joe. She found listening to Skyler had eased something and wasn't ready to send her away. Besides that, if it was urgent, she might need Skyler to relay instructions to the crew while she got herself together.

Iza started to play the message from her bed, but when the face of Raquel Calveras appeared, Iza froze the video and climbed out of the bed to move closer to the viewscreen.

"Who's that?" Skyler asked.

The woman had convinced her she was a genuine friend. They hadn't seen each other since Raquel had thrown Iza through the Gate to test a theory that Iza's genetics would protect her. In the end, she had been okay, but neither of them knew that until she returned.

"A lying snake," Iza answered. "CACI, continue playback."

Raquel's message resumed. There were dark smudges under her eyes and her hair looked like it had been days since she'd used a comb.

"Izzy, I know you don't want to hear from me—"

Got that right.

"—so, I'll get straight to the point."

Iza hated the way the nickname rolled off her tongue. Raquel was less than an enemy and had no right. She'd forever hate the sound of it, and she'd make sure no one else ever called her by that name. Iza couldn't stand the sight of her. Besides, Raquel didn't have anything to say that Iza wanted to hear. She reached to turn off the image, but Raquel looked over her shoulder and back again as if nervous she might get caught.

"Arvonen has Joe. Your Joe. He took him from Earth a few days ago, and he's been running memory experiments on him. I don't know what he's after anymore, but Joe's life is in danger. Arvonen will do anything—go through anyone, remove any obstacle—on his way to get at the Gate and you. He believes that with control of the Gates, he'll rule the Taran Empire. He's mad of course, you've met him, but this time he's close. He also has a man we believe to be your cousin. His DNA has the exact same distinct markers as yours. Whether you knew about Joe's abduction or not, you shouldn't try to mount a rescue for either man. Get as far away from Arvonen as possible. And if you have access to one of the Gate generators, keep it hidden."

Iza huffed. You honestly expect me to believe a bomaxed liar? My aunt said the Gatekeepers had her son. Was she wrong? Raquel's face moved a couple centimeters closer to the camera and she blinked twice.

"I know you don't trust me, and I've given you no reason to, but I'm sending you a video recorded yesterday of Joe as proof."

The image flashed over her screen, and she saw a man dressed in black strapped to a vertically inclined bed with a silver helmet fastened to his head. Beneath the contraption, his eyes were closed, dark, and smudged as if the fatigue had seeped out onto the skin, tinting it blue. There was the faint rapid eye movement beneath the lids and a quick intake of breath.

Joe, it's him and he's alive. Iza's hand lifted as if to touch the image. What have they done to you?

Then, Raquel's face replaced the image, and Iza dropped her hand back to her side. "I'm sorry, I haven't been able to get close to your cousin, but I know he's here." Raquel looked down the regret in the slump of her shoulders. "I know because I was the one who helped Arvonen find him. Please, you have to stop him. If I knew how, I would tell you. Joe isn't going to last long in this condition. I just wanted you to know. I'm doing what I can here, but if I'm caught…" Her voice faded as if that was answer enough, and it was. "Well, you know what he'll do to me. Contact the TSS; they'll know how to save Joe. My only advice is to hurry before Arvonen destroys us all." The message ended

Skyler paced the room like a caged animal as she mumbled something under her breath. Even with the visual evidence, Iza wasn't sure she could believe a word out of the digger's mouth. She was next on the Gatekeepers' list now that her aunt was dead. They were transforming planets left and right—

seemingly at random. They wouldn't hesitate to destroy her or her cousin if they were caught. The TSS expected her to go after Arvonen, but if Raquel was right, she'd be walking into a trap.

"I'm going to contact the TSS and let them know we've heard from Arvonen," Skyler said, heading for the door.

"I wouldn't put too much credit on what that woman says."

"You don't trust her, but she might be telling the truth." Skyler rolled her eyes to the ceiling. For the first time, Iza realized she might be ready to break. The sight of Joe in that machine had turned her stomach. No doubt his older sister had a similar reaction.

"That's right. Go to the flight deck and tell Braedon to start cracking the code on that message. He might be able to do a back trace since it originated on one of his father's ships."

"You're going track down Joe, anyway?" Skyler asked.

"Of course."

"Even though it might be a trap?"

"It most certainly is a trap, and yes. As you said, Joe is a part of this family, and we don't leave family behind."

Skyler nodded and turned to open the door just as someone knocked on the other side.

"CACI, close messages," Iza instructed.

The door opened, and she saw Trix standing there. Skyler moved passed her and the door closed behind her as Trix stepped in.

"I deduced that an encoded message might have distressed you."

"You were right, it seems."

"Your blood pressure is elevated and your breathing irregular. The encrypted message held bad news."

"Excellent deduction. So what? You didn't need my biometrics to know that."

"No, but it does indicate that your emotional health is still out of alignment.."

Iza shook her head. "I'm not sure there's anything I can do about it."

Trix tilted her head waiting for Iza to continue.

"Raquel sent the message to tell me that Arvonen is torturing Joe."

"His life is in imminent danger?"

"I don't trust Raquel. She's an excellent actress, fit for the Sensationals. I should know. But, my cousin, Jaidyn, is also missing. Reagan thinks the aliens took him. But Raquel swears he's also on board the *Arvonen One*."

Trix tilted her head. "You do not believe her?"

"I don't know who to believe anymore. I saw what the Gatekeepers can do. However, I don't think they would take him; they'd just strike him down the way they did Reagan. They don't seem to have any regard for life. Arvonen, on the other hand, is different. He's the only one obsessed with the spheres enough to put everyone I know in danger. Besides that, if Raquel is right in her research, my cousin and I are the only ones who can pass through the Gates. It's a strong motivation for keeping my cousin alive. But, even she didn't know what Arvonen wants with Joe."

"What are you going to do?"

Wasn't that the million-credit question? Iza sat back down on the bed and tucked her feet up under her. She needed to think. There weren't many options, but there was one action she knew in her heart she'd need to take, though she didn't want to do it alone. *If Joe were here, he'd know exactly what to say and do to get me fired up. I'm not sure I can live in a universe where he doesn't exist.*

Iza answered the question with more conviction than she was feeling. "I'm going to figure out a way to get Joe and my cousin without getting myself and everyone else killed."

"It will be a dangerous venture with little probability of success."

"True."

"Are you afraid?" Trix asked.

It was the first time she hadn't used Iza's biometrics to surmise her emotional state. Iza was probably more afraid than she'd ever been on her own. Iza fell back onto the bed and stared up at the ceiling.

"Yeah, I'm scared. Scared of losing Joe forever. Scared of what information about my family died with my aunt. I'm scared my father and uncle might be alive somewhere. I'm scared of what I'll have to tell my cousin if I find him."

Iza kept her cousin's necklace in her jacket that hung from a hook beside the door. She couldn't stop her eyes from filling as she remembered the look on Reagan's face as she'd pressed the necklace into her hands. Then, again, the horror on her face just before her death. Iza rolled to one side so she could look at Trix. From where she lay, she could see the duffle on the floor near her nightstand. She couldn't imagine having the courage to go through his things.

"I never wanted a family. I only wanted my freedom. Now, I'd trade the little bit of independence I have for what's left of the little family I've got."

Trix nodded as if she understood.

"You were always independent. Even as a small child."

Iza sat up in the bed and threw her legs over the side to look closer at Trix who's innocent eyes stared right back.

"Are you malfunctioning again? By the time I bumped into you on the streets, I'd already been on my own for a full year, remember?"

"That is the first time that *you* remember meeting me, but that is not the first time that we met," Trix said.

"How is that possible?"

"Your mother insisted that I be a part of your life when you were small. She and I were close friends once. You were so curious about the world and at times a danger to yourself as you liked jumping off ledges and putting your hands into things that could harm you, like fire."

"You've never mentioned that before. When we met, you acted like it was the first time. You introduced yourself and everything."

Iza remembered that day. She'd almost been caught again by local Enforcers for stealing. The hunger and desperation had stirred in her belly, pushing her toward the convenience store. She had known that the owner took out the trash at about the same time every day. She had planned to wait for him to leave, then sneak in and grab a few food bars. Iza had been at the front door of the store when she'd heard the kids in the alley across the street shouting.

Iza had made her way over to see if it was a fight among anyone she knew. She'd found Trix being hassled by some local street kids, no one she'd seen before. Iza had pulled out the pocketknife she kept in her boot, then strolled up to the largest of them. He'd had greasy black hair and a zit on his nose beaming like a neon target. She'd threatened to cut his throat if he didn't leave Trix alone. She'd only had to slice at his arm with the small pocketknife to get him to leave. The other two bullies had made the smart decision to follow their zit-faced leader. She and Trix had been together ever since.

"You are correct, I did introduce myself to you then," Trix acknowledged. "It is because, at that time, I had already experienced a reboot of my systems. The moment your father was recaptured by his people, I was set to self-destruct. Before that could happen, there was a back-door code entered into my system to preserve my life. I believe it was your mother who placed it there. At the same time, it preserved the lie and the truth about who you were and who your father was. I do not believe he anticipated that we would be separated, thus I didn't know my protocol until we met that day in the alley."

"So, the Gatekeepers tried to destroy you, but my mother saved you so you could look out for me."

It all made sense, why Trix had been there when she was so young. The protocol would overrule everything else, including self-preservation. She didn't want to think about what would have happened to them both had they not found each other again.

"Does that have anything to do with why you speak the way you do?"

"No," Trix answered quickly. Iza waited a full minute for Trix to continue. "As I said, your mother and I were friends once. She and I took care of you when your father was away. By then, we knew who and what he was. Then, one day, he was gone. He'd warned us and prepared me for the hunters that would be looking for you. Eventually, they came. Your mother was desperate to save you. Though I tried to convince her it was a mistake, she felt that Leaving was the only answer."

"So, why didn't you stay with me?"

"You were a Gatekeeper-Taran hybrid child. I'm Lynaedan. I did not think I was capable of caring for you in the way necessary for your mental well-being. My friendship with your mother made me wary of forming such a strong bond with you. Seeing so much of her emotional turmoil in you, I did not think I could survive it if you also left me."

Iza stared at Trix, not sure what to do with her hands. She stood up so they were face-to-face as she spoke. "But you came back."

"Yes, I monitored your transition to the new family. When I saw you were too headstrong to stay with them, I restored my duty protocols and followed you. It's been my responsibility to stand by you no matter what happened. As my attachment to you increased, I thought if you did not grow too dependent on my companionship, I could preserve you from emotional harm if anything were to happen to me."

Iza took a step toward her and grasped Trix's hands in her own and looked up into her eyes. She was close enough to see the circuitry behind the irises.

"Is that what you think? That because of your manner, that I would never become attached to you?" Iza took a breath and let it out, not sure how to say what she knew Trix needed to hear. "I'm pretty sure that if anything happened to you, I'd be permanently damaged along with the rest of the crew. Braedon was in love with you the minute he laid eyes on you. If not for Cierra, he might have tried to date you." Iza laughed at her joke but Trix continued to regard her with some confusion. Iza continued, "You've saved us more times than I can count, and you care more than anyone I've ever met. You are my family, no matter how you choose to communicate. Do you understand?"

Trix nodded. "Yes, I think so."

Iza blinked twice. Trix's tone had changed from robotic to something more natural and Iza felt the sting of tears behind her eyes and she took a step back to gather herself.

Then, Iza was struck with a solution to her current problem. She stood up and grabbed Trix, throwing her arms around her in a hug before releasing her. "You're amazing. Head to the flight deck, and I'll meet you there. I think I know how to defeat Arvonen and get Joe back."

JOE ADMIRED IZA as she sat on the edge of his bed looking out the window. He liked that she'd chosen a side that first night, as if she were going to stay there forever. *How many days has it been?* They'd been together… he'd lost track of the days they'd stayed in his apartment. Today, she had an expression on her face he didn't recognize.

From behind, Joe wrapped his arms around her, pulling her against him. She snuggled his neck and turned her head to place a light kiss on his cheek before she resumed staring out the window at the cloudless sky.

"What's wrong?" he asked.

"Nothing, I'm fine."

"Said no person who was ever fine, ever," Joe teased, giving her a gentle kiss on her temple. "Tell me."

"I'm worried. I feel like things aren't over. They're never going to be over until Arvonen gets that sphere back. He'll never really leave us alone."

"Don't worry about him, he can't bother us here."

Iza pulled away so she could stand with her back to him as she leaned against the window's edge.

"We're not going to be safe until we have the sphere back

and he can't touch it."

"I promise, the sphere is someplace he'd never find it."

"You're smart, Joe, but you don't have many places to hide something like that sphere. Any place you kept it would be discovered once the electrical systems started acting up."

"The sphere is safely hidden in a box like the one it came in. With no one to activate it, there's no danger of it affecting any of the computer's systems in Headquarters."

Iza turned and moved to sit beside him on the bed again.

"You left it in TSS Headquarters?"

"Of course. Where else could it remain hidden and protected at the same time? There's no chance that Arvonen can get through the Agents there or the High Commander. Now, will you stop worrying and come over here and let me love you?" Joe pulled her back onto the bed. Only, instead of the soft give of the mattress, there was a clunk like metal on metal. "Wait, did you hear that?"

Iza's eyebrows drew together. "Hear what?"

Joe inched up the bed and when he didn't hear the sound again, he threw himself on top of Iza, and she giggled. Then, he heard the clank again.

"You don't hear that?" Joe asked again, sitting up.

"I have no idea what you're talking about. Maybe you can describe the sound?"

"It's like someone dragging a heavy piece of metal on the deck of a ship."

Iza let out a giggle that she reserved for their time in bed before she grabbed him by the neck and pulled him in for a kiss.

The kiss started slow and gentle before it went hard. Then her teeth bit down hard on his lip. Startled, he pulled back. She was smiling at him, but he reached up and touched his lip with two fingers pulling them away again and saw she'd drawn blood.

"What's the matter with you?" he demanded.

Joe raised his eyes from his fingers to see what had possessed her to bite him so hard when the room around him shifted and what had been his apartment was now a laboratory. Clean metal lines on every surface. The room was cold and when he looked down at himself, he saw he was wearing nothing more than a medical gown. His legs and wrists were held down with restraints.

"What's going on here? Where am I?" His tongue was heavy in his mouth, slurring his words. His throat hurt as if he'd been yelling for days, making his voice sound far away even to his own ears. There was no one in the room and though it hurt to move his head even a centimeter he took in everything around him and tried to listen for people in the vicinity. His telepathy was off, as he couldn't make out anyone else near or around the area until the door swung open, and a technician—presumably not expecting to find him awake— came in, took one look at him, and ran back out.

"Somebody better bomaxed tell me where I am and what I'm doing here!" he called out. This time, though his throat was scratchy, the sound carried further than it had before.

"Agent Anderson, you're going to be fine," Raquel said as she slid into the room. Her eyes were heavy as if she hadn't slept, but she was carrying a food tray filled with vials of liquid and a large syringe.

He narrowed his eyes at her, then tried to read her thoughts and found his own mind so scattered he couldn't grab onto anything tangible. "What are you doing? Why am I here?" he asked out loud instead.

"You have something Mr. Arvonen wants. You're going to be here until he gets it. I'm sorry to do this to you, but, again, it's best if you don't fight it."

Raquel filled the syringe from one of the red vials and held it up to his neck. Joe whipped his head back and forth, making it impossible for her to get too close. So, she jabbed the syringe into his thigh. The pinch made him wince.

"You're going to pay for th—"

The lab around him faded back to his apartment like brush strokes on an oil painting, revealing Iza on the bed beside him gazing up at him expectedly.

"Are you just going to sit there staring at me or are you going to hold me?"

Joe reached up again and touched his lip. It was dry and no blood came away on his fingers. He stared at his hand in confusion. Then, his eyes met Iza's and he smiled.

"I'm going to hold you and I'm never letting you go."

— — —

Iza and Trix came onto the flight deck together. Braedon was sitting at the helm with his comic on his lap and Skyler had taken Joe's former position. She nodded to Iza as they entered.

"Hey, Iz, you look great," Braedon said.

"That's a sweet lie. Any word from your father?"

"No, but I'm serious when I say I'm glad you're feeling better. Do we have a destination?" He swiveled in his seat as she sat down in the captain's chair. Atano followed her in, and Trix remained standing on her right.

"Thanks, I hope so. I want you to do your coding magic on that encrypted message I received. It was from Raquel Calveras, allegedly from on board the *Arvonen One.*"

"What did she want?"

"To tell me something I already suspected. Arvonen has Joe, and he's hurting him."

"Hurting how?" Braedon asked.

"Some kind of memory experiments. I wouldn't trust a word of anything she says, though she did send over a vid with Joe strapped to a medical bed with a metal device on his head. I want to see if you can trace the message back to where it originated. If it's not too much trouble, also send a copy of it over to Skyler for her review."

He glanced at Skyler a moment then nodded. Something seemed to be resolved between them while Iza had been grieving. Good. Skyler wasn't half-bad as an Agent, and she'd need her if the plan was going to work.

Braedon cracked his knuckles. "Haven't done a solid encryption crack in a while. This may take some time. Whoever's working on the encryption is good enough that the authorities haven't been able to trace them."

"Just do what you can, the sooner the better. Skyler, I want to talk retrieval options. I know not all Agents are equal or whatever, but I'm hoping you can use some of your TSS training to get us onto the ship unnoticed once we're within range."

"I can't make your ship invisible," Skyler said, holding up her hands, "but I'll do what I can. What did you have in mind?"

"There's another call coming through," Trix interrupted. "It's coded for Cierra." The others turned to look at her. She'd used a more natural-sounding voice, and though Iza understood why, the others had no idea why she'd made the change. When there was no response, Trix added, "It's marked 'urgent'."

"Um, sure, signal her cabin and tell her to come up here if she doesn't want to take it there," Iza said at last.

"Wait, what just happened here? I've been trying to get you to— Then all of a sudden— When did this happen? I mean I can't believe it." Braedon stood up waving his hands in circles then slapping them on either side of his face. His amazement was so comical it made Iza laugh.

"I've decided to make a change," Trix responded. "I hope that's all right with everyone. If not, I can always return to speaking the way I did before."

"No!" they all said at once.

The flight deck door opened, and Cierra rushed in. For a woman who was normally well put together and calm, she looked harried and about ready to cry.

"Do you want some privacy or…?" Iza gave her a moment to take in the bodies on the flight deck.

Cierra waved it away. "It's fine, I don't care if the crew knows."

Iza glanced at Skyler, wondering what she thought of being called crew. Her expression gave nothing away.

"Are you expecting any news?" Braedon asked.

"No, which means it can only be bad," Cierra replied.

"Trix, bring it up on the main display," Iza said.

The stars of the viewport turned to white and Cierra's parents filled the screen. Her father had the same greenish eyes and her mother the curls. Today the curls were wild, framing her anxious face. Their expressions, tight and filled with worry, reminded Iza too much of her aunt just before— Even mentally, she couldn't finish the thought.

Cierra's eyes were pleading. "Mama, Baba, what's wrong?"

Her father was the first to speak. "You must come home, now. Something is happening here. We can't explain it." He waved his hand in the air as if looking for the words. That's when Iza noticed his shoulders were covered with a blanket, as was his wife's.

"Our world is so cold. There isn't a location that's not covered with snow," her mother added. The camera panned to the window and they all gasped at the sight of all the white snow falling. They would be covered in a matter of hours.

Cierra's eyes widened in horror as she turned back to Iza.

With a nod to Trix, they would be ready to leave on her mark.

"I'm on my way," Cierra said.

"We can't get a hold of your sister." her mother's eyes filled. "We love you, Biscuit. Please, tell your sister we love her, too."

"You're going to tell her yourself. Hold on, we're coming," Cierra said holding her hands up to the viewscreen as if she could keep them there.

"One planet of ice, another wracked with storms, and a desert blossoming into a paradise," Skyler mumbled. "What's the connection?"

Iza was doing a mental count of the planets altered so far; and, the TSS seemed to know about more than she'd heard about. The only common thread she could see was that the worlds were ill-equipped to handle the changes. In particular, Leveckis wasn't equipped for extreme cold; the snow would destroy all the plant life they spent decades growing.

"Trix, get a message out to Douketis and put in the coordinates for Leveckis. Tell him there's a job in it for him if he hurries."

"Wouldn't the truth be better in this case?" Braedon asked.

"No, it would not. He wouldn't go to Leveckis just for Viper. And, worse, he might ignore the message altogether. Better yet, get Karter to send it; he can still pull Douketis' strings. Trix, as soon as that message is sent, jump up to Leveckis."

"Wait!" Skyler shouted, looking at the faces on the flight deck. "You've seen what Arvonen is doing to my brother. He won't make it much longer, from the looks of things. We need to find him."

"Without a lead on Arvonen, we can't do anything other

than wait," Iza said. "Whatever he's got planned it involves me. He'll find us. We're not trying to hide."

"How can you be so sure?" Skyler asked.

Iza shrugged. "You saw the message. Something has that lying archaeologist scared. She thinks if I show up, Arvonen will be able to make a play. So, he'll find us; he's done it before. While I'm arguing the point with you, Cierra's parents are freezing to death. Do you mind if we get on our way, or would you like to have another discussion about how you haven't been there for your brother in years and you want to use my ship to make up for lost time?"

The two women glared at each other unblinkingly.

"Message sent, Captain."

Iza didn't flinch as she continued to stare down Skyler. "Jump!"

—

Everyone was on the flight deck when they reached Leveckis. From the captain's chair, Iza watched Cierra pacing back and forth. She couldn't blame her; after her own recent loss, it seemed too soon to be losing anyone else. The Gatekeepers had to be stopped, but she wasn't sure she could tackle that particular problem on her own. Her cousin and Joe were at the mercy of Arvonen in some unknown region of Taran space. When had she stopped running and become the pursuer?

Iza spoke the question Cierra no doubt was thinking. "Trix, what's our ETA?"

"We're approximately five minutes from orbit of Leveckis."

Karter stared at her a moment, his shock at her change of tone obvious. But, instead of raving the way Braedon had, he shrugged and lifted one eyebrow at Iza. She shrugged back at him. Trix made her own decisions; he didn't need to know the reasons why.

"Any sign of other ships in the area?" Karter asked.

"None," Trix answered.

Iza nodded to Karter, a measured sign of respect. He didn't have to do it, but in this case, it had helped to light a fire under Douketis to get them there before it was too late. Whether they made it or not, Karter had tried and for that, she and the rest of the crew would always be grateful.

"We're in visual range of the planet," Braedon said. "You're going to want to get a look at this."

Iza stood up and took a step forward. "Pull up visuals and magnify by ten."

Leveckis wasn't a particularly lush planet. Most of the continents had moderate climates. Colonists with extreme preservation and naturalistic values had claimed a part of the land to grow vegetation and food to return to a more basic way of living. Those parts of the world had been tamed through backbreaking work. But, there was no sign of those decades of effort now. The only thing they could see on the magnified display were the tops of the mountain range under a thick blanket of white powder.

"There is reason to move quickly," Trix said.

Cierra sneered. "Other than the fact that my parents are down there?"

"Yes," Trix continued as if she hadn't been demeaned, "the entire planet is covered in snow and the ground beneath is frozen. However, that's not our biggest problem. There's a massive storm approaching, so in addition to the snow there will be freezing rain."

"That's bad I take it," Braedon said with a nervous look to Trix.

"If my analysis is correct, a layer of ice over three centimeters thick will cover the top of everything in the vicinity of your parents' home. The density of the mass of icepack on the surface of the planet has already grown twenty percent in the last thirty minutes, according to documented satellite readings," Trix said.

"How much time do we have?" Cierra asked.

"There are no perceivable communications from the surface. The orbital satellites are the only things left transmitting, which means survivors will be difficult to find without infrared scanning."

"I've got a ship coming in hot," Braedon called out.

"Is it the *Iron Dog*?" Iza asked.

"No," Braedon swiveled in his chair. "It's the local Enforcers."

"They couldn't have worse timing," Iza said, running a hand over her hair and wanting to tug at the ends to steady her racing thoughts. If they went for Cierra's parents, they might draw unwanted attention to themselves, or worse they might be accused of interfering with a rescue operation. If they left, the Quetzalis could die in this. *Why can't anything ever go my way?* "Are they broadcasting an open communication or messaging us?"

"No, the Enforcer ship is not currently transmitting. They are, however, prepping to send shuttles to the surface," Trix answered.

"Maybe they'll be too busy looking for survivors to worry about us," Braedon said.

"There's also another ship in orbit," Trix said. "It's Viper. She's heading for the surface in a shuttle."

"We need to hurry, Captain," Cierra urged, gripping the back of Braedon's chair with one hand and pressing her teeth down on her bottom lip.

"Well, let's go. Braedon, you're with me and Cierra. Trix considering the effect that the spheres seem to have on you, it would be best if you stayed on the *Verity*."

"What about me?" Karter asked.

"Someone has to deal with Douketis. I'm pretty sure he realizes now he was duped into coming here. Keep him here and don't let him or the Enforcers anywhere near my ship."

Karter nodded.

Braedon stood up to throw his arms around Cierra in support and whisper something in her hair. "No matter what happens I'll be right there," he said when they parted.

"I know, I'll find them. You'll love my dad," Cierra wiped at her eyes and raced off the flight deck without looking to see if anyone was following. Braedon had to run to keep up.

"Captain?" Skyler asked.

Iza had forgotten about her.

"You'll probably be of more help to me with the Enforcers than with the rescue."

"Take the Agent with you," Karter said. "I can handle the Enforcers. My cousin is an Investigator, after all. Not to mention my dynastic credentials." He smirked.

Iza wondered if Karter didn't want Skyler on board because he had something else to hide. *What is he up to, now?* She nodded to Skyler and raced toward the cargo hold.

23

IZA FOUND OUT why Cierra had been in a hurry to get off the flight deck when they met at the shuttle in the cargo hold. Cierra had grabbed her emergency boots and had put on at least two layers of clothing, wrapping her head and face in a thicker purple cloth with gold edging. She'd also wrapped one of the long scarves around Braedon's neck and had another ready to hand to Iza.

"You'll need this," she said.

"Thanks," Iza said, draping the blue cloth around her neck and thinking of how much it reminded her of the color of Joe's eyes. Arvonen would keep him alive as long as he could to get the information he needed. She had to get to him soon, but with Viper on the surface to help her parents and Braedon's connection to the family, neither of her hackers would be working on cracking the code to reach Arvonen. Maybe Iza could convince the TSS to take a more direct approach once they located the *Arvonen One*.

Iza noted Cierra carried more blankets on board the shuttle, placing them beside the bench seat. They were an array of colors like she'd never seen before. Most of the standard equipment they kept on board was the color of metal or at best black.

"Where did you get those?" Iza asked.

"They were gifts." Cierra sat behind Braedon, resting one hand on his shoulder.

Iza couldn't fathom how Cierra had so much stored in her small cabin, but she had more pressing concerns. She sat down next to Braedon, who'd already initiated the pre-launch sequence, and Skyler took the seat behind Iza.

Moments later, they were speeding toward the planet's surface. Thanks to Trix, they had the proper coordinates of the Quetzalis' original broadcasting location and didn't have to depend on their eyes to see through the blowing white winds.

A call came in, and Iza knew it must be the Enforcers, so she answered audio-only.

"This is Captain Brontes to the unidentified shuttle craft preparing to touch down on the surface of Leveckis. You are interfering with an Enforcer rescue mission. I advise you to return to your ship and await further instructions."

Cierra's eyes widened and she clutched Braedon's shoulders as she stared at Iza waiting to see how she answered.

"This is Captain Iza Sundari of the *Verity*. The shuttle belongs to me, and we are retrieving our people from the surface before they freeze to death. I hope that won't be a problem for you this time, Captain Brontes."

"Captain Sundari, why is it whenever there's a planet under complete transformation, you seem to be nearby?"

"Bad luck?"

"I doubt that. In either case, we can't afford to have civilians getting themselves killed out here. Please, get yourselves to safety."

"You wouldn't leave one of your officers behind if there was a chance to save them?" Iza pleaded. "You have my authorization to relieve yourself of any responsibility for losing us in all this white, but I'm not turning back without my people."

"The fact remains, the danger is too great."

Skyler stood up and leaned over Iza's shoulder to speak into the transmitter. "Captain Brontes, this is Agent Skyler Anderson, representing the TSS on this mission. We understand your position, but I must insist that we be permitted passage. We won't impede your rescue operations."

There was an awkward pause. "Noted and recorded, Agent Anderson. You are on your own, as requested. Be careful of those updrafts; they're knocking our shuttle around all over the place, so you'll need to compensate. Brontes out."

Cierra let out a sigh as if she'd been holding her breath.

Iza nodded to Skyler. Thanks to her, they wouldn't have to deal with the Enforcers at all. Now, to track down Cierra's parents. "At the risk of sounding like a petulant child, are we there yet?" Iza asked.

"I don't recognize anything other than the mountain there in the east. We're going the right way, but there's nothing here." Cierra frowned at the viewport.

"Bring us down as close to the signal's coordinates as you can manage, but mind the structures; I don't want to collapse a house by accident," Iza said as she unstrapped and moved to the back of the shuttle. It jolted to one side, and she was thrown against the hull. "Hold her steady."

"I'm doing the best I can," Braedon called out. "The winds are picking up and that snow is mixed with hail. The hull's going to get pummeled unless we keep the shield up."

As if on cue, large pieces of thumb-sized hail pelted the shield of the hull.

"There!" Cierra said pointing to something out the viewport. "That shuttle there. It's Viper."

"Who's Viper?" Skyler asked in a low whisper.

Iza answered, "Cierra's sister, and one of the best hackers in the Taran Empire."

"Hey!" Braedon complained.

"Well, didn't she beat you once?" Iza smiled, knowing it would get him riled up. She needed him alert and ready for anything.

All around them was a barren and frozen wasteland. Where the civilizations and gardens had been, there was now only snow covering everything and blowing all around them. None of the lush green trees, forests, or grass showed through the sheet of ice. The trees that remained were now weighed down with snow and icicles, bending near their breaking point.

"Grab whatever you can to help us get through the ice," Iza instructed.

"You've got it, Iz," Braedon said, climbing out of the pilot's seat.

Frigid wind whipped into the shuttle the moment the hatch opened. Iza shielded her face from it with her arm, thankful for Cierra's warm scarf. She stomped forward into the ice-covered snow, breaking through the top surface with each exhausting step, sinking in up past her knees.

They were forging a path to the house when the other shuttle landed nearby. Its hatch opened and out jumped Viper. Her black jacket was sealed up to the neck and she wore a cap that came down to her ears but didn't hide the jagged green haircut underneath. She began her own trudge through the snow toward the house.

Iza clutched her scarf to her face and wished she had enough fabric to wrap her entire body as the snow and ice beat against her head and shoulders.

"Hurry!" Cierra yelled above the storm.

When their path intersected with Viper's, Cierra and Viper clutched each other and pushed forward together. They were walking headfirst into the wind, inhibiting to their forward progress. Iza had her head tilted so far forward she didn't notice when they came to a complete stop until she ran into Cierra's back.

The small house was barely visible in front of them, with only bits of yellow and green peeking through the snow. They got to work using their boots to stamp down the snowdrift at the door while the hail bounced off their backs.

Iza's teeth were already chattering underneath her scarf. The thing was drenched from the hail and freezing rain. Any longer in the wind, and it would be too stiff to move as it would be frozen to her face.

From the outside, the house looked a lot like the size and shape of the small cottage where Cierra had lived. More of the green and yellow of the door showed through after they'd brushed the snow off. There was a wreath frozen to the front and small flower boxes on the windowsills It might've been warm and cozy once, though it was hard to tell with everything covered in ice and snow.

"Do we have anything that can break through this ice?" Iza asked.

Viper immediately pulled the glove off of her mechanical hand and placed it on the door handle then ripped it off, leaving a gaping hole.

"You're modified," Skyler said, her mouth hanging open.

"Good observation, Agent Obvious," Viper said, then turned to Iza. "Where did you get this one?"

The door was stuck at the hinges. Skylar stepped in to use her abilities to melt away the ice enough to telekinetically swing it open. The faint, lingering scent of a fire wafted out through the open doorway. The kitchen table and chairs had been broken to bits and placed int the middle of the dining room to make a small fire. Iza's eyes were burning from the smoke and she coughed to clear her throat. But in the room, there was no one bundled next to the pile of burning debris.

Cierra and Viper ran around the entire house looking for their parents.

"Where are they?" Braedon asked, still turning in a circle.

"They're here," Cierra said with certainty.

"Close, but not in any of the rooms," Viper said.

"There's someone above us," Skyler said pointing to the ceiling.

"I didn't see any stairs," Braedon said, coming back from the kitchen and rubbing his hands together.

Cierra and Viper made eye contact, and sometime during the ten-second silent conversation, they remembered something. They moved to what looked like a small storage door in the middle of the largest wall. Viper pulled it open, revealing a crawl space. Cierra went through first, and before long, Iza could hear the distinct sound of climbing.

Viper went in next, her boots clomping heavily against the stairs as she climbed. Braedon waited for Iza to go next, still waving a hand in front of his watering eyes. Iza slipped in and found the small crawl space opened up into the wall and a set of small stairs. It looked like a place for children as there were still toys strewn about. The space was too short to stand in, forcing an adult to climb on hands and knees to take the stairs.

Above her head, she heard Cierra let out an exclamation. Iza wasn't sure if it was relief or grief until she reached the top of the stairs where a hidden room filled with children's toys and things remained almost untouched. In one corner was a bundle of blankets and sheets where her mother and father had gathered themselves to feel the heat from the floor below but not be engulfed by the smoke. Overall the room was warmer but without someone to tend to the fire in the dining room it had died out, leaving them almost blue with cold, but they were alive.

Iza imagined if they hadn't come straight away, they might not have made it.

"I thought they grew up on an Aesir space station," Iza said under her breath to Braedon who was standing awkwardly at her side.

"They lived here during a few of their summers," he answered, his voice lowered in respect.

"We need to get them back to the ship, right away," Cierra said as she worked to re-wrap and tie clothing around her mother's feet. Neither of them wore shoes, as was their custom here.

Cierra and Viper helped their parents out of their attic and down the stairs of their home. The thick smoke on the main floor made it difficult to breathe. Iza rewrapped her shawl and took a hold of Braedon's arm as he stood at the door ready to lead them out. She could feel Skyler's hand on her back as she grabbed onto her while the girls sandwiched their parents between them. As one, they shuffled out the door and toward the shuttles. Iza dared not even look up to check their positioning.

She heard Braedon mumble something.

"What is it?" Iza asked.

"The bomaxed shuttles are gone. We have to go back to the house."

"That's impossible," she stared in disbelief over his shoulder, even as he turned to move them backward. Iza saw the faint green of the flattened grass underneath the snow-covered area where the shuttles had been. The drift would soon hide any trace of them. It wouldn't be long before their tracks were indistinguishable from everything else around them. She gripped the boiling anger inside to keep warm as she turned back the snow clinging to her hair and face.

"What's going on?" Viper asked.

"No shuttles. We have to go back."

Viper roared over the storm. She screamed curses into the wind that made them all cringe before her mother pulled her close, muttering something in her ear. Whatever she said calmed her down enough to be guided back to the house.

"I should have known. Why else would Reis insist on coming with us?"

"Reis came down in the shuttle with you?" Iza asked.

"Yes, her and Mack. You don't need more than two, but she acted like she had to come," Viper beat at the snow on her shoulders with one gloved hand, dropping it onto the tiled kitchen floor.

"That means that bomaxed dog-faced Douketis has my shuttle," Iza said.

"Why would someone take your shuttle?" Mr. Quetzali asked.

"Revenge. I should have seen it coming. He's been biding his time to get back at me for what happened on Phiris. I'll deal with him later. For now, we have to get more of this smoke out."

Braedon used the shovel he'd brought—normally for handling livestock manure on the *Verity*—and went to work putting out the smoking fire with snow. As soon as he was finished, he used the wrap around his neck against the bottom edge of the door.

"That's the last of our fire, we'll freeze to death," Cierra's father looked ready to pummel him and for a minute Iza wondered if Viper hadn't inherited a little more than just his straight hair and fair skin.

"We'll suffocate long before we freeze to death if we don't get rid of this smoke." Braedon walked to the kitchen then returned, going through the few things left on the floor and then putting them back down. He walked to the door to the attic and swung it on its hinges a few times. "Viper, can you give me a hand with this?"

After she ripped the door from the hinges, he continued over the noise of them breaking it into pieces. "You've never had to deal with the cold weather down here before. There's another way to heat the entire house without setting it on fire. I used to take camping trips with my older brother out into the woods. One year, we waited so late that it was snowing by evening. The two of us had to make camp or risk getting lost and freezing to death on our way back home. I picked up a few survival tricks. We should be able to weather the storm here if we keep the cold air out and the warmth inside. Snow is a natural insulator. At this point, even the snow up against the windows is a good thing; it means there's no air blowing in. All we need now is something to burn."

Then, he gathered up the pieces and flashed his heart-breaking smile on the room. "Give me ten minutes and we'll have another fire going and you'll be warm in no time."

Iza was glad he knew what to do because she couldn't feel her toes anymore and her breath didn't seem to be warming her hands enough.

Skyler pulled out her handheld.

"Agent Anderson for Captain Brontes."

"Sorry, Agent, he's not available at the moment. He's in the middle of evac on Leveckis."

"I'm aware of that. Who are you?"

"Lieutenant Mathers, communications officer," he said.

"Lieutenant, we've got a situation here. Your captain is aware of our presence on the surface. However, our circumstances have changed. We've been stranded here. We're going to need assistance immediately."

"Every available person is out searching for survivors.

There's nothing I can do."

"As soon as you have his ear, relay these coordinates to your captain. Let him know that we found our people, but our shuttle was hijacked."

"Hijacked. Who would do that at a time like this?"

"Doesn't much matter, does it? It's been taken and we're stuck until you can get us help. Can you do that, Lieutenant?"

"Yes, ma'am."

Iza listened while she watched Braedon and Viper fill the stove in the kitchen with wood, which Skyler then ignited using some manner of telekinesis. While the fire was making some progress, Iza stood beside Skyler and the others huddling for warmth. She felt her anger fading as her teeth chattered together. Most of them were wet where the snow had settled into their clothes and hair. From the look of Mrs. Quetzali, she wouldn't last long wet and cold. She clung to her husband, but her lips were losing color.

"Hurry it up in there," Iza urged Braedon.

"We're all set. The heat is blazing in here."

To Iza's surprise, it was. They all clamored for space in the tiny kitchen. The heat radiated out of the stove and the smoke escaped through the ventilation pipe. They'd managed to get almost everything they could find for the fire in a neat pile of combustible pieces beside the stove. The warmth washed over them. She thought she heard Cierra sigh in contentment. They were all so happy to be warm that no one spoke for a full minute, not even Braedon. Before long, however, Iza's face started to burn before her feet had time to thaw.

She moved to the door furthest from the heat and pulled out her handheld. As much as she hated to rely on him, Karter might now be their best bet for rescue, with the Enforcers otherwise occupied. It was a longshot, but she had to try.

24

KARTER WASN'T ABOUT to miss the opportunity to settle things with Douketis. The man had been trailing him for months, had repeatedly caused trouble for Iza, and was all around the worst kind of lowlife. He never would have thought that way before, but Karter realized that life on board the *Verity* had altered his perceptions. There really *was* more to life than having someone who made their lease payments on time and fulfilled contracts. There was a way to do things *right*, and the Taran Empire could benefit from more conscientiousness and fewer people like Douketis. *People like me,* Karter admitted, recognizing that he used to only care about the bottom line, himself. But he vowed to be better, and that started with trying to make things right.

"Trix, message the *Iron Dog*, I'd like to speak with its captain," Karter requested.

"Yes, Mr. Hyttinen," Trix said. "However, let me warn you that Captain Douketis isn't welcome on board the *Verity*. Should you choose to meet with him, please do so on his ship."

Well, isn't she demanding for an android? "Of course," Karter said dryly. He stepped forward and waited until the viewport of the ship transitioned to an image of Captain

Douketis' less than attractive face.

"Karter, if I'd known you were on board, I would have sent my regards sooner."

"I'm sure that's not true, Captain," Karter replied. "How are things?"

"Well, business has been slow, as you know. With these new regulations following the regime change on Tararia, times are tough for traditional haulers like me. We don't all have Iza's connections."

It was a subtle dig at his relationship with her, and Karter wasn't about to let it pass.

"My relationship with Iza is none of your business. However, your continued payments to me are. If you're having difficulty making your monthly installments for the loan you took out two years ago, I'd be happy to offer you an extension. I'll have my assistant draft the forms for you immediately."

It was about time he made out on the deal again, anyway. Douketis would owe him for the rest of his life.

"It just so happens I have your assistant on board, and she's requesting an opportunity to meet with you."

Becca's face came into view, and she nodded to the screen as she would to him if they were face-to-face.

Karter's chest tightened at the sight of her and had to lightly clear his throat to get his voice back. "Becca, you're there. What are you doing out here?"

"There's been a development. Permission to come on board?"

Karter turned to Trix and waited for the android to slowly turn to face him. "Is my assistant permitted to board?"

"I believe that can be allowed as she's not a member of the Douketis crew."

"Wait, what? I'm not invited?" Douketis had the audacity to sound offended.

"You and I will have plenty of time to chat. Let me speak with my assistant about redrafting our current contract, terms pending."

"That won't be necessary."

Karter lifted an eyebrow. Since when was Douketis uninterested in a new deal? "What exactly does that mean?"

"I believe your assistant has the details. As I said, I'm willing to drop her off, but we haven't got all day."

"Fine, you have permission to dock one of your shuttles temporarily. I'll be waiting for Becca. Please see her safely to the *Verity*."

Karter made his way to the cargo hold to wait. He didn't like the cocky manner in which Douketis spoke to him, as if the man wasn't in his debt. There was something amiss with him and the sooner he learned what the 'development' was the better.

Becca was prompt to arrive and dressed in all black the way he liked all of his employees. Her ensemble, like always, was a little more original than the rest of the office workers managed. She gravitated toward black on black geometric patterns, which aligned with her personality. She strolled across the hold carrying nothing but her handheld. Her hair was pulled back in a tight bun made her look so severe, but the bare legs under her skirt reminded him she could relax when she wanted. Her eyes were alight and playful but with her shoulders back and her chin high, he knew she was ready to discuss business. He wanted nothing more than to throw propriety to the side and scoop her up and carry her back to his cabin. Instead, he held up his hand in formal greeting and she did the same.

Once she was in speaking distance, she gave him a curt nod as they waited for the sound of the Douketis shuttle to disengage from the cargo airlock.

"Report," he said.

She passed him the handheld, and he looked down at the document displayed on the screen. She remained silent as he read.

Karter's brow furrowed. "What is this?"

"It's my document of termination, signed by your mother. It was a hostile takeover. I didn't have time to send backups to your private server. But per your request, each evening they were updated. So, you're missing only what happened during the day of the takeover and beyond. I was locked out of all access to Apex Manufacturing and most of the staff was dismissed."

"When?"

"Yesterday. Douketis was on the premises—a meeting with your mother, I believe—and I persuaded him to let me hitch a ride. He was hoping to see your face when I delivered the news."

"That's why he was so smug."

"Yes, Phaedra has renewed contracts with all of your freighters and cargo ships. Your investors have already been informed of the leadership change. Mr. Arvonen was among the investors siding with your mother; I believe they're working on something else together. She was arranging transport with one of the ships as I was being escorted out of the building."

Karter bit the inside of his cheek while he considered her words. If his mother had already swayed the investors, it was too late to make any kind of power play. His mother would have to be forcibly removed, and he couldn't do that sitting on the *Verity*. Of course, she wouldn't go down easy, but once he was rid of her, he'd be free to make his own choices.

His eyes met Becca's briefly, searching her face for a reaction. If she was upset by the recent events, she didn't show it on her face. Instead, she kept level pace with him as he walked toward the flight deck.

Becca took in the ship as she continued her report. "Douketis is in dire straits. He wasn't exaggerating when he said they couldn't find work. His interest in starting a new contract was more because of some poor business choices than his lack of hauling opportunities. In good time, teaching him a lesson might do him well."

He liked the way she thought. "Yes, indeed. I want a list of everyone quick to follow my mother and any who were reluctant to side with her. Also, I want a list of all terminations. Those are no doubt my people, and those who didn't bend to her will."

"That would be accurate, though I would say she was threatened most by me."

"Why do you say that?" Though he thought he already knew the answer.

"Phaedra was quick to remove me first, and she did so personally."

"That sounds like her," he said dryly.

"She also accused me of trying to entrap you," Becca said, her face firm.

"Entrap me?" Karter couldn't hold back the laugh. If she only knew.

"She believes that my efficiency or demand for perfection is in some way tied to my need for approval from you and a desire for your love. Something she assures me you will never give, and she would never approve of," Becca's voice dropped.

There it is. The glimmer that he'd hoped to see was there now. Just behind her eyes, a bit of fire. *Is she telling me because she wants to know where I stand?*

"My mother has a nasty habit of putting her nose where it doesn't belong. Never mind her opinions, you work for me. My approval is the only one that matters," Karter said. Then he dared to try something new. He stopped in the corridor and reached out and rested his hand on her shoulder and her eyes flew to his face. Her green irises burned with desire. It would have knocked him back if his own longing wasn't rising to meet it.

"Becks you're the best thing that's ever happened to me. I need you now more than ever. If you will agree, I would prefer you to stay on board the *Verity* until this business with Arvonen is finished. And I believe we're very close."

"Do you think Phaedra is with him?"

"I'm counting on it. If he's still after those spheres and planning to use them, then my mother will be at his side when we take him down."

"You mentioned that Anderson's sister is on board." Becca looked around as if expecting to see her. "Does she know about Iza?"

"Yes, though she claims to be here for her brother. Though, I'm not so sure that the TSS isn't after something else. The question is, how far are they willing to go to get it?"

"I doubt they're willing to go as far as you are." There was a smirk on her mouth he wanted to kiss.

"You know me better than most."

The grin spread across her mouth. It was radiant and filled with the kind of hope every man wants to see in a woman he has feelings for.

"Let's head in. The others will be returning shortly, and we'll be on our way." Karter led her to the flight deck and Becca kept pace with him step for step.

"What about Iza? You haven't mentioned her," Becca asked, reaching out a hand on his arm.

He resisted the urge to look down at it for fear she'd let go. "What is it you want to know?"

"Do you think she'll have a problem with me being here?"

He paused to look at her; the smile was gone, replaced with the kind of worry that reached her furrowed eyebrows. He lifted his hand to stroke her cheek with the back of his fingers. *I promise there will be a time when that worry is gone from your face forever.* The words never left his lips instead he answered her question. "No, I don't think she'll have a problem with you being here at all."

They entered the flight deck. Trix turned with her hands clasped behind her back to regard them. Karter couldn't read her expression, but the android seemed to be mentally calculating or perhaps she was scanning them for something out of the ordinary. Whatever it was, he shifted his stance to one of authority and Becca did the same.

Iza's dog bounded over to them, sniffing at Becca's bare legs. She giggled then bent to touch him but stopped with hand three centimeters from his head as if remembering herself and straightened. Then she addressed Trix. "It's a pleasure to see you again," she said with a nod at the android.

Trix didn't answer, but her head tilted to one side, before she spoke, "There's an incoming message for you, Mr. Hyttinen. From Iza." She didn't wait for his response as the front viewscreen shifted from stars to white before the captain's face appeared. Her head was uncovered the dark room around her a direct contrast to the orange light on her face.

"Karter, there's a problem," she said without preamble. "It looks like Douketis stole my shuttle out from under me and we've got no way back to the ship."

"How long have you got before you run out of heat?" Karter asked, taking out his handheld.

"I'm not sure. An hour or two? Most of the household items that are flammable have already been burned. I told the Enforcers we wouldn't need them, but it seems that we do.

We've put in a call. Is there anything you can do?"

Karter looked to Trix.

"It would be unwise to try to land the ship without some idea of what's underneath the snow," the android stated.

Iza nodded. "That was my thinking, too. I don't want to lose the whole ship. At the same time, it's no good to me if I'm a popsicle."

"Sit tight, I'll see if I can rush them along. The rescue efforts have increased as another Enforcer ship has arrived to look for survivors."

"Thank you, Karter. I see we have company," Iza said with a knowing smile on her lips. He didn't like it, but there wasn't much he could do.

"Yes, my assistant, Becca will be joining us until our business with Arvonen is concluded. It seems my mother has made her final play for the dynasty, and I'll need to work from here for the time being."

"Huh, interesting timing. I take it Douketis has bolted by now?"

"Yes, he left immediately after dropping off my assistant. I'm sorry, if I had known, I would have handled things differently."

"No, I'll catch up to that bull-dog later. But for now, we're going to need another shuttle."

Karter sighed. Without his normal hold on his fleet of transport vehicles, there wasn't much he could do. It was unfortunate that he'd returned the Q Maximus to its owner at Hubyria. There was his cousin, though he doubted she'd do him the favor. In fact, with their last falling out, she might be siding with his mother for the moment. "I'll do what I can."

"Trix, make sure our new guest is comfortable and off my flight deck by the time I return. End transmission."

Karter placed a light hand on Becca's back and led her off

the flight deck.

"I guess she does have a problem with me being here," she said with a hint of bitterness.

Karter shook his head. "It's not that. Iza has a thing about her personal space, that includes the flight deck. If she were upset about you being here, she wouldn't hesitate to have her android throw you off."

IT WAS OVER two hours before Captain Brontes responded to Skyler's request for assistance and another forty minutes before a shuttle arrived to take them. By then, the group of them were huddled close to the dwindling fire and beginning to audibly shiver. The Quetzalis were returning to the idea of burning the entire first floor for heat.

The sound of the shuttle's engines made Iza's heart flutter, and she bounded for the door before Skyler caught up to her and put a hand on her shoulder.

"Let me go first, Captain," she said as she pulled up her collar and opened the door.

Iza was right behind her, tightening the wrap around her head and neck as she went. The snow wasn't blowing as hard but there was still a steady fall of flakes that landed on her cheeks and nose. The Enforcers had arrived in full gear, helmets on their heads, and gloves over their hands. Iza couldn't tell one from the other.

"Captain Brontes," Skyler said before he could speak through the helmet he wore. He lifted the visor and looked to Skyler than grimaced at Iza.

"Agent Anderson, Captain Sundari." He inclined his head

toward them. "I thought you assured me you wouldn't try to get yourselves killed out here."

"We did our best. If you'd be so kind as to escort us to our ship, we'd be very grateful," Skyler said.

Iza couldn't see behind her black shades, but she knew that Skyler had the ability to read thoughts and intentions before they were spoken. But she wasn't sure Skyler would try it on these men. It seemed her TSS rank was more than enough to get them moving.

"Very well," he said in a gruff voice. "Baelsen, Korsek, make room for the survivors and get them loaded and ready for takeoff."

"Yes, sir," they said in unison.

Brontes helped Iza through the hatch and Skyler followed close behind. Soon, their entire group was seated in next to the Enforcers. The Quetzali parents were the most gracious, thanking the officers for coming for them. The shuttle ride to the *Verity* was short, and before long, they were docking with her ship.

The familiar smells of the cargo hold washed over her as soon as the hatch door opened, and Iza's eyes landed on the empty space where her AS-225 shuttle used to sit. The small ship was old and weathered, but it was hers. Douketis was going to pay dearly for taking it. There must have been something on her face because Captain Brontes cleared his throat and questioned her.

"Do you want to file a formal complaint for the theft of your shuttle?"

"No," Iza said rather quickly. Then, she remembered she was dealing with an Enforcer after all. They had very different ideas about justice. "No, sir. I already know who took it and I know how to get it back. Your services aren't required."

"Well then, I guess that concludes our business. We need

to be off, there are a lot more civilians who need help. I would appreciate it if you would be on your way. We've got a lot of work to do."

"Thank you again, Captain and I owe you one."

"Not at all. We're just doing our duty."

Iza and the others made their way off the shuttle and the Enforcers undocked, leaving her with the Quetzalis and the rest of her crew. Atano was the first to welcome them back, bounding forward. He stopped short when he caught the scent of the new Quetzalis. After a quick pass of Iza, he moved to press his nose to their wrapped feet and legs.

Karter must have been waiting for them because he stepped forward with Becca at his side. She looked wary, though Iza couldn't imagine why. She was off of her flight deck, so for the moment, Becca didn't have anything to worry about. It was a good opportunity for introductions.

"Welcome aboard. Let me introduce everyone. We have Joe's sister, Agent Skyler Anderson," who nodded in acknowledgement, "the Quetzalis," she said, waving a hand in the direction of the family. Both parents and Cierra all lifting a hand in greeting. "We also have Karter's assistant from Apex Manufacturing joining us."

"Becca Drejas, a pleasure," she said, lifting a hand in return.

Mrs. Quetzali nodded with one hand still on her husband's arm. "Thank you for coming for us, I don't know what we'd have done if you hadn't come." Her eyes filled and she bowed her head to hide her tears.

"I'm only sorry you lost the house and all your things," Iza said thinking of all the items that had been either destroyed or left in the small house.

"Those were only material items. The most important things are right here with us," Mr. Quetzali said, reaching out for both his daughters. Cierra was under his arm, but Viper had to be pulled in by her mother and she didn't look particularly thrilled about it.

"And you brought us here. If you hadn't agreed to move so swiftly…" Cierra couldn't finish her sentence as the tears welled up in her eyes, making Iza more uncomfortable. She fought off the urge to tear up thinking of her own lost family.

"I hope you can accommodate us for a bit, Captain," Mr. Quetzali said with a beaming smile on his face. "We promise not to be too much trouble."

"I think we can fit you all, though we're going to have to double up with so many people on board. Viper, your room is still available. It's up to you and Cierra to figure out which to give your parents. But you're welcome to stay as long as you have need."

"Thank you, Captain," Viper said. She stood, shifting her weight from one foot to the other as she stared at the floor as if embarrassed to meet her gaze. The kid was a virtual genius, but she'd have to remind her that she wasn't on board the *Iron Dog* anymore. Viper didn't have to grovel in front of her to avoid being berated.

Then, Iza turned to Karter. "I hope it's not too much trouble to put your assistant in with you." Becca's pale cheeks flushed under Karter's gaze, and Iza knew she'd done the right thing. "The only other available space is with Skyler or Braedon, so work it out amongst yourselves."

Becca nodded without saying a word.

Cierra was anxious, it seemed, to be out of her boots and had already slipped them off, carrying them in one hand and turning toward her cabin while her parents, Viper, and Braedon followed behind her. The Quetzali family chattered about the ship and asked questions as they went.

Iza, exhausted after being in the cold for so long, dragged

herself through the ship toward her cabin to get into dry clothing. Trix had been notably absent in the greeting party, no doubt on the flight deck, and she wanted to check on her friend. By the time she'd changed and stepped out into the corridor, it seemed everyone was getting settled.

Viper's music reached the corridor, but it didn't seem to be bothering anyone else. Iza passed Cierra with a bundle of clothing and coverings in her arms, heading for Braedon's room. Iza averted her eyes. *I don't even want to know.* The Quetzalis had, apparently, taken over her room, and they were still exclaiming about how wonderful and at home it smelled.

On the flight deck, Trix stood looking out at the stars alone. Atano followed Iza in as she sat down in the captain's chair, where he curled up. She was thankful for his heat, still feeling a bit chilled from her ordeal on Leveckis.

"Hey, I'm back," she said as if the android didn't know. "Any news?"

"Nothing you don't already know," Trix said, her voice still in its natural tone instead of the robotic one she'd grown accustomed to hearing.

Iza's mouth clamped closed, unsure what to say.

"It appears that Mr. Hyttinen's assistant will be staying with us for some time," Trix said.

"Yes, and Viper's back along with her parents. We've got a full ship."

"Your heart rate and blood pressure have returned to a normal range. Are you not still missing Joe?"

"No, I am, but to be honest. I'm preparing myself for the worst. If Arvonen is still hurting him, he may never come back, and I have to be ready for it."

"I see."

There was a slight change in her tone that Iza didn't miss. "What?"

"It seems you and I are similar that way. We are always preparing for the worst."

Iza regarded Trix more closely. She'd changed her hair recently. Instead of the low ponytail over one shoulder, she'd taken it out of the binder all together and her hair hung down her back. She wasn't just using a different tone of voice. Trix seemed all-around more relaxed.

Braedon came onto the bridge with Viper following close behind.

"Permission to enter the flight deck?" Viper asked when she saw Iza in the chair.

"It depends. What are you two up to?"

"I want to show Viper the message we got from Raquel. I've been running a tracing program in the background on the ship and it came back with an interesting tag."

Iza nodded her assent. "Where did it originate?" she asked, leaning forward in her seat.

"It can't be right. I mean, I did what I would normally do, but the result is so strange it can't be. I want Viper to double check my calculations." Braedon gestured to his station at the helm, and Viper sat down at the console to begin going over the trace while he stood by looking over her shoulder.

"Fine, but where did the signal come from?" Iza asked again, growing impatient.

Braedon ignored her question as Viper stopped tapping and looked up at him with a strange expression on her face. "This is the trace I would have used. It's not wrong."

Braedon finally looked up from the console and turned to Iza. "It originated from right here. In orbit of Leveckis."

"What?" Iza was standing up again. "How can that be?"

"At the time she sent the message, she was right here," Braedon said again.

"When?"

"Just a few hours before the transformation of the planet began."

Iza ran her hands over her face.

"Is there any way to figure out where they went next? Joe's running out of time."

"No," Braedon said.

At the same time Viper said, "Yes."

They all turned to look at her as she put up the message Raquel had sent on the front display. Viper tapped out something on the console and the image was replaced with what looked like random red dots connected with red lines on the screen.

"She sent an export of data from the nav console, but it was disguised in the metadata of image file attachments. All the places they planned to go."

Braedon stared at her incredulously. "How did…?"

"Honestly, Little Lamb, I'm disappointed in you," Viper ribbed him.

Iza dared let her heart lift with a glimmer of hope. "Where were they heading after Leveckis?"

The image on the viewscreen changed again. This time, Viper placed a star chart overlay onto the red dots and she saw it.

"There," she said, swiveling out of Braedon's chair and standing up to pat him on the shoulder. "Someday, you might just be as good as me."

Braedon crossed his arms with a huff.

Iza grinned. "Trix, plot a course for those coordinates. We're going after Joe."

— — —

Ian Mandren filed into the conference room next door to

the High Commander's office with the group of TSS officers colloquially known as the Inner Circle. Most had trained directly with Wil as the first cohort of Primus Elites, and a few others were close friends who'd played a significant role in their lives and had won a place at the table.

Ian sat near the door with a view of the holopaintings depicting a space backdrop, which called out to him whenever he entered. Ian normally enjoyed getting together with his team. It was like 'old times'—the good times before the war when they trained, ate, and slept together. Ian knew more about the people in this room sitting around the broad oval table than he knew about anyone else in the Taran Empire. They were his family. Of course, some of them already had grown children, but he'd been content to find his family among them and now the circle extended to his trainees. It was no wonder he was so worried about Joe. After what he'd just seen, he couldn't trust the assignment to anyone else, he was going after him, the meeting was only a formality.

Wil Sietinen, their High Commander, led the meeting. In general, he'd never liked meetings, and it was usually obvious by the roll of his bioluminescent blue eyes and the way he slumped in his chair. But, the boring reports of the day brought them all together, and for that Ian couldn't be happier. Today, however, was going to be different. Ian had just handed him the latest news on the *Verity* only minutes before.

Wil gave them all a nod of acknowledgment. "By now, you are all familiar with the disturbances happening in the Outer Colonies. Based on information relayed from the *Verity*, it appears it may be an act of warfare on the part of a race known as the Gatekeepers. Several of our planets have already been transformed, some from hot to cold, from cold to hot, and others from dry to wet. Some believed the locations to be random. I don't."

Ian leaned forward as the room of Agents clamped down on their questions waiting for more details as they'd been trained to do.

"I know you have questions, but we don't have a lot of time. The planets where the transformations have occurred all correlate with one ship's movements. We now believe that the Gatekeepers have found a way to target Victor Arvonen. How? I'm not sure, but I believe there are at least some Gatekeepers living in our system and posing as Tarans."

"What?" Ethan couldn't hold back his questions any longer and it was as if the room was released and the others started in on their own concerns.

"Where is he going next?" Curtis asked.

"Are more planets at stake?" Tom chimed in.

"What about the treaty?" Michael asked, his voice last and thus carrying over the others.

Wil held up a hand and they quieted again.

"I don't have all the answers yet. Most importantly, the *Arvonen One* has been found and they aren't going anywhere for the moment. We have a chance to catch up to him and bring him in while rescuing one of our former Agent, who was taken captive during his escapades. If the Gatekeepers have caught up to him, we need to be prepared for anything."

"We?" Ian spoke the question aloud before he had a chance to think.

"Yes, Saera and I will be going with you, Ian. I know you've been running point on this, so I'll defer to your knowledge of the players, but when it comes to the Gatekeepers, I need to be there. This could be the end of a peace treaty that's held for millennia, and we didn't even know it was in place until days ago. Until people had already gone rogue with selfish actions that may have irrevocably violated it. It's my hope that we can quell any misunderstandings on the part of our people and maintain the peace."

Ian gulped down whatever he was going to say and settled back into his seat after the blow to his chest. *Another war? Could it really come to that?* Then he saw the twinkle in Wil's eye. He was excited, which could also be interpreted as a bad thing. Everyone knew the High Commander had the ability to do more than fight. *What are we in for this time?*

"What about the rest of us?" Ethan asked.

"Michael will oversee operations here at Headquarters while Saera and I are away. I trust you collectively can handle anything else that might arise." It was more a statement than a question, but the Agents all nodded.

"Good. Curtis, I'd also like you to come along on the *Conquest.* I'll be back with answers as soon as I can. Dismissed."

Ian hurriedly packed for the trip. When he arrived at the TSS spacedock, he found the *Conquest* was already powered up and ready to go. It seemed like ages since he'd been aboard. Walking toward the ship, he heard the sound of boots running to catch up to him. He sucked in a breath. He knew who it was, and he had his answer ready before he turned to greet the younger man.

Emery Valackas' dark hair and baby-faced features hadn't changed much since his days in training.

"Emery!"

"Sir, it's good to see you." He raised his hand in formal greeting. Emery, unlike Joe, had done considerably well as a trainee and had even taken the time to help Joe progress in their off hours. Ian knew it was because of his attention and help that Joe had made friends and had completed the training at all.

"I wish I could chat, but at the moment, I'm heading out." Ian didn't want to get into the dangers or what they might be facing.

"I know, that's why I'm here. I'd like to join you on your mission."

"Emery—"

He held up a hand and continued to speak. "Before you dismiss me out of hand, you need to understand something. My best friend and my future wife are in danger. If you're going with the High Commander, then there's something else at stake. I want to be a part of it, because I can't just sit here while you go off and deal with whatever is. If you wind up deploying two teams of Agents to deal with the rescue and retrieval, I would be a familiar face to both of them. I'm begging you to take me with you."

Ian looked at the young man he'd trained and knew his skills. Emery was no Primus Elite, but he'd been one of the best trained Agents in his graduating group. Given his bond with Skyler, without a doubt he wouldn't be dead weight on a mission like this one.

He nodded. "All right, I need to clear it with the High Commander, but I agree you could be an asset."

"Thank you, sir." Emery's face beamed as he boarded the ship.

Ian rolled his eyes to the ceiling and hoped he wasn't making a huge bomaxed mistake.

26

IZA GATHERED EVERYONE in the galley to reveal her plan. Once she had explained what she was willing to do to get Joe back, the others were quiet, no doubt processing the implications. Whatever they were expecting this wasn't it. Iza wanted to assuage their fears, but she didn't have the gift of foresight. There was a chance that the plan would fail. She couldn't guarantee they'd all survive. But it was for Joe, so she had to try. The question was, would they be willing to trust her one more time?

The Quetzalis were on the far end of the table with their daughters on each side, silhouetted against the bright backdrop of subspace visible through the viewport. Skyler and Trix stood with their backs to the cabinets. Braedon sat on Iza's left, tapping out a repetitive beat on his thighs with his thumbs, while Karter sat on her right with Becca on the other side of him. The room didn't feel overcrowded with everyone there, though it should have since some of them had to stand. Iza stood fighting the nerves as she spoke, all eyes on her.

"You all know where we're going. I'll be straight with you: this is about as real as it gets. Each and every one of you has become a part of this crew. I'd be lying if I said I hadn't considered doing this without you. But, the truth is, I need you. It's taken me a long time to admit that sometimes I need to rely on others, so here we are. I *can't* do this alone. But I also can't ask you to keep putting yourselves in danger for me. I understand if you don't want to do this." She nodded in the direction of Mr. and Mrs. Quetzali. "We can find a place for your parents to wait for us, and when everything is done, we can go back for them if you prefer."

"We're not leaving our daughters," Mr. Quetzali said, wrapping an arm around his wife. Their faces were determined as each reached for a hand of their daughters.

There was a pregnant pause before Braedon spoke up. "We're family now, Iz. We're in this together."

Trix nodded, and the others murmured their agreement.

Iza's heart swelled, seeing the determination on their faces. On her own, she was stubborn, and that sheer force of will had been enough to get her by in life. Now, though, she needed her team's skills and their emotional support. She was stronger with them. She never thought she'd admit it, but knowing they were counting on her as a leader made her try that much harder. Together, she knew they could accomplish anything.

She gave a resolute nod. "Then it's decided. I'll keep Arvonen distracted while you get our people."

"We won't know until we get in there if Joe and your cousin are being held in the same place," Viper said. "What if it comes down to us only being able to get one?"

It was a valid question and one Iza wasn't ready to answer, except in the vaguest of terms. "If things go my way, we won't have to choose."

"I don't believe Joe would like your plan," Trix said. "There is far too much risk to you."

"Yes, he probably wouldn't if he were here, but he's not. Any other objections?" Iza asked.

"Not an objection really, just a word of advice from the son of a madman," Braedon said. "He'll destroy anything that gets in the way of his domination of the Gate and our worlds."

"Why, what does he hope to gain?" Mr. Quetzali asked.

"Something he thinks he's never had. Relevance," Karter said. "There's a reason he's working with my mother. The Lower Dynasty families are little more than business leaders. High Dynasties get a seat at the big table and make the decisions that affect us all."

"He wants to sit at the table," Mr. Quetzali said nodding in understanding.

Braedon shook his head and smiled. "No, he doesn't want a seat. He wants the whole table."

Karter nodded in agreement.

"Destroying our worlds isn't going to help him," Mrs. Quetzali said, her eyes hard as stone.

"Arvonen isn't the one destroying our worlds," Iza corrected. "His pursuit of this Gate has brought unwanted attention from an alien race that would like to keep as much separation between us as possible. It's an entirely different problem, but we'll avoid them if we can. I'd rather not have them kill me, too."

"Why would they want you?" Mr. Quetzali asked.

"It's a long story, but suffice it to say, it's a family dispute."

Iza looked up at Skyler; she nodded, though her arms were now crossed over her body. The others sat in silence taking it all in.

"Any plan that involves you being bait is too risky," Karter spat.

"That's a risk I'm willing to take," Iza said. "Once we have Joe and my cousin back, we're going to want to be on the good side of the TSS. That's why Joe's sister is here."

Iza gestured in Skyler's direction with one hand and they

turned to look at her, but it was Trix who spoke.

"I have to agree with Karter, as much as it displeases me. Sacrificing yourself is no guarantee of your success," Trix said.

Iza knew that, but she didn't have a quick retort or anything light to say. It was true; she was bait for both the Gatekeepers and Arvonen, and everyone knew what happened to bait. Iza closed her eyes and focused on her breathing as a tremendous weight settled into her chest. She let out a long exhale and met their eyes. "It's only a sacrifice if you don't do exactly what I say. My plans don't include getting killed, but I didn't want to preclude the possibility in case you were wondering if I was insane."

"That's still up for debate," Viper said.

"This is madness," Karter said. "Though, I think you got the best deal you could in the circumstances. However, I could offer you something more substantial and immediate. We are still contractually engaged. I know I don't have anything, but perhaps if we made it official, we could—"

"You already know I'd rather die than actually marry you, but thanks for the offer." Atano growled under his breath at the perceived infraction echoing Iza's sentiments.

He reached across the table and grabbed both her hands in his soft warm ones.

Iza saw Becca stiffen beside him, but she clamped her mouth closed on whatever protest she was about to make. *Is he putting on a show for her or me?*

"I'm serious," Karter continued. "You don't have to do this. We can find another way. The losses would be too great to overcome if you fail."

He was right. If things didn't go according to plan, not only would Arvonen have her, they could wind up being dragged into some kind of power struggle with the Gatekeepers. They'd already taken her father and killed her aunt and probably her mother. But when she thought of the alternative, leaving Joe and Jaidyn on their own—leaving the outer colonies defenseless against the transformations… She pulled her hands away from Karter's. She wasn't willing to give up.

"This is happening, and if you don't want to get your pretty face injured, now would be a good time to take Becca and go."

Karter glanced at Becca and firmed his lips. Something invisible passed between them that Iza couldn't decipher. Then, he squared his shoulders. "I'll stand with you."

Skyler unfolded her arms. She seemed satisfied now that everyone else had spoken up.

"I still think we should wait for TSS backup to arrive."

"Look, we don't sit around waiting for the TSS to save us. You want to know why?"

"They never make it on time," Trix finished for her.

"They arrest you like a criminal even if you're just an innocent bystander," Braedon continued.

"They get in your way," Viper added.

Iza stared back at Skyler with an eyebrow raised in challenge.

"This is my brother we're talking about," the Agent said. "Not to mention, the galactic-scale implications if things go wrong. We're not going in there without a plan."

"We do have a plan," Iza said as she stood up from her chair and placed her hands on her hips.

"What you have is a hunch," Skyler countered. She bowed her head in frustration. "You don't know what you're doing, marching in there making demands while the rest of us sneak in. Too may things could go wrong. We need back up."

"That's why we have you."

"There's only so much I can do. We don't even have a shuttle, so we can't pick Joe up even if we wanted to. We'll have to rely on Arvonen to not only release him but to deliver him to us. Besides, you're betting a lot he's going to want you and your cousin more than Joe."

"It's a *fact* that he does," Braedon said. "It's not 'betting' when you're certain you have the advantage."

Iza nodded. "Exactly. I'm what Arvonen needs to complete his plan, not Joe. Braedon and Viper have hacked the *Arvonen One* before. Plus, he has no idea you're with us. All things considered, things are stacked in our favor."

"If Arvonen wants you so badly," Skyler said, "then he would be chasing you instead of the other way around. He knows he's got you as long as he holds my brother."

"It's all a game to him. You'll have to trust me, Agent Anderson."

There was an electric current of energy flowing between them, but neither woman was willing to back down.

"We've almost reached the coordinates of the *Arvonen One*." Trix said moving for the door and breaking the tense silence in the room.

"Last chance to save your own butts," Iza said as she glanced around the galley one more time. No one spoke up; they'd made their decision.

It was time to make a move, and she had to be the one to do it.

—

They dropped out from subspace in the middle of nowhere at the edge of the Taran Empire. The nearest planet wasn't even fit for habitation. Only the magnified image of the *Arvonen One* broke up the endless starscape on the front display.

Skyler stood at Joe's tactical position, fuming. Things hadn't gone her way and she wasn't happy about it. She'd just have to get over it.

Iza hadn't become the captain of her own ship so she could do someone else's bidding. She didn't answer to the TSS. They were using her to get to Arvonen and the Gatekeepers, so she was going to fulfill her obligations on her own terms. Arvonen was the enemy she knew quite well, and he'd do anything to get her on board his ship, including a trade for Joe. In fact, she was so sure she was willing to bet her life on it. But, as Braedon said, it wasn't a bet if you held the advantage.

All non-essentials and civilians were banned from the flight deck. Viper had stormed off several minutes ago; she was still just a kid. A genius for sure, but she was too young for this fight, and with her parents on board, Iza didn't want anything to happen to either of their daughters. Karter had protested, too, but she didn't need the businessman on the flight deck. His bad blood with Arvonen would only be a distraction. It was enough his son would be sitting at the helm. Cierra was in the infirmary prepping for casualties, as instructed.

Trix stood on Iza's right. Atano moved to the captain's chair and sat waiting for Iza to sit down.

"Why aren't they responding?" Iza asked again when the *Arvonen One* had yet to acknowledge their communication attempt.

"I'm not sure, but I know they're aware of us. They brought their weapons online almost the moment we arrived," Trix said.

"Can you get into their system?" Iza asked Braedon.

"No, they've revamped everything since our last encounter. It would take ages to figure it out on my own." He was hinting at including Viper, but Iza was determined to leave the girl out of it.

Iza stood up to pace.

"Captain, you're distressed," Trix said. Iza noted she hadn't led with her vitals and that was a nice change. "You need to relax so you can be clear headed when they do signal us."

"Any sign of the Taran Super-slow Service?"

Skyler pursed her lips as if tasting something fowl. "Not yet, but they'll be here."

"I'm sure you won't be surprised if I don't wait," Iza said. "Braedon, can you send a message back through the line that Raquel used?"

His head snapped up and he turned to look at her confusion in his eyes. "Why would you want to contact her? She's most likely with my father."

"I'm counting on it."

"I hope you know what you're doing, Iz," Braedon said loud enough for her to hear.

"I do, and it's going to take everything I've got and more to get it done, so do as I say," Iza said with a glance to Skyler. "Let me know as soon as she answers."

"She'll do whatever my father wants, you know. I hope you don't think you can turn her."

"I'm not trying to turn her," Iza said keeping her eyes on the front display.

"Captain, she's responding. Putting it through now," Trix said.

Iza waited with anticipation for the video feed overlaid on the front viewport to resolve. Raquel's face appeared; her eyes were hollow, and her brows drawn together. When Raquel saw Iza standing on the *Verity*'s flight deck, she took in all of them and then she spoke in a low growl to Iza.

"What do you think you're doing?"

"Arvonen appears to be busy. I'd like you to arrange a meeting for me."

"What? Are you out of your—" Raquel's voice rose jointly with her frustration, but she quickly recovered. "He's going to ask me questions about how you got my transmission signal and our location. You were supposed to run. Other than the Gate, the only other thing in this universe he wants more is you."

Iza raised an eyebrow. That statement confirmed at least one thing.

"Tell your boss, I'd like to meet with him to discuss a trade. Let him know I have something he's been looking for."

"Izzy, don't do this."

"Don't call me that, ever," Iza insisted. "Tell Arvonen I'd like to trade."

"Fine, but do you think trading your life for Joe's is the answer? You can't be serious."

"Will you relay the message or not?" Iza kept her eyes steady on the holodisplay.

Raquel hissed, "I gave you the map as a warning, not get you all killed."

"Braedon prepare to end transmission," Iza said with a wave of her hand.

"Wait." Raquel glanced over her left shoulder then back at the camera and sighed. "Fine."

"Excellent, have him on screen as soon as it's convenient."

27

IZA GREW IMPATIENT as she waited for Arvonen to speak with her directly. A full seven minutes had gone by without a word from him or the 'digger', as Braedon called Raquel. Instead of sitting in her seat, Iza worked off the excess energy by pacing back and forth across the flight deck. Braedon was again tapping a mindless beat on his knee and Skyler drummed her fingers against the console. The only ones unaffected were Trix and Atano. Iza stared at the *Arvonen One*'s specs on her console, going over the potential locations they might be keeping Joe.

"There's a gravity shift in the area off the stern of Arvonen's ship. It could be a stealth ship," Trix said.

"TSS?" Iza asked with a glance at Skyler.

Skyler shook her head. "Believe me, you'll know when they arrive."

Iza frowned. "Any sign of that stealthed ship heading for us?"

"Not at this time," Trix reported. She came to attention. "Captain, we're getting an incoming call from the *Arvonen One*."

"Keep an eye on that stealth ship—or whatever it is—for any changes." Iza started to bite her bottom lip but stopped herself. Instead, she squared her shoulders and sat down with the dog on her lap as if she hadn't a care in the world.

"Put the call through to main display."

A breath later, Victor Arvonen himself stared back at her. It never ceased to amaze her how different Braedon's features looked on his father. The hair streaked with white and the wrinkles around his hawk-like eyes, which didn't miss anything. She saw the disdain in them as he took in her crew one by one before landing on her.

"Captain Sundari, to what do I owe the pleasure?"

"Pleasure? I certainly hope not."

"I'm a very busy man. Is there something I can do for you?"

"Yes—"

"Dad, listen." Braedon jumped in. He stared up at his father's image. "This obsession of yours has gone too far. You have my friend on board that ship, and we want him back."

Iza resisted wiping a hand over her face. This was not at all how this was supposed to go. She'd planned to broach the subject, after a bit of banter and insults. Though it had knocked her out of her flow, his interruption had also thrown his father.

"I have no idea what you're talking about," Victor Arvonen answered. There wasn't even a shift in his eyes when he lied, Iza noted.

"Memory going already, old man?" Braedon sneered. "Let me remind you. You have Joe Anderson, a former TSS Agent, on your ship, and you've been torturing him for information on Iza and the sphere. I gave you several chances to step away from this." Then it was as if his next words were stuck in his throat. "Mother, she wouldn't—"

Arvonen's finger came up in front of his face, pointing at Braedon through the screen. "Don't you dare, speak to me about her. You don't have the right."

Braedon rushed to his feet, now unable to stay seated.

"I *will* speak of her! One of us has to. Just because you've forgotten what kind of person she was doesn't mean I will."

"I'll never forget your mother. She's the reason I'm doing all of this." Arvonen spread his arms wide to either side. "She always wanted you boys to have more than we had. A real chance at a High Dynasty life. I can give you that now. Not running around on some hauling ship with a people who are beneath you."

Iza opened her mouth to speak, but again Braedon cut her off.

"Mother would be ashamed of you." Braedon spat the words, and his father flinched as if he'd been slapped.

Uh oh, we're losing him. Iza needed to get this back on its original trajectory, but how?

Karter stepped onto the flight deck and walked over to stand beside Braedon as if she'd summoned him.

"Karter!" Iza hissed. This was all wrong. *What are they doing?* It was like some kind of conspiracy against her. Didn't they understand making him angry wasn't going to get them any closer to Joe? Karter ignored her, speaking directly to Arvonen.

"You can't just make yourself High Dynasty. If it was that easy, don't you think I would have tried that already? Your son is right. This pursuit is damaging your reputation beyond repair. There is no place for you in real society circles anymore. You just can't come back from what you've done."

Then, as if she'd been waiting for Karter to speak, his mother stepped into view beside Arvonen. Karter flinched but didn't waver. Iza watched with one hand half covering her face. It was like witnessing a horrible Sensationals reenactment of what not to do during a negotiation.

"And what would you know about society circles?" Phaedra asked. The same look of disdain that Arvonen wore mirrored on her face. "You've done everything you can to avoid them."

"Phaedra," Karter said not taking his eyes off of his mother. "I see you've aligned yourself with this madman as well as threatening the future of your own dynasty. That doesn't bode well for business relations."

"How dare you speak to me of my dynasty when you would go out of your way to squander your own? Being engaged to that girl isn't at all what I wanted for you, and you know it. She's too important. I thought you understood that."

Iza sat forward, wondering what his mother meant by her being too important. *Does she know about my mother and father?* She looked over at Karter, but he didn't meet her stare.

"Tell me she knows who her family is at last," Phaedra said.

There it was, she *did* know. Karter had known, too—perhaps before she'd even known herself. Iza glanced to Karter for confirmation. This time, he did meet her gaze. It was there in his eyes, guilt and even regret. Karter refocused his attention on the front display.

"Of course, she knows who her family is. But, that doesn't change who she is as a person. She's not going to help you."

"That remains to be seen," Arvonen said, stepping forward.

Phaedra huffed, crossing her arms over her chest.

Arvonen, however, seemed to be staring at Iza. "You know what I want. I'll accept the exchange: you for your boyfriend."

Iza blinked.

His lips curled into a smirk. "If you're thinking about getting help once you bring me what I want, I can guarantee that won't happen." At his nod, one of his guards moved off-screen and came back dragging Jaidyn, bound, and beaten. "So, you see, you'll have to deal with me and me alone to get him back. I'll let you have him, if you agree to come aboard my ship of your own free will, alone."

The sight of Jaidyn's bloody and bruised face, with his eyes rolling to the back of his head, made Iza a little sick. *Hadn't I prepared for this? Wasn't this the reason I made sure it was me making the trade?* She shook her head to clear it. *Focus. Joe needs me. Everyone is counting on me.*

"I want to see him," Iza stated, resolute.

"What, you don't recognize your kin?"

"Not him. Joe."

Arvonen tightened his jaw and then nodded to the same guard who'd dragged Jaidyn forward. He disappeared and the display went black before stars filled the viewport, the connection severed.

"Captain, we've received a coded signal." Skyler smiled and it lit up her face. "It's the TSS."

"Where are they?" Iza demanded.

"Close, and monitoring the situation."

Iza swore under her breath. *For once, they arrive on time, but now they're not doing a bomaxed thing.* She realized, then, that they were only there to find a way to interface with the Gatekeepers. The interpersonal matters regarding the Arvonen and Hyttinen Dynasties weren't their concern. As long as Arvonen didn't get his hands on a Gate, the civilians were on their own to resolve the other issues.

"Captain…" Trix said softly. "I've been studying that ship near the *Arvonen One*. It's not Taran." She whirled around, her eyes wide.

Before Iza could react, Trix was suddenly thrown across the flight deck. It took Iza a split-second to realize that a figure had appeared and was running toward her.

What the…?

A white light of energy surrounded him, filling the flight deck. Iza felt weighed down, unable to get to her feet.

Skyler tried to lift a hand, but she too was thrown back against the far wall. The thwack of her head hitting the bulkhead was enough render her unconscious. Braedon and Karter remained immobilized by the crushing energy coming from the mysterious figure.

Iza gasped when he turned his face to hers, the eyes black and expressionless. Though he'd looked Taran at first glance, he wasn't. He jumped forward and tackled her.

A silent scream filled her throat. But before Iza could release the sound, a new wave of white light swirled around her.

One minute she'd been sitting on the flight deck of the *Verity*. Now she was on the floor of another ship. The figure who'd tackled her stood up, looking down at her.

The people occupying the stations on the flight deck had the same dark, expressionless eyes as the first. In her gut, she knew. These were the Gatekeeper hybrids—advanced beings wearing Taran skins. She could feel their power, enticing and terrifying at the same time.

Still on her hands and knees, Iza prepared to fight back as the man in the captain's chair moved toward her. The man in front of her had features as familiar to her as her own. *How could I have forgotten his face?* She'd know it anywhere now.

The man stopped in front of her and spoke her name, the words dripping with contempt. "Iza Sundari."

She gasped as she tried to make sense of what she was seeing with her own eyes. "Dad?"

—   —   —

On board the *Conquest* their team, seemed more excited

than nervous. Ian had to admit he hadn't seen any action in years, and this was the closest they would come since they had a new generation of trained Agents to do this sort of thing so they wouldn't have to anymore.

However, Wil had made it clear this particular mission was something different. The fact that he'd brought Saera and Curtis along was confirmation. He hadn't liked the idea of bringing Emery along, but he respected Ian and didn't overturn his decision.

It took them less than five hours to reach the destination. The holographic display wrapping around the spherical Command Center in the heart of the ship showed both the *Verity* and the *Arvonen One*. Wil had stopped their ship out of sensor range from the civilian vessels, waiting for something, though Ian wasn't sure what, exactly.

Wil stared out at the holographic rendering of space enveloping the Command Center. Though he appeared to be looking at the image, Ian know better. He was using his advanced abilities to evaluate the situation in a way the ship's systems couldn't.

"The Gatekeepers are here," Wil said. "A small cabal of them never left, it seems. It's their ship that we picked up near the *Arvonen One*."

"It makes you wonder what other groups are operating in the shadows," Saera murmured.

As Wil's wife and now Lead Agent of the TSS, she was the honorary twenty-first member of the Primus Elites. She and Wil were a formidable team, and if they were going up against the Gatekeepers, they'd need every advantage.

"What do you want us to do?" Ian asked.

"I need everyone to stay calm. I'm going to initiate contact with them. Maybe we can avoid any more damage to Taran worlds."

Wil closed his eyes and reach out telepathically. He opened them several seconds later. "Well, they know we've arrived."

"Now what?" Curtis asked.

"We wait." Wil sat down in his seat in the middle of the Command Center, watching the remote feed of the two ships facing off.

Then, before their eyes, an egg-shaped ship appeared next to the *Arvonen One*.

Ian's mouth fell open involuntarily.

"Stars…" Curtis breathed.

Wil and Saera exchanged a knowing glance, and he focused ahead. "Now we find out what they have to say."

"WAIT, WHAT JUST happened?" Braedon said, staring at the spot where Iza had been a moment before. He scratched his head in confusion. When he looked to the others for an answer, he saw only mirrored bewilderment on their faces.

"Someone took her," Karter said.

Atano, who'd been frightened by the white light, now cautiously crept out from behind the captain's chair, sniffing for his master.

"Can the TSS do that?" Braedon asked, racing over to the place Iza had been.

"I do not believe that was an Agent," Trix stated.

Karter shook his head. "I figured he'd come from your father's ship." He bent down to pick up Atano who was shivering with fear and tucked him under one arm.

Braedon scoffed. "My father? No way. That ship doesn't have that kind of tech. I've never seen anything like that outside of a Dark Net game."

"I'm revising my statement. I'm going to guess it was them." Karter pointed through the viewport to where the gravity signature had identified.

The dark starscape warped and shimmered as an egg-shaped ship appeared. Its sleek design was unlike anything Braedon had seen around the Taran worlds, both in terms of the body design and materials. Its teardrop reflective surface had no visible windows or hatches.

"Are those the…" Braedon began, then looked over at Karter for confirmation.

"Yes, I suspect those are the Gatekeepers."

"Arvonen is messaging us again, demanding to speak to Iza," Trix said. "What should I tell him?"

"Put him on the display. I'll speak to him," Karter said.

"Wait. Who put you in charge? When Iza's not here, you don't become captain," Braedon said, crossing his arms.

"Neither do you," Karter said. "But we don't know where she is or if she's alive, which as the vessel's lessor, means the responsibility of this ship and everything on it falls to me." Karter took a step toward the captain's seat.

Braedon shook his head, ignoring him as he bent beside Skyler to check her pulse. It was faint but still there. "Trix, call Cierra and Viper, and tell them to get up here with a medkit right now. Joe's sister needs help,"

He then turned back to Karter. "You can't just replace her. My father will know something's up, and we'll lose our chance to get Joe."

"He's no longer our priority; getting Iza back is. We knew how to get her back from your father, but the Gatekeepers taking her wasn't part of the plan. They'll kill her, and they could very likely wipe us all out before we could even consider jumping away."

"None of you are second-in-command," Trix said, asserting her position in front of the captain's chair. "As I have been with Iza the longest, the task of caring for the ship falls to me. As I am already integrated with the ship, I'll do the talking until Iza returns."

Braedon glanced at Karter. He couldn't be sure she was, in fact, herself and not functioning as a mouthpiece of the Gatekeepers. Trix had insisted that she was now able to block the aliens from taking her over, but he'd never seen her like this before.

Trix held up her hand. "Please, be quiet. Arvonen is calling. We'll be audio only."

Braedon turned in time to see his father's face on the display beside two large men holding Joe up to the camera. Joe's eyes were red-rimmed and unfocused but open. He was pale and seemed weak, but he was alive.

Braedon heard Cierra gasp behind him, and his jaw tightened. She and Viper had come onto the flight deck to help Skyler and were now staring at the display along with the rest of them.

"Is that how you treat my friends, father?" Braeden's anger bubbled over and couldn't be contained. "You're a monster, and I'm glad I left when I had the chance."

"I hear you, son, but I don't see you. Why are you hiding?"

"We're not hiding," Trix said in a perfect imitation of Iza's voice. "You don't need to see us. We only needed visual confirmation that Joe is alive, and now we have. So, let's talk about an exchange."

Braedon whirled around to stare at Trix as did the others. *Of course! Why didn't I think of that?* He wanted to hug the android for her brilliant approach to the situation, but he thought better of doing so in front of Cierra.

"You and you alone are welcome to come over to the *Arvonen One* for the exchange." There was a twitch in his father's eye; Braedon saw it and recognized it's meaning. He was planning something, but before he could say so, Trix spoke up.

"There's no reason for me to come aboard your ship. Send Joe over here," Trix continued in Iza's voice.

"Also, I suggest you avoid letting Karter advise you in these negotiations; it won't bode well for you."

"If she'd listened to me, we wouldn't be anywhere near you. She's on her own," Karter said.

"I'm no fool, Arvonen," Trix continued as Iza. "If you want me, you're going to have to come and get me."

Arvonen terminated his video feed, going to audio-only as Iza had done. "Then we are at an impasse," he said. "I know they took him. Somehow, they found out he was here, and you managed to get them to help you take him off the ship without us knowing."

"Took who?"

"The two of you are the only ones capable of operating the Gate. I'm not leaving here without one of you. Make your choice."

"Though I'm not sure what you mean, I'll give you thirty minutes to consider my original offer, then we'll let the TSS deal with you." Trix terminated the call.

"Well, this is a bomaxed disaster," Braedon moaned.

"All it not lost," Trix said in her own voice. "I'm only attempting to stall him while determining what happened to Iza."

"Is the TSS still out there?" Braedon asked.

"Yes. I believe they may be waiting for a signal from Skyler. Please attend to her; she may be our last hope of getting the TSS to intervene, and they are now our best chance of getting Iza and her cousin back alive."

Viper helped Cierra position Skyler and placed a blanket over her to keep her warm on the floor of the flight deck. Cierra indicating it wasn't safe to move her yet.

"Doesn't their Agent being rendered unconscious by an

alien attack justify action?" Karter asked. "Let's inform the TSS of our situation and see if they are prepared to move forward without Iza."

"I will apprise them of the situation," Trix confirmed. She got a distant look in her eyes as he prepared the message to the distant ship.

"Well?" Braedon prompted.

Before Trix could respond, Cierra froze in place, her expression changing from fear to wonder. "They— the TSS just made telepathic contact with me," she whispered. "Stars! These minds are so powerful." The hint of tears glistened in her eyes.

She stood in silence for several moments, and then her gaze flew to Braedon's, and he knew she was going to ask him to do something he wasn't going to like. "They want you and Trix to go to your father's ship with a group of Agents."

"Why them?" Karter asked, his tone incredulous.

You know why. Cierra's voice filled Braedon's mind.

He didn't want to think about what it meant that despite all of their planning, it came down to him. "Because I'm his son. I may be the only other person besides Iza who can get close to him."

"Not to sound harsh, but he doesn't care about you, kid. All that matters to him is Iza and without her, you might as well be walking to your death."

Cierra reached up to stroke Braedon's face. The warmth of it lingered even as she continued. "You won't be walking in empty-handed. They brought the sphere. It's enough to get you close, which is all they need to get Joe."

"Wait, how are we going to get over there?" Braedon asked.

"A TSS shuttle. While you're keeping your father busy, they're going to try communicating with the Gatekeepers. The rest of us will wait and tend to Agent Anderson. Trix, we're counting on your imitation of Iza to get the shuttle into Arvonen's docking bay. Can you do it?"

"I believe that's the first time you've addressed me by name," Trix said. There was wonder in her voice, as if she couldn't quite believe it. "Yes, I can do it."

Cierra nodded. "Good."

"I don't think I would believe it if I didn't see it with my own eyes." Viper gave her sister a poke. "Are you softening toward tech?"

Cierra made a face her sister seemed to recognize. "No, not tech. Just Trix; she's different."

"I'm not sure about this." Braedon asked lifting a hand to wipe the sheen of sweat on his forehead. "What about Iza? We can't just leave her on that alien ship!"

"The TSS assured me they're going to get her out and renegotiate a peace with the aliens. All we can do is our parts. She would want you to get Joe if you could."

Braedon nodded. Cierra was right, of course, but it didn't make what they were doing any easier. He turned to Karter.

"I hope one of you can fly this thing, because you may have to defend the ship if the Arvonen or the alien ship starts firing on it. Trix and I won't be here to help you."

Karter waved his hand. "Oh, please. I started flight lessons as soon as I was tall enough to see over the console, same as you as a dynastic heir. You can't believe I'd sell starships without being able to fly them? It won't be a problem for me," he said. As if to prove it, he removed his jacket and rolled up his sleeves, taking Braedon's seat.

"Besides, he's got us," Viper said moving to stand at the tactical station.

"Don't get too comfortable. I'll be back," Braedon cautioned.

"I wouldn't dream of it, kid," Karter said with a snicker.

"Well, let's go get Joe and hope by the time we do, Iza's back here," Braedon said. It was time to stop his father and get the rest of them home.

— — —

His sister's reception was more fun than Joe could have imagined with Iza there. She was gorgeous in her red dress; though she swore she'd been trying to blend in, all she did was stand out. Of course, the bride and groom were glowing in a bubble of their love, but Joe's eyes kept returning to Iza.

"I'm so glad you both could make it." Emery lifted his glass to Iza, who was talking with someone Joe didn't recognize

She turned and flashed Joe a smile that made his knees weak, and he wished they were back on Earth in the bedroom of his little apartment. "I wouldn't have missed this for anything," he said with a reassuring grip on Emery's shoulder. "You two look amazing together. I never thought I'd say it, but you couldn't be more perfect for each other."

"I'm glad you came around. Skylar would have moved mountains to make sure you came."

"By the way, where is my sister?"

Emery shrugged, lifting the glass to his lips. Then out behind him, Joe saw Mandren and two other Agents with serious expressions on their faces headed their way. They crossed the dance floor without regard for the guests and there were a few mumbles of protest in their wake.

"What are they doing here?" Joe asked.

"Who?" Emery spun around just as Agent Mandren reached them.

"Agent Anderson, a moment of your time, please."

"I guess that's my cue to go and find my bride. See you later my friend," Emery said with a grin.

"That won't be necessary. We'd like to speak someplace more private," Mandren said to Joe.

What is this is all about?

As if reading his thoughts Emery asked, "What is this all about?"

"This is official business, Agent Valackas. I apologize for the inconvenience and disturbing your big day."

Mandren didn't wait for an answer, only turning on one heel and marching out of the room. The other two Agents waited for Joe to follow and stepped in line after him. He was being escorted out of his sister's wedding.

What day is it? Why didn't they wait to speak with me until after the reception? Joe tried to focus his thoughts on the wedding, but he couldn't remember any of the details. Had he seen his best friend and his sister speak their vows to one another?

They reached the office of the High Commander and the two guards took their stations on either side of the doorway while Joe followed Mandren inside. Joe tried to remember how they got there. He'd been at the reception with Iza, now he was at Headquarters. The High Commander was seated at the desk. He waved his hand at the two chairs in front of him.

"I apologize for the theatrics. It seemed necessary in this case, to make this an official inquiry."

The High Commander and Ian Mandren shared a look that Joe didn't understand.

"Official inquiry? What is this about?" Joe questioned.

"This is about your activities and your report from the *Verity*. It seems that not only have you been involved in some questionable behavior, but you've blown your cover." The High Commander rested his elbows on the desk and ran a hand through his hair. He looked tired; more tired than Joe had ever seen him before. "You went too far. Too many people know about your mission in the Outer Colonies. We warned you. The crew can't know what your true mission is, however, it looks like you have told them. Why?"

Joe thought back. It had been gradual at first. One crewmember and then another. Iza had been the last to know. *Why can't I remember telling her?*

"You don't understand, things are not as black-and-white in the colonies as they are here," Joe said.

"You are a TSS Agent, and you violated protocol when you told your entire crew on board the *Verity* who you really are. Don't you see that?" Ian asked. The disappointment was written in the lines of his face.

"I didn't do anything wrong. I can trust them," Joe said.

"This isn't about trust. This isn't about your trust in them. This is about our trust in you," the High Commander said. "This mission you were given was supposed to be covert. Everything depended on it. Now that you've announced who you are to everyone, we can't use you."

This isn't exactly how this happened. I've had this conversation before.

Joe tried to make sense of what he was hearing and the time between him telling the crew and attending his sister's wedding. He'd served his time on Earth. *Why were they threatening to send me back to exile?*

"You wanted me to be a part of the crew," he heard himself say. "You want me to live and breathe and work in the colonies. I can't do that and hide who I am from the people who have my back. I'm all alone out there. Without them, I've got nothing. You would have me lie to the people closest to me?"

"That's exactly what you were supposed to do, Agent Anderson. Your failure to comply is a breach of security," Ian said, his tone firm as he stood up. He glanced at the High Commander as he stood up as well.

"Wait, what are you saying?"

It was the High Commander's turn to speak. "You're being shipped back to Earth. Effective immediately, you are no longer an Agent of the TSS. Due to your reckless behavior including, but not limited to the breach of your cover, the leaking of TSS procedures and technology, but also failure to comply with the local laws of the government. You are hereby stripped of your agency and position. The guards outside will see you to your transport."

Joe's world spun in dizzy-making circles. He had no idea what to do next. He didn't want to get on a transport ship and leave Iza and the crew behind without a word. He needed to get a message to them, let them know what happened.

"Stop thinking that way, Joe," Mandren said. "You cannot and will not inform your family and friends of where you are and where you're going."

How did he know what I was thinking?

"But, sirs —"

"This decision is final. Under our laws, you will not speak of this matter to anyone, here or on Earth. If you cannot maintain silence, in this case, we will find a suitable cell where you can spend the rest of your days." Mandren gestured to the door.

Joe stared at him, and then looked at the High Commander.

"I don't know what's going on here. Or what's happened to you," Joe stammered. "You once stood by each other even in dark times. Even if it meant breaking a few rules you kept your friends close. You trusted each other. It was a trust built over time, based on mutual loyalty. You can't ask the people under you to do anything less."

He wasn't sure if he'd gotten through to them, but it suddenly occurred to him he had something with which to bargain. The sphere was in his hand now, the etched sphere cool against the palm of his hand his fingers wrapping comfortably around it. "Take this but leave Iza and the rest of them alone. They are no threat to you, and without this, they'll be safe from Arvonen." He tossed the sphere to Mandren who caught it deftly and handed it off to the High Commander.

That's not what happened. I would never have thrown the sphere at him. He didn't have time to argue as he was dragged out into the corridor by the guards who'd been waiting for the order. Not long after, he was thrown into a shuttle leaving Earth's moon and headed for the planet's surface. He was strapped to a chair and prepared for launch when something jarred his seat.

Joe's eyes snapped open. *What is this?* He was on the floor. *How did I get down here?* There were two Agents in the room fighting a couple of large security guards. *Were we trying to apprehend them on an op? No, I'm not TSS anymore.* Joe's mind circled around the event, trying to make sense of what he was seeing. The floor beneath him shook and there was a consistent blaring coming from somewhere behind him. It got louder as his vision cleared so he shut his eyes, but it didn't dull the noise. An urgent voice spoke in his head, lifting him off the ground.

"Come on, let's get you on your feet. We need to get out of here." The sound of the man's voice was familiar. He tried to place the sound of the voice with the name of the man but couldn't grasp it.

"What's going on?" The question burned his throat as he asked it aloud.

"We're trying to rescue you; no time to catch up. If we don't get you out of here, I'm pretty sure Skyler is never going to marry me."

"I don't understand. Skyler?"

"Joe." The man patted him on the face with one open hand

to getting him to open his eyes.

That's when Joe saw the familiar blue eyes of his friend who it was holding him upright. "Emery."

"Yes, glad you still know me. After what they've done to you, it's surprising you know your own name. Now, let's get out of here before Arvonen kills you."

Another Agent lifted Joe's other arm, and the two of them dragged Joe to the door.

A bundle of disconnected memories resurfaced as Joe looked around the familiar room. He'd been in a lab strapped to a chair. They were combing through his memories, looking for something. He should have been dead already. *Why am I still alive? I gave them everything.*

"Let's not worry about that now. We need to get to the shuttle. Just keep your feet under you the best you can."

Joe had only meant to think the question. *Did I say that out loud?*

Joe's breathing was fast and jagged, and he was having a hard time staying on his feet as he'd been asked. But, he did his best, swaying as they fought their way through the corridor.

A guard caught up to them. He fired from behind, seeking cover in the recess of a doorway along the corridor.

Emery and his partner used their bodies to block Joe while the other Agent lifted a hand and telekinetically pushed the assailant down the corridor until he slammed against a closed door. Then, the two each grabbed a hold of one of Joe's arms, again lifting him enough to get his feet under him and raced for their shuttle.

Upon reaching the craft, they strapped him into a seat, and he heard them discussing whether to leave someone or go for them. They eventually reached some kind of consensus because they arguing stopped, and the shuttle was prepped to leave. *I wonder how they're going to get off of this ship with the docking doors closed?*

"You're going to need help to come back from this. The memories—everything you've been experiencing was a lie."

Joe tried to focus on the words in his head, but soon his eyelids were too heavy to keep open.

Emery's words filtered into the dark comfort of his mind. *"Don't worry, my friend, we'll get you the help you need."*

29

IZA REACHED OUT her arms to gain her balance as she tried to get her feet under her. One arm was caught in the warm hand of someone else. The man holding her up had her father's face.

She stared at him with her mouth open. *How can it be? How can every one of them have the same face?* No, his eyes were different, not the warmth of her father's that she remembered, but dead and lifeless. None of them had his quick smile or the glow of pure joy she'd once seen in her father's features. How had she forgotten his warm eyes and wide smile until this moment?

A whimper in the corner caught her attention. That's when she saw her cousin lying unconscious on the floor. He was starting to wake up after whatever they'd done to him.

"Who are you? What did you do to my cousin?" Iza demanded of her captors.

"You know who we are. Do not pretend you are ignorant of our existence."

"Yes, I mean, no. Are you the one in charge?"

"We have taken this form to communicate with you in your limited manner. Our natural form and nature are too much for you to consume."

They spoke Taran, but the words flowed in a mix of the old and the new dialects as if they couldn't decide which era to be from.

What did he mean 'consume'? Limited? What was he talking about?

Iza looked around the flight deck—a perfect replica of the *Verity*; however, nothing in the space seemed to be functional. An empty captain's chair, a communications station, and tactical console; only the front helm station, normally occupied by Braedon, was occupied. Iza and the first Gatekeeper stood in the middle of the space with her cousin crumpled on the deck next to the captain's chair. Using the *Verity*, the place that was her home, like a set put her on edge.

"How about you explain why in the bomaxed universe you took me off of my ship and brought me here?"

"You have broken the peace."

"What peace?" Iza had gained feeling in her arms and legs again, though the humming she'd once experienced only in the presence of the sphere was coming from all sides as if the room were filled with spheres.

"The treaty. We made it clear that violating the terms would mean your destruction. You had all of this time to learn and grow, yet you squandered the opportunity. Why delay the inevitable war for this long only to break the truce when you are at such a disadvantage?"

Iza tried to wrap her mind around what he was saying. The statements seemed to line up with what little she'd learned from the TSS. "Did you open the Gates on those worlds to change their climates?" Iza asked. She kept her eyes averted from the man's blank stare.

"You Tarans are inferior and frail. We should have ended you before when you tried to interfere. Now, at last, you will pay the price."

Iza's chest tightened. The transformation of the worlds were starting to make sense. The Gatekeepers were altering the planets to be the opposite of their present environments in order to exterminate the people living there. All the effectiveness of a weapon of mass destruction without mess of traditional tools of warfare. Arvonen had used their tech without permission, and so every world he'd touched had gotten a target painted on it. The Gatekeepers were efficient in exacting their brand of punishment, justified or not.

Despite the galactic implications, she was more focused on what the Gatekeepers meant to her own life. "Why did you choose his face?" she blurted out, since she probably would never get another chance to ask.

The Gatekeeper's lip curled up in disgust before he spat out the words. "We know about the abomination."

"Abomination?"

"You should not exist. He cannot exist."

Iza glanced down her cousin, still lying crumpled on the floor. He'd stopped whimpering, and there was no further sign of him rousing. "What have you done to him?" her voice went shrill. She tried to move toward him, but the man blocked her path.

The man took a step forward and the electricity moved with him, reaching out like tendrils toward her. Iza raised her hands in front of her in defense. Her mind racing to think of some way to stall. Her cousin might already be dead, but she needed to know for sure.

"We did not do this to him. The Taran held him, and we took him from the ship as we took you." He continued to block her path. "He cannot exist."

"What do you want with us?"

The man glanced between her and Jaidyn. He shrugged.

"You will be disposed of, as soon as we're finished with you."

"Why? We've done nothing to you!"

"You have passed through a Gate, going places you have no right to enter. We want nothing else with the Taran form and will dispose of all abominations."

Jaidyn moaned on the floor, and the tension in her shoulders eased as she leveled her gaze at the man in front of her. She'd dealt with bullies before, and that's exactly what these Gatekeepers were. Galactic bullies who were trying to bend them to their will. Iza never did like being bullied.

"It was a mistake to choose the form of my father," Iza said, squaring her shoulders.

"You do not like the reminder of how you came to be, abomination?" The man's mouth formed a smile, but it was not due to pleasure.

"No, it's not that. I could never be afraid of my father, and I'm not afraid of you."

Iza took a step forward. The electrical crackling intensified and the man took a step back. Iza could feel the charge in the room as if it were a part of her. She reached out with her senses, touching it, playing with it. Each new sensation gave her more confidence to wield it as she pleased. The electricity could be shot out in any direction she chose, like bolts of lightning.

An overwhelming rush of emotions washed over her, but they weren't her own. They were coming from the man—a mixture of horror and despair.

The man took another unsteady step back before his head tilted to one side. "There are more Tarans coming," said the man sitting in Braedon's chair behind her.

Iza watched through the front viewport as a TSS ship came into view. It was a much larger and more menacing ship than she'd been expecting, but it was, for the first time in her life, a welcome sight. *Better late than never.*

"Oh, yeah, did I forget to mention I didn't come alone? They're with me. You see, we don't particularly like being taken and killed."

"It doesn't matter. We will return to our realm. They cannot follow."

"You're making a mistake. I may not be able to do anything to hurt you, but the Agents on that ship can."

"It is the leader," the man who sat the helm looked back, his eyes seemed wider than before.

Are they scared? Good. It's about time.

— — —

Ian was getting antsy. Wil had been scowling at the view of space, his mind extended beyond his physical form, for too long. Something was wrong.

"The Gatekeepers have grabbed the woman and her cousin," Wil reported, at last. "It's time we stepped in."

Saera nodded her agreement. "How?"

"Be as diplomatic as possible." Wil took a deep breath and closed his eyes in a slow blink.

Ian knew from experience that he'd initiated a direct neural link with the ship in preparation for a jump. The cloud of subspace momentarily swirled across the panoramic viewscreen surrounding the Command Center as the *Conquest* jumped to the location of the other three vessels. The TSS warship dropped down at the center of the grouping, creating a physical barrier between the *Verity* and two enemy craft.

As soon as they were in position, Wil opened a general comm channel to the alien ship. "I come here as a representative of the Taran Empire. I wish to speak with you regarding the treaty."

Ian waited for a verbal reply. Instead, a swirl of white light appeared next to Wil. A man was inexplicably inside the white light, and he reached out to Wil.

Wil stood still, offering no resistance as the man all but tackled him. Instinctively, Ian dove to protect his commander. In a flash, he and Wil disappeared off of the ship in another swirl of white energy.

They reappeared on what looked like the flight deck of a traditional Taran vessel. Ian dropped to the deck, half on top of Wil and the strange man.

He quickly picked himself up. "Sorry, I—"

"I appreciate the sentiment, Ian, but I actually had a plan," Wil said with a slight smile.

"Never go in alone. You taught me that," Ian said telepathically.

His friend nodded. *"Follow my lead."*

Based on the sight out the front viewport—which Ian wasn't sure was real or simulated—he surmised that they were inside the Gatekeeper ship near the *Arvonen One*. Besides the Gatekeeper who'd pulled them from the *Conquest*, there was another Gatekeeper seated at the helm of the flight deck, and Iza and her cousin were near the captain's chair.

Wil looked around. "Fascinating. Is that transporter tech your own, or did you adopt it in the way you did these Taran forms?" he asked the aliens.

"That's not what we're here to discuss," the Gatekeeper at the center of the room stated. The other rose from his seat to stand next to the front console, his attention focused on Ian.

There was an intense hum of energy in the air, the way it felt when powerful Agents were using their abilities. Ian didn't sense such abilities in the Gatekeepers in the way he normally could with the Gifted among the Taran population, but there was no doubt that they were different. In particular, their minds were completely walled off to him, the way Iza's was.

The dark, empty eyes drove home the impression that they were mere vessels—a face to make communications easier with Tarans. It gave him hope that they could find common ground and resolve the misunderstanding; if the beings had appeared in their true form, whatever that may be, it would have been a sign that they'd already abandoned the possibility of a continued relationship.

Captain Iza Sundari seemed shocked to see them. She was kneeling next to a young, beaten man with long hair tied at the nape of his neck, who must be her cousin; he seemed semi-unconscious. Ian wanted to reassure her, but she was telepathically resistant as was the man beside her. Instead, Ian turned his attention to supporting Wil.

The High Commander squared his shoulders and lifted one hand in greeting. "Welcome back to the Taran Empire. Now, may we speak with you about this treaty?"

—   —   —

Iza gawked at the two Agents who had appeared on the flight deck of the Gatekeeper ship. They'd been brought as she had, by one of the Gatekeepers in a swirl of light, and then dropped unceremoniously in the middle of the room. From their expressions, she could see they'd been just as surprised to be there as she'd been, but they were quicker to recover. The one she recognized from her visit to TSS Headquarters, Ian Mandren, glanced in her direction and grimaced, as if torn between going over to them or staying put. Mandren must have thought better of it, as he returned his attention to the aliens. His face was tight and his bright eyes focused with stone-like determination.

The man beside him was known to every Taran civilian. It seemed whenever someone wanted to take over the Empire, the man was there. As she understood it, Wil Sietinen had abdicated his political position in the Sietinen Dynasty, so his daughter was next in line, but his role as both TSS High Commander and son of the Head of the Sietinen Dynasty made him one of the most influential people alive. She'd seen his face on several news feeds as well as in the Sensationals.

In person, he held the impressive commanding presence she imagined the leader of the TSS would carry. She'd never been in a room with someone connected to High Dynasty before, and that lineage no doubt added to his proud stance. However, he didn't wear the entitlement that Karter flaunted, though she doubted he'd been denied much of anything. She could hardly imagine what it must have been like being born into a High Dynasty on Tararia, raised alongside the rest of the wealthy; he certainly had no idea of how people like her lived. Even so, he stood there with Mandren at his side, squaring off across from the Gatekeepers.

It gave Iza comfort to know she'd been wrong. The TSS hadn't abandoned them, after all. Whatever was accomplished here, they'd go on to stop Arvonen, and that's what mattered most. That, and getting Joe back alive.

While the Gatekeepers were distracted by the TSS Agents, Iza took the opportunity to check on her cousin. She lifted Jaidyn's head to rest on her lap and bent her head down to whisper to him. "Are you all right?"

"Arvonen," Jaidyn croaked. "He took me from Hubyria, I think he was planning to use me to go through a Gate. But the Gatekeepers, brought me here. If they get the chance, they'll kill us. We have to get away."

Iza shook her head. They weren't going anywhere. Despite the design of this flight deck for their benefit, she could see no way off of the ship.

Iza's attention returned to the men as Wil Sietinen spoke

aloud to the aliens asking for permission to begin the discussion. She'd have preferred a more direct rescue, but she could only assume they were doing what they could, which meant they were at a disadvantage.

The man who stood before the captain's seat wearing her father's face was the one who spoke, addressing the TSS High Commander. "You speak for all Tarans?"

"Yes, because someone must. You've been living among us. I think you know who I am, and that's why we're having this conversation now."

"We do. But even your power pales in comparison to ours."

"From what little I've seen of your capabilities, I don't doubt it. But I don't think we'd be standing here together if a peaceful resolution was entirely off the table."

The Gatekeeper weighed this response. "It remains that you have broken the peace between our peoples. You have stolen a Gate and used it to enter our territory. There must be a punishment and a consequence for such disrespect." The last words spat out of his mouth.

Iza wedged herself behind her cousin, helping him to a seated position. He held his head and groaned but didn't speak. He seemed as transfixed on what was going on as she was.

Sietinen inclined his head. "A misunderstanding. There has been no intentional hostility by our government against yours, and we apologize for the unsanctioned actions of a small group of our citizens. We have no further plans to use your technology," he stated, calm and measured.

"It's too late." The Gatekeeper moved to the captain's chair and produced a brown shoe—no, a boot, well-worn and faded. Iza's boot. He held it up for them to see. "The responsibility of the broken treaty is on you." He tossed the boot aside and it landed near her cousin's foot. Iza stared at it in disbelief.

It was very the boot she'd lost when she'd been pushed through the Gate had been found leading them straight back to her. She was the reason they'd declared war on the Taran Empire. She'd inadvertently gotten thousands—millions—of people killed, including her aunt. Iza glanced down at the top of Jaidyn's head. His hair as thick as her own, strands of it coming out of the binder at the base of his skull. He would never forgive her once he knew the truth. The weight of the knowledge settled in her gut and made her wish she'd skipped her last meal.

Sietinen gestured toward the viewscreen displaying the *Arvonen One* in front of them, unmoving even in the face of the aliens. "As I said, the actions of a few—"

"No!" the Gatekeeper roared, interrupting Sietinen. "You don't realize what you've done. We're not the ones you should be worried about. All we've wanted was to be left alone. But no justice we can serve today will satisfy the others. You sealed your fate the moment you used the Gate." He shook his head and scoffed.

"Then please, explain it to us."

"If it means so little that you've forgotten, then you aren't worthy of our assistance."

The High Commander looked down and took a slow breath. "You're right. A race is measured by the actions of *all* its members. We have disrespected you, and for that we deeply apologize. However, we're at a crossroads. We can either launch all-out war beginning this moment, or we can seek the path of peace. So, I asked you, will you stop transforming our planets by use of the Gates?"

The alien man glanced at Iza, and a shiver crawled up her spine and latch on to her neck. *We're not the enemy. Haven't they taken enough from us?*

"It doesn't matter what we do now," the Gatekeeper said.

"The damage is already done; they'll think it was you."

The High Commander's brow furrowed. "I don't understand."

"You will, in time."

Iza couldn't take it anymore. All of the loss, the anger, the pain of having her life stripped from her welled up in her chest until she burst. "No, enough!" she shouted. She was on her feet before she knew what she was doing.

The two TSS Agents stood motionless as she stormed toward the Gatekeeper.

"Why are you doing this to us?" Iza demanded. "It was *you* who came into the Taran Empire and started messing with us. I can't help who my father was. Now, you put on his face to mock me. If you want to hold all Tarans responsible for what Arvonen and his cronies are doing with your tech, then I say all Gatekeepers are responsible for my father and uncle going rogue and causing this mess in the first place. For such an allegedly advanced race, you sure don't understand a lot if you can't see the hypocrisy in your judgments."

The alien's mouth turned in disgust, regarding her as if her life meant as little to him as an insect. "So much talk for one so weak."

Iza stretched to her full height. "I'm not weak. If you don't know that character is the true measure of a person's strength, then you've learned nothing in all your studies."

The Gatekeeper leveled his gaze on her, his dark eyes narrowed to near slits. He was assessing her; she could feel it. But she wouldn't back down. She'd rather die here taking a stand than let these monsters take anyone else from her.

Sietinen pulled out a box from his overcoat and held it out toward the alien; it was the right size to contain one of the Gate spheres. "Take your tech and leave. This doesn't need to come to war."

The air around them crackled to life and Iza felt it pulse through her, as if she were a part of the fight. The silent rise of electricity lifted the hair on the back of her neck.

Sietinen and Mandren held steady, but there was a shift in the air, a decrease in the intensity. Mandren glanced in her direction, his eyebrows drawn in confusion. Then, the energy dissipated like a deep breath exhaled.

The Gatekeeper took the box from the High Commander's outstretched hand. "We will spare these two. The others must pay."

In the space of a heartbeat, Iza saw the flash of light from the viewscreen as the *Arvonen One* disappeared into dust. The aftershock sent ripples through space, but instead of disturbing the alien ship they rocked forward and back as if riding a swell of water on a lake. There was so little debris, in fact, it was like someone had thrown sand on the ship's shielding. There was nothing left.

"Joe!" the word was a cry and gasp through her lips. Tears filling her eyes and a sickening burn filled her chest.

A dark cloud passed over Sietinen's face, but his voice remained measured. "That wasn't necessary. We are capable of bringing our own people to justice. You have killed innocents."

"There are no innocents aboard that ship. Our objective is complete. We are done with you, Taran. But the others won't be as forgiving about the violations. They'll be your end."

One of the men stepped forward and gripped Iza. Just like when she'd been brought to the ship, her vision blurred in the white light of energy surrounding her. The oppressive weight of the Gatekeepers' instantaneous travel pressed down on her shoulders as if the man had pushed against her to make the return trip, disappearing almost as quickly as he'd appeared the first time.

The energy subsided on the *Verity*'s flight deck, but the

despair within Iza made her drop to the floor next to her cousin. Viper and the others rushed to her side. Iza still couldn't feel her legs.

"Oh, Iza," Cierra said checking her for physical injuries.

There wouldn't be anything for her to see. They'd ripped out her heart, yet the remains throbbed against her ribcage.

The two elder Quetzalis were repositioning her cousin to the floor and tending to his wounds. She heard the soft murmur of Cierra's mother making him more comfortable.

Karter stepped forward and lifted Iza from the floor, so she didn't have to walk over to the captain's chair. She couldn't focus her eyes on any of them. She kept her gaze on the viewscreen and the dust particles still passing in front of them.

"Iza, what happened over there?" Karter asked.

Her eyes focused for a second as she took in their worried faces. Her cousin was on the floor, but they were all looking to her for answers. The Agents, she assumed, were back on their own ship. The one face she'd wanted to see was nowhere to be found. She answered the question, her bottom lip quivering with emotion.

"The TSS made peace with them."

IZA'S EYES WERE beginning to adjust to the ship and she was starting to take in all the faces. *When had Becca been allowed on the flight deck?* She was holding Atano in her arms, and he was watching everything with rapt attention.

Viper stepped away from her and the ship's alarms ceased.

"I'm fine" Iza said. "Please, help, my cousin. They roughed him up on the *Arvonen One*."

"It looks worse than it is," Jaidyn said. "Just got—"

His words cut off as Cierra pressed her hands against his chest, forcing him down flat. Then, she closed her eyes and placed her hands four millimeters above him, hover over the length of him. Her eyes snapped opened and she blushed.

"You're like her," she said. "I can't read you. I'll have to do a visual examination. I'll make you a tea that will help the headache as soon as I'm done."

"I can help with that," Mrs. Quetzali said, gathering up her robes. They were a pale blue and looked like something she must have borrowed from her daughter who was not quite her height.

Jaidyn frowned at her. "I thought you couldn't read me."

"Not in the telepathic sense. Everyone's body tells a story. You winced at the minimal light in the room, and you're speaking in a low voice. The physical injuries are making your muscles tense which also causes headaches."

Cierra turned to her father, "I'd like to get him to the infirmary as soon as possible."

—   —   —

Braedon sat staring at the side of the shuttle's hull the violence of what he'd just seen replaying over in his mind like a vid stuck on repeat.

Everything had gone according to plan. Trix had spoken as Iza to get them docked in the hangar of the *Arvonen One*. He'd shown his father the Gate within the box as proof of the trade from within the shuttle before he disembarked. The Agents had removed the device, leaving him with the empty box to bring to his father. The Agents hadn't trusted his father to make good on the trade; instead, they'd snuck aboard to hunt him up themselves, leaving Braedon and Trix to keep his father distracted long enough to get Joe out.

They'd been escorted to the flight deck by three of his security guards. The large thugs were twice Braedon's size, but he'd seen what Trix could do and wasn't at all concerned. The three of them would have to dismantle her to beat her and they hadn't brought the tools. When they had reached the flight deck, his father had held out his hands for the box.

"Dad, please. Don't you understand what this is doing to you? Think about the rest of the family," Braedon had said. He didn't have to feign the emotion in his voice every word was soaked with it. Once the TSS took him into custody, he might not ever see him again.

The older man had ignored the sentiment and snatched the

box from his hand. He'd looked inside the now-empty box, confirming what he'd already suspected. "You are the biggest disappointment of my life." He'd thrown the box to the flight deck in anger. "Take him."

Trix had saved Braedon's life. When the men came from all sides, she'd stood between them. She'd almost lost a hand in the fight, when one of his father's security used what looked like a jagged sword against her. The antique must have been part of some collection. Braedon was surprised to see the thing cut into Trix, exposing the wiring and metal components inside her wrist. She'd grabbed him by the back of the shirt with her good hand and practically dragged him back to the docking bay. When their exit was blocked by another team of guards, it was the Digger who'd come to their rescue. In a surprising turn, Raquel had fired off accurate pulse shots at the men blocking their path, dropping them to the deck so Braedon and Trix could escape.

Trix had said the words before he could, "You're not coming with us to the *Verity*."

"Wow, what happened to your voice?" Raquel had stared at her in awe.

Braedon hadn't been able to help the half-smile that came to his face, as it sounded almost like something Iza herself would say.

Then, she'd seemed to take in the words and lifted one shoulder before letting it drop as she answered. "I don't care. Just get me off this ship."

He'd noted the dark beneath Raquel's eyes from lack of sleep. Her blonde hair had been a disheveled mass hanging in disarray, with rogue wisps sticking to the sweat on her brow. Then, there was the bruising on both her bare arms, as if she'd been held too tight by someone much larger. Braedon had been grateful for her assistance, but he'd never tell her so.

The Agent had launched the shuttle the moment they were on board. Thankfully, he hadn't been piloting when the explosion happened. Even as the remains of the *Arvonen One* dusted the outer shielding, he'd asked the question.

"What just happened? Was that my father's ship?"

The older Agent at the helm looked back at Emery and then to Braedon, hesitating. Then he stumbled over the words as if wanting to be rid of them as quickly as possible. "Uh— Yes, it's gone."

Braedon hadn't been able to wrap his head around the loss and the bizarre sense of relief that came with it. His father couldn't be gone. He could still hear the disappointment and curses ringing in his ears from moments ago. Braedon tried not to think about his family's dynasty and what it would mean for all of them once his brother took over his father's business interests. There would be a funeral ceremony, but there would be no physical body to view or burn.

Even now, Raquel still sat on the floor with her head on the bench seat, sobbing. Why she was crying, he had no idea. She hadn't even tried to resist when the Agents had put the stasis cuffs on her.

Trix sat on Braedon's left, her expression neutral. But if he knew her like he thought he did, she was concerned for Joe. He'd caught her scanning him again as they prepared to dock with the TSS ship.

Joe's friend, Emery, leaned forward in the seat across from Joe. "Are you going to be all right, kid?" he asked Braedon.

Braedon nodded. For once, not trusting himself to speak.

"Thanks for your help in there. As soon as we get Joe to the infirmary, we'll see you back to your ship."

Braedon didn't move. Not even when they filed off of the shuttle with Joe lying flat on a medical transport bed. Trix was silent as they waited for the pilot to return. He didn't want to talk about what they'd just witnessed; he only wanted to close his eyes and forget what he'd seen.

—   —   —

"Well, that didn't exactly go as planned," Ian scoffed once they were securely back in the Command Center of the *Conquest*. He felt the wobble of the Gatekeepers peculiar transport system but compensated for it once he took in his surroundings. The sensation was like being back in one of the academy going through one of the gravity locks into a freefall training room.

"No, it seems we may have traded one malcontent for another," Wil said, running a hand through his hair.

Saera stood at Wil's elbow, waiting patiently for their account but not pressing them for information right away. Her eyebrows were drawn in concern.

"I get the feeling this is just the beginning," Ian said, breaking the uncomfortable silence.

"I think you're right." Wil looked to his wife. "What about Joe? Did we retrieve him in time?"

Saera nodded. "Yes, they docked only a few moments before you arrived. He's in the infirmary with Emery."

"And the *Verity*?" Wil asked.

This time, Saera pursed her lips. "We haven't had any contact since the explosion. I believe that's because Skyler is still unconscious. They may have injured."

"Emery will probably want to go over to get her himself," Ian said, "I'll deliver the news and accompany him."

Ian made his way to the infirmary, remembering the last time he'd seen it. He shook of the remnants of memory and entered. Joe was conscious, it seemed; that was a good sign.

"Good to see my two troublemakers are still at it," Ian said.

He plastered a smile on his face though he'd never seen Joe looking so bad. He was gaunt and the bruising on his cheek and around one eye made him ball his hands into fists.

"Sir." Emery straightened when he saw Ian approaching. "We were just catching up."

Ian nodded. "Your fiancée was injured on board the *Verity*. I thought you might want to accompany me over to assess her situation."

"Skyler?" Joe croaked. "She's here?"

"Yes, as is your old crew. Do you feel ready to go back? We can give you some time with them before we discuss your future." Ian didn't want to allude to anything in particular. He wasn't entirely sure what Wil had in mind, only that he'd said Joe would be more useful to the TSS on the *Verity* than anywhere else in the Taran Empire. No doubt it had to do with the fact that his girlfriend was a hybrid Gatekeeper.

Joe shook his head though, his eyes clouding over. "No, not like this."

Ian swallowed. Of course, he wouldn't want to go back in this state. He cleared his throat. "I'll let them know you'll be returning with us for your medical care."

Joe's face relaxed as if the thought had eased some internal pain.

Ian nodded to Emery in signal to follow him out. Once they were halfway to the shuttle, he broached the subject. "How is he, really?"

"Not well. His telepathy is—well—it's like he's defenseless. He keeps slipping into dreams and waking up disoriented. They did a number on him over there. I'm not sure what their end goal was, but he's a mess." Emery put a hand to the back of his neck as if to cool it. "About Skyler, do we know what happened to her?"

"Yes, it seems she was only knocked about by one of the

Gatekeepers when she tried to prevent them from taking the captain. From what I know, she took a pretty heavy hit to the head and she's been recovering in their infirmary." At the sight of Emery's wide eyes, he hastily added, "They have a Healer on board. I'm sure she's doing all right."

Joe would get the help he needed from the doctors at Headquarters. Perhaps they'd even learn the truth about what Arvonen was really after.

— — —

Once she had the strength to stand, Iza went down to check on Jaidyn sleeping in the infirmary. He deserved to know the truth about what happened to his mother as soon as possible. Three candles lit the dim room, and whatever Cierra had given him had eased the pain, as the grimace that had seemed permanently etched on his face had now faded into a more peaceful expression.

She hated to disturb his rest, but it needed to be done. She was reaching out to touch his shoulder when Cierra appeared in the doorway and spoke.

"Let him sleep for now. Whatever you need to say to him can wait. Braedon and Trix are back."

Iza leaped to her feet, and Atano followed her out close on her ankles as she dashed toward the cargo hold. A TSS shuttle was docked and Trix was among the four individuals waiting for her when she arrived.

Iza ran forward, hoping that the fourth person was Joe, but she knew from his stature it wasn't him. Joe was taller and his hair much straighter. Though she was glad to see Trix and said so.

"Thank you, it's nice to be back. We were able to retrieve Joe Anderson from the ship before it exploded."

"You did?" Relief flooded over Iza. *Then why do I still feel hollow?* She was grateful for Trix's candor and at the same time surprised that he wasn't with them. "Where is he?"

This time, Mandren spoke removing his dark glasses so she could read the entirety of his face. "He chose to stay on board the *Conquest*. He needs medical care—the kind he can only receive at TSS Headquarters."

"I want to see him," she demanded, unable to control the sound of desperation in her voice. A moment ago, she'd thought him dead. Now, they were saying he was alive but on their ship.

Ian raised a hand as if to slow her down. "He's asked for some time to recover before he returns."

"What?" Iza couldn't put the words he was saying with Joe's face. "I don't believe you."

"In truth, after we retrieved him, he remained unconscious most of the ride back to the TSS ship and he was taken directly to their infirmary," Trix confirmed.

Iza nodded, though she didn't understand. She dropped her gaze to the deck; she didn't want him to see the anguish on her face after spending her first hour in shock and now learning he was alive but didn't want to come back to the *Verity*. She wasn't sure how to deal with all the emotions she couldn't quite hide.

"I know how you must be feeling. I've been in a war, and there are always casualties, even in the small battles," Agent Mandren said. "Don't forget, this was a win. We got our people to safety and we averted a war. Eventually, Joe will be ready to see you again. You just need to be patient."

The younger Agent with him stepped forward to greet her. "I'm Emery Valackas, Skyler's fiancé. I was hoping I could see her."

"Yes, of course," Iza said leading him to the infirmary.

"And don't worry," Emery added, "we'll get Joe fixed up. I know he's missed you like crazy."

Iza swallowed the lump in her throat.

When they arrived at the infirmary, she found that her cousin was awake but Skyler was still unconscious.

Emery rushed to her bedside. He stroked her hair and kissed her forehead—the kind of loving reunion Iza had hoped to have with Joe. Her heart stung, seeing them together.

After a minute of standing at her bedside, Ian spoke up. "We'll arrange to transfer her to the *Conquest*. Thank you for the care you've provided."

"My pleasure," Cierra said, inclining her head respectfully.

Emery turned to Iza. "Joe didn't exaggerate when he described you."

"Oh, thanks," Iza said not sure what kind of answer he was expecting.

"I know you don't know me, but believe me when I say, I'll take care of them both."

The Agents left with Skyler.

Cierra came in to clean up and light a new candle, the spicey scent tickling Iza's nose. Then, she turned her administrations on Jaidyn, who couldn't seem to keep his eyes on anyone else when she was in the room.

Braedon must have noticed it, too, when he joined her in the doorway. Iza watched him glare at Jaidyn with his eyebrows drawn close together as Cierra lifted his clothing to apply a salve to the abrasions on his skin.

"You still need more rest," Cierra said to Jaidyn. "I'm going to insist that you stay here in the infirmary for a few hours so I can monitor your progress." She turned to tend to the plants in the room with the same care she'd handled his injuries.

Iza cleared her throat to get Braedon's attention, motioning him out into the corridor. "So, what happened?"

Braedon pulled his gaze away from Cierra and Jaidyn, focusing on Iza. "Well, when you disappeared, we didn't know what to do. Instead of panicking we figured sticking with the plan would be better than going off on some random side mission. The TSS would back us up if we played our part, right?" He lifted his hands and paced the floor as he got into the story. "Once we figured out who had you, we had to choose a path. We didn't know exactly what kind of danger you might be facing, so we moved fast. The goal was to get Joe off the *Arvonen One* as quickly as possible."

"You got to him before the explosion. For that, I'll always be grateful."

Braedon's face fell and his eyes darkened. His father had been on that ship.

How could I be so callous thinking only of Joe? "I'm sorry about your father," she said hasty to make amends for her insensitive comment.

Braedon stared down at the floor as if he could see the man. "He wouldn't listen. I tried to save him but, in the end, even when he knew it meant his life, he ignored me. The thing I'll never get over is that he took all those people with him."

Iza clamped her mouth closed, letting Braedon get through the story at his own pace.

"If it hadn't been for Trix, Raquel, and the TSS, we never would have made it out alive," he said.

"Raquel?" The ire rose up in her at the name.

Trix, Viper joined Iza in the corridor listening to Braedon's account.

"It's a long story, but she helped us, and we couldn't leave her behind. We didn't know what was going to happen, but we knew the TSS would have questions for her. They took her into their custody as soon as we arrived."

"Joe was another matter altogether," Trix said, jumping in

to help Braedon with the story.

"Why didn't he come back with you?" Viper asked.

"It's complicated," Braedon said, avoiding Iza's stare. "They really messed him up, Iz. They basically tore open his mind, planted false memories. The TSS thinks my fa—" he swallowed, "that my father was planning to use him against you. But even they're not sure."

"His friend, Emery, said Joe's mind was in pieces," Trix added.

Braedon shook his head, "He wanted to go with the TSS, and I'm not surprised. If it were me, I don't think I'd be ready to step back into my old life, either."

"There are a lot of changes to adjust to," Karter murmured.

Iza's heart threatened to shatter. She took a steadying breath, trying to keep her mind focused on business. "We need to retrieve my shuttle from Douketis."

"Agreed." Karter nodded, quieter and more pensively than his usual confident self.

Viper rubbed her hands together. "Ooh, won't that be fun. A new encounter for your comic book, Braedon?"

He shrugged. "We'll see how exciting it is."

"Speaking of which, now that we're not all about to die, you owe me a peek at it."

"Yeah, I guess you've earned it," he yielded.

"Well, I'll make the necessary arrangements to reacquire the shuttle," Karter said. "I suggest we set a course for Beurias; Apex will make a suitable location for the handoff. And, now that my mother is gone, I'll have to deal with the fallout of her hostile takeover."

Iza realized what he was saying. She'd forgotten his mother had also been on the *Arvonen One* when it was destroyed. He didn't seem to be taking it as hard as Braedon, but they all grieved in their own ways.

Iza wasn't sure what the appropriate level of sympathy was required when an estranged or absentee parent was killed by aliens. She settled on the easiest response. "I'm sorry."

Karter waved a dismissive hand in her direction. "She lived a good life. Though she'd gone rogue in the end, I admit I already feel the loss. I'll have a lot of questions to field from our investors."

Iza saw the pain in his eyes, despite his calm demeanor. It was fortunate that Becca was there with him.

"Captain," Trix cut in, "I'm receiving a call from the TSS ship—for you, specifically."

Is Joe calling? "I'll take it in my cabin," she said and jogged down the corridor.

When she answered on her viewscreen in her room, she was surprised to find herself face-to-face with the TSS High Commander—the High Dynasty heir himself. She struggled to gather herself.

"Um, sir, I—"

"Please, that formality's not necessary," he assured her. "I wanted to reach out, because I suspect you've had a rather poor opinion of me before today. And, despite what I hope have been some redeeming moments in the last few hours, I'm now about to leave again with the person you care about most in the universe."

He's astute, I'll give him that. Iza simply nodded in response.

"I know this may be difficult to believe, but I understand what you're feeling right now."

"Sure," she managed to force out.

"You were used for terrible ends. It's an awful feeling."

The emotion welled up in her chest again. Is that what he was trying to do—to get her to break? She fought back the tears. "It's my fault all of those people are dead."

"No," he said, resolute. "I know something about the weight of guilt, when you're caught up in a mess others created. It's a horrible burden to bear. But I've come to understand that living the best life I can, and helping as many people as possible along the way, is how to best honor those who've died. When you're placed in an impossible situation, there is no win-win. You were used, and it's those who put you in that position who are to blame, not you."

"Why are you telling me this?"

"Because you need to hear it, and I don't know that you have anyone else in your life who understands the situation well enough to say it. I was lucky to have amazing people to help me through my darkest time. Don't shove others away when you need them most."

She looked down, not sure what to say.

"I won't keep Joe from you," he said after a pause.

Her heart skipped a beat. "You mean…?

"When he's recovered, he's free to return to the *Verity* as a civilian. At the time I sent him to Earth, I didn't realize the bond he had with you. If you're willing to trade him for that independent jump drive, you'll be free to go on your way."

"Yes! Of course. And I'm sorry about that… I didn't even know he'd had it installed until—"

"I know. No hard feelings." He looked away before turning his attention back to the camera. "Joe's had a hard life, and I get the impression you have, too. I hope that together, things will be better for both of you."

"Thanks. I hope so," she said. "I need to talk to him, before you go. I need to hear for myself that he's okay."

"I'll pass on the message. Take care."

Iza stood motionless, trying to decide if the conversation had actually happened the way she heard it. She'd expected him to be a hardened military commander, completely out of touch with an average person's reality. *If that's the man leading the TSS, no one ever needs to worry about them.*

She stumbled out into the corridor, still dumbstruck by the conversation.

Karter was stilling lingering in the corridor outside his cabin, and he gave her a questioning look. "What is it?"

"I just got off a vidcall with Wil Sietinen."

Braedon, who was chatting with Cierra near the infirmary, jumped to attention. "You *what*?"

"Yeah, really nice guy, it turns out."

Karter's jaw practically hit the floor. "You didn't happen to mention Apex, did you? A connection with Sietinen could—"

"No, Karter," Iza cut him off. "Not everything is about business. Sometimes, you just need to connect with another person. In the end, we're all just people trying to get through life."

"Yeah, I guess so," Braedon said reflectively.

"Speaking of which, our parents will be wanting to settle soon," Cierra said with a glance at Viper. "If it's all right with you, Captain, we'll arrange to have them dropped off someplace safe."

Iza shrugged. "Yes, whatever you like. Just inform Trix of your plans and she'll adjust our course."

With a nod, Cierra left to see to her parents.

"In the meantime, Trix, get us on our way," Iza continued. "And if Viper's sticking around, find her something to do on the flight deck."

Viper beamed. "Thank you, Captain."

The two of them headed toward the flight deck, leaving Iza alone with Karter.

"I assume you and Becca will remain on Beurias," Iza said.

"Yes, now that my mother will no longer be a problem, I believe it is safe to return."

"What about Becca? Will you do the right thing now?"

Karter's mouth lifted in one corner. "It was a pleasure riding with you, Sundari. Take care of my ship," he said turning on his heel.

"*My* ship," Iza called after him with a smile on her face. With the contract fulfilled, now it really was *hers*, free and clear.

31

"HOW'D IT GO?" Ian asked when Wil emerged from his office next off of the Command Center.

"Well. She's strong. I think she'll be okay, but see if you can get Joe to give her a call, Ian."

"I will," he acknowledged.

"It was nice of you to call her like that," Saera said, rubbing his shoulder.

"I know better than most what she's going through. It was the right thing to do."

Ian nodded. "The other courses of action are less straightforward."

"Yes, I keep running through that conversation with the Gatekeepers, and I'm left with more questions than answers," Wil admitted.

"Like, what did he mean by, 'they'll think it was us'?" Ian asked. "And there were several times he mentioned 'others'."

"Could he have been referencing the third race the Aesir said were mentioned in that treaty?" Saera mused.

"Maybe." Wil shook his head. "I need to study the original text of that treaty, if the Aesir can find it. There's too much nuance at play here to rely on secondhand accounts."

"What about the changes to the affected planets?" Curtis jumped in.

"That will take longer to assess," Wil replied. "Preliminary reports rolling in seem to concur that the Gate activity has ceased; it seems like they gathered up their tech and left, as promised. I suspect the changes to the planets' environments are permanent, though, at least for the foreseeable future."

Saera pursed her lips. "I wish we could study the tech behind the transformations. Though, even if we had access to a Gate, it wouldn't be worth upsetting the treaty, whatever it is."

"In any case, we won the battle," Ian said.

Wil gave a solemn nod. "But the war, perhaps, hasn't even yet begun."

Ian chuckled. "I should have known it wasn't going to be one-and-done for us."

"Oh," Wil said, cracking a smile, "don't you know? Once it's in your job description to save the galaxy, the cosmic forces make sure you're kept busy."

— — —

A TSS ship was the last place Joe had expected to find himself again. The infirmary seemed too shiny after his time on Earth, filled with sophisticated equipment that would only be fiction on his homeworld. Part of him had missed having access to such things, but the tech was secondary to the hole that had been left when he was torn away from Iza.

He wished he was with her now, in the way he'd been in the fantasies within his mind. It had been so effortless being together. Even now, the memories of their love filled his heart. But, he wasn't sure where the true memories ended and the fantasies began.

Surely, their real relationship wasn't so carefree. Nothing was *that* easy. It was the conflicts that made things real—working through those problems together. Going through those tests is what strengthened a relationship to last a lifetime. In his fantasies, he and Iza had only each other, wrapped in bliss. What he had with the real version of her was so much deeper. They'd faced death side-by-side and come out stronger.

Joe wished he'd been able to run to her the moment he was freed from Arvonen, but he didn't want Iza to see him so broken. He needed time to sort out his memories from fantasies and allow his body to heal. She'd risked everything for him, and he wanted their reunion to be one of joy, not worry.

The infirmary door slid open, and Ian entered.

Joe tensed, inadvertently sending a jolt of pain through his bruised ribs from where one of Arvonen's guards had kneed him.

"Don't worry, I'm not here for discipline," Ian said, sensing his mood. He sat down on the empty bed to Joe's right.

"I didn't mean for any of this to happen," Joe murmured.

"I know you didn't. Some people have their own gravity, and crazy things happen when we get sucked into their orbit. I think Iza is one of those people."

Joe cracked a smile. "Yeah, she's something else."

His former mentor fell silent for several seconds. "I wish you'd had the courage to simply resign your commission rather than carrying on how you did."

Joe swallowed. "I've thought about that a lot over the last few months. I'm sorry. You taught me to be better than that, and I was selfish."

"I also was stubborn in my own ways. Your heart wasn't in this career path, but I was determined to make an Agent out of you all the same. That's not what the TSS is about. I should have guided you toward something that would have made you happy. I won't make that mistake with others, and I thank you for teaching me how I can a better advocate for our trainees going forward."

"You always were good at spinning things."

Ian chuckled. "When you've been through as much as I have, you learn to look for the little wins."

Joe stared down at his hands before meeting Ian's gaze. "What happens now?"

"We fix you up as best we can, and then you're free to go."

"Free? Are you serious?"

"I am," Ian confirmed. "It's always a challenge, when Agents leave us. We lost a lot after the war, of course; people can only take in so much death before it eats away at them and they need to get out. Others, like you, have fallen in love and want a lifestyle other than what they can have in the TSS. Each case is a little different, and we need to weigh how best to handle it. Yes, we could lock you up for violating your oaths to serve, but what would that accomplish? Ultimately, you were acting to protect people in need—and *that's* what the TSS is about. Sure, you went against the mission, but from a moral standpoint, you weren't in the wrong. So, in your case Joe, the closest thing we have to a win-win is to let you walk away and live your life."

"Thank you," Joe managed, barely above a whisper. The reprieve was more of a gift than he'd dared hope for.

"We're heading back to Headquarters soon, but Iza would like to talk with you before we go."

Joe shook his head. "No, not like this."

"She made the request straight to the High Commander."

"What? How—"

"Talk to her, Joe." Ian set down a handheld on the bed next

to him. "Take care of yourself." He got up and left without another word.

Joe took a deep breath, letting the words sink in. Upon reflection, he was being self-centered to deny Iza contact. She'd risked her life for him. It wasn't fair to rebuff her, but it remained that he didn't want her first sense of him, after so much time apart, to be of him in such a fragile state. He wanted to be a hero in her eyes. The trust and vulnerability could come with time—not like this. Perhaps there was a compromise.

As soon as he got up the nerve, he put through a voice-only call to her private line.

"Who is this?" Iza asked as soon as the call connected.

Joe's heart leaped at the sound of her voice. He cradled the phone to his ear. "I know you tend to get into trouble when you're left unattended. But the brink of galactic war? You've outdone yourself, Iza."

"Joe…" The relief and love poured from her voice as she said his name. It was everything he'd dreamed of hearing over the past three months.

"I've missed you so much," he said as tears stung at his eyes. "I'm sorry for all the trouble."

"I should have come for you sooner." She sniffed, her voice cracking slightly. "So much has happened, Joe."

"Soon, we'll have all the time in the universe to talk about it."

"I want to see you," she said.

"I know, and I can't wait to have you in my arms. But I need some time to recover, Iza. I need the kind of treatment that only the TSS can provide, to help me get over what Arvonen did. Right now, I can't be the partner I want to be for you. I need to get the help now, while I can. Then, I'm all yours."

She took a shaky breath. "I've learned it takes a lot of courage to ask for help. Take the time you need. I'll be here whenever you're ready."

"I'm looking forward to coming home."

— — —

Iza had hoped to see Joe, but hearing his voice had revitalized her, filling the void in her chest that had been there for months. The love was still there, as strong as ever. She respected him for recognizing he needed time to recover, so she would give him that space. But stars, she hoped she wouldn't have to wait long.

In the meantime, she had other important conversations to have. The encounter with the Gatekeepers had given her new perspective on her aunt's death, and she needed to share the loss with her cousin.

When Iza returned to the infirmary, Jaidyn was staring up at the ceiling. He spoke without looking at her. "Interesting crew you have here," He'd no doubt been listening to everything the crew had been saying out the corridor.

"Yeah, well, we didn't find each other in the traditional way."

Iza climbed up on the vacant bed next to him and lay back, staring at the ceiling in the same way. She became fixated on the pattern of tiles she'd never noticed before.

"Your mother reached out to me when you went missing," Iza began. "She told me more about our history and our fathers."

"That's how you got the necklace."

As much as she wanted to pursue the story tangent, she needed to tell him about what had happened to his mother. He deserved to know the truth before they discussed anything else.

"No, I already had this one. The one in your pocket I got from your mother," she said.

He pulled it out of his pocket and tied it around his own neck wincing with the movement.

"She should have kept it." There was more frustration in his voice than anger.

"Reagan was worried about you, and she made me take it just before—" Iza gathered her courage and spilled the rest. "Before the Gatekeepers killed her."

"I know," he said, his expression unchanged. "I knew the moment she was dead."

"How? Were you there?"

"In a manner of speaking. I had this very vivid dream. My mother was there telling me that she was going to save me no matter what."

"You have the dreams, too? What do they mean?" she asked as she shifted to one side so she could look at him.

Jaidyn's head turned to meet her gaze. "They only started once I was near the Gate on Hubyria. Before that, I'd never had one. Then, when you got angry a few minutes ago," he pressed a fist to his chest. "I felt it here. I think it all might have something to do with them."

Iza turned her head to face the ceiling again. "When I was near the sphere, I would have these dreams. Some of the things happened, but not in the way I dreamed them."

"I don't think it's precognition, but more like intuition. Dealing with things happening in our world but not always as they really are. I had a dream about chasing someone, for example. It didn't happen the way it did in the dream, but it did happen."

Iza nodded. She knew what he meant, but it seemed he didn't understand it any better than her. "Is that why you were following me?"

"No, not at first. I wanted to see you. See what kind of person you were. The dreams came later."

That made sense. She continued, "There was a Gate sphere there for a while. It seems to have an effect on electrical systems and our dreams. It emits a humming or buzzing like on the ship, only more focused."

"Yes." Jaidyn's eyes lit up as he spoke, "I could feel the energy on that ship coursing through my body as if I could control it myself."

Iza understood the feeling but didn't have a clue what that meant. It might have had something to do with the Gatekeepers and their technology, but since none of it remained, they wouldn't be able to test that theory. Neither of them was going to have any satisfying answers, it seemed.

"Your mom said something to me about our fathers—that they might be alive in some way. Do you believe that, too?"

"No," he said, but the way he bit down on the word too quickly made her suspect he hadn't always thought that way.

"What are you going to do now that they're gone?"

"I don't know."

"The *Verity's* not so bad," she said. "We've got hauling work to keep us busy most days. The ship belongs to me, and the crew follows my lead without a lot of complaints. It's not much, but you're welcome to stay here."

"I don't think so. I need to go home."

"In my cabin, there's a duffle bag your mother gave to me. I think it's meant for you."

Jaidyn didn't say anything, but she could feel his gratitude to know that. She wondered if that's what telepathy was like to those who had that ability. Everyone they had ever loved now was gone. *I wonder if he feels as close to me as I do him.*

"I won't be here long. I like being on my own."

Iza sighed. "I used to feel the same way, but if you change your mind, you can always come back here."

"Thank you."

32

AFTER A WEEK of tests, probing, and mental repair Joe was finally able to keep his thoughts in the present. The 'dreams', as the doctors had referred to them, were remnants of the time he'd spent in Arvonen's machine—a device designed to create false memories with the end goal of gathering information about real people and places.

He'd walked Arvonen and his people into the TSS and showed them who he'd given the sphere to and where he thought it might be. Thankfully, getting into TSS Headquarters was more difficult than robbing a bank. Arvonen wasn't able to get to the sphere, but his end goal wasn't only the sphere but getting to Iza. That meant more time in the machine while they crawled over every piece of information they had on Iza that they could use against her.

"How are you feeling today?" the doctor asked him from the plush chair across from him.

Why did they always ask the most redundant questions? He put one arm up on the back of the couch where he was sitting, trying to look casual. "I'm fine."

"There's a bit of hesitation there. Was it the question, or is there something you want to share?"

The telepaths in medicine were beyond belief. He hated to have them prying into his thoughts. It was another form of the machine. It forced out the feelings he didn't want shared. But it was a necessary process if he was ever going to be allowed to leave. They had to believe he was compliant.

"I abhor the question. But I'm fine. I feel as good as I did three days ago when I said the fog in my thoughts had lifted."

"You'll forgive me for going over old territory, then," she said. "You understand we need to be thorough, and as much as I'd like to accept your assurances, let me be the judge of whether or not you're well enough to be discharged."

"I'm not an Agent and I don't work for the TSS. I'm here so that they can see I'm a Taran citizen with nothing to hide. I've given you everything I remember of the incident, and now that Arvonen is dead, I don't think there will be any more issues."

He was getting sick of the temporary quarters where he had been recuperating within TSS Headquarters. The suite was identical to his former residence as an Agent, but the tiny cabin on the *Verity* was the only home he wanted now. These house calls to check on him had become tedious.

"You said once that you'd kill Arvonen yourself if you got the chance," the doctor observed. "That could put you on the path to hurt anyone connected to him." The doctor looked at him intently, waiting for a reaction.

"Yes, I'm aware of transference, but I don't have any of those inclinations. Arvonen was the one who ordered me into the machine and demanded that the scientists he'd abducted do his bidding. In fact, his son and I are good friends."

"What about the archaeologist? Raquel," she flipped through her notes on her tablet, looking for the name all too familiar to Joe, "Raquel Calveras. Do you have any residual feelings toward her?"

"Of course I have an issue with her. She helped Arvonen capture me and hold me hostage. However, when she realized I had nothing more to give, she was there to see that I spent little to no time in the machine, and when they forgot to feed me, she was there. She helped in my escape. In the end, I owe her my life."

"You understand these questions are procedural in nature. You seem upset by them, but you needn't be."

The doctor's soothing tone was giving Joe a headache. He reached his hands up to his head rubbing at his temples before dropping his hand back into his lap.

"Does your head hurt? I can give you something for it."

"No, I already took something; I'm just waiting for it to take effect. Is that all?"

"Are you going to be able to work with Raquel when the time comes?"

Joe's jaw tightened and he forced his teeth apart to keep from grinding them. *They'd saved her life, wasn't that enough?* They wanted more out of her—out of him. The deal was simple, and he'd do whatever it took to get back to Iza.

"I'll do what I must," he said, his tone even.

"I suppose that settles things, then," the doctor said. "I will warn you that the false memories will take time to fade. They became a part of your conscious mind and no doubt appeared as real as the conversation we're having today."

More real.

"Does that mean you're going to sign off on my treatment?" he asked, keeping the eagerness out of his eyes.

"Yes. However, I would like to continue to see you for a monthly check-up. Nothing too serious, and I'll do my best not to ask you how you're doing." She smiled. "You do have some visitors here who have been waiting patiently to see you. I suggested that you all meet here just in case it became too overwhelming for you. Can I send them in?"

Iza, would they let her in? Did she come to see if I'm still alive? Joe nodded. "Yes."

"Great, I'll get them." She moved to the door and let herself out.

Joe stared at it, willing Iza to come through. Instead, he saw his friend Emery peek around the corner, followed by Skyler. Joe jumped to his feet to greet them. They both rushed to his side, but it was Emery who threw his arms around him and squeezed until Joe almost couldn't take a breath.

"Okay, okay, release," Joe said, trying to make light of the fact they were two grown men with tears in their eyes.

"I thought we'd lost you for real, man. But your sister, she wouldn't give up. She made them go after you." Emery stepped aside, allowing space for Skyler.

His eyes filled again at the sight of her with tears streaming down her face, waiting for him to make the first move. *We've been through so much. Why did I push her away for all those years?* Now, it seemed silly and petty. He wanted her to know it. Joe reached out for her hands and then pulled her against his chest holding her as she sobbed. Then, as if he couldn't bear it a second longer, Emery came up behind her and wrapped his arms around them both. The three of them held each other for a long moment.

When they pulled away, Joe wiped a sleeve across his eyes and laughed as he did. Then he moved to the chair leaving them the couch to sit together in front of him.

"Tell me everything I missed. How was the wedding?" Joe asked.

They looked at each other and back to Joe.

"There was no wedding. You think we'd get married if you couldn't be there?" Emery said.

"Oh, I'm sorry you postponed it."

"It doesn't matter. We'll have it now that you're back," Skyler said.

"I'm not really back. Now that my treatment is over, they'll probably ship me back to Earth."

"No, they won't. The High Commander made arrangements for you to return to the *Verity*," Skyler said.

"Why?"

Emery and Skyler looked from each other back at Joe and then at the ceiling where an observation camera was mounted. He'd almost forgotten that his doctor was probably watching everything he did. He'd gotten used to it.

"Can we speak freely here?" Skyler asked, slipping into his thoughts like she belonged there. He missed the sound of her internal voice.

"Yes, they know everything. It's not like I could have hidden anything from them, even if I wanted to."

"I think they decided you've paid your due," Emery said aloud. "You can go anywhere in the Taran worlds you want now."

"We hoped you'd still want to come to our wedding. We're planning it for next week, and we insist you be a part of it," Skyler said, her lips firming in a straight line. The expression was so much like their mother, Joe had to look away; she probably had no idea.

"Of course, I'll be there."

"Does that mean you'll stand up for us?" Emery asked, looking between Joe and Skyler.

"Yes, I'd be honored," Joe learned across the gap between the furniture and grabbed his sister's hand. "I wouldn't want to be anywhere else on your big day."

"Good, because we already resent the invitations," Emery said with a giant sigh of relief. "Your friends are invited, of course. They were good to Skyler while she was with them."

"Iza, knows?" Joe asked, not sure how he felt about sharing her.

"Yes, and she's just like you described," Emery said aloud. *"I mean, it makes sense why you chose her over the TSS."*

Skyler nudged him in the ribs, and he flinched.

"They were good to me," Skyler said. "While I was there, they took care of me like one of their own. You could do a lot worse."

"She's special," Joe said to them.

"We know."

They nodded.

"Either way, they're welcome," Skyler said aloud. Emery took the other hand balled in her lap and lifted it to his lips. Joe watched the stress drain from his sister's face. He was glad he hadn't missed their wedding.

"After the wedding, where will you go?" Joe asked.

"Undecided. We've been offered a joint assignment at an outpost. We're considering it," Skyler said. *"We're going to miss you."*

"I'm going to miss you, too. But I won't be far, no matter where we all end up," Joe said to them, then he spoke aloud, "I can't wait to settle a bet I've got with Emery. He swears he can dance, but I've never seen it."

"It's going to be epic. You might want to get something a little more formal," Emery said as he eyed the material of Joe's casual shirt.

They departed after a few more minutes of light conversation.

The doctor returned, and she gently probed his mind. He could keep her out now; he had that much strength again. He reveled in it, but he didn't let it show on his face. Instead, he clenched his jaw, waiting for this final analysis to be over.

"You didn't tell them."

"Tell them what?"

"Why you chose to be here. Why you didn't return to the

Verity immediately."

"It doesn't matter. I'm here now, and I'll be there for them when they need me most. That's what matters."

"They might have been sympathetic, even understanding of your feelings, but you chose not to share them."

"I didn't want them to know."

"Because you're afraid of being judged?"

"No, I don't want *anyone* to know how much that machine took from me."

—   —   —

The time in the Apex ship port on Beurias was the perfect opportunity for the TSS to reclaim their independent jump drive. Iza hated watching them do surgery on her ship, but it was a small price to pay for Joe's freedom.

After several days of waiting, she'd finally received the message Joe was ready to come back. He had agreed to meet them on Beurias at the service port. Iza had hardly slept the night before from the excitement.

Karter had come through and arranged for Douketis to return her shuttle. She was still livid he had swiped it and left her for dead in the middle of a blizzard. Karter served as their mediator so she wouldn't have to deal with Douketis directly. Though, she would have loved to see the look on his face when Karter told him about the revised contract he'd be working under. She heard Douketis had thrown his hat to the ground and stomped on it in his fury.

While on Beurias, she and Karter also made the dissolution of their engagement final and public. She owned the *Verity* free and clear, and Karter was now free to court Becca. Iza couldn't help but smile at the idea that they'd probably make the Sensationals as the new power couple of the year.

The clang of metal on metal got Iza's attention. *Who thought it was a bright idea to start a metal band?* Atano kept to her side, his tail wagging, and unfazed with the racket as she made her way to the cargo hold where the noise was concentrated.

As it turned out, Trix and Braedon were smoothing out the dents on the outside of the AS-225 shuttle, and Cierra was adding paint to a panel they'd already flattened out. It would never look brand new, but it didn't look like it was going to fall out of the sky anymore.

"Good morning, Captain," Trix said in her chipper new tone of voice.

"What are you doing here?" Iza yelled out over the clanging.

Trix and Braedon stopped what they were doing. Viper climbed out of the inside and stood next to her sister.

"Morning, Iz," Braedon said dropping his hammer and moving over to present the shuttle as if it were his own. "I couldn't sleep last night so Cierra and I got to talking about how we might help out with the shuttle. We started about an hour ago, and Trix wouldn't leave us alone, so we put her to work. Viper stumbled inside about twenty minutes ago."

Viper stared down at her shuffling feet, sounding excited but not meeting her gaze. "I'm working on the controls. You've got some glitchy components that I thought could use some attention," she said. "I hope that's okay."

Iza's thoughts were racing to keep up with the information they were throwing at her, but her eye landed on the side of the shuttle where Cierra had been working.

"What's that?"

"We know how much you loathe naming things, so we thought a symbol would be the best way to identify the shuttle. Your necklace holds significance, so we chose that for the hull. If you hate it, we can paint over it, but I did spend some time trying to get it right with help from Trix."

Speechless, Iza stood staring at what they'd done. Then someone entered the cargo hold behind her. Before she could turn around, the familiar voice spoke.

"I kind of like it," Joe said.

"Well, look who's back," Braedon said, beaming, and passing her to grip Joe's arm. "I thought you'd decided to reintegrate yourself with the TSS and abandon us criminals for an honest life as an Agent dressed in black."

"Robin Hood," he said, then flashed a smile at the others. "Little John, Maid Marian, Will Scarlet."

"Pause, are you in beta?" Viper asked then faced Braedon. "What's he talking about?"

Iza watched them each welcome him back, her eyes never leaving his face. Joe was thinner than he'd been before, though the color of his skin was back to normal. When his blue eyes met hers, it was like a bolt of energy passing between them. Dozens of missed conversations from the last few months filled her thoughts, but nothing came out. Questions she didn't need answers to occupied her mind. *How have you been? What did they do to you? Did you think about me?* No, none of that mattered anymore. He was standing here in front of her, and she couldn't think.

Somewhere behind her, she heard Braedon call the rest of the crew back to work.

Iza went to the shuttle and climbed inside. She'd been fantasizing about leaping into Joe's arms the moment she saw him, but now that they were together, she found herself overcome with nerves.

Joe followed her in.

"I need to re-program this component, it's going to take at least an hour to get the code re-tested," Viper grumbled as she passed them and climbed out.

Iza needed to give herself a little time to get used to Joe being close to her again, so she picked up the closest available project to keep herself from fidgeting. The front console lay open, the wiring exposed. She got down on the floor and slid underneath to pick up where Viper had left off.

"It's going to look brand new once it's all finished," Joe said, breaking the silence.

"Yeah, I don't care about how it looks. I want it to run like new more than anything. I just need to rewire the navigation controls so we can keep her steady on exit and entry. I need to bypass a few other systems to make it work. Pass me those wire cutters, will you?"

Joe knelt down and passed her the cutters, but he stayed on the floor at her side. Iza didn't want to meet his gaze yet. Having him near was enough to turn her insides to jelly.

"All of the paperwork has been filed. I'm a free man of the Taran Empire."

Iza's heart lifted. She busied her hands focusing on realigning the wires in front of her. "The soldering gun should be over there. Can you grab it?"

He dug around in the pile of abandoned tools and found the soldering gun and held it out for her. Iza reached for it, and he held on forcing her to look at him. "I think we've spent enough time dancing around things. I'd like to take you on a proper date."

Her heart fluttered. "Is that so?"

"In fact, I was hoping you accompany me to my sister's wedding next week. I'm supposed to stand up for them. They want the crew to come, too. It seems you all left quite the impression on her and Emery." He was rattling on the way Braedon did, which meant he was nervous. She couldn't help but find it endearing.

Determined to play it cool, Iza lifted one shoulder. "Sounds like a good time."

She pulled at the tool again, but Joe put it down out of reach so he could cradle her face with both hands.

Iza placed one hand on his chest. "I've missed you."

"I've missed you, too. More than I thought one person could ever miss another."

It was what she wanted to hear, but she needed to know what was behind the words. *Is he ready to go all-in the way I am?* She searched his eyes, looking for lingering signs of what he'd been through. "Are you okay?" she asked.

Joe tilted his head to one side. He seemed to be listening to the pounding and steady conversation outside the shuttle. He smiled and shook his head. "No, I'm not." He pulled her in and kissed her senseless. When he pulled back to get his breath, he touched his forehead to hers. "But with you, I will be."

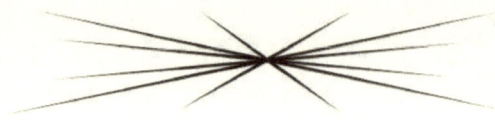

ADDITIONAL READING

Cadicle Space Opera Series by A.K. DuBoff
Book 1: Rumors of War (Vol. 1-3)
Book 2: Web of Truth (Vol. 4)
Book 3: Crossroads of Fate (Vol. 5)
Book 4: Path of Justice (Vol. 6)
Book 5: Scions of Change (Vol. 7)

Shadowed Space Series by Lucinda Pebre & A.K. DuBoff
Book 1: Shadow Behind the Stars
Book 2: Shadow Rising
Book 3: Shadow Beyond the Reach

Mindspace Series by A.K. DuBoff
Book 1: Infiltration
Book 2: Conspiracy
Book 3: Offensive
Book 4: Endgame

Dark Stars Trilogy by A.K. DuBoff
Book 1: Crystalline Space
Book 2: A Light in the Dark
Book 3: Masters of Fate

AUTHORS' NOTES

From T.S. Valmond:

Dear reader, thank you for picking up this series and giving it a read. I know you have plenty of other things going on in your life, this year in particular, and it means so much that you shared this journey with me.

This has been the most fun I've ever had writing with someone else, and I have to thank Amy. Without her, this amazing universe wouldn't exist. As you probably know, finding people with whom you can cohesively work on a single project can be a challenge. My time working with Amy has been awe-inspiring and a true joy. With a guiding hand and an open heart she helped me bring this story out of chaos and seamlessly into her world. I'll always be grateful to her for her insights and care with my characters and ideas.

A special thanks to the entire team for taking time out of your busy lives to help make this book the best it can be. Thank you to our elite beta readers who've been with us throughout the entire series. I couldn't be happier, you're all sensational! I appreciate so much the proofers who sniffed out the typos big and small, you're the best!

Thank you to my wonderful husband, Matthew, for standing by me and being there at all times of the night to listen as I worked through the story. I couldn't have done it without your support.

Thanks again to the readers. I'm so grateful to have shared this story with you. There's a lot more in me yet, and I can't wait for you to see what's next.

An additional note from A.K. DuBoff:

Thank you for reading this third book in the Verity Chronicles! This little trio of books has been great fun to work on with Shelina, and I hope that you've enjoyed reading them as much as we've enjoyed writing them.

The ending of this book leaves a bit of a cliffhanger for these 'others' and what may come, but rest assured that there are big plans for this open storyline. The Taran Empire Saga will blow the Cadicle Universe wide open in scope, so stay tuned for that. It's been great being able to add alien entities into the universe, and I'm looking forward to exploring these threads further.

Thank you to Shelina for bringing such great characters into the Cadicle Universe and for bringing new dimension to my characters from the original series, such as Ian. It's been a great experience working on this together!

Many thanks also to our amazing beta readers and proofers—John, Taria, Steve, Doug, Leo, Eric, David, Gil, Manie, Bryan, and Diane—for their valuable feedback, great ideas, and assistance adding the final polish. These books are truly a team effort, and I feel so luck to work with such incredible people. '

Until next time, happy adventuring!

ABOUT THE AUTHORS

T.S. VALMOND

T.S. Valmond isn't an author (despite the claims). More like a glorified reporter delivering the news from far away worlds. She'll tell you she doesn't write books she's building a universe but don't believe the hype; she also thinks she's a Jedi. She resides in Canada with her husband and dog in an undisclosed location. One can never be too careful when exposing the secrets of powerful governments, intergalactic worlds, and illegal aliens. (Yes, they're watching.)

www.tsvalmond.com

A.K. DUBOFF

A.K. (Amy) DuBoff has always loved science fiction in all its forms—books, movies, shows and games. If it involves outer space, even better! She is a Nebula Award finalist and USA Today bestselling author most known for her Cadicle Universe, but she's also written a variety of space fantasy and comedic sci-fi. Now a full-time author, Amy can frequently be found traveling the world. When she's not writing, she enjoys wine tasting, binge-watching TV series, and playing epic strategy board games.

www.amyduboff.com